JUGGLER *of* WORLDS

Larry Niven

AND

Edward M. Lerner

A TOM DOHERTY ASSOCIATES BOOK • NEW YORK

JUGGLER OF WORLDS

A Tor Book
Published by Tom Doherty Associates, LLC
175 Fifth Avenue
New York, NY 10010

www.tor-forge.com

Tor® is a registered trademark of Tom Doherty Associates, LLC.

ISBN 978-1-250-20897-2

First Edition: September 2008
First Mass Market Edition: June 2009

P1

Praise for *Fleet of Worlds*

"A far-future SF mystery/adventure set two centuries before the discovery of the Ringworld by humans . . . intriguing human and alien characters and lucid scientific detail."
—*Library Journal*

"A new Known Space book, particularly one with new information about Puppeteers and their doings behind the scenes of human history, needs recommending within the science fiction community about as much as a new Harry Potter novel does—well, anywhere. But Niven and Lerner have produced a novel that can stand on its own as well as part of the Known Space franchise." —*Locus*

"If you're a Niven fan, just go buy the book. It's that good! . . . It's the finest Known Space work in many, many years that I've had the pleasure to read. This is an essential read for anyone interested in how good science fiction can be."
—*The Green Man Review*

"A very worthy addition to the ongoing Known Space future history."
—*Sci Fi Weekly*

"As we have long expected from Niven, it's a great read, and Lerner—as *Analog* readers know—has the knack as well. You'll enjoy this one."
—*Analog Science Fiction and Fact*

"Larry Niven and Edward M. Lerner have teamed up to write the prequel [to *Ringworld*], and it's well worth reading, whether you've read *Ringworld* and its subsequent books or not."
—*SFRevu*

"If a little knowledge is a dangerous thing, a lot of knowledge can rock worlds." —*The Kansas City Star*

TOR BOOKS BY LARRY NIVEN
AND EDWARD M. LERNER

Fleet of Worlds
Juggler of Worlds
Destroyer of Worlds
Betrayer of Worlds
Fate of Worlds

TOR BOOKS BY LARRY NIVEN

Stars and Gods
N-Space
Playgrounds of the Mind
Destiny's Road
Rainbow Mars
Scatterbrain
The Draco Tavern
Ringworld's Children

WITH STEVEN BARNES

Achilles' Choice
The Descent of Anansi
Saturn's Race

WITH JERRY POURNELLE AND STEVEN BARNES

The Legacy of Heorot
Beowulf's Children

WITH BRENDA COOPER

Building Harlequin's Moon

TOR BOOKS BY EDWARD M. LERNER

Fools' Experiments
Small Miracles

To the readers who work on a book long after it's closed, and really get their money's worth: Thanks for the help.

CONTENTS

DRAMATIS PERSONAE

KNOWN-SPACE HUMANS*	ROLE
Max Addeo	*Amalgamated Regional Militia (ARM) exec, later high-ranking United Nations (UN) official*
Sigmund Ausfaller	*ARM agent*
Fiona ("Feather") Filip	*ARM agent*
Julian Forward	*Physicist (native of Jinx, in the Sirius system)*
Andrea Girard	*ARM agent*
Dianna Guthrie	*Girlfriend of Gregory Pelton*
Sharrol Janss	*Wife (at separate times) to Beowulf Shaeffer and Carlos Wu*
Sangeeta Kudrin	*High-ranking UN official*
Calista Melencamp	*Secretary-General of the UN*
Anne-Marie Papandreou	*Crew of* Court Jester; *wife of Jason Papandreou (native of Wunderland, in the Alpha Centauri system)*
Jason Papandreou	*Owner-pilot of* Court Jester *(a ship chartered by Nessus)*
Gregory Pelton	*Wealthy industrialist*
Beowulf Shaeffer	*Starship pilot and xenophile (native of We Made It, in the Procyon system)*
Ander Smittarasheed	*Freelance writer; sometimes agent of Sigmund Ausfaller*
Carlos Wu	*Physicist and all-around genius*

OTHER HUMANS	ROLE
Sabrina Gomez-Vanderhoff	*Governor of Nature Preserve 4 (NP4)/New Terra*
Sven Hebert-Draskovics	*NP4 archivist*

*Earth resident, unless otherwise noted.

Eric Huang-Mbeke	*Member of NP4's independence movement; engineer*
Penelope Mitchell-Draskovics	*Sven's cousin; government agronomist*
Kirsten Quinn-Kovacs	*Member of NP4's independence movement; navigator and a math whiz*
Omar Tanaka-Singh	*Member of NP4's independence movement*

KZINTI*	ROLE
Chuft-Captain	*Commanding officer of the spy ship* Traitor's Claw; *has earned a partial name*
Maintainer-of-Equipment	*Renegade citizen of the colony world Spearpoint*
Slaverstudent	*Crewman on* Traitor's Claw
Telepath	*Crewman on* Traitor's Claw

PUPPETEERS	ROLE
Achilles	*Concordance scout (first known to Ausfaller as Adonis)*
Baedeker	*Engineer at General Products Corporation*
Nessus	*Concordance scout*
Nike	*Leader of "Permanent Emergency" faction of the Experimentalist party / later, Hindmost*
Vesta	*Nike's aide*

*Unless otherwise noted, a low-status individual yet to earn a name.

THEY

Earth date: 2637

• 1 •

Sigmund Ausfaller woke up shivering, prone on a cold floor. His head pounded. Tape bound his wrists and ankles to plasteel chains.

He had always known it would end horribly. Only the when, where, how, why, and by whom of it all had eluded him.

That fog was beginning to lift.

How had he gotten here, wherever *here* was? As though from a great distance, Sigmund watched himself quest for recent memories. Why was it such a struggle?

He remembered the pedestrian concourse of an open-air mall, shoppers streaming. They wore every color of the rainbow, clothing and hair and skin, in every conceivable combination and pattern. Overhead, fluffy clouds scudded across a clear blue sky. The sun was warm on his face. Work, for once, had been laid aside. He'd been content.

Happiness is the sworn enemy of vigilance. How could he have been so careless?

Sigmund forced open his eyes. He was in a nearly featureless room. Its walls, floor, and ceiling were resilient plastic. Light came from one wall. I could be anywhere, Sigmund thought—and then two details grabbed his attention.

The room wasn't quite a box. The glowing wall had a bit of a curve to it.

There were recessed handholds in walls, floor, and ceiling.

Panic struck. He was on a *spaceship*! Was gravity a hair higher than usual? Lower? He couldn't tell.

Plasteel chains clattered dully as Sigmund sat up. He had watched enough old movies to expect chains to clink. Even as the room spun around him and everything faded to black, he found the energy to feel cheated.

COLD PLASTIC PRESSED against Sigmund's cheek. He opened his eyes a crack to see the same spartan room. Cell.

This time he noticed that one link of his chains had been fused to a handhold in the deck.

Had he passed out from a panic attack? *Where was he?*

Sigmund forced himself to breathe slowly and deeply until the new episode receded. Fear could only muddy his thoughts. More deep breaths.

He had never before blacked out from panic. He could not believe that *this* blackout stemmed from panic. Yes, his faint had closely followed the thought he might be aboard a spaceship. It *also* had occurred just after he had sat up. Sigmund remembered his thoughts having been fuzzy. They seemed sharper now.

He'd been drugged! Doped up and barely awake, he'd sat up too fast. *That* was why he had passed out.

More cautiously this time, Sigmund got into a sitting position. His head throbbed. He considered the pain dispassionately. Less disabling than the last time, he decided. Perhaps the drugs were wearing off.

Some odd corner of his mind felt shamed by his panic attacks. Most Earthborn had flatland phobia worse than he, and so what? True, he'd been born on Earth, but his parents had been all over Known Space. Somehow they took pleasure in strange scents, unfamiliar night skies, and wrong gravity.

On principle, Sigmund had been to the moon twice. He had had to know: Could he leave Earth should the need ever arise? The second time, it was to make sure the success of that first trip wasn't a fluke.

He listened carefully. The soft whir of a ventilation fan. Hints of conversation, unintelligible. His own heartbeat. None of the background power-plant hum that permeated the spaceships he'd been on. Gravity felt as normal as his senses could judge.

Recognizing facts, spotting patterns, drawing inferences . . . he managed, but slowly, as though his thoughts swam through syrup. Traces of drugs remained in his system. He forced himself to concentrate.

If this was a ship, it was still on Earth. Someone *meant* to panic him, Sigmund decided. Someone wanted something from him. Until they got it, he'd probably remain alive.

They.

For as long as Sigmund could remember, there had always been some *they* to worry about.

But even as Sigmund formed that thought, he knew "always" wasn't quite correct. . . .

IN THE BEGINNING, *they* were unambiguous enough: the Kzinti.

The Third Man-Kzin War broke out in 2490, the year Sigmund was born. He was five before he knew what a Kzin was—something like an upright orange cat, taller and much bulkier than a man, with a naked, rat-like tail. By then, the aliens had been defeated. The Kzinti Patriarchy ceded two colony worlds to the humans as reparations. In Sigmund's lifetime, they had attacked human worlds three more times. They'd lost those wars, too.

Fafnir was one of the worlds that changed hands after the third war. His parents had wanderlust and not a trace of flatland phobia. They left him in the care of an aunt, and went to Fafnir in 2500 for an adventure.

And found one.

Conflict erupted that year between humans on Fafnir and the Kzinti settlers who had remained behind. His parents vanished, in hostilities that failed to rise to the level of a numeral in the official reckoning of Man-Kzin Wars. It was a mere "border incident."

Everyone knew the Kzinti ate their prey.

So *they,* for a long time, were Kzinti. Sigmund hated the ratcats, and everyone understood. And he hated his parents for abandoning him. The grief counselors told his aunt that that was normal. And he hated his aunt, as much as she reminded him of Mom—or perhaps because she did—for allowing Mom and Dad to leave him with her.

The same year his parents disappeared, the Puppeteers emerged from beyond the rim of Human Space. A species more unlike the Kzinti could not be imagined. Puppeteers looked like two-headed, three-legged, wingless ostriches. The heads on their sinuous necks reminded him of sock puppets. The brain, Aunt Susan told him, hid under the thick mop of mane between the massive shoulders.

So *they* came to include these other aliens, these harmless-seeming newcomers, because Sigmund didn't believe in coincidence. And then *they* came to include *all* aliens—because, really, how could anyone truly know otherwise?

That was when Aunt Susan took him to a psychotherapist. Sigmund remembered the stunned look on her face after his first session. After she spoke alone with the therapist. Sigmund remembered her sobbing all that night in her bedroom.

He had a sickness, or sicknesses, he couldn't spell, much less understand: a paranoid personality disorder. Monothematic delusion with delusional misidentification syndrome. He didn't know if he believed the supposed silver lining: that it was treatable.

What Sigmund did believe was the other consolation Dr. Swenson offered Aunt Susan—that paranoia is an affliction of the brightest.

In time, Sigmund understood. Trauma can cause stress can cause biochemical imbalances can cause mental illness. A day and a night asleep in an autodoc corrected the biochemical imbalance in his brain. But a single chemical tweak wasn't enough: Knowing the world is out to get you is its own stress. Three months of therapy with Dr. Swenson addressed the paranoid behaviors Sigmund had already learned.

Dr. Swenson was right: Sigmund *was* very smart. Smart enough to figure out what the therapist wanted to hear. Smart enough to learn what thoughts to keep to himself.

TREMBLING, SIGMUND TRIED again to shake off the drugs. Reliving old horrors served no useful purpose—especially now. He needed to focus.

Start with *them.* They weren't Kzinti: The room was too small. Kzinti would have gone crazy.

They wanted something from him; how he responded might be the only control he had in this situation. Who might *they* be?

Others might see in him only a middle-aged, midlevel financial analyst. A United Nations bureaucrat. A misanthrope dressed always in black, in a world where everyone else wore vibrant colors.

Sigmund saw more. All those years ago, Dr. Swenson had been far more correct than he knew. Sigmund was more than bright. He was brilliant—in the mind, where it counted, not in gaudy display.

Who were *they*? Probably somebody Sigmund was investigating. That narrowed it down. The bribe-taking customs officials at Quito Spaceport? The sysadmin at the UN ID data center who moonlighted in identity laundering?

Sigmund's gut said otherwise. It was his other ongoing investigation: the Trojan Mafia. The gang, known by its reputed base in the Trojan Asteroids, engaged in every kind of smuggling, from artworks to weapons to experimental medicines. They killed for hire—and, more often, just to keep the authorities at bay. They were into extortion, money laundering . . . everything. Every other analyst in Investigations refused to touch them.

Surely that was *who.*

How was more speculative. A "chance" encounter in the pedestrian mall near his home, he guessed, by someone with a fast-acting hypo-sedative. He stumbles; his assailant, to all appearances a Good Samaritan, helps him to the nearest transfer booth.

Where? Other than somewhere on Earth, Sigmund wasn't prepared to guess. On a world bristling with transfer booths, he could have been teleported instantaneously almost anywhere.

And when? Blinking to de-blur his vision, Sigmund raised his hands. His left wrist hurt—not much, but it hurt. The time display had frozen. Ironic that, since the subcutaneous control pips felt melted: tiny beads beneath his thumb. Clock, weather, compass, calculator, maps, all the utility functions he normally summoned by fingernail pressure . . . all gone. He guessed his implant had been fried with a magnetic pulse. It fit the program of disorientation.

They weren't as smart as they thought. The room had no sanitary facilities, not so much as a chamber pot, and so far he felt no need to pee. His black suit was clean, if rumpled. It wasn't an ironclad case, but Sigmund guessed he had been snatched from that pedestrian mall no more than a few hours ago.

Footsteps! They approached along the unseen corridor beyond the out-of-reach door. The door flew open.

A tall figure, easily two meters tall, stood in the doorway. A tall fringe of hair bobbed on an otherwise bald head: a Belter crest. And did not Hector, mightiest of the Trojans, famously wear a helmet with a plume of horsehair?

It all fit with the Trojan Mafia.

Sigmund blinked in the suddenly bright light, unable to make out details.

"Good," the Belter said. "I see you're awake. There's someone who wants to speak with you."

• • •

"YOU SEEM UNSURPRISED, Mr. Ausfaller."

An eerie calm came over Sigmund. "Someone had to put through all the requests for reassignment. Someone had to tolerate one unproductive investigation after another."

"Your boss," his captor said.

"Someone had to authorize those transfers. Someone had to accept the department's persistent failures." Sigmund mustered all the irony he could. "Sir."

"Meaning me." Ben Grimaldi, Undersecretary-General for Inspections, leaned casually against the wall. Body language somehow added, Your suspicions make this easier.

That was self-justifying nonsense, of course. Grimaldi would not have shown himself had there been any chance Sigmund would be let free.

Grimaldi broke a lengthening silence. "I need to learn what you know. More importantly, I need to know how."

Once I reveal that, Sigmund thought, I'm dead. He shifted position, his chains clicking dully. Change the subject. "Why the Trojans?"

Grimaldi smiled humorlessly. "We prefer Achilles. The Trojans were losers."

The Trojan Asteroids fell into two groups, those orbiting the L4 Lagrange point, 60 degrees ahead of Jupiter in its orbit, and those orbiting the L5 point, 60 degrees behind. The Greek Camp and the Trojan Camp, as they were sometimes called. Achilles was among the largest asteroids in the Greek Camp. Of course Hector *also* orbited there, so named before the labeling convention began. . . .

Sigmund pinched his leg, desperate to unmuddle his thoughts. "How much dope did you give me?" he demanded.

"Enough." Grimaldi looked pointedly at his wrist implant. "I must be going soon. Your stay here will be much more pleasant if you answer our questions voluntarily."

More pleasant, perhaps. Also shorter? Did buying time matter? "Why the Trojans?"

"Why would you think, Ausfaller? They made a generous offer for my assistance. Official scrutiny is bad for their business.

"You're an odd one, Sigmund, but I admit you're capable. Persistent. I truly wish I thought we could buy you. Sadly, you inherited piles of money. You still chose to work for a pittance at the UN." Grimaldi shook his head. "You live like a monk. You dress like a monk. Why offer you money when you ignore the wealth you already have? It seems too likely you have principles."

And there it was, the memory Sigmund had struggled for. Money. He tried and failed to blink away the fuzziness. "Perhaps *I* can pay *you.*"

A reflexive flash of contempt—and then, more slowly, an expression of low cunning. Grimaldi said, "You'd still have to tell everything you've learned about me and my associates. And every detail about *how* you learned. It won't do for someone else to discover what you did."

"Understood."

"You wouldn't try to trick me, now would you?" Grimaldi asked.

"Of course not," Sigmund answered.

Grimaldi smacked his hands together; strangely, that assurance had sufficed. "Stet. There will be no negotiation. One million stars, transferred into the numbered Belter account I will give you. Don't bother to protest. I know you're good for it. When your weekly reports began to show progress, I made it a point to learn about you. Here's the deal, Mr. Ausfaller. You pay. You tell all. Then we let you go."

He'd never be let go, but Sigmund acted as though he believed. Anyway, the million-and-change he thought Grimaldi could trace was merely the fraction of Sigmund's wealth he intended to be visible—and it wasn't as though there were anyone to leave his money to. At worst, the charade might make his final hours less unpleasant.

Sigmund raised his arms, clanking on purpose. "For a million stars, I want these off. I want a nicer room. A suite with plumbing would be good."

"We'll see about that after the funds clear. Until then, maybe a pot." Grimaldi took a sonic stunner and a handheld computer from pockets of his bodysuit. He whispered inaudibly into the handheld, set it on the deck, and then slid it with his shoe tip toward Sigmund. Handheld and foot never came within Sigmund's reach. The sonic stunner was fixed on him.

"I'm logged into an anonymous account. All other comm functions are locked out. Moments after my funds are received, they'll be shifted elsewhere." Grimaldi laughed. "My colleagues, as I'm sure you know, are skilled in anonymous transfers."

My funds. Sigmund held in his anger. "Funds transfer from Bank of North America." He paused for the voiceprint check. "Account: five . . . four . . . one. . . ." He articulated slowly and distinctly, leaving no chance for misinterpretation. Account number. Subaccount. Access codes.

The good news was the response time. He was still on Earth.

The stunner never wavered. He'd be lucky to utter a suspicious syllable without being zapped. "Four . . . two . . . niner. . . ."

The bank AI spoke a challenge code. Grimaldi snorted in disgust. He wiggled the stunner, just a bit, in warning.

Sigmund shrugged. Clank. With the challenge-response feature set, a bank would accept transfer authorizations only in real time. Challenge-response defeated coerced recordings. What rational person *didn't* configure his account this way?

Sigmund could authorize the transfer with a duress

code. That would alert his bank, but so what? Money laundering was big business for the Trojans. Within minutes of the money's release, it would be laundered through a dozen shell companies, off-world tax havens, and other anonymous venues. The duress code would accomplish nothing.

If he purposefully aborted the transfer, Grimaldi would know instantly—and the coming questioning could become a *lot* less pleasant. Or—

Dr. Swenson had been right: Sigmund *was* paranoid. And now, he thought, we'll see if I've been paranoid *enough.*

SIGMUND REMAINED IN chains, but he'd been offered a chair, an improvised chamber pot, and a greasy drinking bulb with tepid water. For a million stars, there should have been at least a leaded-glass tumbler and ice.

Grimaldi was long gone. He had delegated the detailed questioning to the lanky Belter Sigmund had met earlier. His interrogator disdained to offer a name. Sigmund chose to think of him as Astyanax: Hector's little boy, hurled from the ramparts of Troy. Like Achilles' son, Sigmund wanted no more kings of Troy.

Slow, pensive sips didn't buy much time.

All crimes lead to tax evasion. Sigmund had concentrated his quest for the Trojans there. He discoursed methodically on forensic techniques in spotting hidden income, waxing ever more pedantic. Whenever Astyanax began looking impatient, Sigmund offered a tidbit about which banking investigations had suggested what line of further investigation. A few such admissions evoked surprisingly astute questions. The Belter was something of an expert himself on income-tax evasion.

A handheld in Astyanax's pocket squawked in alarm. There was sudden pandemonium in the corridor. Thudding footsteps. Thudding bodies? The unmistakable zap of sonic stunners.

Astyanax dropped his own stunner, and took a utility knife from his belt. Low-tech but lethal.

"Don't," Sigmund said. "You'll only make it wor—"

He gasped in shock at the sudden agony in his stomach. His shirt and Astyanax's hand were bright red. Lifeblood red.

"Nothing personal," Astyanax said.

As Sigmund slumped, a squad of battle-armored ARMs burst through the door. To the frying-bacon sound of stunners, as everything went dark, Sigmund thought: Too late. . . .

• 2 •

Sigmund awoke. The incredible pain in his gut was gone. His wrists and ankles no longer throbbed from tight restraints. He was clearheaded and full of energy. Rested. Content.

It scared the hell out of him.

He opened his eyes. A transparent dome hung centimeters from his face. Reflected LEDs shone steadily, all in green.

He was in an autodoc.

Readouts told Sigmund that the 'doc had replaced his heart and part of his liver! And two liters of blood, and—he stopped reading. He raised the massive lid and sat up, to echoes of pain in his chest and belly. Logically, those pangs were in his head, since the 'doc had declared him healed. They hurt regardless.

The room seemed chilly, but that might only be because he wasn't wearing anything. You never did in an autodoc.

"Welcome back."

His head swiveled. A stranger in a drab bodysuit occupied the room's only chair. She was lean, almost gaunt, but also massively muscled. He guessed she worked out obsessively. She would have been striking, if not exactly pretty, if she didn't scare the bejesus out of him.

The stranger stood and handed Sigmund the robe that hung from a hook on the door. She did not turn her back. "You'll want this, I expect. Then we should talk."

"Where are we?" Sigmund asked.

Instead of answering, she waved a blue disc at him. A holo shimmered, Earth, and a bit of text: Special Agent Fiona Filip.

It appeared to be an ARM ident. Perhaps she had answered him.

The Amalgamated Regional Militia was the unassuming name for the UN military forces. Understatement sufficed when merely to see an ARM made most people quail. Everyone knew the militia was how the United Nations maintained control, not just civil order.

Sigmund slipped on his robe and climbed out of the autodoc. Everyone knew what someone meant everyone to know. Grimaldi? The people for whom Grimaldi worked? Maybe the rescue had been staged, Sigmund's stabbing a bit of theater for credibility, to hear what he'd tell those he thought were the authorities. To see whom he'd contact next.

"Sigmund, this will be hard for you. I understand better than you can know." The stranger sighed. "Let's start over. I'm Fiona Filip. My friends call me Feather. I'm an ARM—but not the kind that extracted you. I prefer to avoid guns and knives. People can get hurt with those things. As you recently learned."

When had they become friends? "Where am I, Agent Filip?"

Her smile looked wrong, somehow. Unpracticed rather than insincere. "A SWAT team extracted you from an interplanetary freighter on the tarmac at Mojave Spaceport.

You were dying of a stab wound. You were also, by the way, pumped full of truth serum.

"They always bring autodocs on raids. The squad leader popped you into a field 'doc and delivered you to the nearest ARM District Office. That's Los Angeles. Hollywood, more precisely, if you know the area."

Sigmund remembered saying he wasn't trying to trick Grimaldi, and the bastard had taken his word for it. Truth serum explained it. He had told the literal truth. He hadn't been *trying* to trick Grimaldi—he *was* tricking him.

If any of this was real, of course.

"I want you to trust me, and that doesn't come easily to you, does it?" Filip turned the chair and sat, legs straddling the back. "I don't expect an answer, by the way. As I said, I understand you. I'll answer the questions you don't dare to ask. For starters, you're not a suspect. Not for anything."

Sigmund's mind raced. Except for the usual fresh-from-the-autodoc burst of energy, he felt normal. Normal for *him,* that was. How could that be? "Then I'm free to go."

She flashed an I-know-something-you-don't-know grin. *This* smile looked natural. "Yes, but you won't, because you need to know more."

If Filip was who she said she was, she must know how he had signaled for help. If she wasn't . . . to even reveal that he *had* signaled could bring on retribution. It would, at a minimum, make the Trojan Mafia hide him better.

"You're dying to know how you were rescued. No, let's be honest. Sigmund, you're wondering *if* you were rescued." She laughed at his twitch of surprise, but it wasn't a cruel laugh. "You're kind of cute in an intense way. Just hear me out.

"You came into a fair amount of money when your parents died, part inheritance, part insurance. You took control of that money once you reached twenty-one.

The interesting thing, Sigmund, is what you've done with that money."

"Nothing." Sigmund willed his voice to stay level. In fact, he'd divvied the money into several accounts, two directly in his name, the rest far more subtly registered. He hadn't broken any laws in doing it—*they* certainly watched for that—but he had, arguably, bent a few. "It's my rainy-day fund."

Filip shook her head. "Hardly. You sloshed your wealth around in very unusual ways. You triggered trip wires in more money-laundering audits than I care to admit." She cut off his objection before he could do more than open his mouth. "Relax. You did nothing illegal. Not quite. You kept the individual funds transfers *just* below the banks' required filing threshold. And once my colleagues determined the ownership of all the blind trusts, they saw none of the money had even changed hands.

"Given what you do—you're very good at it, by the way—you knew exactly what would happen. You knew the pattern of activities would flag those accounts. Sigmund, you went to a lot of trouble to create bank accounts the authorities would forever watch."

Sigmund shrugged. He could feign nonchalance all he wanted, but were sensors even now picking up the pounding of his brand-new heart?

"Rainy-day fund? It apparently poured yesterday in the Mojave," Filip said. "From an account long idle, suddenly there's a million-star transfer into a numbered account in a Belter bank haven. It set off all kinds of alarms. I wondered: If you *wanted* attention, why not just make the transfer using a duress code?"

Because a duress alarm wouldn't say enough! If a duress code caught your eye, you might not look any further. Wasn't that obvious?

"I dug a bit deeper," Filip said. "You could have used any of those red-flag accounts. Did your choice matter? Banks assign account numbers, but account owners choose their own access codes. So: I ran your access codes through crypto software. Each of your funny accounts had its PIN derived from the name of a high official in the UN Inspections Directorate. The PINs changed, but not the pattern." She patted Sigmund's arm and he flinched. "The PIN that released those funds decrypted as 'Grimaldi.' He was at Mojave Spaceport when you authorized the payoff."

Sigmund couldn't help shivering. He pulled his thin robe more tightly closed, but he doubted it fooled her. Then it *was* true: ARMs traced people through the transfer-booth system. He'd always worried about that. Transfers had to tie back somehow to people, for billing purposes.

Or the Trojans were even cleverer than he'd feared. Grimaldi might have recorded his PIN as he authorized the transfer. If Trojans had decrypted his code, they might be testing him now. . . .

"Sigmund! Come back." She laughed, somehow kindly this time. "Who but a paranoid sets traps with the ARMs to implicate their co-workers? You came out of the autodoc as paranoid as you went in. I see it in your eyes. Surely *you* noticed. Have you asked yourself: Why?"

He sat still, afraid to speak. Why *hadn't* the autodoc reset his brain chemistry?

Filip said, "Here's where we become friends, Sigmund. You've heard the rumors. Senior ARM agents are paranoids. It helps us with the job. We get that way chemically. We're pumped up for the workweek, and pumped out when we go off-duty. Most ARMs, that is. Like you, I'm a natural schiz. I'm drugged before they send me home for the weekend.

"The thing is, today is Wednesday. A workday. After your little mishap, you went into an autodoc. Ours see nothing unusual with a bit of schizo brain chemistry. It's no accident you're as messed up as ever.

"Sigmund, that's the reason I understand you. We're the *same*."

He wanted to believe. Of course, he'd heard the stories. Who hadn't? The thing was—

"Sigmund," she snapped. "Stay with me. You're thinking: ARMs put out the rumor that they're paranoid to trick you into revealing that you're paranoid. I did, too."

For the first time since Sigmund had climbed out of the autodoc, she peered directly into his eyes. "Bright and paranoid is a license to be miserable and alone. Miserable maybe I can't help. But alone—that's something else."

He accepted the new ident chip she offered him. When he held it just right, a blue globe and his name shimmered above it. It was supposedly keyed to his DNA and would get him into the ARM academy in London. He struggled into the plain, black suit she whisked from a cabinet. It didn't surprise him that it had been synthed to his size and preferred style.

He admitted nothing, promised nothing. He was, finally, apparently free.

Free to go? Free to be followed? Festooned with tiny cameras?

Beyond the clinic door, an office buzzed with activity. No one paid Sigmund any attention. Ignoring the transfer booths, he found his way outside. Large five-pointed stars shone in the pedestrian walkway. Grauman's Chinese Theatre stood across and just down the street.

He turned. Above the double doors through which he had just exited, stone-carved letters read: Amalgamated Regional Militia, Los Angeles District. A faux ARM office could hardly be fabricated in such a public place.

Sigmund fingered the ident chip Agent Filip—Feather—had given him. It suddenly seemed possible, after more than a century alone, that he had finally discovered a place where he could fit in.

A MISSION OF GRAVITY

EARTH DATE: 2641

· 3 ·

"Eerie, don't you think?" Without waiting for an answer, Trisha Schwartz cranked the bridge telescope's holo to max magnification. Her voice brimmed with curiosity and impatience.

Nessus marveled. Their ship was not even a minute out of hyperspace. Curiosity explained why she and her colleague were here; there was much to be learned in this place. Their impatience explained why *he* was. Someone had to show judgment.

She *should* be eager. This was, theoretically, a rescue mission. Nessus kept his pessimism to himself.

Distorted and curdled starlight rushed at him and vanished, replaced by . . . nothing. Vertigo washed over him. Nessus braced himself against the nearest bulkhead and sought meaning in the amplified hologram display.

Trisha said, "It shows in the mass pointer. Its magnetic field is enormous. It's unmistakable on deep radar. And here"—she poked a hand into the center of the projection—"nothing."

Beside her, a crash couch creaked as Raul Miller shifted his considerable bulk. "Just wait," he said. A tiny circle of light flashed and disappeared. Seconds later a second halo flickered.

Trisha was delighted. "See? Gravity lensing as stars pass directly behind it. We're still not seeing *it*. It's eerie, I tell you. Don't you agree, Nessus?"

Nessus was a label of convenience. His real name was only reproducible by paired throats or a wind ensemble. Unaware he was in listening range (why reveal how acute his hearing truly was?), Trisha had once described his name as an industrial accident set to waltz time.

That was no worse, Nessus supposed, than what humans called all his race: Puppeteers.

"I sense nothing supernatural here," Nessus said, choosing his words with caution. He did everything with caution. "Scary, I'll grant you."

That got the chuckle Nessus knew it would. Puppeteers were widely seen as cowards—which, essentially, was why this ship flew with a human crew.

Alas, Nessus thought, I'm just crazy enough to be assigned to lead them.

KNOWLEDGE IS POWER. On that all intelligent species concurred.

Species differed on how best to acquire knowledge. Among Nessus' kind, it was agreed that exploration was madness. It could not be otherwise, when to leave home world and herd was insanity.

Hence these humans.

Trial and error had shown humans made excellent explorers. Humans didn't know about the experiments, of course. Nessus had no intention of revealing them. He didn't dare. No Puppeteer would.

The invisible *it* they distantly orbited was a recently discovered neutron star, designated BVS-1. Like every neutron star, BVS-1 was the extremely compressed remains of a supernova. Implosion had crushed the stellar slag, more massive than many a normal star, into a sphere just 17 kilometers in diameter. Its own gravity kept it that small. A film of ordinary matter coated a slightly thicker layer of free-ranging subatomic particles, which covered—no one knew what, exactly. That inner orb approached the density of an atomic nucleus. Physicists called the core material neutronium or neutron-degenerate matter. Engineers called it unobtainium. Both argued heatedly about its properties.

Most neutron stars shouted their presence across

light-years, transforming cosmic dust and gas into cataclysmic X-ray blasts or gamma-ray bursts. But it wasn't radiation that kept explorers away from neutron stars and a close look at the mysterious neutronium. It was those in-spiraling clouds of dust and gas themselves, accelerated to relativistic speeds as they were sucked in. No matter how impervious the hull, the pummeling would be fatal to instruments or crew.

And then there was BVS-1, cold and dark, its presence recently revealed by a gravitational anomaly.

BVS-1 had long ago devoured its accretion disc and ceased to pulse. Its surface temperature, scarcely warmer than empty space itself, implied it had been a neutron star for at least a billion years. That made it approachable—

Or so the theory went.

THEY CIRCLED BVS-1 at the presumed safe distance of two million kilometers. Nessus tried not to dwell on that presumption. Peter and Sonya Laskin had monitored BVS-1 for days from a closer orbit, reporting regularly by hyperwave radio, before swooping in for a close look.

The *Hal Clement* had not been heard from since.

"Any signs of them?" Nessus asked. His calm tone was a lie. Every instinct demanded that he flee—if not from the astronomical enigma, then at least from the unpredictable humans. He wanted to lock himself into his cabin, to curl into a ball, his heads tucked tightly inside, and hide from the universe.

Trisha shook her head. "No response to our broadcasts. Nothing on radar."

"Could be interference," Raul said hopefully. "Or simple equipment breakdown."

True, the Laskins' comm gear might have failed. That didn't explain the lack of a radar sighting. "Keep trying," Nessus ordered. He fought the urge to pluck at his already-disheveled mane. Something had gone badly wrong here.

This was why his people didn't explore.

Raul broke the lengthening silence, his manner apologetic. "Still nothing."

Nessus settled astraddle the Y-shaped padded bench that was his post on the bridge. With his lip nodes, far nimbler than human fingers, he operated a human computer console. The Laskins' planned course was as he remembered. Their hyperbolic plunge would have them skim within two kilometers of BVS-1's mysterious surface. If their autopilot had erred only slightly and they had somehow impacted . . .

If he could contemplate *that* malfunction, why not others? Nessus contemplated the planned hairpin turn, the ship hurled back into space. It had been days since the Laskins went missing. "What if the autopilot didn't resume orbit after the dive? How far would they coast?"

Trisha plopped onto an empty crash couch. Her body blocked whatever she did with her console. "I'll expand our radar search."

She found the ship adrift, millions of kilometers from where they had searched. It did not answer hails. Raul brought them alongside.

Through his view port, Nessus studied the *Hal Clement.* It had a ferocious spin. Why had the Laskins spun up their ship like that?

"We can't board for a look while it's spinning," Nessus said. "Any ideas?"

Raul rubbed his chin. "Nessus, are the landing struts on the other ship steel? Ours are."

Nessus retrieved the specs. "Steel, yes."

"Then we use our magnetic docking couplers for drag. Like all our equipment, the couplers are way overengineered. We slow the *Hal Clement*'s spin while our attitude thrusters keep us at a safe distance."

There were several bursts of keyboarding, and then

Raul slapped the console in frustration. "Tanj! It's going to take a while."

Of course their systems were overengineered. Nessus would not otherwise have set hoof aboard. "Proceed," he said.

And so Raul managed the braking pulses, adjusting the pulse rate as spin bled away. Trisha and the nav computer muttered to each other. Nessus . . . fretted.

Until—

Trisha whistled. "*That's* why they're spinning and so far off-course. The rotation of a massive object—tiny though it is, BVS-1 outmasses Sol—warps nearby space. I ran the numbers and it comes down to this. The spin the *Hal Clement* picked up and the kink from its planned trajectory show BVS-1 rotates about every two and a half minutes."

"Interesting," Nessus said atonally. In truth, he couldn't imagine how knowing the spin of the neutron star could possibly matter. If his kind had any curiosity, though, they'd probably be as foolishly brave as these humans.

All that interested Nessus at that moment was the still silent ship. It had finally slowed down enough for meaningful observation—and cautious boarding. Its landing struts looked *odd* somehow. That had to be in his imagination. Peter and Sonya could not possibly have landed. If they had, they could not have launched.

Trisha and Nessus checked Raul's suit gauges twice before allowing him into the air lock. Their comm link checked out. So did his helmet cam. Holding a gas pistol, Raul jetted the few meters to the derelict. A dimple of curdled sky, where gravity bent even starlight, showed the general location of BVS-1.

Something was terribly wrong. Nessus could tell Trisha felt it, too. She leaned forward anxiously as Raul disappeared into the air lock of the Laskins' ship.

"Nessus, Trish, are you there?" Raul's camera relayed the inner hatch of the air lock. They watched his gloved finger stretch toward the controls. Status lamps flashed. The hatch began to cycle. "Life-support systems all register nominal."

"We're here," Nessus said. "I suggest you keep your suit sealed anyway."

"Will do," Raul said.

Nessus watched the inner hatch open. Raul and camera moved inward, panned along a corridor, turned a corner—

The next thing Nessus saw, as his heads whipped uncontrollably to a point of safety between his front legs, was the underside of his belly.

• 4 •

Sigmund sat alone at a small table in the packed ship's lounge. Beyond his left elbow lay a coat of blue paint, a supposedly impregnable hull, and an unknowable amount of . . . he didn't know what.

No one did.

The good thing about hyperspace was hyperdrive. Hyperdrive travel corresponded, in normal space, to a light-year every three days. The bad thing about hyperspace was no one knew what it was. Every so often, a hyperdrive ship disappeared. Scientists declaimed learnedly that the pilot must have flown too close to a mathematical singularity, the warping of space near a stellar mass.

What happened in such cases was unclear. Perhaps the errant ship fell down a wormhole, only to emerge unreachably, incommunicably, far, far away. Perhaps the ship became trapped forever in hyperspace. Or, just maybe, the ship ceased to exist. The math was ambiguous.

Compared to the less-than-nothingness centimeters away, odd scents and strange constellations were inconsequential. Sigmund yearned for a world. Any world.

He took more comfort from the beer in his drink bulb than in General Products Corporation's assurances about indestructible-hull technology. Invulnerability hardly sufficed when his whole ship could disappear.

General Products being a Puppeteer company, and Puppeteers being Puppeteers, little was known about the hull material beyond its truly impressive warranty. Die because of a GP hull failure and your heirs would become very rich.

Well, not *his* heirs. Sigmund had none. He expected none. He didn't take it personally—the Fertility Board felt that way about all natural paranoids. Truth be told, 18 billion people on Earth were several billion too many. He couldn't fault the board for preferring sane progeny.

That didn't mean he liked it. He sucked on his beer bulb, hunting for happier thoughts.

The sudden collapse of Nakamura Lines meant ships everywhere were filled to capacity. Every stateroom aboard was taken. Passengers stood three deep at the small bar. Only Sigmund and a battle-scarred Kzin had tables to themselves. Even the Jinxians shared their tiny tables.

Jinxians: *That* wasn't a happy thought, but Sigmund tried to keep his expression neutral.

Jinx was the human-colonized moon, marginally habitable, of a gas-giant planet orbiting Sirius A. The surface gravity on Jinx was 1.78 standard. Living there *shaped* a person. Jinxians were built like boulders, short and squat, with arms as thick as Sigmund's legs, and legs like old tree trunks.

Why would anyone live there? Raise families there? Flatlanders and spacers alike chalked it up to Jinxian craziness.

Not Sigmund. Jinx was the kind of world on which to raise an army of supermen.

A waiter came by, insinuating himself with admirable grace through milling crowds and between full tables.

Sigmund accepted a fresh beer bulb while the opportunity presented itself, but his dark thoughts remained fixed on Jinx.

Not even supermen could threaten Earth—not without first defeating Earth's vastly larger fleets. Hence, the unsubstantiated certainty that had set Sigmund onto this trip. Where better for the Jinxians to seek technological superiority than in that world's immodestly named Institute of Knowledge?

The institute's sprawling museum and vast public data banks suggested openness, but much of its research remained "proprietary" to its scientists. That secrecy seemed not to bother people. Why would it, what with the institute being a public, not-for-profit organization? A myriad of endowments, corporate sponsorships, academic alliances, and government grants funded its operations.

Sigmund took a long sip of beer, and resisted the urge to smile. He'd once been one hell of a forensic financial analyst. And so, on Jinx, he'd mined the public record.

He had not braved hyperspace and alien worlds for nothing.

Most of the institute's academic alliances were with government-run Jinxian universities. Much of the corporate sponsorship came from businesses holding Jinxian government contracts. The endowments came from the Jinxian elites, with countless ties to current and retired officials.

Money laundering was money laundering.

With a mind of its own, Sigmund's left hand crept to his stomach. Autodocs only removed physical scars.

Passengers kept wandering in and out of the lounge. The ratcat bared his teeth when anyone approached him. Sigmund's scowl was a pale substitute. He wasn't surprised when a shadow fell across his table.

"Mind if I join you?"

Sigmund looked up to a willowy blonde with twinkling green eyes. Earth willowy, not Belter skeletal. Her voice had a throaty quality. She eyed him frankly.

He pointed to an empty seat. "Help yourself."

She sat. "I'm Pamela," she said. "I've never met a Wunderlander."

"Sigmund." He stroked the beard he'd grown for the trip. More than a home world, the beard implied a station in life. The beard's most prominent feature was a waxed spike sprouting from the right side of his jaw. Close-cropped stubble covered the rest of his chin. He had dyed his whiskers snow-white to contrast with his black suit. "Ah, the beard. Funny story, that."

A funny style, as well. Its singular "virtue" was the absurd amount of time required for its maintenance. On Wunderland, the human-settled planet orbiting Alpha Centauri A, asymmetric beards were all the rage among the idle rich. Pamela probably thought he was from one of the Nineteen Families of original settlers—parasites all.

"I'd love to hear it." Pamela smiled at the returning waiter. "Vurguuz."

Vurguuz was a Wunderland concoction. Sigmund had tried it. Once. Years ago. He remembered a fist to the solar plexus and a minty-sweet aftertaste.

So Pamela wanted to impress him. . . .

"An interesting choice," he said. "It makes my story even droller." He said no more until her order arrived and she took a squeeze. Her eyes grew round.

Sigmund handed her his spare beer. She sucked the bulb dry in one convulsive swig. "I'm from Earth," Sigmund said. "I just liked the exotic look. Wunderland is the final stop on my grand tour. When in Rome, and all that." Jinx was neither the first nor the last stop on his itinerary, neither the shortest nor the longest stopover, the better to disguise his interest. He signaled for two more beers.

"That *is* funny." Pamela coughed, her eyes tearing. "Two flatlanders. Still, I like the beard."

The best disguises are simple, Sigmund thought. Across Human Space, most people disdained the Wunderlander aristos. At home, revolutionaries fought to overthrow them. Only an oblivious buffoon would travel aping one.

Who'd ever suspect him of being an ARM on a covert mission?

The brazen twinkle had returned to Pamela's eyes. She laid a warm hand on Sigmund's arm. "Sigmund, tell me about your grand tour."

Starships offered few diversions. Drinking shipboard was expensive. The obvious alternative for consenting adults was free. Sigmund couldn't imagine perky little Pamela matching the athletic send-off Feather had given him—nor that Feather would expect him to abstain. He patted Pamela's hand. "It's so crowded here. Perhaps we could adjourn—"

Pamela was looking past him. The whole lounge had fallen silent. Glancing over his shoulder, Sigmund saw the ship's captain approaching. Sigmund had taken his turn at the captain's dinner table. It was hard to see the genial host chatting up his first-class customers in the grim-faced man now approaching.

"Ausfaller?" the captain said.

"Yes." Sigmund's reflexive thought was of the Kzin passenger. There had been six Man-Kzin Wars. Why not a seventh? ARM HQ might expect him to take custody of the alien.

"Come with me, sir."

Sigmund followed the captain to the liner's bridge. And once Sigmund had decoded the priority hyperwave radio message from ARM HQ, he felt like he'd had the vurguuz.

· 5 ·

Arching one neck, the Puppeteer accepted the proffered ID. It set the disc on its desk and began a thorough examination. Apart from the few padded, backless benches and the oval desk, the office suited We Made It norms. The wall holos all showed scenes of human worlds.

The mundane decor didn't surprise Sigmund. Puppeteers didn't give clues about their worlds—never a name or description, much less a location or representation.

He trusted the aliens as little as they trusted him.

Sigmund had never met a Puppeteer in person until today. The flunkies and functionaries had passed him along, one to the next, and now to this latest one, almost too fast to form impressions. What had struck him was how everyone in the outer offices appeared to have assumed a humanized name. Satyrs and centaurs, fates and furies, heroes and muses . . . when time permitted, he intended to ponder the aliens' evident fascination with human myths.

This one, Sigmund decided, was a decision maker. Standing, it matched Sigmund's height. That was the only similarity.

The Puppeteer stood on two forelegs set far apart and one complexly jointed hind leg. Two long and flexible necks emerged from between its muscular shoulders. Each flat, triangular head had an ear, an eye, and a mouth whose tongue and knobbed lips also served as a hand. Its leathery skin was off-white with patches of tan. Its elaborately coiffed and ornamented brown mane covered the bony braincase between those sinuous necks.

Apparently Sigmund's ID passed inspection. "You

are quite far from home, Mr. Ausfaller. I do not understand the United Nations interest." Like the Puppeteers in the outer office, it spoke perfect Interworld in a startling contralto.

It? Puppeteer genders were as mysterious as their origins. Despite their feminine voices, all were addressed as he. "Might I ask your name?" Sigmund asked.

Heads turned; for a moment, the Puppeteer looked himself in the eyes.

The mannerism meant nothing to Sigmund. Nor did its aural accompaniment, like a large glass window shattering in slow motion.

"More relevant is my responsibility within General Products Corporation. In human terms, I am the regional president here on We Made it."

If the Puppeteer chose not to offer a name, Sigmund did not mind assigning one. Broken Glass seemed the obvious choice, but for the many demigods in the outer office.

Sigmund's work and personality alike demanded attention to detail, and he'd noted many subtle distinctions among the aliens. Black, brown, and green eyes. Variations in height and build. Dissimilar skin patterns, in patches of brown, tan, and white.

The *big* disparity was in manes. Passing from worker to worker—up the corporate ladder?—mane styles became ever more elaborate. Like the aristo Wunderlander beards, an elaborate mane style denoted social status. This boss Puppeteer, Sigmund decided, his mane resplendent, will be Adonis.

"Again, Mr. Ausfaller, I do not understand UN interest."

You conniving weasel, Sigmund thought. Perhaps one new human spaceship in 20 *isn't* built in an exorbitantly priced General Products hull, reliant on claims of invulnerability.

Adonis stepped out from behind his melted-looking desk. He gave a wide berth to the row of human chairs, and the "dangerous" edges on their legs. To show Sigmund the exit?

Sigmund said, "It has come to our attention that a Sol system citizen died recently in a GP-supported experiment." Not that there were Sol system citizenships, but it sounded plausible, and Peter Laskin had been a Belter.

"Ah, the Laskins." The Puppeteer lightly pawed the floor with one forehoof. "I'm now doubly surprised. Their ship was only very recently recovered. A tragedy, to be sure."

Other ARMs had studied Puppeteers. Pawing the floor was believed to be a flight reflex.

Hyperwave radio was a wonderful thing. It was instantaneous where it worked: everywhere except deep within gravity wells. Comm buoys in the comet belts of all settled solar systems converted between radio waves and laser beams for intrasystem messaging and hyperwaves for interstellar messaging.

The ARM placed a *very* high priority on infiltrating General Products. Did Adonis suspect? How surprised would he be to know Raul Miller secretly worked for the ARM? That while piloting the salvaged *Hal Clement* home from BVS-1 Miller reported back to Earth?

Thereafter, it made perfect sense that ARM HQ had notified Sigmund, already en route from Jinx to We Made It. Both Laskins held research grants from the Institute of Knowledge.

"Very tragic," Sigmund agreed. He ignored Adonis' implied question. "But their deaths are only a part of our concern. What most interests me is how they died inside one of General Products' supposedly impregnable hulls."

THE PUPPETEER PROFESSED bafflement.

His idiom and accent were flawless. Sigmund did not doubt the Puppeteer's acting skills. "Show me the ship," Sigmund demanded.

"Why not." The Puppeteer looked himself in the eyes again. "We also want to understand what happened. If you can explain, so much the better. Come with me."

Adonis had a transfer booth in his office. They stepped through. Outside the destination booth, a spaceship rested on its side. It was about one hundred meters long and pointed at both ends. General Products sold only four hull versions; this was the #2 model. One end was painted, the rest left transparent, just as it—as all GP hulls—had been delivered.

Then Sigmund made the mistake of looking up.

We Made It was among the most inhospitable of the human-settled worlds. Summers and winters, the surface winds approached 250 kilometers per hour. The colonists built underground.

Hotels catering to the tourist trade had gravity generators. Elsewhere there was no ignoring the paltry gravity, a mere six-tenths gee, or the Belter-gangly natives, but Sigmund could—and did—stay indoors.

This wasn't a hangar.

He stood on a ground-level roof. The ship was the only structure of any kind. Featureless desert stretched to the horizon in every direction. Although it was spring, he couldn't see even the smallest speck of greenery—seasonal winds scoured the land clean of life. In a too-bright sky, above the blazing, too-blue sun, hung the piercing red spark that was Procyon B.

His heart pounded. His hands shook. Sigmund told himself the crawling on his skin was only the arid desert air.

Eyes cast down, he strode toward the ship. Its hull was transparent, but massive apparatuses inside cast long shadows. He stopped for a closer look in a comforting pool of shade beneath the stern.

Things appeared—wrong. The landing shocks were bent. Panels and equipment looked like they had melted and been forced aft under tremendous pressure.

A gust of wind flapped Sigmund's trousers. Dust and

gravel spattered off the hull. The breeze smelled—wrong. He hurried into the air lock.

He was in the main crew quarters when Adonis joined him. Something had torn loose the acceleration couches and sent them crashing into the ship's nose. Instruments and chairs alike had crumpled. Walls, decks, ceiling—everything toward the bow—were thickly spattered in something brown.

Sigmund knew the answer before he asked. "These brown splashes?"

"That," said the Puppeteer, "is the Laskins."

ALIEN SKY SUDDENLY didn't feel like a problem. Gulping, Sigmund walked back to the air lock. He and Adonis cycled through.

In the windbreak under the hull, Sigmund demanded, "What did that?"

The Puppeteer plucked at his mane. "Are you familiar with BVS-1?"

"No," Sigmund lied. Until recently, the statement would have been true. Since Raul Miller's relayed message, though, Sigmund had read everything on the subject that he could find.

"An old, dead neutron star, scarcely a light-year away, recently discovered by the Institute of Knowledge. They wished to study it up close, but lacked funding. We offered them a suitable ship, with the usual guarantees, if they shared their findings."

Having died, the Laskins weren't sharing.

The Puppeteer was suddenly at a loss for words. Bit by bit, Sigmund coaxed out the story. Nothing contradicted the report from Miller: Prepping the *Hal Clement* on We Made It, because Peter Laskin, a Belter, refused to set foot on Jinx. The short flight to BVS-1. The initial, unremarkable observations from a distance, reported by hyperwave. The suspension-become-cessation of communications for the dive into the singularity. Whatever the Laskins learned, lost. The rescue turned salvage mission.

GP hulls were supposedly indestructible. Nothing got through but visible light—customers painted any parts they wanted opaque. And if it was learned that mysterious forces could kill right through the hulls? Sigmund understood Adonis' dilemma. General Products might be ruined.

Not his problem.

This was: Suppose the Institute of Knowledge suspected this vulnerability. Suppose the so-called research project was somehow a test of a Jinxian weapon. He imagined death rays that penetrated the hulls of Earth's fleet, impregnable no more.

"What did this?" Sigmund hissed.

"We do not know." More pawing at the ground. "As you can imagine, we very much desire an explanation. As you might also imagine, no one, for any amount of money, will repeat the Laskins' voyage."

Didn't know? Sigmund refused to accept that.

To believe what little they disclosed about themselves, Puppeteers were herbivores and herd animals. To those who felt kindly toward them, the Puppeteers were supremely cautious. Everyone else called the aliens cowards—and Puppeteers took that as a compliment.

They nonetheless sold supposedly impregnable hulls to other races. Those sales *might* reflect unshakable confidence that their worlds would never be revealed. It seemed far more likely they had secret ways to disable any of their own hulls turned against them.

Wind whipped around the hull and clutched at Sigmund's clothes. The feeble pull of this world seemed unequal to the task of holding him down. Stubbornly, Sigmund denied his fear.

Whether or not Adonis truly sought answers, he must cooperate fully with an ARM investigation. Anything less would show General Products already understood the undisclosed vulnerability—and sold the hulls regardless.

Something about Sigmund's flight to We Made It prodded his subconscious. Pamela? Vurguuz?

Overcrowding. "Have you asked pilots laid off by Nakamura Lines?"

"Among others," Adonis said. "All have declined. Their reticence, however problematical, is logical. Assuring their silence thereafter has cost us a small fortune."

Once more, Sigmund pictured an enemy fleet equipped with whatever slaughtered the Laskins without harm to their ship's hull. Jinxians. Kzinti. Belters. The adversary hardly mattered. What was intolerable was Earth's sudden exposure.

The ARM had resources Puppeteers did not. "If I find a volunteer, I trust you'll provide us a ship on the same terms you offered the Jinxians."

It wasn't a question, because Adonis had no choice.

• 6 •

Sigmund had his pilot, although to call Beowulf Shaeffer a volunteer was a stretch.

At Sigmund's insistence, General Products made Shaeffer the same offer 11 pilots had earlier rejected. Shaeffer made that an even dozen.

And then Shaeffer, too, discovered he had no choice.

Sigmund had selected Shaeffer by data mining the financial records of out-of-work pilots. On Earth, Sigmund would have completed such a search in minutes. Here on We Made It, it could have been done almost as quickly with a bit of hacking. Instead, he obtained access from the local authorities. Professional courtesy (although not total candor).

Interstellar cruise lines paid their pilots well, and

Shaeffer chose to maintain his standard of living after the Nakamura Lines folded. Now, months later, Shaeffer was mired in debt. Despite the artfulness with which he fudged his loan applications, rolled old debts over into new loans, and dribbled out partial payments to his creditors, the moment of financial truth loomed.

A million stars or debtor's prison—that was the offer Sigmund had advised Adonis to extend.

For two weeks, Sigmund had kept watch from a discreet distance. Shaeffer spent his days here in the GP building, supervising the Puppeteer engineers configuring a new #2 hull to his specifications. He'd named his ship *Skydiver.* Tomorrow, Shaeffer left.

I had no choice, Sigmund told himself. If not Shaeffer, then whom?

Sigmund had followed Shaeffer into the GP tavern. Its clientele were mostly Puppeteers. The barroom chatter sounded like dueling orchestras warming up.

Shaeffer grew up on We Made It. He stood well over two meters tall, merely average here. He massed about 70 kilos, scrawny by Earth standards but stocky for a local. Commercial spaceships generally maintained artificial gravity at a standard gee; Shaeffer must have worked out to handle the gravity aboard his own ship. Like many on this planet of mole people, he was an albino.

One other thing about Shaeffer—he had a mind of his own.

And so Sigmund kept postponing this conversation. It was better that Shaeffer maintain his illusion of free will.

Sigmund crossed the bar. Without asking, he sat at Shaeffer's table. Shaeffer's face froze, and he shoved back his chair and stood.

"Sit down, Mr. Shaeffer," Sigmund said.

"Why?"

Sigmund offered his ARM badge. Shaeffer tilted the disc this way and that. From the time he devoted to the task, he was stalling. "My name is Sigmund Ausfaller. I wish to say a few words concerning your assignment on behalf of General Products."

Shaeffer stayed.

"A record of your verbal contract was sent to us as a matter of course," Sigmund said. That sounded better than: I set you up. "I noticed some peculiar things about it. Mr. Shaeffer, will you really take such a risk for only five hundred thousand stars?"

"I'm getting twice that."

"But you only keep half of it. The rest goes to pay debts. Then there are taxes. . . . But never mind. What occurred to me was that a spaceship is a spaceship, and yours is very well armed and has powerful legs." The planned armaments had struck Sigmund as soon as Adonis passed along Shaeffer's specs. Without knowing what had killed the Laskins, weapons made sense. But defense wasn't the only explanation. "An admirable fighting ship, if you were moved to sell it."

"But it isn't mine."

"There are those who would not ask. On Canyon, for example. Or"—Sigmund theatrically stroked the spike of his beard—"the Isolationist party of Wunderland."

Shaeffer said nothing, but metaphorical wheels turned behind those spooky red eyes. No doubt about it—he'd thought of running.

Unacceptable. Earth was in danger; it needed a pilot. Sigmund pressed on. "Or you might be planning a career of piracy. A risky business, piracy, and I don't take the notion seriously." The hell he didn't.

"What I would like to say is this, Mr. Shaeffer. A single entrepreneur, if he were sufficiently dishonest, could do terrible damage to the reputation of all human beings everywhere. Most species find it necessary to police the ethics of their own members, and we are no exception. It occurred to me that you might not take your ship to the neutron star at all, that you would take it elsewhere and sell it. The Puppeteers do not make invulnerable war vessels. They are pacifists. Your *Skydiver* is unique."

More lies, of course. Planetary governments outfitted GP hulls as warships all the time. *Skydiver* was unique nonetheless—a warship about to be released into the control of a single civilian. Judging by his run-up of debt, Shaeffer didn't mind cutting a few corners. . . .

In the cause of Earth's defense, neither did Sigmund. "Hence, I have asked General Products to allow me to install a remote-control bomb in *Skydiver.* Since it is inside the hull, the hull cannot protect you. I had it installed this afternoon.

"Now, notice! If you have not reported within a week, I will set off the bomb. There are several worlds within a week's hyperspace flight of here, but all recognize the dominion of Earth. If you flee, you must leave your ship within a week, so I hardly think you will land on a nonhabitable world. Clear?"

Shaeffer stiffened. After a long while he said, softly, "Clear."

"If I am wrong, you may take a lie-detector test and prove it. Then you may punch me in the nose, and I will apologize handsomely."

Shaeffer shook his head.

Feeling only twinges of guilt, Sigmund stood and walked from the bar.

• 7 •

Through surveillance cameras, Sigmund watched Shaeffer float between sleeping plates. He wasn't sleeping. Shaeffer's hands and face were flaming red and blistered. Whether from sunburn—how, from a cold, dead star, eluded Sigmund—or other reasons, his newly returned pilot was obviously in pain.

The man belonged in an autodoc, or at least pumped full of painkiller. This once, Adonis refused Sigmund's demands. "Answers, first," the Puppeteer said. Turning his back on Sigmund, Adonis cantered next door into the sickroom.

Shaeffer looked up. "What can get through a General Products hull?"

"I hoped you would tell me." The room lacked Puppeteer furniture. Adonis leaned back on his single hind leg, looking ill at ease.

"And so I will. Gravity."

"Do not play with me, Beowulf Shaeffer. This matter is vital."

"I'm not playing," Shaeffer said. "Does your world have a moon?"

"That information is classified," Adonis replied. Any other answer would have shocked Sigmund.

Shaeffer's shrug became a wince. "Do you know what happens when a moon gets too close to its primary?"

"It falls apart."

"Why?"

"I do not know," Adonis said. Nor, for that matter, did Sigmund.

"Tides."

"What is a tide?" the Puppeteer asked.

Sigmund started. A very interesting piece of data had just fallen into his lap.

It seemed Shaeffer had gotten it, too. He was quiet for a long time. "I'm going to try to tell you. The Earth's moon is almost thirty-five hundred kilometers in diameter and does not rotate with respect to Earth. I want you to pick two rocks on the moon, one at the point nearest the Earth, one at the point farthest away."

"Very well," Adonis said.

"Now, isn't it obvious that if those rocks were left to themselves, they'd fall away from each other? They're in two different orbits, mind you, concentric orbits, one almost thirty-five hundred kilometers outside the other.

Yet those rocks are forced to move at the same orbital speed."

"The one outside is moving faster."

"Good point," Shaeffer acknowledged. "So there is a force trying to pull the moon apart. Gravity holds it together. Bring the moon close enough to Earth and those two rocks would simply float away."

"I see. Then this 'tide' tried to pull your ship apart. It was powerful enough in the lifesystem of the institute ship to pull the acceleration chairs out of their mounts."

"And to crush a human being. Picture it. The ship's nose was just a few kilometers from the center of BVS-1. The tail was a hundred meters farther out. Left to themselves, they'd have gone in completely different orbits. My head and feet tried to do the same thing when I got close enough."

Sigmund's mind flashed to the recovered video from cameras hidden aboard *Skydiver,* video hastily scanned as GP personnel settled Shaeffer in next door.

Water bulbs, clipboards, voice recorder, all the loose paraphernalia on the bridge, shifting and vibrating as though with minds of their own. The panicked look on Shaeffer's face as understanding struck. His doomed attempts to pull out of the ship's hyperbolic plunge. His mad scramble up the main access tube to the ship's center of gravity, where tidal effects would be almost nil. Shaeffer spread-eagled, his spider-like limbs atremble, pressing against the smooth sides of the access tube. Slipping, slipping . . .

Starlight blazing brighter and brighter through the transparent hull as the ship plummeted toward the neutron star: gravitational lensing. Hah! *That* was the cause of the sunburn.

In the vacated cabin, those same water bulbs, clipboards, voice recorder now, one by one, hurtling into the bow. The impregnable hull ringing like a gong with each blow. Acceleration couches ripping loose to follow, each collision tolling like a great cathedral bell.

Shaeffer slipping, slipping, a muscle tremor away from plummeting half the ship's length—splat!—to join them.

But Shaeffer had only almost been torn loose, torn apart, to be daubed like paint across the ship's bow. *That's* why Shaeffer was in such pain.

Sigmund shook his head, his thoughts churning. Guilt? Certainly! But also exultation! Tides were no weapon. Jinx could hardly threaten Earth's fleets with a neutron star, and any gravity generator must surely crush itself before attaining such field strength.

Adonis had remained on his script. "We have deposited the residue of your pay with the Bank of We Made It. One Sigmund Ausfaller, human, has frozen the account until your taxes are computed."

"Figures," Shaeffer said.

If Adonis understood his pilot's disgusted look, the Puppeteer kept it to himself. "If you will talk to reporters now, explaining what happened to the institute ship, we will pay you ten thousand stars. We will pay cash so that you may use it immediately. It is urgent. There have been rumors."

"Bring 'em in." As though in an afterthought, Shaeffer said, "I can also tell them that your world is moonless. That should be good for a footnote somewhere."

"I do not understand." But two long necks had recoiled, and the Puppeteer clearly fought not to paw the sickroom floor.

"You'd know what a tide was if you had a moon. You couldn't avoid it."

"Would you be interested in—," Adonis began.

"A million stars? I'd be fascinated." Shaeffer beamed beatifically. "I'll even sign a contract if it states what we're hiding. How do you like being blackmailed for a change?"

In the seclusion of the surveillance room, Sigmund felt his guilt had been assuaged just a bit.

THE THRONGS ABOARD the Earth-bound ship rivaled the worst Sigmund had encountered. For once, the crowding didn't faze him. He rubbed his chin, smooth shaven again, and counted the days until home.

The lounge was jammed. He bellied up to the bar. All things come to he who waits. Bored beauties. Cold beer.

And answers. . . .

Crushing debt was the essential reason Sigmund had picked Beowulf Shaeffer. All those obligations left the out-of-work pilot subject to manipulation. But debt was not the only reason.

The rumors Adonis feared were rumors no longer. The Laskins' deaths were common knowledge, and one press conference was not enough. General Products needed a very public—and demonstrably independent—explanation. They needed people to feel safe in a GP hull.

And Sigmund . . . *he* needed a full account as well. He wanted all the details, including the ones you didn't volunteer to the ARM who coerced you into a suicide mission.

Hence, in the hopes his pilot would survive whatever had killed the Laskins, Sigmund had a second criterion for picking Shaeffer.

In person, Shaeffer was slick enough. He oozed an easy charm Sigmund could only envy. But old school records showed plainly: *Writing* made Beowulf freeze. Make the message formal and the man couldn't string two words together.

The hero of the hour went straight from his press conference to the autodoc to writer's block. He'd already been paid by General Products for the article. He had to write *something.*

"Your order, sir?"

Sigmund looked up. A Jinxian bartender waited to do his bidding. Sigmund named a microbrewery beer he'd grown fond of on We Made It.

If you knew to look for it—and Sigmund did—the anonymous ad revealed its desperate author.

Wouldn't Beowulf be astonished to know Sigmund was the true employer of the very detail-oriented ghost-writer so quick to respond to Bey's ad?

INTO THIN SPACE

EARTH DATE: 2645

· 8 ·

General Products Tower loomed over greater Los Angeles. From Nessus' vantage on its park-like rooftop terrace, arcologies and office buildings stretched in every direction as far as the eye could see. City lights bleached the stars from the night sky. On the streets and walkways far below, unseen human multitudes teemed. Most of them, just as most like Nessus, could never bear to leave their home world.

The superficial resemblance to home made Nessus miss Hearth all the more.

He didn't actually see those alien myriads eight hundred stories beneath his hooves. He wasn't about to approach the terrace's edge, despite its chest-high parapet.

His heads swiveled inward, and Nessus looked himself in the eyes: an ironic laugh. He had once approached a *neutron star.* He'd come orders of magnitude closer to it than any other of his kind.

There was an important difference, of course. He'd run *that* risk for a reason.

Recovering the *Hal Clement* wasn't like staring into a kilometers-deep abyss for "fun." And though the BVS-1 mission had failed to rise to Nike's personal attention, someone in Clandestine Directorate had taken notice. It had earned Nessus reassignment to Earth. Perhaps here, with his expanded responsibilities, he'd have the opportunity to reap Nike's trust. . . .

A two-throated warble ended Nessus' reverie. He pivoted. He had company.

"Beyond this point be monsters." Puck theatrically craned a neck as though to peer over the distant parapet. He'd entered Human Space more than a century ago, among the first. He knew the idioms. "Also, in the main lobby."

The breeze riffled Nessus' aide's yellow-and-brown mane and tangled his decorative ribbons. Nessus said, "Then my callers have arrived?"

"Right," Puck said. He untwisted a few ribbons with a mouth. "Shall I tell them you're briefly delayed?"

"Escort them to the cargo-floater lab. I'll join you there."

Puck cantered to the nearest transfer booth. Nessus took a moment longer to absorb the droning murmur of the city. Earth in its entirety bore a population less than some cities on Hearth, and yet humans had spread across many solar systems. They were an insane and ambitious people. It was best to remember that.

He stepped through the transfer booth into the lab, brushing flanks companionably with technicians as he made his way to where Puck and two humans stood beside a grounded cargo floater. They looked up at the clicking of his hooves. Nessus read the insignia—Procurement Division, if the emblems could be trusted—and name badges on their ARM uniforms. "Colonel Kim. Major Robles. I am Nessus. How may I help you?"

Kim was a tall, big-boned man with large ears and a broad forehead. He extended a hand in greeting, and then reclaimed it with an embarrassed look on his face. "Habit. You're in business development, Nessus. Is that correct?"

"Correct," Nessus agreed. *Business development* sounded so much more innocuous than *threat assessment*.

Or *spy*.

THE CARGO FLOATER hovered half a meter above the lab floor. It did not as much as quiver as water sloshed back and forth in the open tank on its deck. More water arced in from the fat hose bucking in Robles's hands. Beads of spray dotted his hair, face, and shirt. "I don't believe it," Robles muttered to himself.

A payload as simple as water. The clear plasteel box whose inside dimensions Robles had measured when empty. As water filled the tank, to know the growing load weight was basic math.

"A recent upgrade," Nessus said modestly.

He had studied human nature during his years on We Made It, and more in his short time here on Earth. Release an improved cargo floater to the commercial market, he had promised, and the ARM will beat a path to General Products' door. So it had come to pass. Not after the first product upgrade, nor the second, nor the third—

And then ARM Research Labs requested an appointment. They would very much like a demonstration of General Products' latest floater products.

"Impressive," Kim said. "The load capacity, of course, but more so the real-time control. I haven't seen a bit of wobble. GP will sell a *lot* of those." He took out a pocket comp and called up a holo filled with text. "I'm interested in adapting it for naval use."

"Naval use?" How would humans expect a confused Puppeteer to act? General Products sold ship hulls. They didn't sell cabin gravity control. Nessus settled for a quizzical inflection. "Oh, I see. Cabin gravity to offset acceleration." He read aloud in his best puzzled tones, " 'Dynamic response. Power efficiency. Form factor. Field uniformity?' "

As Kim scrolled through his long list of specs, Nessus struggled not to wriggle his lip nodes in delight. Learn the limits of cabin gravity and you knew the crew constraints on flight performance.

ARM Research Labs had extrapolated capabilities from cargo-floater gravity control to cabin gravity control. Nessus wasn't technical; he left it to General

Products' specialists to reverse-engineer the process. He understood what was important.

The ARM's formula, applied to the specs of the newest export-model floater, implied cabin-gravity improvements beyond the present, very secret, naval standard. That was why these men were here. The specs of the previous model had generated no ARM interest.

Between those limits, "business development" had just nicely bracketed a key parameter of ARM naval capability.

Nessus' lips again struggled to wriggle. After some days of delay to feign interest, he'd reluctantly tell Colonel Kim that the GP engineers couldn't build to these specifi—

Wall speakers trilled, pitched far above human audible range. The chords summoned everyone to the main auditorium for an announcement by the regional president. Grace notes indicated urgency rather than emergency.

"I'll check," Puck offered in the same voice register. "Excuse me," he added for the humans' benefit. He joined the engineers and technicians suddenly queuing for the lab's transfer booths.

"They're going to a departmental meeting," Nessus dissembled. "Please continue."

"Would General Products be interested in adopting its floater technology"—Kim gestured at the cargo carrier, its man-tall tank nearly full—"to shipboard use? The ARM would pay well for exclusivity."

"I'm in marketing. Of course I'll say we're interested," Nessus said. He paused for Kim's chuckle. "Our engineers will need to review the requirements." Lab security cameras had captured Kim's holo, of course, but the underlying records would add details.

Water now lapped the top of the tank, ripples going over the edges and down the sides. Robles twisted the nozzle shut. He wiped spray from his face with a sleeve, still muttering his disbelief.

Puck and the last of the techs had vanished. The alert tones finally stopped. What was happening?

"You'll want to talk alone about the demo." Nessus led his visitors to an empty alcove where they could consult about how best to transfer the technical specs. He withdrew to a polite distance. The illusion of privacy would let them activate discreetly whatever antieavesdropping devices they carried.

Puck finally returned through the transfer booth. Looking relieved to find Nessus alone, he trotted over. His usually neat mane was disheveled. He managed to look himself in the eyes and paw the floor at the same time.

The day must inevitably come when humans understood Citizen speech. Had the ARMs carried bugs? *He* would have. Nessus dipped a head into a pocket of his utility belt to activate a jammer. "Puck, what's going on?"

"I have good news and bad news," Puck said. He tugged at one of the few ribbons left in his mane. "The good news is, we're going home."

Home! That was excellent news! Images of Nike popped unbidden into Nessus' mind's eye. Still, it made no sense. Didn't General Products—didn't Clandestine Directorate—need a presence on the main human world?

How bad could the bad news be? Surely not BVS-1 bad, and he'd survived that. And Puck was *here*, not curled into a ball in the main auditorium.

"And the bad news?" Nessus prompted.

With a shudder, Puck shook the remaining hints of order from his usually meticulously coiffed mane. "The bad news is, the galaxy is dying."

· 9 ·

Earth had been at peace too long.

Sigmund stood and stretched, thoroughly bored. When he'd signed up four years ago, ARMs were expected to dope down—or, for naturals like him, dope up—on weekends. Paranoia at work, sanity at play. For six months now, the policy had extended to *all* time off. They waived the rule while you stayed in ARM facilities.

No one wanted to yo-yo daily.

He shared the off-duty lounge this evening with Feather, a very foul-tempered Conan Murphy, and a pinch-faced newbie named Andrea Girard. The newbie snored softly on the couch. Murphy and Feather watched soccer, the vid sound turned low.

Murphy was always in a foul mood. Maybe it was his assignment. The Kdatlyno *looked* scary, a bit like scaly, wingless dragons, but they *loved* humans. They'd been Kzinti slaves until humans freed their worlds during the Second Man-Kzin War. You watched the Kdatlyno because this was the Bureau of Alien Affairs and they were aliens. Not even the most dedicated paranoid had ever found cause for worry about them.

Sleeping Beauty had been assigned to watching Puppeteers. You could tell she still saw them as sock puppets selling pricy toys. For all Sigmund knew, she was right—he just didn't believe it. Puppeteers were secretive. They had tech far beyond humans and Kzinti. They didn't mind being called Puppeteers, for tanj sake.

And he'd never gotten over the feeling Adonis had pulled one over on him back on We Made It.

He'd rather be working.

Sigmund had been killing time online in a massively

multiplayer quest game. His ranking tonight stank, but that might soon change. For motivation he'd overridden the other players' avatar choices. In his holo views, from now on, the wizards and treasure hunters would appear as Kzinti and Jinxians. Never mind that he watched Jinxians for a living. He watched Kzinti, too, but unofficially. ARM higher-ups doubted his objectivity.

Maybe someone botched a play. "Futz this," Feather announced. She caught Sigmund's eye and then glanced at the door to the small sleeping area. Sigmund and sleeping area. Sigmund and sleeping area.

Feather had never mastered subtlety. She hadn't ever tried. "What about Murphy?" Sigmund mouthed. Murphy, oblivious, kept watching his vid.

"You're such a prude," she said loudly. "Murphy, can I borrow your body for a while? Sigmund won't play."

Sigmund sighed, embarrassed. "I've reconsidered."

Murphy ignored them both.

Sigmund let her tow him into the nap nook. It didn't matter that *he* was quiet, and he imagined Murphy and the awakened newbie exchanging grins. After, floating between the sleeper plates, Sigmund said, "You and Murphy?"

"Or the new girl, if you men both fail me." Feather laughed. "You're actually jealous."

"No, I'm actually paranoid." He loved being able to say that aloud. And maybe he was jealous, too, although he knew Feather was yanking his chain. It was time to change the subject. "Things seem quiet tonight."

"Every night." She raked her fingers through her hair, tonight emerald green with silver sparkles. It went with her mint green skin dye job. She favored colors as much as he avoided them. "We're all fossils. Eventually even Kzinti know when they're defeated."

Feather would know. She kept an eye on the ratcats.

She was trembling! Feather, who could rip a limb from a Kzin with her bare hands. Sigmund pecked her bare shoulder, just above where the contraceptive crystal was implanted. They both knew where ARMs got redirected when things got slow.

"I know," he said softly.

"I *hate* mother hunts!" Feather burst out. "Those poor, scared women."

Desperate for a baby. Desperate enough to hide for months while their contraceptive implants dissolved. Desperate enough to forfeit their own lives if caught with an unlicensed child.

"I know." What else could he say? He put an arm around her.

Enforcing the Fertility Laws meant mother hunts, parental executions, and sterilization of the unlicensed offspring. Not enforcing the laws would mean utter chaos. You needed more than good genes to get a birthright license from the Fertility Board. You needed persistence. For a short while, he'd once read, Earth's population appeared to stabilize. During that period, the people without an aching need for children voluntarily thinned their ranks. After a lull, after the ambivalent, like the space-eager, had withdrawn themselves from the gene pool, Earth's population had exploded with a vengeance.

Unchecked, today's 18 billion could double in a generation.

"I want a child," Feather whispered. "I need a child."

They were both natural paranoids. The Fertility Board had never—ever—licensed a child to a paranoid parent. He kissed the nape of her neck. "I know."

THE SQUAD ROOM was as relaxed as Sigmund had left it after his last shift. People moseyed, or sat with their feet on their desks, or shot the breeze.

Boredom is the sworn enemy of vigilance. He sifted through the latest intel, surveillance of recently arrived visiting Jinxians. He saw only business meetings and a club-wrecking night on the town. He skimmed recent publication abstracts from the Institute of Knowledge. He ordered a statistical survey of Jinxian emigration patterns.

Newbie was also back on-shift, lazily painting her fingernails. She hadn't spent enough time in Alien Affairs to earn her boredom. He strolled over. "What are the Puppeteers up to, Girard?"

She fanned a hand, fingers spread, the wet polish gleaming. "Not a thing."

"How do you know?" Sigmund asked. She seemed far too relaxed. Calibrating meds was an art. The right dose for training wasn't necessarily the right dose on the job.

Andrea Girard swung her feet from her desk. Maybe she'd gotten the message. "Honest, Sigmund, I'm doing my job. Look." She twiddled with her comp, and a graphic appeared. "Transfer-booth usage by Puppeteers. I watch North America, but I've asked around. The pattern's the same, down, worldwide. The Puppeteers are in their office buildings, minding their own business."

Sigmund's lips twitched at her little joke. The Puppeteers did nothing *but* business. General Products had a presence in Known Space. Of the Puppeteer government, or governments, humans, Kzinti, and Kdatlyno alike knew the same: nothing. "How long have they been doing whatever they're doing?" he asked.

"It's been quiet for days," she said.

Days of unexplained new behavior? Girard's meds definitely needed a tweak. "Who have you informed?" he demanded. She named names, and Sigmund couldn't argue, so he turned back to her holo. "The transfer-booth traffic looks about normal at the main spaceports."

"Meeting incoming ships? They're importers, Sigmund." She blew on her fingernails. "Don't you have Jinxians to watch?"

Behind him, people sniggered. Was no one working today? Sigmund suddenly knew it wasn't only Newbie whose meds were too low. The 'docs had been dialed down. Without any threats on the horizon, why manufacture paranoia?

That's just what Earth's enemies *wanted* the ARM to think.

Maybe mother hunts weren't the worst thing.

He kept studying the holo, ignoring the squad-room laughter. "Mojave Spaceport has a lull in visitors. Why is that?"

A hand came down heavily on his shoulder. Conan Murphy said, "Give it a rest, Sigmund. Let the woman do her job."

Sigmund returned to his desk. The Jinxians had done nothing suspicious in the minutes he'd been gone. (Lying low, like the Puppeteers? In conspiracy with the Puppeteers?)

He leapt from his chair. To anyone in the room who might be listening, he explained, "Puppeteers are cowards. Who or what are they avoiding?"

No one answered—and no one laughed. He perched on a corner of Newbie's desk. "Andrea, you say the Puppeteers are all in GP buildings. Now tell me what they're doing."

She couldn't.

From what did Earth's Puppeteers hide? Sigmund surfed the Net, looking for inspiration. Riots after the World Cup semifinals. A teleportation-system malfunction in Phoenix, some kind of a data-collection problem. The ongoing corruption scandal in the Beijing city council. Starving mountain lions had attacked a hiker camped on Mount Shasta. Celebrity gossip.

"What's the extent of the transfer-booth outage?" Sigmund asked. Others had silently gathered to watch. Someone reached past him to call up a map. A blotchy area ebbed and flowed, amoeba-like: the time-lapse view of the service disruption. Sporadically, a pseudopod reached out to graze Mojave Spaceport.

Mojave was the only spaceport Puppeteers seemed to be avoiding. Because, cowards that they were, they shunned the area affected by the outage?

Things aren't always what they seem. Were Puppeteers gathering in GP buildings? Were they avoiding Mojave Spaceport?

A sick conviction seized Sigmund. A data-collection malfunction needn't mean the system couldn't work. It was a billing problem—and, by extension, a problem with tracking people's movements. Or Puppeteers' movements. "Any unusual flight activity at Mojave in the last few days?"

General Products had long stored an unsold colony ship at Mojave. Like all modern colony ships, it used GP's largest-model hull. Sigmund had seen #4s, and they were monsters, spheres a good third of a kilometer in diameter. A ship like that would carry a *lot* of Puppeteers. Every Puppeteer on Earth, perhaps? Boarded unseen through transfer booths?

The colony ship had taken off yesterday.

When inspectors began reporting back that GP buildings around the planet were empty, Sigmund wasn't at all surprised.

MURMURS AND MUTTERS, intense whispers and heartfelt cussing, purposefully quick footsteps—all the sounds of a major investigation. Fear and dread gnawed at Sigmund's gut.

He found the time to smile at Feather. They wouldn't be sent on a mother hunt anytime soon.

· 10 ·

The vastness commonly referred to as Known Space encompassed an approximate sphere of about 60 light-years in diameter.

To apply that description, *known,* took breathtaking hubris. Few solar systems in that enormous volume had ever been surveyed, much less settled. The gulfs between stars were, since the advent of hyperdrive, circumvented rather than traversed. Most of "Known Space" remained defiantly *un*known—including, in a timely example, the location, presumably somewhere in the region, of the Puppeteer world or worlds.

To our ignorance, Sigmund mused, we can add a new mystery. All the Puppeteers who once visited the settled worlds of Known Space—worlds of all races, not only humans—had vanished. No one could say to where.

Jinx, abruptly, was no longer Sigmund's designated worry. As the reports trickled in, sometimes unsolicited, as often triggered by Earth's frantic hyperwave queries, ARM HQ had decreed the need for a special task force to investigate the Puppeteer disappearances.

And they had named Sigmund to direct it.

He'd reported as ordered to HQ in New York. His new office was barren, as ascetic as his black suit. He set the walls to window mode, and gazed out over Manhattan. Freighters clogged the harbor. Cargo planes filled the skies over the bustling megalopolis. It seemed normal, and yet—

A few klicks to the south, amid the tallest of Manhattan's office towers, the biggest stock market in Sol system was imploding.

Sun glinted from the kilometers-tall spires of the financial community. People said that once you reached terminal velocity, the final seconds before impact were peaceful. No one could tell Sigmund how they knew that.

That wasn't a constructive train of thought. He blanked the walls again, wondering where to start. Three-Vs droned in neighboring offices.

Across Known Space, slow-motion catastrophe unfolded. General Products had wiped out three races' hull-production industries—and now GP was gone. Rebuilding the lost construction capacity would be the labor of years.

Economic crisis began with starship builders and interstellar cruise lines. It spread to their subcontractors and investors. And to all their employees, of course. Then to clothing stores, restaurants, realtors, utilities . . .

Soon enough, the pain would spread worlds wide.

In a sudden cascade, the 3-V murmurings blended into a louder and louder roar: news bots tuning in a breaking story. Sigmund had yet to download his preferences to the new office comp. He stuck his head into the hall. He couldn't quite place the voice on the newscast.

"Come in, Ausfaller," a neighbor said. She was a petite Eurasian woman with too many facial piercings and a fondness for blue.

Samantha? Selena? Sangeeta? Sigmund had met two dozen people that morning. At this point, he couldn't remember anyone's name. He nodded.

Some astronomical phenomenon occupied the holo. A nebula perhaps, but painfully bright and speckled with black.

"Will you look at those radiation readings," Sangeeta(?) said. "It's like the inside of a solar flare, and the ship is still thousands of light-years away from it. And listen to the cabin ventilation fans whine."

Away from it. Away from what? Sigmund wondered. The voice he couldn't quite place continued. ". . . Chain reaction of supernova events, long ago. Those dark motes are stars. They look black because they block the much hotter and brighter light streaming from behind."

The corner logo read, in an ornate logo, JBC. The Jinx Broadcasting Company. Sigmund knew it well, long tracked by hyperwave. Was this a science show? An educational simulation? Why would something like that trigger significance filters here in ARM HQ?

"We're fortunate to live a good twenty thousand light-years away. We wouldn't even know, except for this truly amazing vessel." A GP #4 hull replaced the glowing patch. At this small scale, machinery filled every bit of the transparent hull. "It embodies an experimental Puppeteer hyperdrive, capable of nearly a light-year every minute. I've returned the ship and made my report to General Products, my employers. Now I'm free to tell all of you."

A light-year per minute! Sigmund was trying to grasp *that* when the crawler restarted at the bottom of the holo. The crawler began, "Galactic core explosion revealed!"

The galactic core had exploded?

Twenty thousand light-years. Had the Puppeteers fled a danger at least twenty thousand years into the future? And the JBC exclusive . . . why the connection with Jinx?

The crawler inched along. "Only on JBC! Coming next: our exclusive interview with the pilot." The holo cut to the pilot, the man whose voice was so familiar. His face was, too: a lean, pointy-chinned albino.

Sigmund shook with fear. Puppeteers. Jinx. And now—

The pilot was Beowulf Shaeffer.

• 11 •

Flee from danger. Gather for protection.

Pawing the floor, Nessus struggled to defy eons of instinct. In the days since the report of the core explosion, Citizens had evacuated Earth, as they had evacuated every other GP outpost. They sped, as fast as the escape vessels could carry them, to Hearth. There to flee again. . . .

Here on Earth *he* must remain, unable to gather or flee.

Nessus hid in one anonymous ship among hundreds on the tarmac at Outback Spaceport. Prying eyes could not see him through the paint that coated the interior of the impregnable hull. The air-lock hatch was fake, bonded to a seamless hull. Access was possible only by transfer booth—and then only if he chose to reconnect the booth to power. His fuel tanks held tritium and deuterium to capacity. Anyone calling would reach only the liveried butler persona to which his uncustomized human comm system defaulted. Given reserves, recycling, and synthesizers, he had air, water, and food more or less indefinitely.

Duty required him to stay. Logic called him safe.

Instinct demanded that he launch immediately and rejoin the herd, and if returning was impossible, to roll himself into a tight little ball of denial.

Instinct be damned. With a shudder of defiance, Nessus placed a call.

THE WAR ROOM hummed. Sigmund got names wrong half the time, and that was progress. He'd gotten Feather assigned to him, because she was good, and Andrea Girard so she could learn something. The rest of the task force were supposedly experts in Puppeteers or General Products technology or both; so far, he had only an ARM computer's word for it.

Surmises lined the display walls, outnumbered by the open questions. Facts, beyond confirmations of the Puppeteers' disappearance, were scarce. Holos flashed over desks. Comms trilled, chittered, and hummed. Knots of conversation formed and broke apart. Occasionally, the ventilation fans emerged from the din. They failed miserably at removing the smells of too many people. In a corner of the war room, two hulking strangers cowered before Feather's wrath. Whatever task they had failed to perform to her satisfaction they would do better the next time. Feather was *not* someone you wanted angry at you.

Above everything hung an aura of dread.

Feather finished administering her tongue-lashing. As she headed his way, Sigmund's pocket comp buzzed with the tooth-rattling buzz that meant he really needed to take the call. His AI assistant did the filtering.

"You should take this, Sigmund," Medusa said. Snakes on her animated head hissed and coiled. His callers didn't face a green-skinned gorgon, of course. They saw a primly coiffed woman named Georgia. "It's a Puppeteer."

Sigmund groaned. Since the United Nations had announced his task force, calls had streamed in by the thousands. All nutcases and cons of one sort or another, claiming to know the whereabouts of Puppeteers—or to *be* a Puppeteer. Every call had to be checked out—but not by *him*. At least the "Puppeteers" with booming basso voices could be disregarded. "I'm sure it's a wonderful simulation, Medusa. Add it to the queue."

"Bear with me." Hiss. "Your caller said he met you on We Made It. The date checks out. And 'he' has a voice Feather would kill for."

Feather reached Sigmund's side. He ushered her to his office and shut the door.

Medusa transferred the call to desktop comm, tracking him through the security cameras. "He said his name is Nessus." Hiss. "It's a known Puppeteer name. It first appears in the *Hal Clement* records. That file has no images of him. The name 'Nessus' pops up regularly in our files for the past three years. The most recent instance is an ARM procurement visit to GP days before the disappearances. There's surveillance imagery from that meeting, and the skin-tone patterns match your caller."

Feather asked, "What's the call trace say?"

Hissssss. "We can trace to Canaveral Spaceport. Triangulation from comm towers only tells us the area of the field. The call could come from any of dozens of vessels. That's showing caution enough that I presume the call originates elsewhere."

Sigmund knew the drill: cascaded anonymizer relays, using accounts opened with many-times-laundered funds. A Puppeteer in hiding would be that cautious. So would a knowledgeable impersonator.

"Most or all of them GP hulls, I presume," Feather said. Medusa did not correct her.

Sigmund found himself pacing. It made sense. If a Puppeteer remained on Earth and chose to reveal himself, inside a GP hull was the safest place to be. But the very Puppeteer who had recovered the derelict at BVS-1? Sigmund shivered. "Put Nessus through."

In an instant, a Puppeteer replaced Medusa—and the new image above the desk might have no more physical basis than the old. To animate an avatar was simple enough.

"Mr. Ausfaller," the Puppeteer said. "You look different without the beard."

That Wunderlander beard! He'd forgotten all about it. He had started growing it on the trip out and taken it off before arriving home. "You say we've met, Nessus."

"A slight exaggeration to get past your AIde," Nessus

said. "We passed each other many times in the General Products building. We were never introduced."

Sigmund floated a trial balloon. "I mostly worked with GP's regional president for We Made It."

Nessus made noises like glass breaking. "He was well above me in the company."

"One moment." Sigmund tapped the mute and blind buttons. "I did have a beard on We Made It. And the Puppeteer I worked with had a name like that. This could be real."

"Assume it is," Feather said. "What does he want?"

"Let's find out." Sigmund unfroze the call. "It seemed all Puppeteers left rather abruptly last week. Now you called. I have to wonder why."

The Puppeteer took a one-head-high, one-head-low stance. The better to watch for danger? "I called, Sigmund Ausfaller, because you represent the UN's response to our Exodus.

"I wish to arrange a private consultation with you."

TINY SPYBOTS COVERED Sigmund; many more lined his pockets. Video, audio, global positioning, environmental—if something could be monitored and recorded in a compact manner, he carried sensors for it. He expected them to be jammed, but occasionally life dealt a pleasant surprise. Better to try and fail than to forever wonder.

"You don't need to do this," Feather said again. She smacked the transfer booth. "Step into a GP hull and you'll get out only if Nessus permits it."

Sigmund hardly needed help finding reasons to worry. "Every Puppeteer in Known Space has withdrawn or gone into hiding. It may well involve a danger to Earth. I can't imagine it's all been done so Nessus could harm me personally." The funny thing was, he meant it. ARM training *had* refocused his paranoia. Before he could have second thoughts, he pressed the transmit button.

The glow panel in the destination booth switched off faster than he could exit. He was trapped! He stepped into what was clearly a cargo hold aboard a spaceship.

He had long marveled how expressions survived the centuries. *A house divided against itself cannot stand. Catch-22. My brother's keeper. Run out of steam.* An overcrowded Earth had long ago eliminated cemeteries, and Sigmund had never seen one—

But suddenly, his skin crawling, he knew what it must mean to whistle past the graveyard.

His heart pounded. At ARM HQ it was easy to say the Puppeteers probably weren't after him personally. It was still him personally here inside an impregnable spaceship, trapped and at the uncertain mercy of a hidden Puppeteer. He remembered Astyanax's knife. . . .

A second transfer booth faced the one Sigmund had just vacated. As he watched, its interior lights activated. An opaque glob masked the address display; he couldn't budge the dried glue, or whatever it was, to read where this booth would send him. He walked in and pressed transmit.

Once more: A booth went dark. Dead.

Behind a transparent partition—GP hull material?—a Puppeteer waited. His skin was cream colored, with a few scattered tan patches. He was one of the scruffier ones Sigmund had ever seen, with little of the mane ornamentation that appeared to denote status. Strikingly, one eye was red, the other yellow. "Nessus, I presume."

"Correct, Mr. Ausfaller. Thank you for coming." The Puppeteer pointed with a briefly straightened neck: a chair. "Please make yourself comfortable." The chair, the remotely deactivated transfer booth, and a standard synthesizer were the only furnishings.

"What if I brought a laser pistol?" In truth, he'd considered it. Any wall he could see through a laser pistol would shoot through—even hull material passed visible light. "Or am I talking to another holo, with all this staging to make me believe otherwise?"

Nessus quivered. "I'm quite real, I assure you. No doubt you carry comm gear. Please take a moment to satisfy yourself it's been jammed.

"Although a scanner in the first ship revealed no weapons, you might have fooled it. If so, before you shoot anyone, consider that only I can reactivate your transfer booth. It is the single way out for you and whatever you hope to learn."

Sigmund got a drink bulb of cold water from the synthesizer and sat. "I'm here to listen, no more. Why did you want to see me?"

MENTION OF A laser pistol made Nessus tremble. If he had kept any order to his mane, he'd have plucked it out now. "You have shown good faith in coming, Mr. Ausfaller."

But for the departed snowy beard, Ausfaller was much as Nessus remembered. Short, middle-aged, and moonfaced. A bit thicker through the middle than four years earlier. He wore his hair natural: black, thick, and wavy. He still dressed in black, all the starker for his pale, undyed skin. An unimpressive specimen—until you saw those dark, dark eyes. Ausfaller's gaze was intense. Piercing.

Unnerving.

"I regret we did not get to know one another on We Made It," Nessus said. "It might make this conversation easier."

Ausfaller shifted his drink bulb from hand to hand. "The Puppeteer I dealt with, the regional president, wanted to keep things between us. I can't begin to reproduce his name, but he had the most elaborate mane in the place. I thought of him as Adonis."

Adonis? Nessus struggled to control his lips. This

was no time for laughter. And if anyone on Earth studied Citizen mannerisms, it would be ARMs. "My apologies, Mr. Ausfaller. Most of us at General Products take human-pronounceable names." So did many Citizens who would not dream of setting hoof off Hearth. Human pseudonyms were quite the popular affectation back home, within the Experimentalist party, at least.

Nessus' onetime boss had such a pseudonym: Achilles. All scouts were crazy, of course, but it took a particular insanity to assume the name of a legendary human warrior. At least Achilles had had the wisdom not to offer *that* name to an ARM. But Adonis? His mane was garish, a fashion nightmare. Then again, what did Citizen scouts, much less humans, know of proper mane styling?

Not that fashion gaffes mattered. Nessus was increasingly of the opinion that all mane ornamentation was a pointless, time-wasting pretension. There was nothing like the coming end of everything to put things into perspective.

Ausfaller squirmed in his chair. "Adonis' real fake name doesn't concern me, Nessus, unless he's on Earth."

"I'll get to the point," Nessus said. "And no, he's not. You are doubtless aware of the recent discovery regarding the galactic core. As many have surmised, General Products personnel have returned home because of that news."

Ausfaller leaned forward. "Why was the recall done in secrecy? Why so hastily? The radiation won't arrive for twenty thousand years."

Flee from danger. Gather for protection. How could it be otherwise? Long before intelligence emerged, those without these instincts died in the mouths of predators. "What one thing does everyone on Earth know about Puppeteers?"

"That you're cowards." Ausfaller took a long swallow from his drink bulb. "No offense."

Nessus said, "I'm not offended. We consider ourselves prudent. Among us, cowardice is a virtue." He paused to synth a beverage, busying his heads when they yearned to pluck the tousled mess that was his mane. Human food lacked nutritional value for him, but warm carrot juice soothed him nonetheless. "We run from danger. We don't wait."

Sigmund considered. "So everyone else went home immediately. How is home, wherever that is, any safer?"

A head defied Nessus' will, plunging to twist and pull at an errant tress. He brought the head back up. "You misunderstand. We must flee the galaxy."

"And hang the consequences to the rest of us."

Hang? Maybe Puck would have understood the metaphor. *The rest of us* was clear enough. "We verge on the purpose of this meeting. Unavoidably, General Products' departure impacts human worlds. It impacts Kzinti worlds, too, although that may concern you less."

"Impact?" Ausfaller snapped. "That's quite the understatement. You were connected enough to ascertain my role and track me down. You must also have seen on the Net what havoc GP's disappearance continues to cause. When I last checked, millions had lost their jobs. A hundred billion stars or more have already evaporated from Sol system's stock markets."

The human was right, but so what? It changed nothing. "We can avoid danger, so we do. You have my regrets, if it matters."

"It matters not at all." Ausfaller's cheek pulsed. "Nor do I believe you arranged a meeting to extend futile apologies."

"I didn't," Nessus said. "My people avoid perils, however remote. ARMs worry about perils, no matter how improbable. Are we so different?"

Ausfaller smiled. "But paranoia isn't normal. Usually, it's treated."

The smile lacked humor, and hostile undertones lurked beneath *treated.* Nessus acknowledged a more personal similarity: Neither of us belongs.

He ignored the pang of empathy. "You wonder if General Products intentionally caused this panic. Maybe you think we hope to exploit the situation. That isn't the case, Mr. Ausfaller. Having left the region, we have no use for human assets."

"I'll try again. Why did you ask to see me?" Ausfaller's tic throbbed.

"Our reputation concerns us, Mr. Ausfaller. We want the United Nations to know we intend to honor our commitments. Various transactions remain to complete. Our many business relationships will require disentanglement."

"And alone among all Puppeteers, you've been picked to stay behind and handle this. Nessus, why sneak away? Why meet even now in secrecy?"

"Because other humans must feel as you do." Nessus pawed at the floor, the motion blocked from Ausfaller's view by a desk. "In the interest of stability, would the UN have interfered with GP's departure if it could? You're thinking that we could have met at your office. Tell me, Sigmund. Would I have been allowed thereafter to leave?"

"So you've been left behind to clean up GP's messes, all to protect the good name of Puppeteers," Ausfaller said. "That's your story."

He hadn't responded to Nessus' questions. That was answer enough.

Hearth's hidden location was its first and main defense. Nessus could not divulge, or be made to divulge, its coordinates. *No* Citizen left Hearth without deep-rooted, autonomic conditioning that would stop his hearts first. Now, in crisis, all Citizens must move—and in flight, surely their risk of discovery swelled.

How Nessus yearned to hide beneath his own belly!

"Protecting our good name is my job, Mr. Ausfaller. Someday, in the distant future, your descendants and mine might meet in a safer neighborhood."

The ARM stood, frowning for reasons that eluded Nessus. "Who are you really, Nessus?"

"I'm with the Warranty Department." It sounded better than a human term Puck had suggested: *rear guard.*

And much, much better than *expendable.*

• 12 •

Carlos Wu was dark and slender, with straight black hair. Curiosity danced around his eyes, and a trace of whimsy.

He seems normal enough, Sigmund thought. Carlos didn't look like someone the Fertility Board had awarded an unlimited parenting license. At age 18, tanj it! There *ain't* no futzy justice! "Thank you for coming, Dr. Wu."

"Just Carlos."

"Then I'm Sigmund." He laced his fingers. "You're probably wondering why I asked you in."

"I'm not often asked to ARM HQ," Carlos answered.

"This doesn't happen often, either." Sigmund called up a holo of the core explosion. "Assuming it has happened."

"So that's why I'm here." Carlos tipped his chair back against the wall. "Oh, it's happened, Sigmund. I've studied the data extensively."

Sigmund couldn't decide whether to be impressed or annoyed. ARM interest nonplussed most people. Even astrophysicists. Until the infamous broadcast from Jinx, Sigmund had gone his entire life without meeting any. "So the report holds up."

"Oh yes." A very toothy smile. "Quite fascinating, really. In twenty thousand years, we'll want to be elsewhere."

Sigmund found it difficult to care—and more difficult not to dislike Wu. How many billion descendants would this genius have by then? "Nearer-term events concern me, Carlos. We're in a deep recession. The economists tell me the Puppeteer Exodus caused it."

The staff exo-psychologists accepted everything Nessus had told him. They said Puppeteers would flee from the supernovae, repercussions to any other species be damned. Market crashes. Recessions. So what?

With a thud, Carlos righted his chair. "Ah. It would be reassuring to know why GP vanished. General Products must be very wealthy. If their purpose were nefarious, they'd have liquidated their assets before disappearing, maybe sold the market short."

Short selling was rather remote from astrophysics. Finance and accounting were Sigmund's fields, but Wu had no way to know that.

Carlos mistook silence for confusion. "Shorting a stock is a bet on its decline. You borrow and sell shares, planning to return shares bought later at a lower price. If Puppeteers *meant* to cause a market panic, they should have shorted a lot of stock."

Rather remote from astrophysics. Also, very perceptive. Sigmund began to like Wu. "We've looked. GP left its assets here, and there's no evidence of short selling."

"Then back to physics, Sigmund. The reported measurements and the instrument calibrations all check out. I assume my peers have told you the same."

Peers. Did Wu *have* peers? "No one I spoke to was supposed to reveal their consultation."

Carlos chuckled. "No one did. I assumed there were others."

Smart-ass.

If the core explosion was real, then the Exodus was, too. There'd be no reason for Puppeteers to try bottom-fishing Earthly stock markets. Sigmund said, "I'd prefer to independently confirm the observations."

"Me, too," Carlos said. "Not me, personally, but

someone. Without the advanced hyperdrive, it's impossible."

"And if we don't have it?" Sigmund asked.

Carlos smiled. "Until then, I'm afraid, you'll have to trust me."

DINERS CHATTED AT antique iron tables arrayed across an uneven redbrick patio. Horse-drawn carriages, cloppedy-clop, made their way down the cobblestone street that fronted the marina bistro. Waves lapped against the shore and rocked the yachts at anchor. Seagulls wheeled overhead.

Night was falling, but Sigmund had teleported in from California. Despite the aromas of peppers, curries, and ginger wafting from the kitchen, he wasn't ready for dinner. He sipped his piña colada, waiting, remembering a time before transfer booths. Since teleportation, nothing but prices stood between tourist hordes and beautiful little Caribbean islands like this. The 20-star drink in his hand didn't faze him. He could afford it. What *did* irk Sigmund was that his companion, now merrily devouring a fresh-caught lobster on Sigmund's tab, couldn't possibly know that.

Ander Smittarasheed was an off-the-books source. He wanted confidentiality and was entitled to it; they never met in an ARM office. Ander had picked both St. Croix and one of the most exclusive eateries on it. Ander's petty greed often correlated with the quality of his findings. Sigmund hoped today was such an occasion.

Finally, Ander set down his fork and belched. He was massive, a weight lifter. Muscle rippled beneath his pink-and-purple bodysuit. The fabric put the sunset to shame, but it fit right in among the diners. "Excellent, Sigmund. You should have joined me. Perhaps you'll reconsider for dessert."

"Perhaps. How was your trip?" Sigmund prompted.

"Interesting." Iron scraping on brick, Ander pulled his chair closer. "Fascinating fellow, young Shaeffer. Quite the sightseer."

"From the beginning, please," Sigmund said.

"Right. I took transport to Jinx. I found Beowulf there, basking in the adulation of the public. The masses usually came to him, though. He likes the gravity control of the finer hotels."

Jinxian gravity was three times that of We Made It. Sigmund tried to picture it. Jinxians short and stout like fireplugs. Shaeffer tall and gaunt. "The adoring women could have snapped him like a twig."

Ander laughed. "His sex life was the one thing I didn't ask about. Here's the short version. Beowulf has a weakness for the finer things. However generously the Puppeteers paid him off four years ago, he seemed determined to burn through it."

A speedboat roaring up to the pier made conversation impossible. Birds screeched their protests. Buoys clanged, softer and softer as the wake dissipated. After a while, Ander said, "So, Sigmund. Four years ago on We Made It, you heard what Bey heard. What did the Puppeteers pay for your silence?"

"Nothing." Sigmund knew Ander wouldn't believe that. It wasn't just that Sigmund hardly needed the money. If he had extorted a bribe, Adonis would have had leverage over him by threat of exposure.

And somehow Sigmund always knew: If anyone anywhere were ever to be caught for corruption, it would be him.

None of which Sigmund had any intention of sharing. "I told him, 'General Products will have to owe me one.' "

"All right then." Ander laughed cynically. "Back to the free-spending Mr. Shaeffer. He was *delighted* to run into me. The Puppeteers probably no longer care whether Bey ever scripts a docudrama of his voyage to the galactic core. Jinx Broadcasting Company is another story. Heh. Shaeffer thumbed an exclusive contract with JBC before he ever set out for the core. *JBC* still wants its show, and their execs were holding his feet to the fire.

"Having told no one I'd ghostwritten the story of his pass past a neutron star, he was running out of ways to stall." Ander drained his mai tai, and began flapping the miniature cocktail umbrella. "It pays to have a distinctive writing style."

Sigmund motioned for a fresh round. Slowly he coaxed out details. Shaeffer with wanderlust and money burning a hole in his pocket. Winding up on Jinx. The inquiry from General Products, to fly an experimental craft. "Ander, did the Puppeteers suspect something like the core explosion?"

"Bey doesn't believe so. The Puppeteer honcho described it as a publicity stunt, something to bring in investors. GP wanted help defraying the cost of miniaturizing the new drive."

In the JBC vid, the ship had looked crammed. "What's the ship like?"

Ander shrugged. "It was long gone when I reached Jinx. Maybe a Puppeteer pilot stayed behind after the Exodus. Someone took off with it as soon as Bey vacated."

Nessus had stayed behind on Earth, unseen. Why not another Puppeteer, on Jinx?

The sky grew dark. Sigmund motioned for another round to keep Ander talking.

Ander had been away for weeks; he had much to report. No one but human custodians in the GP building. A long talk with an astrophysicist in the Institute of Knowledge, a Dr. Julian Forward. Forward repeated what Earth's scientists said: The data Shaeffer brought back with him were self-consistent and without anomaly. The observations didn't in every respect match existing theory, but, according to Forward, "reality is sometimes stubbornly like that."

"My man Bey doesn't much like the execs at General Products," Ander continued. "Funny as hell listening to Beowulf talking about them. The regional president on Jinx was—"

"Why Jinx?" Sigmund interrupted. He could no longer hold back the question. "Why did this expedition launch from Jinx?"

"The short answer: I don't know. Shaeffer doesn't know." Ander scratched his long nose, considering. "Beowulf was told the GP shipyard on Jinx had idle capacity when it was needed. The Puppeteers weren't eager to fly an experimental vessel, so the new drive was assembled in Human Space, counting on getting a human test pilot. Bey assumes GP approached him because he happened to be there and was in corporate files from the BVS-1 incident."

"Purely hearsay and speculation."

"For sure," Ander said cheerfully. "You know, all this talking makes a man hungry. I'm told the crème brûlée here is excellent."

Churning mind. Roiling stomach. "Not for me, but go ahead." Sigmund waited for the waiter to take and return with Ander's order. "So perhaps the choice of Jinx has meaning. How can we know?"

Ander tore into his dessert, leaving Sigmund alone again with his thoughts. Truthfully, he saw no reason for Puppeteers to conspire with Jinxians. Or Beowulf to conspire with either.

Shaeffer fit in—somehow. Of that, Sigmund was certain. But *he* had picked Shaeffer back on We Made It. What was he missing now? "Might the mission to the core have flown from Jinx simply because that's where Shaeffer happened to be?"

"Maybe. A ship that can go to the core goes across Known Space in no time flat." Ander blotted his lips with his napkin. "With absolutely no data to back me up, I bet you're right. I know about Beowulf's blackmail scam because you told me, but there's no hint he ever told anyone. He certainly said nothing to me when I ghostwrote the BVS-1 saga. Since Puppeteers consider blackmail a normal business practice, GP probably considers him reliable."

They finally left the café, Ander a noticeably wealthier man than when he entered. Sigmund walked Ander to a transfer booth, then settled onto one of the benches at the end of an old wooden dock.

He stared out to sea. The waves shattered the moon's reflection into a million pieces. An enormous jigsaw puzzle, it taunted him.

Like Puppeteers, Jinxians, and Beowulf Shaeffer. . . .

MOST UNUSUAL

EARTH DATE: 2645

• 13 •

A sharp tap-tap made Sigmund look up. Andrea Girard, grinning, stood just outside his office.

He wondered why she was so pleased with herself. "Come in. What have you got?"

"Surprise!" Andrea said. She shut the door behind herself and sat. "Beowulf Shaeffer is here on Earth."

Sigmund felt gut-punched. "How? When?"

Andrea, oblivious, cracked her knuckles. "He arrived on a commercial liner from Jinx a week ago last Thursday. The passenger manifest listed Shaffner, comma, B. Wolf. The name-correlation software at Customs didn't recognize that as a person of interest. My AIde just flagged it."

She held up her pocket comp, projecting a surveillance shot. A shock of snow-white hair leapt from the image, on a head that jutted high above the crowd. Red eyes glared from a tanned face. "Outback Spaceport. Feature matching says that's your buddy, at better than ninety-nine percent confidence. He's apparently using tannin pills, not necessarily as a disguise. He would need those just to go outside."

That was Shaeffer, all right. "Barely enough of a name change not to trigger our entry protocols," Sigmund said. Also, plausibly deniable as an honest mistake. It sounded too subtle for Shaeffer. "Jinxian connivance?"

Andrea shook her head. "What do Jinxians know of Old English epic poems? My grandma always says, 'Never attribute to malice what can be as easily attributed to stupidity.' "

Sigmund guessed her grandma wasn't an ARM. He got up from his chair, planting both hands flat on his desk, in what Feather called his let-me-explain-this-to-you-in-words-of-one-syllable-or-less stance. "Andrea, think about it. This task force worries about Puppeteers. Where they went. What it means. We don't know many things for sure.

"One is that the Puppeteer disappearing act *hurt Earth.* Another is that Beowulf Shaeffer is a serial accomplice of Puppeteers. He's possibly the cause of their flight from Known Space. Third, there's but one Puppeteer known to be left on Earth. Nessus claims to know me from the General Products building on We Made It. Shaeffer was there at exactly the same time.

"Andrea, tanj it, you *should* have been tracking Shaeffer at this task force's top priority level. This has nothing to do with—not that it's any of your business—my past interest in Jinx." He glowered at her. "Are we clear?"

She had the good sense to stay quiet.

Sigmund sat back down. He took several deep, calming breaths. "That's water under the bridge. Where is Shaeffer now?"

She looked down. "It's unclear. There's no record of him since a few hours after he arrived."

"Come *on,* Andrea." A vein throbbed in Sigmund's temple. "Follow the money. Hotel, transfer booths. This is basic."

"I *know,* Sigmund. I tried to trace it. Honest. Shaeffer made an Earth friend on the ship. I traced Shaeffer to the friend's home. If the friend has been picking up the tab, it'd explain Shaeffer disappearing from the grid."

She's here because you wanted to train her, Sigmund reminded himself. "Judging from my experience, he'd also be off the grid if he were conferring with Nessus. Shaeffer's situation isn't 'unclear,' Andrea. Tanj it, you've lost him."

"Aren't you curious about the friend?" Andrea asked. Was that a trace of a smile? "It's Gregory Pelton."

Sigmund watched aliens, human and other, not his fellow flatlanders. Pelton was a common-enough name, and it took a moment to click. "*The* Gregory Pelton?"

"The very same." Andrea reclaimed a trace of her former bravado. "One of the richest men on the planet."

SIGMUND FLOATED, EXHAUSTED, a wild-eyed Feather draped across him. He'd once come across an odd saying: "Make love, not war." Feather tended to split the difference. Tonight was one of those nights.

"How is she?" Feather said abruptly.

"She?"

"Andrea. Surely your little protégée has made it all better after her lapse." A hand snaked up his bare thigh, lest he be obtuse. "Better."

He jerked, and not only because of her hand. "Hardly."

"Hardly?" Feather rolled onto her back, stretching luxuriously. "Because you don't play with your co-workers? Somehow, that seems weak."

How about because Andrea was a dumb kid, a century younger than him? No, that also pointed out how much younger Andrea was than Feather. "Drop it, please."

Her hand remained, more personal than ever. "You know, that's too bad. There's always room for one more."

She resumed a state of intimate hostilities without waiting for an answer.

PELTON'S VESTIBULE WAS a good five meters tall, with a bigger footprint than Sigmund's entire home. The personal transfer booth, which for most people who could afford one was a token of wealth, seemed lost in a corner. Sigmund admired the decor while he waited for Andrea Girard. Massage chairs. Pale, plush carpet. Holo art. Gourmet synthesizer. Two-story, polished brass doors dominated one wall.

Andrea stepped from the transfer booth. She almost managed not to gape. "I guess he believes his booth address is private."

Pelton was rich enough, and connected enough, that Sigmund hadn't dared pull his teleportation records without a subpoena. Half a century earlier, Pelton's great-great, et cetera, grandmother had invented the transfer-booth system. Gregory, as far as the public record showed, was a ne'er-do-well enjoying her money.

Perhaps no one was home. Sigmund had not called ahead. If Pelton were there, he could have been gone, and Shaeffer with him, given any warning.

And *if* Pelton was inside, he was now on the wrong side of the Emerald City–sized doors from his transfer booth.

A flatscreen intercom was flush-mounted in the wall near the brass doors. Sigmund showed it his ARM ident. "I'm here on official ARM business to speak with Mr. Gregory Pelton."

"Someone will be right with you, sir." The unctuous tone sounded like an AI butler program. The flatscreen remained dark.

A brass door soon opened. Two women stood inside, wearing robes. One was short and petite, with a red dye job to her skin and improbably silver hair flowing to her waist. The other was taller and, if only in comparison, stocky, with elaborately dyed, highlighted, and coiffed hair. Sigmund wondered inanely what Nessus would think of that hair.

"I'm Dianna Guthrie," the shorter woman said. Her hand remained on an ornately carved door handle. "This is Sharrol Janss. We're friends of Ele . . . Gregory. What is this about?"

"I'm Agent Ausfaller." He tipped his head at Andrea.

"This is Agent Girard. We'd like to speak with Mr. Pelton. Also, Beowulf Shaeffer, if he's still here."

The taller one, Janss, started at the mention of Shaeffer. Only Guthrie's name had popped out of the computer as a Pelton associate. Janss must be Guthrie's friend.

"Are they here?" Sigmund prodded.

"Sorry, no." Guthrie stepped forward, pulling the door closed behind her. Perhaps not coincidentally, she closed Janss inside. "What's this about?"

Sigmund shrugged inwardly. You never knew what might be lying out in plain sight at someone's residence.

"We're with the ARM task force investigating the so-called Puppeteer Exodus." Sigmund stopped, waiting to see if Guthrie filled awkward silence with anything interesting.

No such luck. She settled into a chair. "I don't see how that involves Gregory."

Sigmund took out his pocket comp to try again. Note taking also rattled some people. "Beowulf Shaeffer, your friend's companion, knows several Puppeteers. Mr. Pelton spent a great deal of time with Shaeffer on their recent flight from Jinx."

"And you thought Gregory could tell you Bey's whereabouts." Guthrie adjusted the position of a holo art frame on a teak side table. "Yes, Bey was here."

Was?

Andrea cleared her throat. "Dianna . . . may I call you that?" She didn't wait for an answer. "Why was Gregory on a commercial liner in the first place?"

Andrea was supposed to just listen—but that was an interesting question. Pelton had a *lot* of money.

Guthrie said, "Gregory has his own ship, as you would expect. He calls it *Slower than Infinity*. He'd planned to take it to Jinx. He was having it refitted for the trip. The overhaul ran slow, I think because of a parts shortage. Yes, that's it. I remember now. A big supplier went bankrupt. Some key parts were hard to come by. It might have been a result of the Puppeteer Exodus, if that matters. Rather than rush the overhaul or postpone his trip, Gregory flew commercial."

Sigmund made a show of taking notes. "What was his urgent business on Jinx?"

Guthrie stiffened. "I don't see that it has anything to do with missing Puppeteers, but I'll tell you. He'd made plans to go on a Bandersnatchi safari. He wasn't about to miss that for anything." She misunderstood Sigmund's reflexive shudder. "I agree. I'm the world's biggest flat phobe."

Sigmund knew all about Bandersnatchi. The white, slug-like Jinxian creatures were the ultimate big game, bigger than brontosauruses. The Bandersnatchi were also intelligent, and hunting licenses were their main source of hard currency. The covenants that governed the safari trade restricted hunters' weapons to those that gave the prey a fair chance.

Roughly 40 percent of hunters didn't make it back.

Pelton must be crazy. "Let's go back a bit," Sigmund said. "You say Shaeffer was here. Where is he now? With Pelton?"

Guthrie shrugged. "I assume they're still together. Where are they? *That's* a more difficult question. Gregory dragged Bey on to another adventure."

Andrea leaned forward confidentially. "Dianna, it's important that we speak with Mr. Shaeffer. How can we get in touch with them?"

Guthrie seemed to wrestle with how much, if anything, to share. "I'm a flatlander. I see nothing wrong with that. Futz, I take pride in it. But Gregory? That's another story.

"He's been all around Sol system. He's been to a dozen other stars. He's hunted Bandersnatchi, and lived to talk about it. And still, to every spacer he meets, he's a flatlander. Being called that irritates the hell out of him." She waved off Sigmund's scowl. "I *am* answering you. Gregory's goal is to go somewhere so unusual, to do something so spectacular, it will demolish anyone who *ever* again dares to call him a flatlander. So that's where he and Bey went. Out to do something famously stupid."

Was it too late? "Medusa!" Sigmund shouted at his pocket comp. "Location of the private space yacht *Slower than Infinity*?"

The familiar snarling-crown-of-snakes head materialized. "It left Earth three days ago, Sigmund. The flight plan took them out of the traffic-control area and then switches to 'open.' "

"A maximum-acceleration flight plan," Andrea guessed. Medusa didn't correct her. "They'd already be out of the singularity."

Into hyperspace, on their way . . . where?

• 14 •

By the hundreds, Citizens leapt, kicked, and pirouetted. Their bejeweled manes sparkled, resplendent. Hooves clicked and clattered against terrazzo, sometimes in unison, sometimes in staccato bursts, sometimes in a rolling, roaring crescendo.

With a discordant trill, Achilles froze the Grand Ballet. He spent more and more time in the holoshow. Most days it was his only company.

If he wasn't careful, someday he would fail to leave.

Windblown grit pelted the hull of *Remembrance*. Visibility out the view ports was scarcely a few ship lengths. A thoroughly unpleasant world, he thought.

Jinx was an enormous egg, tidally locked with its gas-giant companion. By human convention, "east" was the direction that permanently faced Primary. East End and West End alike protruded above the atmosphere, home to vacuum-based industries.

Jinx's midlatitudes were habitable, if you could

abide, or compensate for, the oppressively strong gravity. Most of the human populace lived in East Band.

Ocean dominated the waist of Jinx, beneath a dense atmosphere. Survival anywhere in the equatorial band took high-pressure gear; few visitors came. Bandersnatchi, the size of mountains, roamed the tropical shorelines.

But Bandersnatchi couldn't *climb* mountains. Jinx's equatorial highlands held nothing to interest anyone—so there Achilles hid.

The turbid atmosphere impeded observation from space. Geysers all about disguised *Remembrance*'s heat signature, their thick, sulfurous fumes an additional disguise.

I could go undetected here for years, he thought, too lonely for the notion to cheer him.

Someone had to unwind General Products' dealings with the Jinxians. And so he did, day after day, through chains of intermediaries, radio relays, and layer upon layer of network anonymizing services.

He remembered calculating that the caretakers who stayed behind on the worlds of Known Space would earn the gratitude of those who led from behind. He remembered the shocked silence when, volunteering, he'd grandly proclaimed, "Achilles was only vulnerable when he presented his heel." *That* was a moment of insane bluster his superiors would not soon forget.

He restarted the dance.

THE HUMAN STARED, wide-eyed, through the impregnable walls of his transparent enclosure. His hands shook. Sweat trickled down his face and neck, and soaked his shirt. He panted for breath.

Molecular filters in the transfer-booth ceiling could as easily supply oxygen as remove it. Achilles had yet to decide whether to bother. He watched in silence.

"You abused my hospitality, Ernest," Achilles finally said, his voice flat with rage. In one mouth he clutched the tiny radio beacon his visitor had thought to smuggle aboard. An earlier stage in the teleportation relay had separated man and device. "You insulted my intelligence."

"It won't happen again," Ernest wheezed softly.

Achilles strained to make out the words. "True," he answered, and fear blossomed on his captive's face.

Someone might deserve to die, but it wasn't this pawn. Someone far above Ernest in the Jinxian Syndicate had given this messenger a beacon.

So much for the supposed emergency that had detained Achilles' customary visitor. She, clearly, had been wise enough not to take the risk.

How much, Achilles wondered, would the government have paid for the location of the last Puppeteer on Jinx?

"It would not have worked anyway," Achilles continued. "Active shielding cancels any unauthorized transmissions from this place."

Ernest's face was pale blue—of hypoxia, not fashion. His eyes darted about desperately. He said nothing, whether recognizing the futility or conserving what little oxygen remained.

Achilles flipped the useless bug into the air and caught it. Tossed and caught. Tossed and caught. "Perhaps your masters thought to trace the path by which visitors arrive." Toss and catch. "My precautionary measures of course extend to that route. Had they sensed any signal beyond their abilities to block, you would not have survived even this long."

Were those precautions sure to forestall the smuggling of beacons—or weapons? Certainty was impossible to prove. Somehow, Achilles managed not to pluck at his mane. *His* doubts must remain secret.

Dead or alive, returning Ernest made a point. Achilles tongued a control console, exchanging the stale air above Ernest's sweat-sodden head with fresh. Inside the tiny cell, a hidden fan whirred to life. The human gulped in air. "Take a message back to your superiors," Achilles said. "They have forfeited any payment from me for a year. Any future dealings will be accomplished solely by vid.

"Tell them." A wriggle of lip nodes sent the mobster on his way. To the solitude of his surroundings, Achilles added a raucous chord of evil music: an old curse.

ACHILLES TRIED TO keep busy. On good days, he lost himself in research. Once, he'd considered himself a physicist.

He'd been posted to Kzin itself, gleaning subtle wisdom from experiments Kzinti scientists were rash enough to perform. Some days, he even found an eerie fascination in Kzinti daring.

And then the BVS-1 expedition had come.

He'd been promoted to We Made It expressly to oversee the neutron-star mission, but there was never time to plumb its findings. Another promotion, from We Made It to the larger General Products office on Jinx, only delayed his research.

Now he had all the time he could ever want to study the BVS-1 data. Every day, he found it harder and harder to care.

Each morning, utterly alone, he hoped his reward—in fame and privileges—would match his sacrifice. Then he would picture the other sacrificial few who had remained behind, one to a solar system. At some time or another, he'd met most of them. They were all misfits—especially that social climber Nessus.

In his hearts Achilles knew: That was how everyone on Hearth would see *him*. And it could only get worse.

Those willing to leave home, the scouts, had always been suspect. Then came the calamitous news, the shock that had plunged almost everyone into despair. He'd been one of the few on Jinx to remain functioning.

How they'd struggled to move the catatonic, belly-hugging hundreds to the embarkation points! How he ached, imagining their unceremonious off-loading from the evacuation ship. The herd would now disdain scouts more than ever.

Somehow, the howling wind sounded lonely. Now that he'd begun to crave even human contact, he did not dare to meet with them.

ACHILLES SYNTHED SOME grasses-and-grain mush. He chewed mechanically, wondering: Is it too early today to resume the dance?

Is it too soon to propose to those who lead from behind that he could safely return home?

An alert chord, strident and vibrato, chased away his introspection. Who could possibly be using this comm ID? He answered, cautiously, "Eight eight three two six seven seven oh."

"My General Products hull has failed," said a human stranger.

Achilles had responded voice only; not so his callers. The man who spoke was unimposing by Jinxian standards but bulky by the norms of every other human world. He looked like a bull next to his spindly companion. Beowulf Shaeffer!

But a hull failure? That was impossible. The coincidence of Shaeffer's presence faded to insignificance. "I beg your pardon?" Achilles said.

"My name is Gregory Pelton. Twelve years ago I bought a number-two hull from General Products. A month and a half ago it failed. We've spent the intervening time limping home. May I speak to a Puppeteer?"

Achilles turned on his camera, wondering if Shaeffer would recognize him. What was it about Shaeffer and unsuspected vulnerabilities in GP hulls?

Achilles tried to ignore the lethally dense atmosphere

outside, and the stampede of doubts whether *Remembrance* would protect him. "This is quite serious. Naturally we will pay the indemnity in full. Would you mind detailing the circumstances?"

Pelton didn't mind at all. He was vehement. He went on at length about the exotic properties of the nascent solar system they'd just explored.

"I see," Achilles said. He did: The two were fools. "Our apologies are insufficient, of course, but you will understand that it was a natural mistake. We did not think that antimatter was available anywhere in the galaxy, especially in such quantity."

The humans twitched. Pelton's voice became curiously soft. "Antimatter?"

"Of course. We have no excuse, of course, but you should have realized it at once. Interstellar gas of normal matter had polished the planet's surface with minuscule explosions, had raised the temperature of the protosun beyond any rational estimate, and was causing a truly incredible radiation hazard. Did you not even wonder about these things? You knew that the system was from beyond the galaxy. Humans are supposed to be highly curious, are they not?"

"The hull," Pelton said. His stunned expression appended a question mark.

"A General Products hull is an artificially generated molecule with interatomic bonds artificially strengthened by a small power plant." Achilles was deep into the explanation before he realized what valuable information he was imparting. How starved he was for companionship! Too late now to stop. "The strengthened molecular bonds are proof against any kind of impact and heat into the hundreds of thousands of degrees. But when enough of the atoms had been obliterated by antimatter explosions, the molecule naturally fell apart."

Pelton nodded, apparently struck speechless.

Achilles said, "When may we expect you to collect

your indemnity? I gather no human was killed; this is fortunate, since our funds are low."

Rather than answer, Pelton broke the connection. Achilles assumed Pelton would call back. Until then, it was unclear whether he or the humans were more appalled.

·15·

Klaxons screamed.

From the holo that suddenly hovered over Sigmund's desk, a grim-faced man spoke rapidly. The name tag on his uniform said: Rickman. "Attention, ARM. Repeat. Attention, ARM. Jinx is under attack."

The vanished Puppeteers demanded all Sigmund's time. He had had to trust others to keep watch on Jinx. Only *very* high-priority matters now made it past his message filter. Rickman's message was coded COSMIC; priorities didn't come any higher.

All the colony worlds were prickly about their independence, Jinx more than most. They would call for ARM help only under the direst of circumstances.

Sigmund killed the audible alarm. Blinking icons in a corner of the holo indicated double encryption, in ARM and Jinx Defense Force standards. He squinted at routing codes beneath the icons. The recording had passed through Southworth Station, the hyperwave relay out past Pluto, and James P. Baen Station, in a similar orbit just outside Sirius A's singularity.

It looked frighteningly authentic.

"We've spotted a ship-sized object plunging into Sirius system at eight-tenths light speed. Repeat, oh-point-eight cee. Preliminary observations suggest that it's altering course."

Aiming?

People filled the hallway outside Sigmund's office. "Kzinti?" someone whispered. Others murmured agreement.

ARM naval forces must be scrambling. If Jinx was under attack, why not also Earth? And who but the ratcats would try it?

Near light speed meant a kinetic-kill weapon. A ship-sized mass going that fast was a planet-buster. How could you stop it? No one would survive the impact. How had the ratcats managed this?

Jinx to Baen, and then Southworth to Earth. Those light-speed crawls in the gravity wells meant almost a day's delay. Was Jinx still there?

"Quiet, everyone," Sigmund snapped. And then—

In the streaming message, a woman in JDF uniform whispered into Rickman's ear. "A moment," Rickman said. He turned his back to the camera. Men and women huddled.

"The transmission is muted," Medusa said. "I lip-read something about a radio contact, presumably with the intruder. Now I can't hear or lip-read."

Sigmund wondered: Who mutes an end-of-the-world message?

Rickman turned back to the camera. Anger had replaced fear in his eyes. "We've just gotten a message from the object. It's owned by a futzy flatlander, name of Gregory Pelton. He's demanding rescue. He's decelerating, so it's probably not an attack. Have you got anything on this yutz?"

Sigmund sent: "Respectable citizen. No record of wrongdoing." Thinking: Respectable until he began consorting with Beowulf Shaeffer. The Jinxians didn't need to know about those suspicions.

But from where was Pelton returning? And how, at eight-tenths of cee in Einstein space?

• • •

THE TRANSFER BOOTH delivered Sigmund from ARM HQ to—Atlantis? Beyond a picture window, a stingray rippled languidly. Coral glistened in crystalline, sunlit waters.

Carlos Wu emerged from a shadowed alcove of the vestibule. "I do apologize, Agent Ausfaller. I enjoy the reactions too much to forewarn guests."

"I thought I was transferring to your home," Sigmund said. He tried to ignore the tons of water pressure striving to crush that window. The lobby decor favored shells, driftwood, fishing nets, and seascapes, like a seafood restaurant designed by a really exclusive interior designer.

"This *is* home." Carlos smiled disingenuously. "It happens to nestle inside the Great Barrier Reef."

It took more than money to live somewhere so ecologically fragile—it took a UN license. One more perk for the genetically golden? Then Feather stepped through, and the confusion on *her* face was priceless. Sigmund excused their host. "Dr. Carlos Wu. Agent Feather Filip."

"Just Carlos." Carlos shook Feather's hand enthusiastically. He offered beverages and snacks, pointed out a lionfish hiding in a crevice of the reef, and generally bubbled with enthusiasm.

Annoyingly charming, Sigmund thought. Or is there more to Wu's animation than that?

A quick data dive had shown Wu used to hang around with Sharrol Janss. Had she contacted him since meeting Shaeffer? "Thanks for seeing us on such short notice, Carlos."

"Sit." Their host gestured at massage chairs. "You're welcome, of course. I'm glad to help. At least I assume I am. You didn't really explain. Not another galactic explosion, I hope."

"Nothing so dramatic," Sigmund said. "Not quite. It may still merit a few minutes' conversation with an astrophysical genius."

The Jinx Defense Force had yet to admit publicly to its brief panic. If no one else revealed the intruder, Sigmund guessed the JDF meant to keep it secret.

Feather shifted in her chair. "Here's a hypothetical question. Say I wanted to accelerate a large object, ship sized, up to, oh, say, eighty percent of light speed. How would I do that?"

"I'd need other parameters." Carlos fidgeted with a conch shell from his coffee table. "But what's the point? Hyperdrive moves ships at faster than light."

"Hypothetical," Feather repeated.

Carlos raised the conch to his lips and blew. A note sounded, deep, resonant, and haunting.

Charm or nerves? Sigmund wondered again. From some random corner of his mind came an image, some Renaissance sketch seen long ago at the Getty Museum. *Triton Blowing a Conch Shell,* he thought it was called. A Caravaggio maybe? No, Carracci.

Every Puppeteer Sigmund had ever met had a name from human mythology, usually Greek. He didn't recall meeting a Triton. That proved nothing. Sigmund was terrible with names.

Carlos lowered his horn. "The obvious answer is a ramscoop. All the early unmanned interstellar probes were ramscoops. After the crew shielding problem was solved, colony ships were also ramscoops. All before we got hyperdrive, of course."

"Of course," Sigmund said.

"And an answer you obviously didn't need me for." Carlos turned the conch over and over in his hands. "How long do I have? To accelerate the ship, that is."

"About three months," Sigmund said. Pelton and Shaeffer were gone from Earth for three months before they came barreling out of space to terrorize Jinx.

"Too little time for a ramscoop." More tuneless, conch-amplified whistling. The stingray grew bored and left. A school of silvery fish zigzagged past. "That's a tough one," Carlos finally decided. "It's too short for thrusters or fusion engines, even assuming a ship could carry enough fuel for the job."

Carlos set down his conch and stood abruptly. "Forgive my manners. Can I get either of you something to drink?"

He'd offered refreshments minutes earlier. Was Wu stalling or just very polite? Maybe it was tough to be a genius and Wu was embarrassed to be without an answer. Sigmund shook his head.

"Nothing for me," Feather said. She stood, too, and went to peer out at the reef. "Very relaxing." She turned away from the window wall. "Too relaxing. Carlos, back to business. Call me a dumb cop, but I don't get it. I've been on ships that go a light-year in three days. Why can't a ship approach light speed in three months? Why not simply slow down less coming out of hyperspace?"

"Hardly dumb, Feather. Those are astute questions." Carlos joined her at the glass. He pointed into the sea. "A fish in water and a fish in air are quite different things. Normal space and hyperspace are different, too."

What was with the trite metaphor? Sigmund wondered. Was Carlos flirting? Women begged to have Wu's children. Women with birthing licenses, of course. Sigmund couldn't imagine Carlos having an interest in an ARM schiz. "Once a ship is out of the singularity, whatever its speed, it can jump to hyperspace. Right?"

"Right," Carlos said.

"And in hyperspace, it moves a light-year in three days," Sigmund went on.

Carlos reached into a seascape beside the window. Frigate and storm vanished, revealing a synthesizer. The unseen sensor restored the holo as his hand withdrew, clasping a glass of water. "Unless it's the *Long Shot.* Then it does a light-year in not much over a minute."

"And when the ship exits hyperspace?" Sigmund asked.

"It has the same speed, neither faster nor slower, as

when it entered. Velocity in Einstein space and hyperspace are independent."

"So it can't be done." Feather smiled. "Hypothetically, that is."

"Unless it *has* happened. Your interest suggests that it has." Carlos sipped slowly. Ice cubes tinkled. "Reality trumps theory every time. So I'm going to venture a guess. I say . . . the Outsiders."

• 16 •

"I have studied your report," Nike said. His voices and bright eyes were distinctive, his build lithe and slight. His hide was pure cream, remarkably free of markings. Plush orange ribbons, Experimentalist colors, adorned his ornately braided mane. "You were correct to request an urgent consultation."

Achilles shivered with surprise. Nike himself! Clandestine Directorate by its nature dealt with off-world hazards, but those who led from behind remained, naturally, on Hearth. But hyperwave radio did not work within the planetary singularity. Nike had traveled deep into space to confer personally.

As had Achilles, although there were none on Jinx to whom *he* might have delegated. In *Remembrance*'s main bridge view port, Sirius burned brightly, a distant spark. "I felt it important that you be made aware."

Pelton claimed to have bought from the Outsiders the coordinates of "the most unusual" world in Known Space. An antimatter world, orbiting an antimatter sun, surely qualified.

Achilles managed to wonder if Nike was suitably impressed with that calm understatement.

With the entire population of six worlds already in flight, *he* had uncovered a new catastrophe in the making. An entire antimatter solar system hurtled through Known Space—and *he* had deduced its existence. *He* had ascertained humans knew its location. The peril was immeasurable, and far closer than the blast front onrushing from the galactic-core explosion.

"There's no question a General Products hull was destroyed?" Nike probed. The undertunes encouraged *any* ambiguity, however small.

Achllles replied with arpeggios of confident certainty, "None, I regret to say. I examined what remains of *Slower than Infinity.* Hyperdrive, lifesystem, fusion reactor, everything—they're covered in a powdery residue. Spectral analysis proves it's remnant hull material. If you doubt the cause, you must still believe the destruction of a General Products hull."

"Very well," Nike answered. "If I must believe that much, and experts here confirm your conclusions, then I must accept these humans encountered vast amounts of antimatter. And they say the Outsiders ferried them to this antimatter solar system?"

Was that a tremor? In *Nike*'s voice? If so, Achilles empathized.

The Outsiders were the galaxy's elder race. Beings of liquid helium, they shunned the warmth favored by every other intelligent species. They traveled the galaxy, trading with everyone, mostly for knowledge. Their science and technology far exceeded that of all others.

They possessed unimaginable power.

And yet, Outsider access to the antimatter solar system wasn't what terrified Achilles. The Outsiders appeared as free of aggression as Citizens themselves.

The same could *not* be said of humans.

Large predators had been exterminated on Hearth millennia ago. Citizens worried about all technically advanced races, of course, but spacefaring *carnivores* evoked instinctive horror. Dread and loathing of the

Kzinti blinded his people to the dangers of other races. Humans were violent, curious, expansionist . . .

Much was forgiven them as a counterweight for the Kzinti.

Too much, Achilles thought.

But humans with antimatter? Achilles shuddered. "The ferry service by the Outsiders is *good* news, Excellency. It implies the antimatter solar system is passing at speeds otherwise inaccessible to the humans."

Nike bobbed heads in cautious agreement. "It would be good to believe that."

If I can convince Nike, Achilles thought, I have done Hearth—and my career—a great service. "Pelton's initial radio contact with me was greatly blue-shifted. That is, the wrecked ship came at Jinx at relativistic speeds." Roughly 0.8 light speed.

"Why is that significant?" Nike trilled. "Ah. With hyperdrive, humans lack a reason to go that fast in normal space. Can they, if they so wish?"

"With a ramscoop certainly, and given several months, but *Slower than Infinity* is no ramscoop. Not with any technology humans currently use. I saw only standard gear in the remains of their ship." Achilles plucked his mane, unable to restrain himself.

Braking to rendezvous speeds had taken Pelton a long time. Again and again the crippled ship, its gravity drag glowing red-hot, had raced through Sirius system. After each passage, perceptibly slowed, the ship had dropped back into hyperspace, circling around Sirius to repeat the process.

Gravity drag didn't work in reverse.

"The Outsiders towed Pelton's ship," Achilles concluded. "That's the only way *Slower than Infinity* could have achieved that speed."

Nike was quiet for a long time, considering. "The reappearance of this Beowulf Shaeffer troubles me."

That had been Achilles' initial reaction. He'd had the

time to conclude otherwise. "Respectfully, Deputy Minister, Shaeffer's presence explains much.

"The ship Shaeffer named the *Long Shot* was experimental, and hideously expensive for General Products to equip. Had something gone wrong on the way to or from the galactic core, our ship would almost certainly have been beyond our ability to recover. Before I dispatched Shaeffer, I personally hyperwaved several Outsider ships. I encouraged them to pass the word. Had the *Long Shot* broken down, the Outsiders might have been able to salvage our ship."

"I see," Nike said. "Then Pelton's distress call used the Net address you had left with the Outsiders for Shaeffer to use."

"Correct."

"And the two humans intend to keep their discovery secret until Pelton can make some grand expedition there."

"So Pelton claims, and he appears sincere," Achilles agreed again. "Regardless, the antimatter system must be moving at such great speed, their knowledge of its existence cannot long be a danger to us."

"A moment, please." Nike's side of the link froze, muted, and Achilles imagined urgent consultation. "My advisors here concur with your well-reasoned assessment. As do I."

Achilles trembled with pride and relief. "Then the matter is—"

"I have one reservation," Nike interrupted. "Agreed, the threat appears short-term. If a human government became involved, however—they might surprise us.

"We must keep an eye on Pelton and Shaeffer."

· 17 ·

Singly and in small groups, Citizens strolled, trotted, and cantered across the display walls of *Gamboler.* The clatter of hooves. The harmonies of fellowship. Well-known faces. Well-remembered mannerisms. Comforting presences.

All gone.

The merest intimation of the looped recording penetrated Nessus' consciousness. If he could, he might never unclench from the limbless ball of flesh he had become. When the air within grew unbearably stale, he loosened just a little, and the sights and sounds briefly returned. Did they console him? Chastise him for having deserted them? Both, perhaps, in equal measure.

All Nessus knew for certain was he could not bear to turn them off.

The evacuation ship was long overdue at Hearth. There was no message. No emergency buoy. No hope. Everyone assumed a pilot too eager for home, or too numbed by the horror of the core explosion, had delayed a moment too long to drop from hyperspace. One more vessel—with all his friends and colleagues—presumed sacrificed to the hungry maw of a singularity.

From the universe outside his belly came Puck's voices, wry and wise. With a wail of despair, Nessus pulled his flesh tight over his heads.

ABANDONMENT *HURT.*

The first time came long before he took on the name Nessus. Did he even know so young that other worlds existed? Other intelligent species? Probably not. He was but three years old then, and scarcely withers high to an adult. He remembered idly peeling the bark from a fallen twig, rolling the crumbs of husk between lip nodes.

"You're odd," someone warbled from the depths of the herd. He couldn't see who. "Odd," echoed another unidentifiable voice. More joined in, "Odd. Odd. Odd." Chanting filled the air. It echoed from the high walls that surrounded the playfield. "Odd. Odd. Odd."

In the distance, adults watched, lips curled in disdain.

"I'm *not* odd," he insisted, unsure of the word. He could not help but understand the herd posture. In all directions, the group receded. Emptiness formed around him. He lowered his heads submissively. "I'm not odd," he gurgled softly, knowing that he must be.

Still the adults did nothing. *Odd* must be a bad thing.

His heads sank lower. He noticed more things than his playmates. Was that bad? He still craved their company. He still needed to belong.

He edged toward flockmates he thought were his friends. "Let's play," he sang.

They whistled dismay and sidled away.

In despair, he fell to the ground. His necks drooped, aching to wrap themselves tightly against his belly.

He had once cut himself on a broken toy. The gash had hurt, but not nearly so much as his parents' paralyzed expressions of horror.

Banishment hurt *far* worse.

Then, with a random glance, his life had changed forever. Through meadowplant tattered by a thousand little hooves, a bit of stone poked. A vein in the rock sparkled. He shifted a head this way and that, studying it. He'd never seen anything like it. "Why does it shine so?" he asked aloud. He ripped at the turf, fascinated, prying the stone free of the entangling roots.

When did the taunts fade to silence? He did not notice. Eventually, he became aware of younglings huddled around him, necks craned to discern why he ignored their shunning.

He learned that day that he would never fit in. And something else: to take solace in the wonders of the world around him. It was, although it would be years before he knew it, the first step toward becoming a scout.

Nessus wasn't yet ready to deal with the world, but he knew: When the time came, salvation must again come from somewhere outside himself.

SCREAMS OF TERROR yanked Nessus, flanks heaving in fear and shock, from the depths of catatonia. His heads darted about, seeking peril.

The message light flickered on his main console. His failure to acknowledge it had set off the shrieking alarm. How overdue was his response? "Alarm off. Play the message."

A hologram appeared. Nike, he noted apathetically. Nike, the leader of Clandestine Directorate. Nike, the rising star of the Experimentalist party. Nike, the charismatic. Nike, for whose notice Nessus had, so far without success, volunteered for one dangerous assignment after another.

That he could be so indifferent shocked Nessus. He forced himself to replay the recording.

The holographic Nike said, "An urgent matter has arisen. Its resolution must be your top priority."

In growing horror, Nessus listened. Limitless quantities of antimatter, the location known only to two humans, now on their way to Earth. *He* needed, somehow, to watch the humans.

The Outsiders also knew the coordinates, of course. They wanted an exorbitant payment to reveal the information. There was no reason to pay them, unless—

"This is most critical, Nessus," Nike stressed. "We *must* know if the humans attempt to return. A repeat expedition would almost surely fail, like the first. And yet . . . my experts believe it is possible, given enough resources, for the humans to return with dangerous amounts of antimatter. We *must* know if that becomes a risk, at least until the antimatter system moves beyond the humans' possible reach. Everyone on Hearth is depending on you."

Damning him to stay here and keep watch, alone, for years.

"YOUR CREDENTIALS ARE satisfactory," the woman called Irina Gorychka told Nessus. As much of her skin as Nessus could see was dyed red and white. Her stripes reminded him of a candy cane. Her companion, the man introduced as Gerald Hauss, had covered his cheeks in stylized yellow stars. Both had shaved their heads.

So General Products' payment, circuitously routed, had cleared. Nessus studied his callers, at once fascinated and appalled. Dealings with aliens always involved stress. *These* were renegades among aliens. How much less trustworthy did that make them?

These were avatars he viewed, not people. Those who might provide the services he sought did not reveal themselves to strangers—especially strangers who refused to reveal themselves.

Nor was Nessus about to disclose himself. He presented only one face now, and it was human. Almost certainly the faces and voices presented to him were as illusory as those he offered. On the other side of the call, they might be two or ten, men or women.

Nessus' human avatar, all the while, stared impassively. "I assured you that I had adequate funds."

"You'll need them," Hauss said. "These are well-connected people. Pelton himself *cannot* be monitored directly. He can afford every kind of protection. From our initial survey, it appears he uses them all. Sentries. Alarm systems: home, office, and on his person. Jammers. Top-notch encryption. AI data sniffers on the prowl for anyone like us. We can only watch associates, and associates of associates, and then try to piece together what Pelton is doing."

Gorychka cleared her throat. "Just so you know, Nessus, this isn't a onetime process. We must constantly track who becomes how close to Pelton. Some people's privacy is protected, or will get that way, by proximity to him. We'll keep adjusting who and how we monitor."

In other words, expect to keep paying.

Somehow, Nessus managed to function. He found it hard to *care.*

Only his friends' deaths mattered. Withdrawal, denial, depression, reunification with the living—those were the stages of grief. Duty had cruelly short-circuited the process. Now he was in some nether state, distant and numb, his inner self in tatters. And if his spirit somehow healed sufficiently to make the attempt, with whom could he bond? Humans?

Maybe. At times he could identify more closely with them than with his own. Except for his fellow scouts, and they—

"I will expect a full accounting," Nessus said. Forcing himself to interact was hard enough; he could not muster the interest to care what the surveillance cost. All he wanted to do was roll up again and hide. "And I demand utter discretion."

• 18 •

The summons was all the more peculiar for the manner of its delivery.

Max Addeo strode into Sigmund's office. Addeo was Sigmund's boss, the ARM Director of Investigations. He was lean and perpetually tanned, with an easy manner, and Sigmund liked him—except as a superior. The man didn't worry enough for Sigmund's taste.

Andrea excused herself, and Addeo shut Sigmund's

office door behind her. "You're expected now, Sigmund."

"That's rather vague, Max." And rather short notice.

"Nonetheless." Addeo handed over a folded sheet of paper. It bore only a booth address. The prefix indicated midtown Manhattan. "I received a message for you. This address and one word: *now*."

"Received from whom?" Sigmund asked.

"It will be clear soon enough." Addeo managed a wan smile. "You went alone to meet the world's last Puppeteer. I think you can manage midtown in midafternoon."

Addeo opened the door. His parting words were, "Now, Sigmund."

Sigmund flicked from the ARM HQ lobby. He stepped from the destination booth and looked around. Snack stands. Milling crowds. Towering buildings.

Directly before him was an ancient redbrick structure a mere seven stories high. The land beneath it, if used for a modern skyscraper, would be worth billions. This building's very existence made a statement.

Sigmund climbed the broad granite stairs. The liveried doorman held open the brass-and-glass door for him.

The concierge ignored the ident Sigmund offered. "That isn't necessary, sir. You are expected. Please follow me."

Across the three-story-tall Common Room, formally suited men and women sipped brandy or coffee, read, and engaged in intimate conversation. It seemed like everyone spoke in whispers, although that might be the acoustics. Huge Oriental rugs covered the age-darkened hardwood floor. Leather-bound books lined the walls to a height of about two meters. From the mahogany paneling above the bookcases stern faces glowered, oil paintings in ornate gilded frames. The occasional squeak sounded as people shifted in their red leather wing chairs. An actual log fire burned in the man-tall masonry fireplace.

In this most exclusive of private, moneyed establishments, Sigmund didn't see a single vid phone or pocket comp in use. No one had asked for his. The members would never tolerate being asked for their comm gear. Instead, there would be suppressors here, banning the distractions and interruptions of ubiquitous networks—and, with them, all bugs and recorders.

"This way, sir," the concierge said. He gestured Sigmund inside a meeting room, appointed like a miniature version of the Common Room.

Beyond the massive claw-footed oak table, a man and woman stood with their backs to Sigmund. He couldn't make out their conversation. The man was short and broad shouldered, almost Jinxian. Gregory Pelton, Sigmund guessed. They had yet to meet, but Sigmund had seen plenty of file images.

The woman was wispy, especially by comparison. Her hair spiraled in alternating braids of gold and platinum. More than eye-poppingly vivid, the turquoise of her bodysuit was a signature color.

Calista Melenkamp, the Secretary-General of the United Nations.

The door closed behind Sigmund with a soft whoosh. The two turned at the sound; the man *was* Pelton. Melenkamp fixed Sigmund with a penetrating stare, then left by another exit without speaking. She didn't need to say a word. Pelton held her confidence. That she delivered that message here, personally, and yet so deniably, said even more.

Pelton glared, his forehead furrowed. Even the close-cropping of his black beard seemed somehow angry. "Agent Ausfaller, your interest in my affairs has become intolerable."

Anger didn't impress Sigmund. It so often was a mask. "Welcome back to Earth, Mr. Pelton. I understand you had an interesting trip."

"True enough." A flicker of a smile. "And that's more information than you had any right to expect. Be happy for it, because it's all you'll get. You *will* cease spying upon and harassing me and my friends."

A silver coffeepot, curls of steam wafting from its gracefully curved spout, waited on a sideboard. A Revere piece, Sigmund guessed. He poured himself a cup. "It's my duty to investigate potential threats to the safety of Earth, Mr. Pelton."

"I'm a patriot, Agent Ausfaller. I've done nothing to endanger Earth. I never will." In Pelton's clenched hands, the padded back of a chair creaked in protest. "Whatever you believe, I will not tolerate groundless intrusion into my affairs. I'm well aware of ARM paranoia. I refuse to be its victim. Unlike most, I have the resources to accomplish that."

Not the least of those resources being the trust of the Secretary-General.

"Understood, Mr. Pelton." Sigmund pulled out a chair. Sitting was less confrontational. "That said, the fate of *Slower than Infinity* concerns me. It's not every day that a General Products hull disintegrates."

"Has one ever?" Pelton jerked out the chair he'd been squeezing and sat. "Okay, I see what this is about. I took a trip in my yacht. On my travels, someone made me an offer I couldn't refuse for the ship. They wanted the hull, mostly; in the hinterlands, GP hulls are much in demand since the Puppeteer Exodus. I sold *Slower than Infinity* and bought something else. That ship's hull *did* fail, teaching me a lesson. Stick with the best."

Had anyone ID'ed the trace powders on the remains of Pelton's ship? Not according to ARM sources on Jinx.

The mystery traces weren't the only anomaly. Serial numbers on the wreck's hyperdrive matched Earth shipyard records for *Slower than Infinity.* Experts said that assembling a hyperdrive inside a hull took time. Disassembly would be the same. Had someone extracted the hyperdrive from the GP hull, the ship-in-a-bottle trick in reverse? Why do it, even if they could?

Or was this all, as Pelton would insist, a bookkeeping mix-up?

Sigmund no more believed that than that Shaeffer's arrival on Earth had been innocently disguised by a spelling error.

He had a head full of questions. He yearned for at least one credible answer. "Where did the profit go from selling your ship?"

Pelton's face flamed. "Listen carefully, Agent Ausfaller. I sold the ship off-world. I deposited the proceeds off-world. The transactions are none of Earth's business. I will be *most* irate if my finances should be examined. You have my word: I will *vigorously* protest any such harassment to the proper authorities."

And to an improper one: the S-G herself.

Sigmund sipped his coffee, letting Pelton fume. Angry people blurted out things they had no intention of saying.

Pelton *had* deposited a huge, so far untraceable, sum into the Third Bank of Sirius Mater. He'd hired people on Jinx, too, all working at an out-of-the-way spot in West End. That much ARM had managed to determine. It would be good to know just what Pelton had going.

"Agent Ausfaller," Pelton said. "You have yet to justify your actions. This is your one opportunity to explain why you are persecuting me and my associates. If you cannot . . . well, for your sake I hope there is a reason I've overlooked."

"How's this?" Sigmund said. "I'd like to better understand your business with the Outsiders."

Pelton blinked. "I purchased information from them."

How had Dianna Guthrie described Pelton's quest? "About the most unusual planet in Known Space."

"Yes." Pelton thrust out his jaw. "I assume that's not a crime."

"Causing a civil-defense panic sort of is," Sigmund answered. Had it happened in Sol system, it *would* have been. Jinx hadn't jailed Pelton, and that was one more bit of alien behavior. Perhaps Pelton had bought them off.

"We went someplace with a very high normal-space velocity. We bought a lift from the Outsiders."

Carlos was right!

Kzinti. Jinxians. Puppeteers. And now the Outsiders? The gathering storm was so vast Sigmund wondered if his brain could encompass it.

But the Outsiders had once *helped* mankind. Hyperdrive was their technology. Had the Outsiders not happened upon a human ship near We Made It, back during the First Man-Kzin War, and sold a hyperspace shunt, the ratcats would have won. Earth itself might now be a slave world to the Kzinti Patriarchy.

The Outsiders were beyond human scale, ancient, unknowable. Maybe he failed to grasp their grand plan. Or maybe that next-to-elder race, the Puppeteers, *did* understand the Outsiders. Had Puppeteers manipulated the Outsiders for General Products' own nefarious purposes?

Sigmund suspected much but knew very little. In one interpretation, a GP hull had dissolved. The evidence, all under cover, remained on Jinx. By Pelton's own admission, the Outsiders were involved.

Pelton and Shaeffer might understand all of this—but Pelton was untouchable, and he'd taken Shaeffer under his wing.

The possibilities were so worrisome Sigmund almost overlooked blurt number one: a pronoun change. *We.* "You and Beowulf Shaeffer."

"Yes." Pelton walked around the table and poured himself coffee. The delicate china cup looked wrong in his massive hand. "Bey had traded before with Outsiders, back when he worked for Nakamura Lines."

"Did you leave him on Jinx?"

Pelton shook his head. "He returned to Earth with me. We're good friends, Agent Ausfaller. More than that, he saved my life on our adventure."

"I'd like to hear that story."

"I'm sure you would." Pelton drained his cup and set it down. "Ausfaller, that's as much of the tale as I mean to share anytime soon. It's innocent. There's no reason for ARM interest. There's no reason to interrogate or spy on me.

"Not me, not my friends, not my associates. There will be no further interest in Dianna Guthrie, or Beowulf Shaeffer, or Sharrol Janss, or Don Cramer, or *anyone* close to me."

Don Cramer? Who was he? Sigmund made a mental note to find out. And Pelton had said *further* interest. Sigmund had no one watching this Cramer. Who else might be watching?

Pelton was on a roll. "Inconvenience any of us again, Ausfaller, and you'd better have proof of something wrong. Do you understand?"

"I completely understand, Mr. Pelton." Sigmund stood and offered his hand. It helped him to avoid rubbing the remembered wound in his gut. An Undersecretary-General once sold him out to the Trojan Mafia. It wasn't the type of experience anyone forgot.

What Sigmund truly understood was that no official, however lofty her rank, was beyond suspicion.

EYE OF THE STORM

EARTH DATE: 2648

• 19 •

"We got a runner," Andrea hissed over the radio. She was hidden in the woods north of the isolated clearing. "Make it two. Man and a woman."

Of course, a man and a woman. That's how you made a baby. "Which way?" Sigmund asked.

"West," Andrea said. "Toward you."

Sigmund saw them now, fear etched on their faces. The mother waddled more than ran, unmistakably pregnant. The presumed father half-supported, half-dragged her. They staggered away from the tumble-down cabin, little more than a shed, really, toward the distant trees.

Floaters bringing the local constabulary were five minutes away. *Local* was a relative term in the Alaskan wilderness. The runners would be long gone when the floaters arrived. The couple would be hard to spot in the woods.

Sigmund saw no sign of the reported laser hunting rifles that had the three ARMs waiting for backup. "Futz," he muttered under his breath. This wasn't why he had become an ARM. Nor Feather—who almost certainly had revealed herself to the would-be parents. Feather was east of the cabin; if the preggers had seen only her, they'd naturally run west.

Eighteen billion were way too many. It was the law. It was his job. Without enforcement, everyone would be off making babies.

Futz.

Sigmund drew his handgun. It carried only mercy darts, slivers of crystallized anesthetic—which mattered not at all. These two would be spare parts in the organ banks, soon enough.

This was *not* why, a year earlier, when Max Addeo disbanded the Puppeteer task force, Sigmund had asked for his core team to be reassigned to the Alaska ARM district.

"WALK WITH ME," Max Addeo said. He looked eerily mottled through the graphic that hung over Sigmund's desk.

"What can I do for you, Max?" Sigmund asked.

"Walk with me," Addeo repeated.

"All right." Sigmund closed the file he had been studying; the holo vanished. He followed his boss to a nearby transfer booth. They emerged onto the front porch of an old home surrounded by a white horse fence. The sun beat down from a cloudless sky. Rolling, grassy hills stretched as far as the eye could see. Hikers dotted the trail that led up to a nearby ridge.

"Where are we, Max?"

"Sky Meadows." Addeo pointed to low mountains in the distance. "That's the Blue Ridge. Shall we walk?"

They walked, Sigmund thinking this was too much of a buildup for good news.

"I'm being promoted," Addeo finally said. "Deputy Undersecretary General for Security Affairs. The official announcement comes out tomorrow."

"Congratulations." Sigmund kept his eyes on the dirt path. "Why tell me first?" *And why tell me here? What's the bad news?*

"I'm closing down the Puppeteer task force."

Sigmund grabbed his boss's sleeve. "Why? When?"

Hikers turned and stared. "It's all right, folks," Addeo said, brushing off Sigmund's hand. He waited for people to walk away. "*That's* why, Sigmund. I imagined you'd respond like this."

"No, futz it! Why terminate the task force?"

"The thing is, Sigmund, it's a Puppeteer task force, only there are no Puppeteers. There haven't been in two years. Even Nessus is long gone."

"You have no reason to think so," Sigmund argued.

"And *you* don't know he's still here! When did you last see or hear from Nessus? More than a year ago, as I recall."

Sigmund's mind raced. "The promotion is *for* shutting down the investigation, isn't it? Pelton always had pull at the UN. Now he's won."

"You're right in a way," Addeo snapped. "A case can be made the shutdown is because of Pelton—because *you* are obsessed with him. Just like you're obsessed with Beowulf Shaeffer. You forgot this was a Puppeteer task force."

How could he forget? Sigmund said, "Don't you see? They're all in it together! Shaeffer gave the Puppeteers their excuse to abandon and betray Known Space. Pelton befriended Shaeffer, making it impossible to investigate Shaeffer."

Addeo glanced up at a passing shadow. Far above, a hawk circled, effortlessly climbing a thermal. The sight seemed to calm Addeo. Sadly, he shook his head. "How is Shaeffer part of a Puppeteer plot, Sigmund? General Products hired Beowulf Shaeffer to go to the core because they had used him before. *You* selected Shaeffer back on We Made It."

Sigmund said nothing.

"Finally," Addeo said. "You recognize reality. Let it go, Sigmund."

That Addeo could not be swayed—that was reality. The noninvolvement of the Puppeteers? That was a different matter entirely.

Pelton was a *very* rich man. Much of his money was off-world, out-system, and very difficult to trace. Impossible, so far, when Sigmund dare not be caught attempting to trace it.

What if Shaeffer were chosen *for* me? Then so much made sense!

Pelton's business interests on Jinx awarded grants to the Institute of Knowledge. The institute initiated the BVS-1 mission. If Pelton then used his wealth to ruin Nakamura Lines, then *Pelton* had guided Sigmund's choice on We Made It toward Shaeffer.

General Products. Pelton. Jinx. Who were the real puppeteers here? And now—

"Sigmund," Addeo said with an edge to his voice. "Stop whatever paranoid fantasy you're concocting to rationalize my promotion."

"Which leaves me where?" Sigmund asked.

Addeo angled downhill off the packed-dirt trail, toward an unoccupied wooden bench. "That's the second matter we're here to discuss. I can influence your next assignment. Your friends' assignments, too."

Which begged the question: What *did* he want?

He wanted to nail Shaeffer and Pelton.

And *that* suggested the barest possibility of a plan. Could he pull it off? "It's awfully warm out here," Sigmund answered. He raised his arms dramatically, emphasizing his ubiquitous black suit. "To be fair, I'm not dressed for here—wherever 'here' is."

"The top of the Shenandoah Valley," Addeo answered. "Northern Virginia."

"It's even hotter than New York," Sigmund muttered. "Tell you what. How about someplace cooler? Maybe Alaska. Is there an opening in Alaska?"

Addeo shrugged. "Hard to imagine there isn't, but it doesn't matter. I'll make room. I owe you that much. The quiet will do you good."

"Thanks," Sigmund said, meaning it, although he deserved any posting he wanted.

Why not close to Nome, where Beowulf was now living with flat phobe Sharrol Janss?

• • •

THE TWO PREGGERS hobbled frantically toward the trees. Sigmund heard them gasping for breath from clear across the glade. Tears streamed down the mother's cheeks.

"They look unarmed, guys," Andrea radioed. "I've got a clear shot. What say I take 'em down and we all go home?"

Feather hadn't said anything. Sigmund didn't expect she would. If asked, she'd deny showing herself to the two fugitives. He said, "Hold your position, Andrea. They're coming my way."

Mom tripped over something unseen in the blowing grass. She fell, shrieking, to her hands and knees. Dad hoisted her back to her feet, and they scrambled unknowingly almost straight toward Sigmund.

Of what, truly, were they guilty? Heeding billions of years of evolution, commanding them to reproduce.

Sigmund wondered: Do I think more or less of Janss for divorcing Shaeffer because the Fertility Board wouldn't approve an albino for a birth license?

As the Fertility Board never—ever—approved natural paranoids. I don't really even want children, Sigmund told himself—but Feather does. And I want a life with Feather.

Nothing had gone according to plan. Janss now lived in the South Pacific, having reacquainted herself with Carlos Wu. Sigmund foresaw babies in *their* future. Shaeffer had left Earth. The last Sigmund had heard, Shaeffer was sightseeing on Gummidgy, in the CY Aquarii system. Pelton continued shuttling between Earth and his clandestine project on Jinx.

And here, Sigmund thought, in the middle of nowhere, *I* remain.

"Sigmund! They're almost into the trees," Andrea shouted, bursting from cover.

"Stay down, Newbie," he ordered. "Their rifles may be stashed in the woods."

Across the clearing, Feather stared. He nodded

slightly. "I've got the shot," Sigmund called out. Pfft. Pfft. Dust and shreds of grass spurted at the runners' feet. "Tanj! Missed."

As their quarry slipped into the trees, Sigmund couldn't help thinking: Perhaps, just for today, there *is* justice.

• 20 •

Snack in hand, Nessus' guest slouched on the armchair behind a partition of hull material. "I wish you'd upgrade your synthesizer," Max Addeo said. "Humans like variety."

Nessus considered, astraddle his padded bench. "Perhaps you're comfortable enough already."

Addeo laughed. "Why am I here today, Nessus? Apart from the money, of course?"

Money was the one resource Nessus had in abundance, all the vast wealth accumulated over the years by General Products. The challenge was in identifying capable yet trustworthy scoundrels to hire.

"I require clarification on your latest report," Nessus said.

Addeo spoke around a mouthful of handmeal. "There are more discreet ways to communicate, you know. I use up a fake ID every time I visit, so that I can't be tracked through the transfer-booth system."

Because I need company, even if it's a human traitor's company. Even if I feel safe only with a wall between us. "Put it on your bill, Max."

Chew, chew, swallow. "What do you want to know, Nessus?"

Outside *Gamboler,* whiteness swirled. What would it be like to cavort in deep drifts of snow? Nessus didn't ask. The question hinted that snow never fell on Hearth. It fell seldom enough on Earth, already in its early stages of industrial overheating. "Why does the ARM continue to look for us, Max? You assured me the task force has been disbanded."

"By *us* I assume you mean General Products." Addeo stood and stretched. "It's only been three years since the Puppeteer Exodus cratered the economy. That's enough of a reason for some, task force or no. Because by *the ARM* you really mean Sigmund."

"Isn't it clear we're gone?" The undertunes of incredulity were wasted on Addeo, but Nessus couldn't stop himself.

"Except you," Addeo said. He laughed at Nessus' worried plucking at his mane. "I don't think Sigmund realizes that. He's seen no trace of you for a long time."

"Then why?" Nessus persisted. "Ausfaller works beneath you. Why don't you stop him?"

"I have stopped him, to the extent I safely can. Let me tell you the story about how Sigmund became an ARM." Addeo fastidiously wiped his hands on a napkin. "Eleven years ago, Sigmund was a financial analyst, a glorified accountant. He was investigating a criminal gang. I remind you, he wasn't yet an ARM.

"Nonetheless, Sigmund was paranoid. He got there the old-fashioned way, without drugs. It was quite the accomplishment to keep his condition secret and untreated. Then the gang he was studying abducted him. Sigmund *should* have died. Now ask why he didn't."

"Why didn't Sigmund die?" Nessus dutifully asked. It was better than talking to himself.

Addeo smiled. "Paranoia. He suspected a corrupt United Nations official must be aiding the mob. He didn't know who. Sigmund set traps, using his own money, for eight different co-workers.

"It turned out Sigmund's boss's boss, a guy named Grimaldi, *was* dirty. When Grimaldi went to gloat, Sigmund offered to ransom himself. The bank transfer identified Grimaldi. ARMs tracked Grimaldi, rescued Sigmund, and broke up the gang. A major coup, Nessus.

"So. Sigmund is savvy and paranoid. Of *course* he was recruited. Now do you see?"

Such convolution! It made Nessus' brain hurt. "Truly? No."

"Sigmund interprets any order to desist—and he *has* gotten that order—as proof of a broader conspiracy. Hopefully, he thinks the command came from the Secretary-General. Neither you nor I wants Sigmund looking too closely at me." Addeo frowned. "But if it should occur to you that Sigmund might meet with an unfortunate accident . . . don't. Based on his history, it's all too likely Ausfaller has made 'in-case-of-my-death' arrangements. There's nothing like an unexpected death to make paranoid ravings suddenly seem not so paranoid."

Jinxians and Puppeteers? UN officials and rich industrialists? Nessus couldn't begin to imagine the plot Ausfaller had constructed from shadows. Mostly from shadows: Addeo did conspire, if not in the way Ausfaller feared.

It was all madness—but loneliness was a kind of madness, too. Nessus desperately needed companionship. The topic hardly mattered. "Explain how Ausfaller ties Jinx into his speculations."

Addeo exhaled loudly, and tipped back his head in thought. "Sigmund's job for years was to worry about Jinx. So he did. In a way, you have to admire his persistence. If there were any real danger there, I'm sure Sigmund would long ago have found it."

"Go on," Nessus said. "Explain his fixation with Beowulf Shaeffer."

"If I can. Until Nakamura Lines folded, Shaeffer shuttled between colony worlds. For excitement, he had his pick of bored woman passengers. All very remunerative and mundane.

"Suddenly, he's had three big adventures. The doomed BVS-1 mission was Jinx funded, and it seemed to involve a weapon that could kill through a General Products hull. Next, Shaeffer leaves *from Jinx* on a mission that discovers the core explosion. He sends Puppeteers into hiding and economies across Known Space reeling. Then, he leaves Earth in a ship built within a GP hull, only to reappear on Jinx with the same hyperdrive but no hull. Was the GP hull sold, like Pelton claims, or somehow destroyed, as Sigmund fears?"

Nessus' heads crept lower and lower. Ausfaller *knew* nothing—and yet much that he *suspected* was at the fringes of the truth. "And Ausfaller's fixation with Pelton?"

"Pretty," Addeo said, now watching the snowstorm. "A projection to disguise this location, of course."

"Of course," Nessus lied. "What about Pelton?"

Addeo turned back toward Nessus. "Many reasons. Guilt by association with Shaeffer, certainly. The disappearing-hull trick. The off-world money that Sigmund can't watch. The secret project—on Jinx. The family's pull. Futz, it doesn't surprise me at all that my man Sigmund distrusts Pelton.

"Then there's a fascinating, decades-old rumor. Lots of folks believe Puppeteers sold Pelton's great-whatever-grandma the core technology for transfer booths. *Sigmund* knows the rumor."

"I see," Nessus said flatly. It suddenly took too much effort to properly inflect human speech. Because it wasn't a rumor. General Products had sold that technology. Puck himself had negotiated the deal. . . .

Puck: Three years later, that wound still throbbed. Nessus dragged his thoughts back to the present. Not even a corrupt ARM must ever suspect that Citizens could compromise the transfer-booth system. "Insanely creative," Nessus said. "It's hard to believe *you're* an ARM."

Addeo laughed. "Earth needs people like Sigmund, but they creep out the powers that be. At my level, the execs are normal. We're buffers."

As I look creepy to my bosses, Nessus thought sadly. Will they ever bring me home?

When Addeo finally teleported away, his report completed, Nessus was more depressed than when his lackey had arrived.

• 21 •

Nessus poked at a tangle of freshly synthed grasses. The imminence of change had him too excited to eat.

Hope had been a long time coming.

He'd expected to be without an appetite, but for other reasons: Dealing with Addeo made Nessus feel dirty. Nor was it only Addeo; it was all his recent contacts. Any honorable human would want to find out what secret goals kept Nessus on Earth. And so he met only with felons and, through their connivance, venal officials. Like Addeo.

It had not always been thus. Once Nessus had worked with *good* humans. Capable humans. Humans to whom he had learned to entrust his safety. Humans with whom he had actually approached a neutron star and lived to tell about it.

What, he wondered, had become of his former crew?

His thoughts fell all too easily into the familiar rut: Those like me, the few able to voyage far from Hearth, had always been a scarce commodity. Always.

And now scarcer.

The core explosion was hardly imaginable to most. Not so the scouts. Its discovery had plunged most scouts into catatonia—and all his friends into a hungry singularity.

Despite everything, reluctantly but obediently, he had stayed behind on Earth, one of a very few remaining scouts. . . .

Who then would guide a trillion Citizens in their flight?

Again and again, his entreaties to help went unanswered. If not me, Nessus had realized, then there must be *someone.* Trish and Raul, his crew so many years earlier, had exhibited great promise—under his guidance, of course. Why not use reliable humans?

And so Nessus had sent home a bold recommendation. Let watching Gregory Pelton be Achilles' duty. Pelton, if he meant ever to return to the antimatter world, made his secretive preparations on Jinx. Even now, Shaeffer might be making his way circuitously back to Jinx.

With a will of its own, a head rose from the shallow bowl of grass. Nessus stared himself in the eyes. What Ausfaller-like reasoning!

Better to be like Ausfaller than Addeo.

And finally, to Nessus' surprise, new orders had arrived. The task of monitoring Pelton and Shaeffer, together with responsibility for Nessus' agents in Sol system, had all been reassigned to Achilles. As for Nessus . . . *he* was recalled home—

To lead the training of a cadre of human scouts.

SIGMUND BROODED IN his darkened living room, eyes shut, immersed in the Mozart Requiem mass. Half a world (and a transfer booth) away waited all the desperate would-be parents of Alaska.

They would be there still for his next shift, and the next, and the next. . . .

"We're not flat phobes. We can leave Earth. Leave Sol system," Feather shouted over the music. And start a family, she didn't bother to articulate. There was no need.

"Not together." Sigmund sighed. "It wouldn't be allowed. We know too much." He opened his eyes. "Medusa, music off. Raise lighting to fifty percent.

"Feather, you know how things work. Suppose we somehow managed to get away and meet up on another world. For the rest of our lives we'd be looking over our shoulders for someone just like us to appear." And when, not if, the ARM found us? Then who would raise our children?

"Tanj it, Sigmund," she snarled. "I can't spend my life on mother hunts. I won't. I only wish I had the guts to risk pregnancy myself."

What could he say? That their latest request for reassignment back to Alien Affairs had been rejected. She knew that. That joining the ARM was a one-way trip? Given how he'd become an ARM, saying so would be an accusation. Anyway, she knew that, too. "Let's go out onto the balcony."

The fronds of his potted palms rustled in the evening breeze. He and Feather stood side by side, hands on the railing, watching the city lights far below.

Everything looked normal; perhaps that was the point. The Puppeteers were long gone—apparently even Nessus. The economy, though not recovered, was finally improving. Shaeffer was somewhere far away.

Pelton, for all his secretive machination, had harmed no one. Possibly he had found his schemes too fraught with complications. Possibly Max Addeo was right all along and Pelton *had* no nefarious plans. Either explanation accounted for the absence of trouble from Pelton.

How pleasant it would be to believe such fairy tales.

"Oh, well," Feather finally said. "Eventually there's bound to be a riot, or a suicidal renegade Kzin, or some other diversion from mother hunts."

Sigmund patted her hand. "Ever the optimist."

"You'll think of something. You're the smartest person I know."

"Hardly," he said. "That's got to be Carlos Wu."

Wu! Lately, Sigmund couldn't get Carlos out of his thoughts. The explosion at the galactic core had been the first of so many dominoes to topple. Every physicist with whom Sigmund had consulted swore to the integrity of the instrument readings Shaeffer brought back on the *Long Shot.* And every physicist also considered Carlos to be the very brightest of their fraternity.

In his mind's eye, Sigmund teetered at the edge of an abyss.

"Feather," he whispered. "What if Carlos Wu fabricated the core-explosion data?"

VINDICATED

Earth date: 2650

• 22 •

Sigmund sipped his coffee, half-awake. A news digest shimmered over the breakfast table. Color-coded by topic, brightened or dimmed according to Medusa's sense of immediacy, inset windows scrolling . . . It would be a challenge to absorb even after the caffeine kicked in. His glance flitted about the projection, steered by Medusa's cues. Little of the information registered. Feather sat across the table, feigning interest in soccer-match highlights, no more prepared than he to speak.

"Stupid Cavaliers," she finally managed, minutes later. Her complaint was directed at the holo, or the coach, or the universe. Not him. She turned up the audio when he looked her way.

Another big mother hunt was imminent—not just regional harassment, for appearances, but a big global push. He couldn't stop it. He couldn't excuse her. He couldn't protect her if anyone else detected her interference.

He couldn't bear her misery.

A green face, crowned with hissing, coiling snakes, popped up over a corner of his news digest. "Turquoise alert," Medusa said softly.

Sigmund pulled his chair closer, instantly alert. "Display." A new window opened, within it an oblique view of a transfer booth. He watched four men emerge and take up positions around the booth. Moments later, Calista Melenkamp appeared. The bodyguards, faces expressionless, swept the Secretary-General up the broad granite stairs into her New York club.

He cleared his throat. "I've got to take care of something."

Feather looked away from the game. "What?"

He stood. "We'll talk later."

Her eyes narrowed. "You're not doing something stupid, are you?"

The jury was still out on that. "Me?" Dialing his destination, he had a moment to appreciate that Feather still cared.

Manhattan was overcast and blustery. As Sigmund climbed the stairs of Melenkamp's private club, the doorman made no move to open the door.

Sigmund halted two stairs from the top. "I have an urgent message for the Secretary-General," he said. It didn't surprise him to find he was unwelcome. Whatever unseen security system had ID'd him was as modern as everything within was antique. That, or the doorman had a very good memory for faces. Either way, Sigmund was impressed.

"I am sorry, sir. Only members and escorted guests are permitted inside."

"I understand." Sigmund took an envelope from his coat pocket. The day's gloom made the melodramatic bloodred drop of sealing wax all the starker. He had carried the missive for weeks awaiting just this opportunity. Melenkamp (at Gregory Pelton's urging?) had seen to it that Sigmund could only communicate with her through channels. The information in his hand must go only, and directly, to the S-G. "It's a matter of global importance. *Solar* importance."

The doorman palmed the sheaf of thousand-sol bills beneath the envelope. "I'll see what I can do, sir. Please wait here." He left Sigmund on the narrow porch.

Ten minutes later, two of Melenkamp's bodyguards appeared to escort him inside.

"LEAVE US," MELENKAMP told her guards. They hesitated just long enough to convey disapproval before backing from the room, closing the massive oaken door behind them. She gestured at a fragile-looking chair. "Sit."

Sigmund sat. The pages of his letter rested, side by side, on the otherwise bare table before her. "I hoped you would be curious."

"How could I not?" She bit off each word. "How long have you been following me, Agent Ausfaller?"

Sigmund had surrounded this establishment with almost invisibly small ARM sensors. No good could come of admitting that. "I've followed money, not people."

"Evasion noted." She poured a cup of coffee from the carafe on the sideboard, then sat at the table by his letter. "Talk about the money you followed."

So he did: Of the almost unimaginable fortune General Products must have earned in Sol system, much of it still untraced. Of the wealth that remained behind after the Puppeteer Exodus five years earlier. Of funds from what ought, logically, to be dormant accounts, still seeping away. Of circuitously routed transfers, passing through conduits as anonymous and untraceable as modern financial engineers could construct. Of—

She exhaled sharply. "Puppeteers were secretive when they were here en masse. So now, with their presence reduced to one lonely Puppeteer in hiding, of *course* they're indirect. I remember the name Nessus, and that he remained behind to settle outstanding obligations. I did read the reports from your task force, Mr. Ausfaller—when you *had* a task force."

He was losing her. He couldn't allow that! He should have begun at the end of the tortuous money trail, not the beginning. At an off-world bank haven in the Belt. "And if a hidden Puppeteer is putting money into a numbered account controlled by one of your deputies?"

"Damn it, Ausfaller, of course I care! That's why you're here, however briefly. That's why you aren't in custody for a years-long rogue investigation. Not yet. I *will* confirm the substance of your accusation—if that's possible. For now, I'll assume you are neither so foolish nor so mad as to stalk me in order to lie to me."

Or Melenkamp meant to find out how much he knew about her, before having him arrested. No, Sigmund lectured himself. You couldn't trace any GP money to her. You have to trust her now. "You *should* check everything out—discreetly. A deposit happens by the tenth of every month. Your man checks his balance between the eleventh and the thirteenth."

Her cheek twitched. "Belter banks will confirm this? In my experience, neither they nor the goldskins are so cooperative."

Belter cops wore yellow vacuum suits; the familiar mention was no accident. Melenkamp's UN career began in the attorney's office. She had prosecuted her share of interworld money-laundering cases. She had surely had her share of run-ins with the goldskins about jurisdiction and sharing evidence.

Admitting to further infractions risked nothing. Either he convinced her he acted for a higher cause or he went, soon enough, into the organ banks. "Some will cooperate," Sigmund said. "It depends who is beholden to whom."

And that, in a nutshell, was why it had taken so long to get here. Five years of offering more information to Belter authorities than was revealed to him. Five years of running interference for naïve Belter tourists, of making behind-the-scenes interventions. "Enough goldskins owe me favors now."

One folded sheet of paper remained in Sigmund's coat; he removed it now. "This is a list of financial analysts in the Office of the Secretariat who probably aren't getting trickle-down payoffs. I suggest you send at least two to the Prague branch of Bank of Ceres."

"Two? Ah, to watch each other." Sighing, she accepted the folded paper from his hand. "You live in a devious world, Ausfaller."

He sensed the stirrings of belief in her response. "Respectfully, the matter we should be addressing is: What next?"

She stared. "Arrest, certainly. Confiscation of every cent of every bribe. Into the organ banks with him, as quickly as it can be arranged."

"No." In Sigmund's mind, the dissent continued: As happy as that would make me. "I've traced some of the money. Some of the downstream recipients. There's so much we *don't* know. I'm skeptical even Max Addeo can tell us everything—knowingly."

Slowly, she smiled. "So for now you'll watch Max."

Sigmund nodded. "As you will. Puppeteers bought access to the innermost circles of the UN for some still-hidden reason. I doubt they would reveal their purposes to Addeo.

"With your influence over what Max sees, reads, and hears in the office hallways, I hope to scare whoever controls General Products' wealth into showing himself."

FEATHER GRUNTED AT Sigmund's approach, more an acknowledgment than a greeting. Her attention remained on her workstation.

"Feather," he said.

She heard something in his voice, and finally looked up. "Big crunch, Sigmund, especially since I was covering for *your* unexplained absence."

"Sorry." He touched her arm lightly. "Five minutes. Come with me."

The skies had opened in Fairbanks, and cold rain fell in torrents. Sigmund dialed Sky Meadows State Park in Virginia. The mid-Atlantic region was sunny and fair, and the venue seemed apt. He led her off a meandering trail into the shade of a solitary and stately pine. Rolling meadow and wooded hills stretched to the horizon.

"Five minutes, huh?" Feather finally said. She ignored him for the spectacular view. "Aren't you in enough trouble already?"

Sigmund bent to retrieve an old fallen pinecone. Evergreens. Verdant fields. The seed in his hands. It all symbolized newfound hope. "Feather, I'm going back to New York. UN Headquarters. I want you there with me."

Her head swiveled round. "Headquarters! Why?"

"Officially, a new special-investigations unit, reporting directly to the S-G. Unofficially . . ."

"Unofficially, what?" she snapped. "Not coordinating futzing mother hunts. I refuse to take *more* responsibility for those."

He kissed the top of her head. "Unofficially, we're back hunting Puppeteers. It turns out they're still around. At least it looks that way, because someone is spending General Products money. *That's* why I've been secretive. If Melenkamp hadn't believed me—or if she were in on it—I didn't want to take you down with me."

A sour look came over her, an expression that said she didn't want or need anyone's protection. "Spending their money on what, Sigmund?"

"For starters, the Deputy Undersecretary General for Security Affairs."

"Addeo," Feather hissed. "That's why the bastard disbanded the task force."

"Addeo," Sigmund agreed. "Working at headquarters, we'll be able to watch him. We'll know who Max talks to. Behind the scenes, working through the Secretary-General, I hope to control everything Addeo is assigned and everything he's told."

Suddenly, it was the old Feather who stood beside him. A happy, predatory glow lit her face. "And Addeo leads us to Nessus."

"Nessus may be gone." Addeo's dirty money, all the payoffs, flowed through the underworld. None of Sigmund's informants had heard from or about Nessus in the past two years. Some had encountered a new name, though, a name the mere thought of which made Sigmund's gut cramp with remembered agony.

Sigmund said, "The criminal mastermind my sources keep reporting is called Achilles."

· 23 ·

From deep in the throat the growl emerged, rolling on and on. A hairless tail lashed from side to side. Ears lay flattened against the head.

Better to fixate on tail and ears and harmless noise than the baring of needle-like fangs. Than the razor-sharp claws that extended from hands like four-fingered black leather gloves.

Achilles stood, alone and unarmed, before the enraged Kzin. "I thank you for coming," he snarled. The snarl carried no aggressive intent; Hero's Tongue could be spoken no other way. "I am Achilles. How should you be called?"

The Kzin retracted his lips still further. Sunset glinted like blood on his teeth. He towered over Achilles. "Address me as Maintainer-of-Equipment."

A title rather than a name, Achilles noted, and a lowly title at that. The Kzin had come to this remote and barren plain for one purpose: to *earn* a name in hand-to-hand combat.

Achilles had, with extreme indirection, posed as a human adventurer. His simple boast to the underclass of this impoverished Kzinti colony world of Spearpoint: to defeat, one by one, all challengers. How wondrous and depressing it was that merely one Kzin had come. Was this warrior race *so* intimidated by the humans? After six disastrous wars, Achilles supposed he was saddened more than surprised. "Maintainer, you are surely disappointed to discover your challenger."

The Kzin's only immediate response was a deeper growl.

"I will explain," Achilles continued. "I seek those prepared to confront our mutual adversary."

Maintainer-of-Equipment's tail scythed the air. "Leaf-eater, I am soiled merely talking with you. Do not presume to speak of anything mutual."

Achilles' legs trembled from the effort not to flee—not that he could possibly outrun this monster. He had come secure in the knowledge that no Kzin would demean himself by attacking an herbivore. "Nonetheless, Maintainer, we share an interest in teaching humility to the humans." And, for our separate reasons, we both desire to pursue our aims discreetly.

Maintainer-of-Equipment turned away, striding for his small airship. "I tasted human in the last great war. I would do so again. And no *leaf-eater* will tell *me* how to hunt."

Maintainer-of-Equipment poured all his rage into his takeoff. The exhaust incinerated a cluster of low-lying leathery shrubs and blasted dust and pebbles across the plain. His airship roared contemptuously low over *Remembrance*, and disappeared.

Achilles stood alone on the undulating plain, with only a few smoldering plants for company. So it had gone on every backwater Kzinti world he had visited. The humans had won: There were no more Heroes. His legs quivered as he made his way back to his ship.

If not even Kzinti still in search of proper names would serve, how could he deflect the unwelcome attentions of the humans?

• 24 •

Nessus was too excited to sleep. The sidelong glances he got at a communal dining hall made plain he was too nervous to show himself in public. As the least worst alternative for coping with his anxiety, he tramped in place within his tiny living unit until his legs ached and sweat dripped from his flanks.

His only company was an unending holographic herd. Companionable warbles and whistles sounded all around him. Only an occasional snippet, never more than a chord or trill, rose to the level of intelligibility. The synthesized voices were quite random. None of it calmed him. The stakes were too high, for him personally—

And for whole worlds.

Finally the time neared for the appointment he had requested. Demanded. Nessus refreshed and dried himself with a quick ultrasonic cleansing. He gathered his mane into a token few braids, whether for credibility with Nike, or for Nike himself, Nessus did not know himself.

He teleported directly from his arcology into the Ministry of Foreign Affairs, emerging into a transparent isolation booth. Still struggling for the notes to articulate his vision, Nessus was startled by the sudden blue light he should have remembered to expect. He swiveled his heads toward the darting beam that sought out his retinal prints. At the same time, hidden sensors searched him for any inappropriate implements.

The booth was a sealed bubble of hull material, of course. At a higher intensity, the light would vaporize him where he stood, right through the unbreakable material. Nessus had a twinge of sympathy for his erstwhile visitors on Earth.

He was teleported without notice into a cozy antechamber. Nessus moved from the stepping disc inlaid on the floor to settle onto a pile of soft cushions. How those earthly visitors would have gaped at a proper stepping disc! Even their primitive closed transfer booths would have been beyond them, but for General Products.

The problem was: He liked humans. Not all of them certainly, but enough. Now he feared that humanity's fate rested in his jaws. Quivering with tension, Nessus worked himself into a manic state. Nike would not be easy to convince.

Nike. A rush of recent memories almost overwhelmed Nessus. An intimate stroll, just the two of them, along a secluded shore. The ballet, enjoyed from Nike's private box. The exclusive party after the dance, introduced there to the cream of Experimentalist party politicians as Nike's personal guest.

Citizens courted with rituals as formal as the ballet. By proper standards, Nike had made no commitment. But did not actions sing as loudly as words?

In his hearts Nessus knew that one such as Nike was schooled to choose every word—those uttered and those withheld—with exquisite care.

And yet.

After striving for *so* many years to be noticed, Nessus had finally been summoned to the ministry to meet Nike—although not for the reason Nessus had expected. His idol had listened politely enough to a report on the experimental scouting program, and the first mission of many that would roam ahead of the Fleet in its journey. But Nike's interests lay not in probing the path ahead, but on the danger close behind: Sigmund Ausfaller's renewed quest for Puppeteers. Only after systematically wringing from Nessus countless details about Earth had Nike asked Nessus to accompany him to the ballet.

I have earned Nike's respect, Nessus concluded. It

was a start. And if, in this time of crisis for the Concordance, I must return to Sol system, then at least I will do it with the full confidence of the Director himself.

And if Nike's personal attentions were meant to soften him for a truly horrifying course of action? Nessus nervously straightened his token braids, eager for and dreading the pending session.

"Come." A tall, green-eyed Citizen had materialized across the room. The green brooch on his utility belt bespoke allegiance to the ruling Conservative faction. "The Deputy Minister will see you now." Then he was gone as abruptly as he had arrived.

Nessus cantered to the temporarily activated stepping disc. He had been to the ministry before; he understood the routine. He stepped after the one he recognized as an aide of Nike's. They made their way through the buzzing office complex that was Clandestine Directorate. Personal ornamentation here was mostly Experimentalist orange. Conservatives ruled, but they lacked the flexibility of thought even to imagine leaving Hearth.

The taciturn aide led Nessus to the entrance of Nike's spacious office. Holo artwork filled the room, and lush meadowplant carpeted the floor. Nike emerged from behind his work surface, his mane breathtakingly coiffed. A string of orange garnets glittered amid his braids. "Please come in," Nike said.

Nessus quivered with nervous energy. The latching of the door behind him by the departing aide scarcely registered. The manic state never lasted long; he must make his proposal quickly. Now. "I have an answer!" he blurted.

"How I envy you. What was the question?"

Nike looked *relieved*! Had he feared Nessus would raise more personal matters? Later, Nessus thought, I must examine that impression. Larger issues now required his attention.

Nessus shifted his weight between front feet. "An answer for the problem with the wild humans. I can save them. That is, I know how to preoccupy them."

"Can you keep the ARM from finding us?" Doubt was plain in Nike's eyes. In flight, the Concordance was more vulnerable than ever. Of all species, the wild humans must not find them.

"Yes, yes!" Nessus bobbed his heads in vigorous alternation. He *must* be compelling. No matter that the chaos he proposed to unleash weighed on his conscience. Failure would bring far more dire consequences. A stealthed General Products hull, accelerated to a high speed, smashing undetected into a populated world. . . .

Shivering, Nessus returned to his proposal. A simple analogy would make things clear. "I was at Harem House and—"

Nike flinched. Choosing of a Bride was obviously not in *his* mind.

Nessus dare not stop. Later he would collapse into a blind lump of embarrassment. For now, the words tumbled out, unstoppable. "The point, Nike, is those on Earth also control their numbers. Unlike us, the humans have chemical means of contraception. Their use is mandatory. Would-be parents require government permission to forego their annual booster doses. Those who have children without permission are executed, and their offspring sterilized."

His left foreleg, with a mind of its own, dug into the meadowplant. "They're not like us, Nike. Earth remains a wilderness, home to a scant few billions. Our arcologies rival in number of residents the largest cities on Earth." Because humans need room. They swarm the nearby solar systems. Nessus kept *those* thoughts to himself. They did not advance his argument. "They reconcile themselves to a repressive government because to them Earth already seems too crowded. That is why discrediting Earth's Fertility Board is the key."

"You propose a scandal to divert the hunt for the Concordance." Nike's necks wobbled skeptically.

Nessus fixed Nike with a two-headed stare, astonished by his own boldness. He *must* demonstrate his absolute conviction. "Imagine if it were suspected Citizens were secretly buying Brides and the right to reproduce. How would our kind react?" To Nike's expression of horror Nessus added, simply, "Exactly."

Nike brought his heads together in thought, doubtless imagining the strife such rumors would cause even among the communal and sociable Citizens. "Is it doable?"

"I believe so, given access to sufficient resources," Nessus answered. "I envision our agents bribing some members of the Fertility Board, and compromising others by creating bank accounts in their names. The economies of the human worlds have yet to recover from the shock of General Products' disappearance. The more wealth people have lost, the quicker they will be to suspect conspiracy. Many will believe the rich are buying birthrights. A bit of innuendo here, some surreptitious funding to political opportunists there . . ."

Nessus found himself lapsing into Interworld for words otherwise absent from his vocabulary. It was unavoidable. For too long he had had none but humans for company.

He could maintain this frenetic audacity for only so long. He *must* convince Nike soon, before he lapsed into the depressed catatonia that was sure to follow.

Nike seemed not to have noticed his flagging concentration. "The retained earnings from the General Products Corporation are adequate to the task?"

"If the approach is valid, money will not be the limiting factor." Nessus could not help tugging at a braid. He knew he was on the edge of collapse.

Nike stood in silence for a long time. Finally, he said, "I am very encouraged, but of course a great deal of detail must remain to be determined. I would like you to make this your top priority. Please get back to me soon with an update."

As Nessus shambled to the closed office door, Nike whistled softly: Stay a moment. He came right up to Nessus, and leaned forward to intimately stroke Nessus' scruffy mane. Too bad his approach seemed stiff and calculated. "Come back soon. I am depending on you."

MEETINGS WERE HELD. Plans evolved. Resources were allocated. Contingencies were categorized and analyzed, and mitigations identified.

Nessus' experimental scouting program, almost as an afterthought, was declared a success. His trainees, unsupervised, must explore the way ahead for the herd. They could hardly be assigned the mission he proposed.

Nessus was not surprised, but was a bit saddened, to get Nike's go-ahead for a return to Sol system in an impersonal recorded message.

• 25 •

Crash. Tinkle. *Crash.* Crash. Clink.

Glass shards flew everywhere. Now the steady rain was mostly bottles, the windows of the nearby buildings having long since been shattered.

Squadrons of copseyes floated overhead, playing hide-and-seek with the hooligans who burst out of the crowd or darted from places of concealment to lob their primitive missiles. The grapefruit-sized bots only carried stunners, but at least two stunned rioters had fallen from windowless offices to their deaths.

One more inarticulate roar burst from the thousands

who filled the square. The cheering drowned out the haranguing from across the plaza.

Sigmund swung his plasteel shield to deflect yet another bottle. He'd done a lot of that; his shield arm was getting very tired. "Futz," he announced. The helmet mike in his riot-control gear was set to a private channel. "Has everyone gone insane?"

A thin line of ARMs in assault armor surrounded the demonstrators, awaiting orders. Sigmund couldn't imagine any orders that could make sense. "Futz," he repeated.

Crash. *Crash.* Tinkle. *Crash.*

"You don't need to be here," Feather snapped. She meant: He wasn't *supposed* to be there. ARM offices worldwide had emptied to help contain the global eruption of violence, but as a unit head he was considered too senior to endanger himself.

Tough. He went where his team went. That had meant three different cities so far today. He thought this was Chicago. "And miss all this?" His eyes maintained their steady sweep.

"But I'm glad you are," Feather added under her breath.

A few more bottles deflected. Men and women shaking their fists. Bobbing placards demanded reproductive justice and the right to bear children. Tanj it, Sigmund thought, the world is already too crowded. This chaos was unacceptable. And yet—

Feather seemed to read his mind. "Of course this is wrong." She meant the riots. "But is their *cause* so wrong?"

Would it really be so wrong if he and Feather had a child?

Not waiting for, or maybe not expecting, a response, she kicked a mound of the refuse from the looted offices and condos. She stomped a torn painting and snapped its gilded frame. "Parasitic bastards. Holo art is too good for them. And now they're buying babies, too."

". . . Ready," Sigmund's earphones announced as another yell burst from the crowd. The latest rabble-rouser, standing on a cargo floater, had just shouted out something about lotteries. A new cheer broke out: "Justice, justice, justice, justice. . . ."

Sigmund barely made out over the chanting, "Clear the square." The line straightened. He locked shields with Feather to one side and Andrea Girard on the other. The second rank raised their shields above their heads. It felt vaguely medieval, or maybe more ancient.

Crash. *Crash. Crash.*

Something tickled his thoughts. An old memory? Whatever it was had to wait. Distraction now would get him killed.

One after another, copseyes thudded onto the plaza, vivid yellow amid the detritus. Sigmund counted five. One or two copseyes might be brought down by beer bottles and dumb luck. This many down, this close together, meant a sniper with a serious weapon, most likely a hunting rifle. They *had* to act, and decisively, before those guns were turned against people. "Oxygen on," came the radioed order. "Sleep gas in ten seconds."

They didn't get even that long. Two ARM squad carriers soared over a building that abutted the square, flashers pulsing, spewing thick clouds of gas. Sigmund winced. Two floaters couldn't begin to take down a crowd this large. It was worse than doing nothing.

Protestors stampeded, shrieking.

Sigmund's earpiece reawakened. "On my mark, advance."

Advance? A human sea washed over the police phalanx. Everywhere, people fell: gassed, stunned by copseyes or ARMs, struck from above by the hail of bottles, or trampled. The thin line burst, the mob scattering the vastly outnumbered ARMs. Coughing rioters fought the ARMs—and then one another—for oxygen masks.

A wild-eyed lunatic rushed at Feather's back. Naught remained of his placard but the sturdy scrap of lumber he now swung like a mace. Sigmund braced his shield, his stunner lost in the melee. As he charged, motion from above caught his eye. He had a brief impression of a chair hurtling down at him—

And then nothing.

SIGMUND JERKED BACK to awareness, unable to see. Someone twisted his helmet. His head and neck throbbed. He flailed, screaming. A boot connected, and someone screamed back.

"Sigmund! It's me!" Feather shouted. "Let me get your helmet off."

He clamped his jaw against the pain and tried to lie still. The helmet turned, and he could see again. Feather, still in full riot-control armor, knelt at his side. She removed his helmet and held it where he could get a good look. One side was crushed. He remembered that chair, flung from who knew how many stories up. The blow that smashed his helmet must have spun it around until the visor was over his right ear.

The few civilians nearby were all on the ground in unnatural poses, apparently entangled in force fields. Mostly they lay very still. It was a good decision, because the restraints got tighter the more you struggled. He almost felt bad about the protestor he'd just kicked.

Feather looked intact. "What's happened?" he croaked. "Where is everyone?"

"The cavalry happened." Feather gestured at the police floater circling the area. "The driver saw you go down and buzzed the crowd. He's been running interference since. Ambulances are on the way. The riots moved uptown, and our guys followed. They're okay."

Sirens wailed from every direction. "Feather, help me up."

"No way. Wait for the ambulance." She patted his hand.

His pocket chimed. He vaguely recollected it had been going on for a while. "Accept the call," he said. Medusa wouldn't forward anything unless it was urgent.

A dim green glow seeped out from under his armored vest. The body armor muffled Medusa's voice so that Sigmund had to strain to hear. "I couldn't trace the delivery," Medusa said. "Whatever that means, it's important."

ARTIFICIAL HERD PHEROMONES, pungent and thick, filled the relax room of *Aegis*. The scent did nothing to help Nessus relax. He was light-years from another of his kind, light-seconds from any ship or settlement. To unwind seemed impossible.

A human broadcast droned in the background, forwarded to his ship by a chain of stealthed relay buoys hidden deep in Sol system. Mostly he monitored Belter stations, since Earth's media appeared to be under heavy United Nations censorship. Belters didn't exactly revel in Earth's misfortune; they didn't sugarcoat it, either.

He had hundreds of deaths on his conscience.

"I brought it on myself," Nessus told himself. "Better this than"—he couldn't help but look at the larger-than-life image of Nike with whom he shared the cabin. He had several. He'd taken this picture at an Experimentalist party rally, soon after Nike first caught his eye. Before he had volunteered for the scouting program in the hope, someday, of catching Nike's eye.

In more innocent times.

Not even Nike's image could soothe Nessus. His mood was too guilty. Better than what? he wondered again.

"What would you have done to keep us safe?" he asked Nike's image. What manner of genocide? On Earth and how many other human worlds?

Perhaps he wasn't being fair. Nike had, after all, endorsed this more subtle action.

A bowl of mixed grasses sat before Nessus, untouched. He had no appetite. The longer he was away, the harder it was to believe Nike ever had sincere feelings for him. The ballet, the party, their time together . . . it was all cajolery to maneuver him into returning to Sol system. At such great distances, all alone, orders meant nothing. Scouts had to be inspired, lest they exercise too *much* initiative.

Strangely, Achilles had taken offense at Nessus' return. No matter that Achilles never wanted responsibility for Sol system; he took it as an affront that someone else now had it.

And still Nike looked at him. "Just you wait," Nessus told the hologram. "Soon enough I'll have proof that the ARM has been thoroughly diverted. Then you'll see the surprise I have planned for you."

SIGMUND WOBBLED DOWN a long corridor at UN Headquarters. Only painkillers and a megadose of stims kept him moving. Feather walked beside him, muttering disapproval, catching him whenever he stumbled.

They still wore riot gear. Trailing anxious bureaucrats and sleep-gas fumes, they came finally to an office suite at the end of the hallway. The plaque next to the glass double doors read: Deputy Undersecretary for Administrative Affairs. Sigmund lurched past protesting aides and factotums in the reception area, into an inner office. Feather slammed the door behind them.

Sangeeta Kudrin shot from her chair. "What happened? No, never mind that. Let's get you into an autodoc."

Sigmund plopped onto her sofa. He would rather

talk to the Secretary-General herself, but Melenkamp was off-world. For cover he routed most progress reports through Sangeeta, anyway. "After I bring you up to date."

"Agent Filip, can't you give me the report?" Sangeeta asked.

"You would think." Feather settled next to Sigmund on the couch. "Except he won't tell me what's on his mind, either."

"Whenever you're ready," he said impatiently.

"Sorry," Sangeeta said. "What's this about?"

"The riots." His side was killing him. A broken rib, he guessed. Somebody got in a good kick under the edge of the vest before his rescue. His med kit still had painkillers, but any more would render him incoherent. "Puppeteers are behind them."

Sangeeta's current dye job involved stylized lightning bolts on her cheeks and dramatically arched faux eyebrows. She somehow managed to look more surprised. "Surely not."

In his mind's ear, the shattering of glass rolled on and on. Far away he'd met a Puppeteer whose name sounded like a window breaking in slow motion, and dubbed him Adonis. Broken Glass's name of convenience was something else, of course. Nessus had admitted as much without sharing a pronounceable pseudonym.

Sigmund would offer good odds that the GP exec he'd met on We Made It went by the name Achilles.

Sangeeta stared. She'd been twitchy since his return to headquarters, obviously trying to hide something from him. She needn't have bothered. Her affair with Calista Melenkamp was the worst-kept secret at headquarters. The Secretary-General's husband might be the only one not in the know; Sigmund doubted even that. It wasn't like Sigmund cared, or, given his own relationship with Feather, could even criticize.

True, Sangeeta had done well in her career since

Sigmund met her back in '45, when they had neighboring offices. Jealous co-workers did whisper about her "connections." He and Sangeeta had been friends of a sort; he chose to believe his respect still mattered to her.

Futz! Why dwell now on this trivia? He'd clearly overachieved on the meds.

He shifted positions again, welcoming the head-clearing stab of pain from abused ribs. "Bear with me. Look at the progression, in the space of a few months. I trace laundered General Products funds to Max Addeo. The S-G lets Max discover that my new Special Investigations Unit is, in fact, the Puppeteer task force reborn. Protests break out against the Fertility Board, by far the worst in centuries. The riots are meant as a distraction." To distract *me.*

"Oh, come on," Feather said. He hadn't shared this epiphany even with her. "The disturbances are about corruption. The Fertility Board took bribes for licenses. It's that simple."

Feather wanted to believe the worst about the board. If she couldn't have a child, at least she could feel the victim. But opportunities for corruption had always been there. Why would they be worse now?

He said, "Spreading rumors is easy. There have always been whispers. We're in this mess because people—surprising people, powerful people—make it possible. They don't condone the violence, but they 'express their sympathy.' They 'welcome the public's input' on the matter. They legitimize the dissent and hopes of change. Tell me this, Sangeeta: Why are so many senators, ministers, and media stars suddenly sympathetic?"

Sangeeta broke eye contact. "Anyone with an ounce of decency has to feel some compassion."

Beside him, Feather tensed. Evidently more than one secret had been poorly kept. "I'm referring to actions, not feelings. More opinion leaders are speaking out about Fertility Board policy, and about *revising* that policy, than have for centuries. I ask you again, why."

"Why," Sangeeta echoed. "I don't *know* why."

"Someone very savvy has gone into the coercion business." Sigmund waved off her objection. "We'll get to who *someone* is."

He fished his pocket comp out from under his armored vest. "Medusa." The gorgon's head appeared, her crown of snakes writhing. "Access Archive AE Two."

"AE Two?" Sangeeta asked.

Alter Ego Two. It was one of six identities Sigmund maintained, fully realized personae who existed only in databases around Sol system. He took special pride in AE Two, an ARM agent who lived beyond his means. "The code name for a source," he said. "Medusa, play back the recent delivery to AE Two."

The gorgon vanished, replaced by a surveillance-camera view into a parcel-delivery transfer booth. Panel lights flickered and an envelope materialized. Projecting from the envelope, in an animated hologram, snarled a three-headed beast.

"Cerberus, the eternally watchful guardian of Hades," Sigmund offered. Did Sangeeta remember that Puppeteers took names from Greek mythology? "My source got it two days ago."

Feather frowned. "What kind of source?"

"A financially disadvantaged ARM," he answered. "That's why he was approached."

Sangeeta turned to gaze out the window. "Help me, Sigmund. A scary envelope. By implication, delivered to someone who can be coerced or bribed. What does this have to do with the riots, or why you're not in an autodoc where you belong? Or with Puppeteers, for tanj sake?"

"I asked Medusa to trace the envelope. That should be easy. As you saw, it came by transfer booth. Medusa?"

"I couldn't." Snakes thrashed and hissed. "The originating coordinates were nulled. The authentication check on the sender ID appears to have been bypassed. And there's no payment record for the teleportation."

"But that's impossible," Feather said. "Isn't it?"

"Oh no." Red-faced, Sangeeta turned toward him. "I see where this is going. The transfer-booth system was meddled with, and Gregory Pelton's family owns a controlling interest in the company. Sigmund, I'm *not* going back to Calis . . . the Secretary-General with wild accusations about the Peltons. You know she won't tolerate that."

He started shaking his head; it hurt and he stopped. "The general public only suspects transfers are traceable. Pelton certainly knows it. There's ARM gear integrated throughout his network. Subverting the system points right back at him. He wouldn't do it. Someone hoping to implicate him might."

Sangeeta crossed her arms across her chest. "Then who?"

He shrugged. Who hadn't heard the rumors that Puppeteers first sold a Pelton the underlying technology?

"What was in the note?" Feather asked.

The stims had started to fade. "An enumeration of AE Two's debt. A list of questionable deposits made into his accounts." Sigmund smiled wearily. He took a perverse pride in the traps he'd set. Each, in its own way, was a thing of beauty.

"That's *it*?" Sangeeta said. "No demands?"

"They'll come later," Feather guessed. "In the next letter. First, someone wants AE Two to sweat."

That would be a neat trick, Sigmund thought. Words grew harder to find, and even harder to get out of his mouth. "Back to the Puppeteers. Feather, I'm going to make a confession here, lest you start a witch hunt while I'm in the autodoc. AE Two is a computerized figment—I wrote him—but as far as personnel records are concerned, he's an ARM who reports directly to me.

"Who but a Puppeteer would work so hard to get a secret source into the Puppeteer task force?"

· 26 ·

Blue and brown and white, the planet hung above the horizon like a priceless jewel. Two small continents and part of a third presented themselves. Cyclonic storms dotted the sea-girt equatorial band. Large ice caps gleamed. The narrow night-side rim glimmered by moonlight.

The cratered moonscape from which Achilles stood observing could not have been more different.

Under other circumstances, the pristine globe overhead would have made an excellent new farm world for the Concordance. It would prove as alluring to Kzinti and humans. By drawing human and Kzinti attention, it would shelter all Citizens in their flight. The herd would never learn what happened here, of course, but he did not doubt their approval. Any Citizen would opt for safety over a bit less synthesized food in his diet.

Achilles busied his mouths with the apparatus before him, its controls awkward through his pressure suit. He had precalibrated all the units aboard *Remembrance*, but each required final tuning on-site. The geometric and geophysical constraints were exacting. He took every factor into account: the precise slope at each position, the exact altitude, the tiny perturbations in surface gravity due to subsurface mass concentrations.

Each painstaking adjustment took time and intense concentration.

The horizon loomed eerily near; the little moon's gravity seemed inadequate to hold him to this spot. Cosmic rays sleeted down. Here outside the impregnable hull of his ship, a meteor might strike at any moment. . . .

A strident polyphony in his headsets jerked Achilles to alertness. "Attention. Danger. Respond," bellowed the synthesized voices of the shipboard computer. "Attention. Danger. Respond."

The terminator line had visibly shifted on the beautiful world overhead, its changing phase a crude but serviceable timepiece. He had lapsed into catatonia too quickly even to notice. The computer had recognized his immobility.

"Acknowledged," Achilles intoned. He made his final, minuscule adjustments. "Apparatus readout?"

"Aligned within tolerance," the computer answered.

He cycled through the air lock. He still wore the pressure suit, since every point on this small moon was close. Three more units to put into position.

The planet set behind the horizon as *Remembrance* arced to where he would emplace the next unit. Fear and worry tugged at him—but so did excitement. What he attempted had never before been done. He was at the boundaries of science. To accomplish what he hoped to achieve here, Nature exploded entire stars. *He* had a defter touch.

How odd it was that the timidity of *Kzinti* had brought him to this threshold! How odd to realize that Maintainer-of-Equipment was among the *bravest* of the current generation. Six disastrous wars had rendered the "Heroes" impotent as a counterweight to the humans.

With a featherlight touch of thrusters, Achilles lowered the ship onto the pale regolith. Dust clouds raised by the landing slowly cleared. Most settled glacially onto the powdery surface; the weak gravity allowed some to dissipate into space.

Clutching a stepping disc, Achilles stepped down gingerly from the air lock, leaving its outer door open. He positioned the disc and stepped back. "Computer, transfer the next unit."

The equipment materialized before him. Disc and device alike embodied technology not meant for other races. It hardly mattered. All would soon be beyond recovery.

He busied himself with delicate adjustments. Sun and planet were absent from the sky, and he worked by the faint light from the open air lock.

Stars shone down, diamond bright and too numerous to count. They were set in blackest night, and the darkness drew his eyes like a bottomless well. Gravity's feeble hold seemed so inadequate. . . .

"Attention. Danger. Respond," the ship wailed.

"I'm fine," Achilles exaggerated. He *had* to finish soon. The wonder was that he had not yet gone irreparably mad. Surely no other Citizen could bear what he had borne: alone, in perilous surroundings, attempting this unprecedented transformation. Who else could have conceived this experiment? Who else fully understood the implications of the BVS-1 expedition? (Not that scientists on Hearth hadn't asked, but he offered them only hints. This would be *his* triumph. No one would try this experiment before him.)

Who else will protect a trillion lives on Hearth? Nessus?

Somehow Achilles managed to complete the deployments. He flew *Remembrance* for safety to the opposite side of the nameless planet. If he had miscalculated, not even an indestructible hull would protect him from the forces he was about to unleash.

The equipment array continued to report its status through relay buoys. In the bridge's main holo tank, a dodecahedron framework enclosed the image of the moon. Each of the twenty vertices marked a precisely configured device.

His limbs shook. Stress and trepidation and loneliness could not be denied for much longer. He *must* attempt the experiment now. Then, success or failure, he would fold into a comforting ball of self to reinvigorate himself.

Or he'd be dead.

"Extra scent," he trilled. The ship thickened the stew of artificial herd pheromones that already permeated the ship's living space. He inhaled deeply, allowing the spiciness to calm him. "Instrumentation status?"

"All instruments online," the ship acknowledged.

"Activate."

A GRAVITY WAVE passed through the pristine world, but the single-celled life-forms that were its only occupants took no notice. The instrumentation aboard *Remembrance* registered a flux of gravitons.

Softly crooning optimism, Achilles sent off a deep-radar ping. Neutrinos scarcely interact with normal matter, and the planet behind which he took shelter appeared in the scan display as the very palest of shadows. Beyond that translucent sphere, however, hung an ebony dot: a tiny region that stopped neutrinos in their tracks.

Achilles warbled in triumph.

He had learned much during his long exile among Kzinti and humans. He understood concepts incomprehensible to even the most sophisticated Citizen on Hearth. They lived too far from nature; they were too many generations remote from a world with predators. But not he.

And so, with the collapse of that moon into a compact mass of neutronium, he had baited his first trap.

· 27 ·

Sigmund stirred scrambled eggs with his fork, while Ander took another pass at the food-laden sideboard. Ander was newly home from Jinx, and to a point Sigmund sympathized: Bulking up for that gravity built a hearty appetite. A colonial-style hunt breakfast in Olde Williamsburg might fill him up.

Ander had dominated most settings even at his

previous size. He now moved through this dining room like a force of nature. Other diners squeezed their chairs close to their tables to make way. The host and hostess, dressed in scratchy-looking woolen colonial garb, stayed out of his path.

Ander eventually returned and set a heaping plate onto the table. *More* eggs, sausages, bacon, ham, fried chicken, biscuits and gravy. He scraped back his chair and sat. "Maybe it's because they eat so tanj much, but Jinxians have practically made food into a religion. I've had my fill of new cuisine, nouvelle cuisine, neo-cuisine, and fusion cuisine. *This* isn't cuisine at all. It's just good, hearty, natural food."

And thus hideously expensive, Sigmund thought, not that any food could compare in price to interstellar travel. "So how is Jinx?"

"Booming again." Ander paused to devour a chicken leg. "Puzzled by flatlander stupidity."

"The riots?" Sigmund guessed.

"The riots," Ander agreed. "The universe is plenty big, they say, and Earth isn't its center. Go elsewhere, they say, and have all the children you want."

Ander's opinion notwithstanding, this inn was hardly genuine colonial. In a bow toward authenticity, it *had* banished 3-V. Of that, Sigmund approved. It was a relief not to hear about Fertility Board corruption, or lynch mobs, or rallies for reproductive emancipation, or pitched battles with protestors. Or about proposals that birthrights be sold openly, on the grounds it would minimize corruption. Or the newest madness in the zeitgeist: gladiator fights. The winner gets a birthright; the loser gets dead; the population stays balanced.

And though, try as he might, he still could not prove it, Sigmund knew Puppeteers had caused it all. He shoved away his plate.

"How's Feather?" Ander asked.

Distant, bitter, and driven. Gone from his life but at

his side every day at work. Obsessed with the children she was not allowed. Angered by the denial of her emigration application. None of which he would discuss. What had possessed him to ever say anything to Ander about his personal life? "She's not on Jinx."

"Just being sociable." Ander shifted his weight, and his chair groaned in protest. "Back to work then.

"For starters, a lot of Jinxians love Gregory Pelton. Well they should. The money he's dropping on Jinx is a big part of why their economy turned around faster than Earth's. Elephant, they call him. Do you know that's his nickname?"

After years of surreptitious watching, Sigmund knew everything about Pelton—except what he was up to on Jinx. "I do."

Ander wasn't deterred. "To a Jinxian, a Bandersnatch is a big land animal. *Elephant* is a diminutive, a term of affection. I find that droll."

"So tell me what Pelton is doing on Jinx," Sigmund prodded.

"It's big," Ander answered. "He employs hundreds on West End. West End was always primitive and poor; that makes Pelton one of the biggest employers."

On Sigmund's long-ago visit to Jinx, West End had had no resources to offer save vacuum. "Paying those hundreds to do what?"

Ander demolished several sausages before answering. "That, I'm afraid, isn't entirely clear. They're very loyal."

A picture emerged through patient question-and-answer. Through intermediaries, Pelton owned a large dome on West End. He was stockpiling provisions for a deep-space mission, destination unknown, bought from enough suppliers to obscure the quantities. The employees didn't talk, and the suppressor field in the dome rendered useless the few sensors Ander managed to smuggle in. Pelton staffed his security team with moonlighting Jinxian police. That was smart, Sigmund conceded, effective in its own right, a guarantee of harmonious relations with officialdom—and a deterrent to any extralegal methods he might otherwise consider.

Whatever Pelton planned, it was *big.*

There were no indications, however, that it was imminent. When the time came, Sigmund guessed, ships would be brought inside Pelton's security perimeter for outfitting.

Taking comfort in that conclusion, Sigmund left Ander, still eating, to address more pressing—and official—matters.

THE ENORMITY OF events sometimes made Sigmund's head spin: All the plots and possibilities, the alliances and marriages of convenience and cynical manipulations, among Earth's numerous adversaries. Outsiders and Jinxians allied with Gregory Pelton. Aggrieved flatlanders unwittingly abetting Puppeteers, even as Puppeteers spied on Sigmund. Pinprick raids by Kzinti renegades on obscure, backwater worlds. Beowulf Shaeffer on a tour, it seemed, of every human-settled world.

It all meant something, surely, and too often the truth of things taunted and eluded Sigmund.

But not today.

FOR HIS EIGHTH birthday, more than anything, Sigmund had wanted a kitten. His normally indulgent parents said no. Dad claimed Sigmund was too young for the responsibility of a pet. Mom didn't want to deal with the mess. He remembered keeping his room clean and orderly to show responsibility. He promised to faithfully put out food, change the water, and empty the litter box. They still said no.

And then, when the day came, the package they

brought him mewed. Something inside scratched and thumped. The box had air holes.

A century and a half later, a simple observation filled him with the same elation.

Setting aside the wars and skirmishes with the Kzinti, all human worlds combined had lost twelve hyperdrive ships. Twelve starships lost in two and a half centuries weren't many. Most incidents happened near Sol system, just as most flights started or ended here. It made sense.

The most recent three losses happened somewhere far to the galactic north, two within the last year. All three ships had vanished without a trace.

Two years ago, it was *from* galactic north that Gregory Pelton's hull-less ship had hurtled at Jinx at 80 percent of light speed. Something very important there awaited discovery.

Sigmund intended to find it.

· 28 ·

"You're the head of Special Investigations," the message from Calista Mellenkamp said. "This is your case." Her first subtext was that she couldn't *not* assign this to him and still maintain the cover for the Puppeteer task force. Her second subtext was that the assignment was not open to discussion.

That suited Sigmund fine. Getting his marching orders electronically also avoided any discussion about how soon he'd arrive in London. Transfer booths would get him there near to instantly, but he had avoided transfer booths since the Cerberus affair began. Redirecting a teleporting passenger en route seemed no more improbable than delivering an envelope without leaving a trace. A suborbital hop and a cab ride would have to be fast enough, Sigmund looking for all the world like another tourist admiring the sights. If anyone asked, he'd allowed the local authorities a few hours to secure and study their crime scene.

No one asked.

Flashing his ARM ident got Sigmund past a line of bobbies and into the British Museum. He showed the holo badge three more times before he reached the burgled exhibit hall. A bobby at its entrance pointed out the man in charge.

Sigmund's footsteps echoed as he walked the length of the hall to where two men stood in conversation. They turned at his approach.

The taller man was sweating copiously despite the exhibit-preserving cool of the museum. Sigmund guessed this was the museum's director of security. If so, he had ample reason to sweat.

"Ah, our ARM expert from New York," the nervous man said. "Cecil Braithwaite, with the museum. Call me Cecil."

"Special Agent Ausfaller."

Cecil winced but took the snub in silence.

"Senior Inspector Owen Bergen, the Yard." Offering his ident, Bergen spoke over Cecil's embarrassment. Bergen's broad forehead and wide-set blue eyes conveyed a mature and observant intelligence.

"I'm pleased to meet you, Senior Inspector," Sigmund said. He had far more confidence in Scotland Yard than a museum cop.

"We've been busy, as you might imagine, Agent Ausfaller." Cecil prattled on about alarms, sensors, and cameras. He expended altogether too many words before concluding, "So you see, the security system gives us nothing to go on."

Bergen shook his head. "I disagree, Cecil. We'll learn something useful from how the criminals defeated the security system."

"You suspect an inside job?" Sigmund asked.

Bergen raised an eyebrow. "Of course. One can't just disable these things from the outside. This is a very secure facility."

"Bypassed sensors account for the thieves going unseen." Sigmund glanced at the empty walls. Only yesterday, the most famous marble sculptures of the ancient world had been displayed here. Just how many tonnes did they weigh? "So the thieves toted everything out past the night guards?"

"Well, no," Cecil admitted. "We see no evidence of tampering with the street surveillance cameras. And even if they, too, were circumvented, we had one bit of good luck. The skies over London were clear last night. We have continuous satellite imagery of the area."

Sigmund felt vaguely disappointed. This was going to be trivial, not a diversion, after all. "Then you have video of the vehicles that carried away the marbles."

"Actually, no," Cecil said.

That left but one way out of the building. Sigmund said, "Then the marbles were removed by transfer booth, direct from the museum to somewhere you couldn't surveil. Where did the thieves teleport?"

Bergen steepled his fingers. "That's exactly the question. There seem to be no transfer records. Interesting, eh?"

Cerberus! It took all Sigmund's willpower not to shout the word. The disappointment he'd been feeling vanished, along with the final shreds of doubt as to who was behind the Cerberus extortions. Sigmund knew *exactly* who had orchestrated the theft of the Elgin Marbles.

Who but the mythology-obsessed Puppeteers would steal the sculpted frieze that once graced the Parthenon?

• 29 •

Danger lurked in simple blue lines.

From heads held far apart Nessus stared into the mass pointer, the transparent sphere that was the heart of *Aegis'* navigational console. Blue lines radiated from the center of the orb, one line for each detectable gravitational singularity. The longer the line segment, the closer and larger—the more perilous—the mass.

Gravitational maws: He felt their hunger.

One line segment, still short, pointed straight at him. When it split into six closely spaced lines, he would be almost home.

In theory, he need check the mass pointer only once or twice every shift. Theory offered little comfort. He had lost too many friends to hyperspace. Had they trusted too much to theory?

With good reason, no sane Citizen would travel by hyperdrive.

Closer to Earth, Nessus had dropped *Aegis* back to normal space a few times to rest. Sleep came grudgingly, but never rest. Too many perils tormented him.

His urgent recall implied much but explained little. The scout ship *Explorer* was missing, Clandestine Directorate had reported, with all heads unaccounted for. The correct term in this context was *all hands.* His chosen scouts—three more friends, though aliens—where? Lost in a singularity, perhaps, or taken prisoner by an unknown power. In a hostile universe, so much could go wrong.

Had he been aboard *Explorer,* would his superior caution have saved them?

But numbers far larger than the three lost crew weighed on his conscience. For what gain had he meddled? Possibly none. His thoughts churned endlessly in a rebellious jumble. His limbs trembled from the strain of catatonia too long denied.

NESSUS FINALLY BOWED to reality, dropping for a time from hyperspace. He staggered past his cabin with its mound of sleep cushions to the packed cargo hold. The last things he saw, before fatigue overcame him, were the stacked crates he was bringing to Hearth. The sight cast a ray of hope into his troubled thoughts.

After Nike received *this* gift, surely he would be the next to mention Brides.

HOMEWARD *AEGIS* FLEW—

Deeper into the galactic north where Ausfaller now cast his uncanny attention. Through his minions, Nessus had learned that much about the ARM's progress.

Nessus pawed the deck, agitated by all that remained hidden. As fear directed a Citizen's actions, so curiosity drove humans. Someone with more arrogance than understanding of humans had drawn the gaze of the Concordance's most implacable adversary. Nike would not identify the scout responsible, but Nessus had his suspicions.

Provoking Ausfaller by accident sounded like something Achilles would do.

At some point Nessus made his way to the ship's relax room. He ordered another serving of whatever he had last synthed. What to eat, at least, was a decision he could simplify. The first bites made his mouths water, and he ate voraciously. Not until the plate was empty did he look up. He had no idea what he'd just consumed.

Ausfaller's shadow haunted Nessus. The ARM *must* be stopped. But how? Ausfaller's own superiors couldn't dissuade him. The riots that troubled Nessus' conscience hadn't deflected him. Achilles' trap had only drawn him.

Nessus filled several drinking bulbs with water, to

carry back to the bridge. The dispenser's shiny front panel reflected a bedraggled, wild-eyed creature. It defied belief that so disreputable a character must carry such responsibility on his shoulders.

Even Nessus' most senior sources in the United Nations feared the ARM.

"You want me to spy on *Ausfaller*?" Sangeeta Kudrin had blurted. She had been sealed at the time within an impregnable bubble, intercepted between two primitive transfer booths, entirely at Nessus' mercy—but it was Ausfaller who terrified her. "The man is a raving paranoid. Maybe you don't understand what that means. It means he suspects *everyone*."

Max Addeo had tried once to explain. Nessus thought, I should have worked harder then to comprehend. Only when Kudrin panicked had Nessus *truly* grasped Ausfaller's evil genius. She'd said, "I'm guessing that you chose your victims, at least some of them, by clever data mining. I don't see how else you could have found *me*. My . . . creative use of UN funds."

Ausfaller had constructed a persona in the personnel files, she had explained, someone with a suspect-looking past, just to entrap anyone trying to coerce ARMs. Unwittingly, Nessus had sent Ausfaller a Cerberus envelope! And Ausfaller had deduced it was Puppeteer meddling. . . .

Nessus blinked, his eyes dry from staring. The mass pointer was a psionic device; it required a conscious mind in the loop. He sensed the approaching singularity. That was normal. But to sense its hunger? He knew that was madness.

It was no less insane to feel Ausfaller's eyes. The ARM was too perceptive to ignore, too dedicated to be corrupted, and too persistent to deflect.

Ausfaller's strength was also his greatest weakness. The paranoia that led to such profound insight evoked, in turn, distaste and distrust among his own kind. Thus weakness became, in turn, strength: Any harm done to

Ausfaller, or even an unsuccessful attempt, would only raise the paranoid's credibility.

And then there were Addeo's warnings about "event-of-my-death" messages.

I'm obsessed with Ausfaller, Nessus realized. In his hearts, alongside the fear and admiration, Nessus acknowledged pangs of empathy. We are both misfits, striving mightily to protect the societies that disdain us.

Nessus' necks ached. He told himself he felt only the strain of physical exhaustion. That was a half-truth, at best. Every instinct demanded he look over his shoulder for his pursuer.

And yet, amid all the self-recrimination, salvation beckoned. Yes, Sigmund Ausfaller remained on the hunt. And yes, Nessus himself had been ordered away from Sol system—

But he was not without his own cunning. An arrogant overconfidence in Concordance science had put all Citizens at risk of discovery. And so, before leaving Sol system, Nessus had enlisted a human ally as complex as Ausfaller and as scientifically gifted as Achilles.

The safety of the Concordance was now in *his* hands.

BESIEGED

EARTH DATE: 2651

· 30 ·

It took the Secretary-General months to discreetly divert the funds for a long-range exploratory mission. It took Sigmund more months to covertly acquire *Hobo Kelly*.

Much can happen in a year.

Ander didn't notice, or paid no heed to, Sigmund's introspection. "Trust me, the normal-world women tourists are eager." It had become Ander's favored theme. "The natives scare the hell out of them. By comparison, I and certainly you, my friend, are of unthreatening bulk."

"Piloting" a starship, it turned out, required surprisingly few skills. The autopilot could be relied on to get you in and out of a solar system. Between solar systems, the mass pointer made navigation entirely straightforward: You merely kept your ship pointed toward the line that pointed at *you*. There were too few stars nearby to permit any confusion.

Not in Known Space, anyway. Perhaps the galactic core had enough stars to confuse things.

Dark thoughts about Beowulf Shaeffer, below the radar for over a year, had one advantage. They distracted Sigmund from Ander's prattling. Sigmund didn't care to discuss why Feather moving out was the best thing that had ever happened to him. Not with anyone. Certainly not with Ander.

". . . And that's how, last trip, I ended up with twins from We Made It," Ander continued.

Fortunately, with just the two of them to cover three shifts, they didn't overlap often. When they did, Sigmund tried not talking.

Ander didn't seem to mind. Or to notice. "Yes, Sigmund, it's my mission to show you the better, by which

I mean baser, fleshpots of Sirius Mater." Ander cackled. "My mission and your pleasure."

It grew harder and harder to remember why he'd brought Ander along on this shakedown cruise when he wanted to take Ander by the throat and shake *him.* It didn't help Sigmund's spirits to know that nothingness lurked outside the hull. He reminded himself often that Ander was good at what he did. Ander was just lousy company.

Finally, their ship reached the outskirts of Sirius system. It was a relief on many levels, not least for the prospect of company other than Ander's, to drop out of hyperspace.

The coded hyperwave message beamed from James P. Baen Station quickly dispelled Sigmund's relief.

SIGMUND REMEMBERED SIRIUS Mater from ten years earlier. It was as dreary as he remembered it. By Earth standards, Jinx's largest city scarcely qualified as a village. Its buildings, like its inhabitants, were short and squat, and for the same reason: the intolerable gravity.

The major hotels offered gravity-controlled comfort—and tourists. Ander was not amused when Sigmund ordered him immediately to West End, decidedly short of off-world visitors, to attempt once more to infiltrate Pelton's project. Tough. The alert from the ARM station chief here had changed everything.

Carlos Wu was on Jinx.

Passport records said this was Wu's first trip off Earth in ten years. Eight ships lost in the vicinity of Sol system in the last ten months and *now* Carlos decides to travel? He'd taken the last passenger ship out before the final cruise line suspended operations in and out of Sol system.

And Carlos had chosen Jinx, of all places. . . .

For anyone other than Ander, the main tourist attraction in Sirius Mater was the museum portion of the Institute of Knowledge. It could only be experienced at Jinx-standard gravity. Sigmund rented a floating travel couch from the one-gee lobby of his hotel, and let it carry him the short distance to the institute. It was time to happen to meet Carlos.

Sigmund wandered through the museum until he came upon the physicist in the art wing. "Small galaxy," Sigmund said.

Carlos was also in a travel chair. Glancing over his shoulder, he did a double take. "Agent Ausfaller. A small galaxy indeed."

They were in a gallery of Jinxian nudes. Sigmund gestured at the nearest one. "*Rubenesque* suddenly seems like another word for 'petite'. And there's no cause for formality. We're a long way from Earth."

"Sigmund, then." Carlos stroked his chin. "Yes, these are *big* people. They have to be, of course."

"So what brings you here, Carlos?" Sigmund said. "To Jinx, I mean."

Carlos kept his eyes on the holos. "Personal reasons."

"Been here long?"

"Long enough." Carlos shrugged. At least he tried to shrug. The casual gesture morphed into a shudder. "I'm more of a flatlander than I realized. I miss home."

"And with the quarantine, you can't get home." Sigmund edged his travel chair closer to a portrait. "I heard you got married. Do I get to meet your wife?"

"We recently divorced. That's kind of why I wanted to get away." Awkward pause. "What brings you to Jinx, Sigmund?"

"Business," Sigmund said. "I can't say much about it."

That was the truth. Ships near Sol system disappearing without a trace. No wreckage. No distress calls. The ARM's working assumption was pirates.

His Puppeteer hunt was delayed until ship disappearances closer to home could be resolved.

He had expected to be quite bored by the time *Hobo*

Kelly completed its final outfitting. An open question in the piracy theory was whether ships were targeted or taken at random. Accomplices employed in shipyards could hide transmitters during a routine overhaul. Hidden beacons might explain why more ships had disappeared outbound from Sol than inbound. Or, the number of disappearances being small, the difference could be meaningless.

Hobo Kelly needed a major refit for its new mission, and Jinx had some of the best shipyards in Human Space. Claiming that a refit in Sol system was too risky gave Sigmund an excuse to take out his ship. He had his reasons. He wanted Ander back on Jinx, despite the quarantine. *Hobo Kelly* needed a shakedown cruise. Sigmund wanted to practice his newly learned piloting skills.

"I can't really talk about it," Sigmund repeated. They'd been floating down the hall. They reached the last of the muscle-bound nudes. "Have you seen the landscape gallery, Carlos?"

"Not yet." Carlos floated under an arch into a new room. He stopped to admire a holo of crescent Primary hanging over East End. "I thought I was on the last ship from Sol system," Carlos commented suddenly. "How'd *you* get here?"

"Some government ships are still flying. In fact, I'm headed back to Earth in a few days." Sigmund had a flash of inspiration. He didn't want to leave Carlos here, unsupervised. "If you wish, you can come back with me."

Carlos looked surprised. "Is it safe?"

"I wouldn't go myself, otherwise." Don't push, Sigmund told himself. "Where are you staying? I'll get in touch when my business is done. You can give me your decision then. I'm at the Sirius Mater Hilton, by the way."

"I'm at the Jinx Towers." Carlos took a deep breath. "I *would* like to get home. I'll think about it."

"Sounds good. Or give me a call sooner when your

schedule permits, and we'll have a drink." Sigmund leaned forward in his travel chair and extended his hand. "It's good to see a familiar face."

"Same here, Sigmund. I may take you up on the drink." They shook hands.

If Carlos noticed the pinprick when Sigmund planted a microbug, he gave no sign.

CARLOS RETURNED TO the institute the next two days. Two hours into the first day, with little to hear but occasional footsteps, presumably those of Jinxian museumgoers, Sigmund delegated listening to Medusa. He split his time between the shipyard and his suite at the Hilton. At least in his room Sigmund could pretend to be on Earth.

He was having lunch in his room, surfing Jinxian 3-V, when, with a chime, Medusa appeared. "Here's a surprise," she said. "Do you recognize the second voice?"

It was familiar, but Sigmund couldn't quite place it. "Who is Carlos talking to?"

All the snakes stopped coiling to stare at Sigmund. "Beowulf Shaeffer."

If only he could have placed a video bug! Alas, Carlos probably took out a new floater each day from his hotel lobby; surely he changed his clothes. A bug planted on *Carlos* had to be subcutaneous, which limited it to audio.

"Here's the interesting part," Medusa continued. "They know each other *really* well."

Sigmund shivered. He had a bad feeling about this. "How well?"

"Carlos fathered the children the Fertility Board denied Beowulf."

THE CAMELOT WAS a sprawling, vaguely Escher-like jumble of boxes, and a landmark in downtown Sirius

Mater. The hotel maintained one-gee gravity throughout, not only in its guest rooms. That made the Camelot's bar the most popular watering hole among off-worlders.

Sigmund claimed a booth. Carlos was meeting him here for a drink, and to talk about the trip to Earth. And although Carlos didn't know Sigmund already knew, they would be talking about another passenger. Carlos had offered Bey a ride.

The two men walked into the bar together, Shaeffer towering over Wu. Sigmund stood. "Beowulf Shaeffer! How good to see you again! I believe it has been eight years or thereabouts. How have you been?"

"I lived," Shaeffer snapped.

Carlos rubbed his hands together briskly. "Sigmund! Why did you bomb Bey's ship?"

Sigmund blinked in feigned surprise. "Did he tell you it was *his* ship? It wasn't. He was thinking of stealing it. I reasoned that he would not steal a ship with a hidden time bomb aboard."

"But how did you come into it?" Carlos slid into the booth beside him. "You're not police. You're in the Extremely Foreign Relations Bureau."

It's called Alien Affairs, Sigmund thought. And I don't need to be told where I work. Worked. Special Investigations wasn't officially part of Alien Affairs.

Sigmund saw no advantage in volunteering information. A partial truth would suffice. "The ship belonged to General Products Corporation, which is owned by Puppeteers, not human beings."

Carlos turned to his . . . friend? Ally? Coconspirator? "Bey! Shame on you."

"Damn it! They were trying to blackmail me into a suicide mission! And Ausfaller let them get away with it!"

"Good thing they soundproof these booths," Carlos said. "Let's order."

Shaeffer finally sat, looking flustered.

No one offered to explain why Shaeffer was here. Sigmund wasn't supposed to know, so he changed the subject. "Well, Carlos, have you changed your mind about coming with me?"

"Yes, if I can take a friend," Carlos answered.

And so the dance began, Shaeffer professing uncertainty.

Something had brought these two to Jinx. Whatever they planned, Sigmund hoped to disrupt it. Least of all did he want to leave Shaeffer behind. Unsupervised or at risk of encountering Ander—either possibility had risks. A possible third chance encounter with Ander after a second chance encounter with him? What suspicions would *that* raise? No, it was better that Shaeffer come along so Sigmund could keep an eye on him.

Shaeffer had tried to steal a warship before. Perhaps another warship could serve as bait. It wasn't hard to steer the conversation to piracy.

"They would not take me so easily," Sigmund declared. "*Hobo Kelly* is deceptive. It seems to be a cargo and passenger ship, but it is a warship, armed and capable of thirty-gees acceleration." At least that was now true, its refitting finally complete. "In normal space we can run from anything we can't fight. We are assuming pirates, are we not? Pirates would insist on robbing a ship before they destroy it."

Shaeffer was intrigued. "Why? Why a disguised warship? Are you *hoping* you'll be attacked?"

"If there are actually pirates, yes, I hope to be attacked. But not when entering Sol system. We plan a substitution. A quite ordinary cargo craft will land on Earth, take on cargo of some value, and depart for Wunderland on a straight-line course. My ship will replace it before it has passed through the asteroids."

Carlos hypothesized weird astrophysical phenomena that could precipitate ships from hyperspace. Shaeffer hypothesized more wildly yet, about hyperspace creatures eating the ships. Sigmund let them ramble, before offering, "I would be glad if you would change your mind and come with us, Mr. Shaeffer."

"Um?" Shaeffer responded in surprise. "Are you sure you want me on the same ship with you?"

"Oh, emphatically! How else may I be sure that you have not hidden a bomb aboard?" Sigmund chuckled at his own joke. "Also, we can use a qualified pilot."

If *Hobo Kelly* was bait, there was no benefit to Beowulf knowing Sigmund could fly his own ship. Let them think him dependent. Lying came easily, especially to these two. If he had to, Sigmund felt confident he could take either or both of his passengers—one bookish, the other a We Made It scarecrow—even without the hidden armory he always carried. It was Sigmund's turn to prattle, flattering Shaeffer for his past exploits.

Shaeffer left the bar claiming he had to sleep on it.

Sigmund wasn't at all surprised when Shaeffer called later that evening to accept.

• 31 •

Shaeffer circled Jinx on the way out. It wasn't necessary, and Sigmund started to object—

Then Primary rose above the horizon. The sight took Sigmund's breath away.

Shaeffer broke the silence a moment later. "Despite appearances, Primary is smaller than Jupiter. It looks bigger from here because Jinx orbits so close to it. But Primary *is* special. It masses more than Jupiter. In fact, Primary masses so much that gravity has compressed its core into degenerate matter."

From the copilot's crash couch, Carlos stared out the view port, grinning from ear to ear.

Shaeffer kept up his patter. "A billion years ago, give

or take, this moon we call Jinx orbited much closer to Primary. That was before tidal drag moved them apart. Jinx was tidally locked then, too, of course. Primary's gravity warped Jinx into the shape that will soon become apparent."

The normal curvature of a receding world became anything *but* normal.

"From space," Shaeffer went on, "this world looks like God's Own Easter Egg. Note the Ends, bone white tinged with yellow, climbing above the atmosphere. Moving in from the poles, we see the brighter glare from rings of glittering ice fields at the limits of the atmosphere. Next come the blues of an Earth-like world, overlaid with more and more cloud as your eyes sweep inward. Finally, we reach the waist, girdled in pure white cloud. Beneath those unbroken clouds, forever hidden, lies the equatorial ocean on whose rocky shores the Bandersnatchi roam."

Throughout his travelogue, Shaeffer's eyes darted from instrument to instrument. His hands never left the controls.

As Jinx shrank into the distance, Sigmund had an epiphany. With a great deal of computer assistance, he thought, I can get a ship from Point A to Point B. I'm competent.

Shaeffer was a *pilot.*

FOR FIVE DAYS, allowing himself only occasional breaks, Shaeffer guided *Hobo Kelly* through the clutter that was Sirius system. The autopilot could have accomplished the same task. It had, inbound. Shaeffer preferred to fly manually and get a feel for the controls.

They still had long periods of time with nothing nearby and no piloting to be done. After they had passed the main asteroid belt, Sigmund took his shipmates for a tour. More than once their eyes widened in surprise.

Hobo Kelly was a belly-lander, a hundred meters long and triangular in cross section. Beneath its uptilted nose were big clamshell doors for cargo. It had adequate belly jets, a big fusion motor at the tail, and a line of windows indicating cabins. It looked harmless—and that was the point. The passenger area was large enough for 40 or 50, but it held cabins for only 4. The cabin windows they'd seen outside before boarding were holograms. Weapons take room.

Hobo Kelly was Sigmund's personal Trojan Horse.

The ship was richly strewn with tiny ARM sensors. Soon enough, when Sigmund was off-shift and in his cabin, Shaeffer went exploring. Medusa woke Sigmund when a hidden camera revealed Shaeffer popping the access panel that covered the controls for the concealed weapons array. Sigmund hurried back to the bridge.

Shaeffer looked up. "I thought you were asleep."

I'm sure you did, Sigmund thought. "I couldn't sleep." He pointed at the open panel. "Let me walk you through what we've got."

They had a lot. A big X-ray laser. Smaller laser cannon set for different frequencies. Four self-guided fusion bombs. A hidden telescope, so powerful that the ostensible ship's telescope was only a finder for it. None of it showed from outside.

Shaeffer lit a cigarette. "I don't know whether to be comforted or terrified. What do you expect to fight?"

Sigmund smiled. "Whatever is there, Shaeffer. Whatever is there."

THEY TALKED ABOUT art and literature, places they'd seen, and countless other topics. They speculated endlessly about what might make ships disappear. That was unproductive; they knew no more than before the trip started. Sigmund mentioned Carlos's spectacular undersea home, which made Carlos ask about Feather. That wound remained raw; Sigmund changed the subject.

When Carlos and Bey thought themselves in private, they talked about Sharrol Janss, and the little boy and girl Bey was so eager to get home to adopt. Sigmund had glimpsed holos through his surveillance network. Louis and Tanya were cute kids.

Bey, not Shaeffer. Alone in his cabin, Sigmund acknowledged the truth. He was losing his detachment. And they had another two weeks together before Sol system.

Bey could have children anywhere but Earth—but the woman he loved was purebred flat phobe. Sharrol *couldn't* leave Earth. Although Bey seemed not to realize it, his friend Carlos loved her, too.

Familiarity cut both ways. Bey alluded once to the one time General Products had paid the warranty on a GP hull, then rushed to change the subject. "Did I ever tell you about the time on Gummidgy that—?"

"Right. That was on your outing in 'forty-five with Elephant," Sigmund interrupted. Interrogation 101: Pretend you know more than you do. "The time your hull dissolved."

"His friends call him Elephant," Bey said coldly. "I don't think you're in that category." Then he'd gone on with his Gummidgy story.

Truth be told, that was an interesting tale.

No one mentioned the riots, and for that Sigmund was grateful. The topic was too painful, for each of them in a different way. I'm as much a victim of the Fertility Laws as Bey. Sigmund thought of Feather, and his own problems. Sometimes the universe sucks.

Especially when his new friends remained his chief suspects, at least of collaborating in secret with Puppeteers.

It wasn't long to his next shift. He gave up on sleep

and headed for the bridge, where Carlos and Bey were again talking about the children. They fell silent at his appearance.

"Hi, Sigmund," Carlos said.

"Gentlemen." From habit, Sigmund checked the mass pointer. Nothing anywhere nearby. "What's our topic this shift?"

"Bey's stories," Carlos said. "He's got a million of them."

Certainly Bey told the most stories. A funny thing, though: Sigmund felt no need to strangle the man. By this point outbound from Earth, Sigmund had been ready to throttle Ander.

A few of Sigmund's stories had actually happened; two had even happened to him. An only slightly censored version of how he'd become an ARM kept their attention. He also told them almost everything about the still-unsolved theft of the Elgin Marbles, omitting only speculations about Cerberus and Puppeteers. The latter incident was a test. That neither of his passengers reacted, Sigmund decided, constituted an inconclusive pass.

Carlos told stories, too—only they mostly involved cosmological arcana or too many dimensions for anyone but Carlos to follow. Sometimes both. Carlos assured them his stories were funny.

So Carlos's answer meant only that Bey was the glib one of the pair.

Bey stalled by lighting a cigarette—which he held between two toes. Maybe everyone from We Made It was that limber, Sigmund didn't know, but never before this trip had he seen anyone smoke using his feet. It bugged the hell out of Sigmund. He guessed Bey enjoyed that more than the cigarette.

Sigmund played along. "Neutron star? Core explosion? Outsiders?"

Bey shot Carlos an annoyed glance.

"Don't give me that, Bey," Carlos said. "Sigmund

and I talked about the Outsiders before you and I ever met."

"True," Sigmund agreed. "When you and Gregory Pelton went barreling into Sirius system six years ago, it seemed pretty obvious you'd gotten a lift from the Outsiders. I'd like to hear that story."

"I was crew on that trip. That makes it Elephant's story, not mine." Bey loved to tell stories, but his tone of voice made it clear this story was an exception. He brought a foot up to his face and took a long drag. "That's not to admit or deny we encountered Outsiders." Puff, puff. "Speaking of the Outsiders, a few months ago I saw a starseed open. *That* was truly amazing."

And Beowulf was off, spinning tales of the galaxy's elder race.

The Outsiders were immensely fragile, looking something like large cat-o'-nine-tails, with a metabolism based on liquid helium. They roamed the galaxy in city-sized ships, shunning the inner solar systems. ("Those amazing ships of theirs have the galaxy's least imaginative names. I had business with one once. It was called Ship Fourteen.") Their civilization was billions of years old, moving to a less than glacial tempo impossible for the warm-world races to imagine.

It had been an Outsider, native to regions outside of solar singularities, in the dawn of time, who discovered hyperspace and perfected the hyperdrive shunt. By selling that technology to the human colony of We Made It ("Not to a relative, though"), the Outsiders indirectly saved humanity from enslavement by the Kzinti. For reasons of their own, Outsiders themselves traveled only in normal space.

Sigmund thought, not for the first time: If Bey wrote half as well as he spoke, Ander would never have gotten his foot in the door.

"Bey?" Carlos interrupted. "Starseeds?"

"I'm getting there. We don't know much about the Outsiders. One of those few things we know is this: They spend their time in pursuit of starseeds." A great smile lit Beowulf's face. "Giant creatures, about two kilometers across. They follow slow migratory patterns from the rim of the galaxy to and from the core.

"That's two klicks across *furled.* Inbound to Gummidgy, our ship passed a starseed. A starseed is mostly gossamer-thin sail, tightly rolled. Imagine that sail, thousands of kilometers across, slowly unfurling. Four muscular shrouds connect the sail to its tiny central kernel. Now picture that great, silvery mirrored sail catching the sun. . . ."

In his mind's eye, Sigmund *did* see the starseed. It was beautiful.

Yes, if Bey could write half as well as he spoke, he'd never have needed Ander.

CARLOS AND BEY had met by accident. Bey had been bound for Earth; the captain of the passenger ship had diverted to Jinx rather than face whatever was eating ships in Sol system.

One "coincidence" explained—it was a start.

Then again, Gregory Pelton could certainly bribe a cruise-line captain. Pelton would scarcely notice the expense.

It was almost time to drop out of hyperspace. Their wide-ranging conversations abruptly focused. Pirates, ship eaters, wandering uncharted planets—theories suddenly ceased to be mere intellectual exercise.

"It boils down to three possibilities," Bey decided abruptly. "Kzinti, Puppeteers, and humans."

Carlos guffawed. "Puppeteers? Puppeteers wouldn't have the guts!"

"I threw them in because they might have some interest in manipulating the interstellar stock market. Look, our hypothetical pirates have set up an embargo, cutting Sol system off from the outside world. The Puppeteers have the capital to take advantage of what that does to the market. And they need money. For their migration."

It was the first theory Sigmund heard that made any sense. He'd had similar thoughts about the Crash when the Puppeteers vanished. Bey—and Carlos?—had been involved then. . . .

Carlos wasn't buying it. "The Puppeteers are philosophical cowards."

"That's right," Bey agreed. "They wouldn't risk robbing the ships or coming anywhere near them. Suppose they can make them disappear from a distance?"

Carlos wasn't laughing now. "That's easier than dropping them out of hyperspace to rob them. It wouldn't take more than a great big gravity generator . . . and we've never known the limits of Puppeteer technology."

So Shaeffer suddenly had a plausible explanation, without any new information. Had he been holding back for the whole trip? Sigmund asked, "You think this is possible?"

Bey nodded. "Just barely. The same goes for the Kzinti. The Kzinti are ferocious enough. Trouble is, if we ever learned they were preying on our ships, we'd raise pluperfect hell. The Kzinti know that, and they know we can beat them. Took them long enough, but they learned."

"So you think it's humans," Carlos said.

Bey looked unhappy. "Yeah. If it's pirates."

IN THE MASS pointer, the narrow line that marked Sol grew longer. Bey claimed the controls as his own. As tense as he looked, he found the energy to chain-smoke with his feet.

The three of them shared the bridge as *Hobo Kelly* penetrated the Oort Cloud. Only twelve hours remained until they returned to normal space. Then it was ten. Five. One.

Bey asked suddenly, "Carlos, just how large a mass would it take to make us disappear?"

Their resident genius didn't hesitate. "Planet size, Mars and up. Beyond that, it depends on how close you get and how dense it is. If it's dense enough, it can be less massive and still flip you out of the universe. But you'd see it in the mass sensor."

"Only for an instant . . . and not then if it's turned off. What if someone turned on a giant gravity generator as we went past?"

"For what? They couldn't rob the ship. Where's their profit?"

"Stocks."

Sigmund shook his head. They'd talked all through this. Was Shaeffer trying to divert them at a critical moment? "The expense of such an operation would be enormous. No group of pirates would have enough additional capital on hand to make it worthwhile. Of the Puppeteers I might believe it."

The long line marking Sol was almost touching the surface of the mass sensor. Bey said, "Breakout in ten minutes."

And the ship lurched savagely.

• 32 •

"Strap down!" Bey yelled. He stared wide-eyed at the hyperdrive controls.

Sigmund stared just as incredulously. The hyperdrive motor was drawing no power. None of the instrument readings made any sense. Unless . . .

Bey had the same thought. He activated the view ports, kept inert in hyperspace. The displays came on, revealing stars.

Somehow, they were in normal space.

"Futz! They got us anyway." Carlos sounded neither frightened nor angry but awed.

The hidden access panel. Why was Bey reaching for it? Sigmund shouted, "Wait!"

Bey threw the red switch anyway. The ship shuddered as explosive bolts blew. A monstrous blip appeared on the radar screen, slowly receding.

That blip was most of the ship: the false hull, their disguise. Now anyone watching would see a GP #2 hull, ringed with weapons. Sigmund cursed in every language he knew.

Shaeffer didn't know the old words, or he didn't care. He lit the main fusion drive and ran it up to full power.

Sigmund squeezed the padded arms of his crash couch, his knuckles white. "Shaeffer, you idiot, you coward!" Or traitor? That was a possibility, too. How could he have considered trusting this man? "We run without knowing what we run from. Now they know exactly what we are. What chance that they will follow us now? This ship was built for a specific purpose, and you have ruined it!"

"I've freed your special instruments," Shaeffer said with aggravating calm. "Why don't you see what you can find?"

There were ships out there. Sigmund got a close-up of them: three space tugs of the Belter type. They were shaped like thick saucers, equipped with oversized drives and powerful electromagnetic generators. Asteroid haulers. With those heavy drives they could probably catch *Hobo Kelly,* assuming they had adequate cabin gravity.

They weren't even trying. They continued on their course, three points of a slow-moving triangle.

Carlos asked, "Bey? What happened?"

"How the futz would I know?" their pilot snapped. It seemed a fair answer. Several hyperdrive indicators had gone wild; the rest looked completely dead. "And the drive's drawing no power at all. I've never heard of anything like this. Carlos, it's still theoretically impossible."

Carlos said, "I'm . . . not so sure of that. I want to look at the drive."

Shaeffer didn't look up from his console. "The access tubes don't have cabin gravity."

On radar, the three innocent-looking tugs receded. Of course, until moments ago *Hobo Kelly* had also looked entirely innocent, not like the warship it was. Rather than scream, Sigmund said, "If there were an enemy, you frightened him away. Shaeffer, this mission and this ship have cost my department an enormous sum, and we have learned nothing at all."

"Not quite nothing," Carlos said. "I still want to see the hyperdrive motor. Bey, would you run us down to one gee?"

"Yeah. But . . . miracles make me nervous, Carlos."

Crawling one by one through the access tunnel, they encountered a miracle.

Their hyperdrive motor had vanished from the ship.

CARLOS BROKE THE stunned silence. "It takes an extremely high gravity gradient. The motor hit that, wrapped space around itself, and took off at some higher level of hyperdrive, one we can't reach. By now it could be well on its way to the edge of the universe."

He seemed very confident for someone without an opinion a few minutes ago.

With some trepidation, they powered up the hyperwave radio. It neither disappeared like the hyperdrive nor exploded. Sigmund relayed a coded query through Southworth Station to get registry data on the three tugs. From the ship to the relay, comm was instantaneous. The link between the station and the inner solar system was another story. There, light-speed crawl was the rule. They'd have a ten-hour round-trip delay for any answer.

Carlos used the comm gear next. He wanted data about cosmology and cosmologists, astronomy and astronomers. There was also something in his request about a meteor strike in Siberia in 1908. What Sigmund found most significant was *who* Carlos asked. The call went to one of Gregory Pelton's unlisted numbers.

Shaeffer didn't understand, either. "I haven't the remotest idea what you're after."

Smiling enigmatically, Carlos went to his cabin.

Sigmund needed urgently to shake answers out of someone—and couldn't. Not without hard proof of a crime. Wu was among Earth's chosen. Shaeffer was under the protection of Gregory Pelton.

Futz.

THEY TOOK TURNS on watch before the answer to Sigmund's message arrived via Southworth Station. The registration check on the tugs was worthless. All were supposedly owned by the Sixth Congregational Church of Rodney—libertarian Belter nonsense. The United Nations would never tolerate such evasions.

Soon after, information began pouring in for Carlos. The physicist refused to share his thinking. The fool would rather be dead than proven wrong. As for the data stream itself, for all the sense it made to Sigmund it might as well have been in hieroglyphics.

Sigmund concentrated on the bit he could understand: the list of Sol system's leading experts in gravity theory. Name after name was paired with a Southworth Station hyperwave comm ID. That put all of them here in the Oort Cloud. Here where ships disappeared.

Where in the Cloud hardly mattered. The fringes of the solar system were practically next door to any hyperdrive-equipped ship. "These people," Sigmund said. "You wish to discuss your theory with one of them?"

Carlos seemed surprised by the question. "That's right, Sigmund."

"Carlos, has it occurred to you that one of these people may have built the ship-eating device?"

"What? You're right. It would take someone who knew something about gravity. But I'd say the Quicksilver Group"—and Carlos gestured at the long block of names that shared a comm ID—"was beyond suspicion. With upwards of ten thousand people at work, how could anyone hide anything?"

One name on the list looked familiar. He knew a gravity theorist? Sigmund couldn't imagine why. Whoever he was, the comm ID showed he wasn't with Quicksilver. "What about this Julian Forward?"

Carlos looked thoughtful. "Forward. Yeah. I've always wanted to meet him."

"You know of him? Who is he?" Shaeffer asked.

"He used to be with the Institute of Knowledge on Jinx. I haven't heard of him in years. He did some work on the gravity waves from the galactic core . . . work that turned out to be wrong. Sigmund, let's give him a call."

Jinx. Sigmund suppressed a shiver. Now he placed the name. Forward was one of the experts who had vouched for the integrity of Shaeffer's galactic-core-explosion data. Ander had spoken to him six years earlier. And now Forward turns up *here*?

"And ask him what?" Shaeffer said pointedly.

"Why . . . ?" Then Carlos remembered the situation. "Oh. You think he might—yeah."

"How well do you know this man?" Sigmund asked.

"I know him by reputation. He's quite famous. I don't see how such a man could go in for mass murder."

Sigmund wondered: How can someone so brilliant be so innocent? "Earlier you said that we were looking for a man skilled in the study of gravitational phenomena."

"Granted."

That was rather grudging, Sigmund thought. "Perhaps we can do no more than talk to him. He could be on the other side of the sun and still head a pirate fleet."

Carlos shook his head. "No. That he could not."

"Think again," Sigmund said. "We are outside the singularity of Sol. A pirate fleet would surely include hyperdrive ships."

"If Julian Forward is the ship eater, he'll have to be nearby. The, uh, device won't move in hyperspace."

Shaeffer had begun to look testy. He said, "Carlos, what we don't know can kill us. Will you quit playing games?" But Carlos kept smiling, shaking his head. "All right, we can still check on Forward. Call him up and ask where he is! Is he likely to know you by reputation?"

"Sure. I'm famous, too."

"Okay," Shaeffer said. "If he's close enough, we might even beg him for a ride home. The way things stand, we'll be at the mercy of any hyperdrive ship for as long as we're out here."

"I hope we are attacked," Sigmund said. "We can outfight—"

"But we can't outrun," Shaeffer interrupted. "They can dodge; we can't."

"Peace, you two. First things first." Carlos sat down at the hyperwave controls and keyed in a comm ID.

One shipmate a foolish genius, the other a coward or a traitor. He couldn't rely on either of them; he didn't trust Forward. Sigmund backed into a corner that the comm gear did not see. "Can you contrive to keep my name out of this exchange? If necessary, you can be the ship's owner."

Before Carlos could answer, the comm display lit. They saw ash-blond hair cut in a Belter crest over a lean white face and an insincere smile.

"Forward Station. Good evening."

"Good evening. This is Carlos Wu of Earth calling. May I speak to Dr. Julian Forward, please?"

"I'll see if he's available." The video froze.

Carlos shouted, "What kind of game are you playing now? How can I explain owning a warship?"

Before anyone could comment, the video unfroze. They saw someone massively muscled, undeniably a Jinxian.

"Carlos Wu!" Forward said with unctuous enthusiasm. "Are you the same Carlos Wu who solved the Sealeyham Limits problem?"

They babbled in tongues. "Well," Forward finally said, "what can I do for you?"

"Julian Forward, meet Beowulf Shaeffer. Bey was giving me a lift home when our hyperdrive motor disappeared."

Shaeffer jumped right in. "Disappeared, futzy right. The hyperdrive motor casing is empty. The motor supports are sheared off. We're stuck out here with no hyperdrive and no idea how it happened."

"Almost true," Carlos said cheerfully. "Dr. Forward, I do have some ideas as to what happened here. I'd like to discuss them with you."

"Where are you now?"

Shaeffer sent Forward their position.

Forward glanced at the coordinates. "You can get here a lot faster than you can get to Earth. Forward Station is ahead of you, within twenty a.u. of your position. You can wait here for the next ferry. Better than going on in a crippled ship."

An icy calm came over Sigmund. Forward was that near? The Jinxian must be involved.

"Good!" Carlos said. "We'll work out a course and let you know when to expect us."

"I welcome the chance to meet Carlos Wu." Forward sent his coordinates and dropped the link.

Carlos turned. "All right, Bey. Now *you* own an armed and disguised warship. You figure out where you got it."

Shaeffer had the sense to look worried. "We've got

worse problems than that. Forward Station is exactly where the ship eater ought to be."

Carlos nodded. But he remained amused with something he still would not share.

"So what's our next move?" Shaeffer persisted. "We can't run from hyperdrive ships. Not now. Is Forward likely to try to kill us?"

"If we don't reach Forward Station on schedule, he might send ships after us. We know too much. We've told him so," Carlos said. "The hyperdrive motor disappeared completely. I know half a dozen people who could figure out how it happened, knowing just that." He smiled suddenly. "That's assuming Forward's the ship eater. We don't know that. I think we have a splendid chance to find out one way or the other."

"How? Just walk in?" Shaeffer asked.

Ideas started to percolate in Sigmund's mind. "Dr. Forward expects you and Carlos to enter his web unsuspecting, leaving an empty ship. I think we can prepare a few surprises for him. For example, he may not have guessed that this is a General Products hull. And I will be aboard to fight."

"So you'll be in the indestructible hull," Shaeffer said cynically, "and we'll be helpless in the base. Very clever. I'd rather run for it myself. But then, you have your career to consider."

Something had reached through *Hobo Kelly*'s hull to remove its hyperdrive motor. A few years ago, tidal forces had reached through *Skydiver*—another GP #2 hull, as it happened, like *this* ship—and almost splatted Shaeffer across the inside of the bow. And between, Shaeffer had almost certainly experienced the complete destruction of a GP hull.

Maybe I should be a little more sympathetic to Beowulf's caution.

"I will not deny it," Sigmund said. "But there are ways in which I can prepare you."

· 33 ·

A lopsided stony mass flecked with ice hung in *Hobo Kelly's* main view port. On magnification, signs of human presence dotted the rock's mottled surface. Sigmund recognized air locks, flush-mounted windows, and antennae. The long, many-jointed metal arm with a bowl at its end? He hadn't a clue.

He returned his attention to the tiny open vehicle crossing the short distance to Forward Station. Two space-suited figures straddled a device that was little more than rocket motor and fuel tanks. Someone in a skintight suit and a bubble helmet waited for them. They moored the taxi to a spur of rock and went inside.

"I'm Harry Moskowitz," their greeter said. "They call me Angel. Dr. Forward is waiting in the laboratory."

Angel's voice was as clear as if Sigmund were on the rock. Sigmund had equipped Bey and Wu with ARM gear.

Sigmund had explained about their borrowed ARM earplugs, "Transmitter and hearing aid with sonic padding between. If you are blasted with sound, as by an explosion or a sonic stunner, the hearing aid will stop transmitting. If you go suddenly deaf, you will know you are under attack." He had seen no need to volunteer that *transmit* also meant *broadcast*. They might fail to act naturally if they knew he was listening.

The earplugs transmitted at very low power across a very broad spectrum—the devices wouldn't reveal themselves by interfering with Forward's equipment. Floating a few hundred meters away, *Hobo Kelly's* long-range comm gear picked up the signals easily.

Carlos and Bey followed Angel inside. As soon as

they removed their space suits, Sigmund had video. One button on each of their jumpers contained a camera, another detail he had seen no reason to mention.

Angel's station tour was anticlimactic: long, boring tunnels such as have laced a thousand asteroid mines—which, supposedly, this rock had once been. Toolrooms. Storerooms. Fusion generators. A space-taxi hangar.

Shaeffer was also getting bored. Admirably casual, he asked, "You use mining tugs?"

"Sure," Angel said. He seemed to think nothing of the question. "We can ship water and metals up from the inner system, but it's cheaper to hunt them down ourselves. In an emergency the tugs could probably get us back to the inner system." The Belter continued his tour before slipping in his own offhanded question. "Speaking of ships, I don't think I've ever seen one like yours. Were those *bombs* lined up along the ventral surface?"

"Some of them," Bey said.

Carlos laughed. "Bey won't tell me how he got it."

"Pick, pick, pick. All right, I stole it. I don't think anyone is going to complain." Bey spun a yarn as only he could, about being hired to pilot a cargo ship to Wunderland. Only it had turned out to be a warship hidden inside a fake shell. "By then I was already afraid that if I tried to back out, I'd be made to disappear."

Angel frowned. "Strange they left you with a working hyperdrive."

"Man, they didn't. They'd ripped out the relays. I had to fix them myself. It's lucky I looked, because they had the relays wired to a little bomb under the control chair." Shaeffer paused, thoughtfully. The man was a born actor. "Maybe I fixed it wrong. You heard what happened? My hyperdrive motor just plain vanished. It must have set off some explosive bolts, because the belly of the ship blew off. It was a dummy. What's left looks to be a pocket bomber."

"That's what I thought," Angel said.

Bey shrugged. "I guess I'll have to turn it in to the goldskin cops when we reach the inner system. Pity."

And then the tour took an interesting turn.

The next tunnel ended in a great hemispherical chamber. A massive column stood at the center of the room, rising through a seal in the curved dome into the enigmatic multijointed arm whose purpose Bey, Carlos, and Sigmund had all tried—and failed—to guess.

Julian Forward sat at the horseshoe-shaped control console near the pillar. "The Grabber," he intoned with mock portentousness.

"Pleased to meet you, Carlos Wu. Beowulf Shaeffer." Forward bounded from his seat, beaming. "The Grabber is our main exhibit here. After the Grabber there's nothing to see."

Bey asked, "What does it do?"

Carlos laughed. "It's beautiful! Why does it have to do anything?"

Forward said, "I've been thinking of entering it in a junk-sculpture show. What it does is manipulate large, dense masses. The cradle at the end of the arm is a complex of electromagnets. I can actually vibrate masses in there to produce polarized gravity waves."

Carlos and Bey leaned back to admire the Grabber. It was huge. Sigmund took in views from their hidden cameras and the telescopic overhead perspective of *Hobo Kelly.* Massive curved girders cut the dome into pie sections. Like the seal, the girders gleamed like mirrors.

Carlos mumbled something about reinforcement by stasis fields. Then he spoke to Forward: "What do you vibrate in there? A megaton of lead?"

"Lead sheathed in soft iron was the test mass. But that was years ago. I haven't worked with the Grabber lately, but we had some satisfactory runs with a sphere of neutronium enclosed in a stasis field. Ten billion metric tons."

Sigmund twitched. Neutronium? It didn't exist outside of neutron stars, did it? He was sure he remembered that from the BVS-1 affair.

Maybe Carlos would have commented, but Bey spoke first. "What's the point?"

"Communication, for one thing," Forward said. "There must be intelligent species all through the galaxy, most of them too far away for our ships. Gravity waves are probably the best way to reach them."

"Gravity waves travel at light speed, don't they? Wouldn't hyperwave be better?"

"We can't count on them having it. Who but the Outsiders would think to do their experimenting this far from a sun? If we want to reach beings who haven't dealt with the Outsiders, we'll have to use gravity waves once we know how."

The conversation lapsed further into technobabble. Sigmund hadn't a clue what any of it meant. It didn't seem threatening.

And it didn't explain why an expert on gravitational theory was here in the wrong place at the wrong time.

Every few sentences, the name of a mutual acquaintance bubbled out of the babble. Many were in the Quicksilver Group. Others were out-system, especially on Jinx, mostly seeking funding from the Institute of Knowledge.

"Are you still with the institute, Doctor?" Carlos asked.

Forward shook his head. "They stopped backing me. Not enough results. But I can continue to use this station, which is institute property. One day they'll sell it and we'll have to move."

This operation couldn't be cheap. If the institute wasn't supporting Forward, Sigmund wondered who was. Or was the Jinxian lying?

The conversation on Forward Station eventually turned to the matter of the mysterious hyperdrive disappearance. Forward dismissed Bey's space-monster theory. Then the physicists were at it again. Gravity, hyperspace physics, and cosmology all tangled in an enigmatic mess.

Sigmund sipped a bulb of coffee, waiting for the conversation to turn comprehensible. He decided he knew three things about cosmology. It attempted to answer questions about the formation of the universe. Theories went in and out of vogue—hardly surprising, since those origins could never be observed. It could not possibly affect him.

That third cosmological fact was wrong.

SIGMUND COULDN'T PARSE the questions, let alone the answers, but he understood people. Carlos was trying to lead the conversation somewhere. Had Wu forgotten he was in a possible pirate's lair, not a graduate colloquium?

Bey shifted in his seat. The tenor of the conversation made him uneasy.

Carlos, oblivious, was speculating again about the ship eater. "That ten billion metric tons of neutronium, now, that you were using for a test mass. That wouldn't be big enough or dense enough to give us enough of a gravity gradient."

Enough to precipitate ships from hyperspace, Sigmund guessed that meant.

"It might, right near the surface." Forward grinned and held his hands close together. "It was about that big."

"And that's as dense as matter gets in this universe. Too bad."

Forward nodded. "Have you ever heard of quantum black holes?"

"Yeah," Carlos said brightly.

"Wrong answer." Forward spoke midleap, casually backhanding Carlos across the face as he passed, and grabbed Bey.

Forward was used to the minuscule local gravity, and

he likely massed twice what Bey did. Shaeffer thrashed without effect. Carlos slumped to the floor.

So much for the disguised weapons, like stun grenades disguised as other buttons, with which Sigmund had equipped them.

Within seconds Carlos and Bey were prisoners, their backs against that central column and their arms tied behind them.

SIGMUND PACED THE bridge. *Hobo Kelly* had the armaments to destroy Forward Station easily enough, but that would not help Carlos and Bey. He could hardly storm the place, even if, miraculously, no one spotted him crossing the gap between ship and station.

And now, except for what could be glimpsed through the dome, he was deaf and dumb. The massive column to which Carlos and Bey were lashed, or the immense metal arm above it, absorbed the signals from the earplug transmitters and button cameras. Sigmund's mind raced as, incredibly, nothing happened. The only motion in the dome was Forward wandering about, as though in conversation.

Then the blat of the proximity alarm gave Sigmund something new to worry about. Three objects were approaching in formation. He checked the radar and wasn't surprised: space tugs. As before, his instruments showed no weapons.

Three tugs in formation when something precipitated *Hobo Kelly* from hyperspace. Three tugs now, in the same equilateral-triangle formation, minutes after Carlos said too much.

The three ships were heading straight toward Sigmund.

Weapons ringed *Hobo Kelly.* Whoever flew those tugs had to know he was armed. Logic insisted they were also armed, even though no weapons registered on his instruments.

Sigmund maneuvered *Hobo Kelly* directly between the tugs and the station. He was stalling for time, searching for an option that did not involve abandoning his shipmates—his friends. The tugs couldn't shoot at him without blowing up their base.

The tugs changed course and kept coming. They must be gambling he would not fire on unarmed ships. On *apparently* unarmed ships.

Would he? "Unidentified ships, this is an ARM patrol vessel. Break off your approach," Sigmund radioed. No response. No deviation. "Unidentified ships, break off or I will fire."

Nothing.

At a minimum, the tug crews were reinforcements if he figured out a way to attempt a rescue. And they'd been warned.

Sigmund fired the main X-ray laser. One ship burst open, spouting gases. Then a second ship. The third ship fled.

He slewed *Hobo Kelly* until its bridge once more faced the station. The Grabber was flailing around. That was presumably Forward's doing, as he was again seated at his horseshoe-shaped console. Angel stood behind Forward.

I'll never have a better chance to rescue them.

The Grabber kept up its writhing as Sigmund struggled into his space suit. What did the Grabber grab?

The drifting wreckage of one of the disabled tugs flashed blue-white. Its disappearance lasted just long enough to give an impression of motion in Sigmund's direction. He lunged for a crash console, half into his space suit, and jetted out of the way of . . . what?

The Grabber compressed suddenly, then recoiled. The bowl at its end still looked empty. It had caught something very massive and very small.

Things happened too quickly to fully take in. Lightning flashed under the dome. A chunk of the Grabber vanished. The dome ruptured. A painfully bright blue-white dot appeared near the break, and Angel fell *up* into it. The scintillating spot of light drifted toward the floor. Forward fell—shot—into it and vanished. The glowing dot sank into the floor.

There was no time to speculate. For the next minute or two, no more, everyone in the base would be busy getting into pressure suits. And in another minute or two, there would be no one left for Sigmund to rescue.

This would be his only chance.

Sigmund put *Hobo Kelly* on autopilot and sealed his helmet. He hit the air lock emergency override; cabin pressure blew him out. He dove into the wrecked dome, his rocket pack on full power. Somehow he managed not to crash.

He whirled in a circle, sighting over a handgun. He found no one but Carlos and Bey, their arms still tied behind them around the central column, bleeding from the ears and nose. Their mouths gaped, screaming silently as the final gas traces burst from their lungs.

Sigmund cut Carlos loose with a hand torch, and helped him into a rescue bag. Once it was zipped and its small oxygen tank began to inflate it, Sigmund did the same for Bey.

Sigmund felt heavier than he expected, and the floor wobbled beneath them. They needed to be someplace else *fast.*

The breach in the dome was too small for him to carry out even one inflated rescue bag. Sigmund set his gun to explosive rounds and blasted a bigger opening.

By then, *Hobo Kelly* had landed on autopilot. He dragged the rescue bags to it, and then pointed at the gaping air lock. Inflated rescue bags wouldn't fit through. He opened his mouth wide as a signal. Bey and Carlos unzipped and crawled into the ship.

Air gushed in as the air lock closed behind Sigmund. Bey and Carlos looked just barely alive. Carlos rasped, "Please don't do that anymore."

Sigmund popped off his helmet and tried to smile

reassuringly. "It should not be necessary anymore. Whatever it was you did, well done. I have two well-equipped autodocs to repair you. While you are healing, I will see about recovering the treasures within the asteroid."

"Forget it," Carlos croaked. "Get us out of here. Now."

He didn't understand. "What—"

"No time. Get us out."

"Very well. First the autodocs." Sigmund turned, but Carlos's hand plucked feebly at his sleeve.

"Futz, no. I want to see this," Carlos whispered.

Sigmund went to the bridge, Carlos and Bey tottering after him.

They strapped down. Sigmund fired the main thruster and took *Hobo Kelly* away from the rock. And from something else. What?

"Far enough," Carlos whispered presently. "Turn us around."

Sigmund nudged the ship around. "What are we looking for?"

"You'll know." Looking half-dead, Carlos somehow managed to smile.

"Carlos, was I right to fire on the tugs?"

"Oh yes."

As they watched, a part of the asteroid collapsed into itself, leaving a deep crater.

"It moves slower at apogee. Picks up more matter," Carlos said. He seemed indifferent to the blood still dribbling from his nose.

"What are you talking about?" A black hole, Sigmund guessed. Mention of one had set Forward off.

"Later, Sigmund. When my throat grows back."

"Forward had a hole in his pocket," Bey said helpfully.

Now the other side of the asteroid collapsed. Lightning briefly flared there. Then the whole ball of rock and ice began to shrink.

Bey coughed. "Sigmund, has this ship got automatic sunscreens?"

"Of course we've got—"

There was a blinding flash. By the time the tears slowed and Sigmund could focus again, nothing showed on his instruments but stars.

· 34 ·

With much assistance, Carlos lowered himself into the autodoc. "Thanks, Sigmund," he said. Breath gurgled in and out of his vacuum-ruined lungs. "I may not want to ride with you after this."

"Don't blame me." Sigmund pushed the close button; the lid started down. He timed his rebuttal to have the last word. "I think it's Bey who's unlucky to fly with."

Lights began blinking on the 'doc. Text scrolled across the display.

Shaeffer had toppled into the remaining autodoc on his own. He had a height advantage. "It's hard to imagine that I used to fly people—safely—for a living."

Given his recent history, Sigmund agreed. "Now it's my turn to fly."

Bey turned his head. The slight motion seemed to hurt. "You don't know what we narrowly escaped." It wasn't unkind, and it wasn't a question.

"I'm not sure," Sigmund admitted. "A black hole?"

"Yeah."

"A quantum black hole?" Sigmund suggested. "Never mind. Tell me after you get out."

"At one time," Bey said. There was no stopping the man midstory. "Did you know quantum black holes can only be created in a Big Bang?" Cough. "True. Forward found it orbiting inside an asteroid. It's a long explanation how, but trust me, he told Carlos and me."

Told them when? Sigmund wondered. Then he remembered losing reception when Bey and Carlos were tied to the base of the Grabber.

Bey hawked a ball of bloody goo into his hand. "Ugh. Quantum black holes are tiny, much smaller than an atom. Since atoms are mostly empty space, a quantum black hole isn't much of a threat. It takes too long for one to eat anything. So he fed his."

"Neutronium." Sigmund appreciated the look of surprise his comment drew.

"Yeah." Cough. "After that, it was large enough to swallow a big asteroid. Followed by all the ships he pirated. It's still microscopic." Cough, cough. "Oh yeah. Early on, also the exhaust from an old ion-drive ship for about a month."

Drive exhaust? "Ah," Sigmund said. "To give it an electrical charge. That's how the tugs could maneuver it into the shipping lanes, and how the Grabber could grab it."

Nothing had somehow compressed the Grabber like a toy spring. Sigmund shivered. "The tugs dropped their black hole after my attack, but Forward caught it. He was going to throw it at *Hobo Kelly.* In a vacuum, it must be invisible. I would never have seen it coming."

Bey coughed again. This time, he couldn't stop. It sounded like he was trying to cough up a lung (and perhaps he was). "Right," he managed to get out. "Until his futzy big electromagnet went *pfft.*" When the racking coughs finally trailed off, Bey donned that ironic half smile that meant: There's more to this story that *maybe* I'll tell you sometime.

That presumed he lived to talk about it. "Bey, we need to start the 'doc. Now."

"You know"—chain of coughs—"that you want to know *how.* You found me still tied up. Did you notice"—cough, hack—"that I'd kicked off my shoes?"

His shoes?

Flat on his back in the open autodoc, Bey raised a foot to his mouth and pantomimed taking a puff.

"You disabled the Grabber with your *toes*?"

This time it was the patient who hit the autodoc control. A devil-may-care smile served Shaeffer as his last word.

NOTHING BUT AN occasional rock for millions of kilometers—and the last rock Sigmund saw had vanished down a black hole. No company. Days away from sunlight and fluffy white clouds and air that didn't taste of recycling.

The autodocs were in use, but Sigmund would have avoided them anyway. He knew how restful it could be to let the 'doc fill his arteries with drugs and let all Earth's enemies fade away into fantasy. It would be like waking from a series of bad dreams. He wanted the rest. But he needed to think, and he needed the distrustful mind Nature had given him.

Days *alone,* with nothing to do but brood.

—About the Jinxian menace. Only a few years ago, the Institute of Knowledge, meaning the Jinxian government, had sponsored that neutron-star mission. He had been so naïve as to convince himself that the Laskins' messy deaths through a GP hull weren't a danger to Earth. He remembered thinking Jinx could hardly threaten Earth's fleet with a neutron star!

Well, a Jinxian had, almost single-handedly, besieged Sol system with a black hole bulked up with neutronium. Operating from a facility owned by the Institute of Knowledge.

—About Gregory Pelton. Pelton had encountered *something* that destroyed GP hulls. Beowulf had as much as admitted it. And now Pelton poured his wealth into research on Jinx. Was he developing the technology?

—And about the Puppeteers. They had enabled the BVS-1 expedition. They knew as much about its findings as the Institute of Knowledge. If Puppeteers had once favored a Pelton with the technology for teleportation, might they not also support *this* generation? Puppeteers were behind the Fertility Law unrest, surely to deflect Sigmund from his quest.

The physics aspects made his head spin. What I do understand, Sigmund thought, is *money*. He must dig even deeper. If Julian Forward had told the truth about losing his institute funding, who funded him at the end? Jinx, merely with more subtlety? Pelton? Puppeteers?

Days alone, with nothing to do but brood.

Sigmund's thoughts swirled, turbulent and inchoate. Like water circling and gurgling down a drain. Like eight innocent crews, and the guilty crews of those space tugs, and Angel and Julian Forward and anyone else who had been on that rock—all sucked down a black hole to oblivion.

Days alone, with nothing to do but brood. . . .

THEY SAID SIGMUND was gibbering and staring at nothing, dehydrated and malnourished, when an ARM cruiser matched courses with and boarded *Hobo Kelly*. They said only occasional words and short phrases were intelligible: *neutronium. Jinx. Conspiracy. Conniving Puppeteers.* Something about mysteries to the north. And one recurring phrase—

No more spaceships.

BECALMED

EARTH DATES: 2652–2653

· 35 ·

The hospital felt unearthly.

Sigmund strode down the corridor. Unfamiliar stimuli assailed him. Medicinal odors. Hushed tones. Pale walls and floor, the better to spot traces of dirt or . . . he chose not to think what else. His skin crawled. I've almost died a couple times, Sigmund thought. Both times an autodoc handled it. People didn't end up in hospitals unless they were *seriously* ill.

Like Carlos.

There was conversation coming from Carlos's room. Laughter. That sounded encouraging. Sigmund tapped on the door frame.

"Good of you to join us," Feather said. She'd been pricklier than ever since his interstellar adventure. She knew tanj well why Sigmund refused to use transfer booths—and that he wouldn't discuss Cerberus in front of Carlos.

Her dig was just one more way to hassle Sigmund. He ignored it, as he tried to ignore the many tubes and instruments connected to Carlos, afloat in a sleeper field. "You're looking much better."

"An attentive guardian helps." Carlos's voice rasped, and fluid gurgled in his lungs. "I'm glad that Feather is here."

She'd arrived only a few hours before Sigmund. The hospital was in Melbourne, and teleporting beat suborbital hops every time. Carlos had been asleep in a hospital 'doc, under round-the-clock specialist supervision, for months. Cloning custom lungs took time.

"What's the prognosis?" Sigmund asked.

"Good, I'm told." Wheeze. "My own damn fault I'm so sick."

"It's Julian Forward's fault," Feather said protectively.

That was true enough, and everyone knew it. Never mind this wasn't the place to be discussing Forward. Carlos knew that, too. "What do you mean, Carlos?"

Wheeze. "For starters, my so-called perfect genes didn't do much for me. Autodoc spares are supposed to work."

They did for most people. Carlos had nearly died in the autodoc on *Hobo Kelly.* His body had massively rejected the replacement lungs on board, and he'd burned through all the immunosuppressant meds before they had crossed Neptune's orbit. Only drugging him into near hibernation, his vacuum-seared lungs scarcely working, had kept Carlos alive.

"Such a modest genius." Feather patted Carlos's arm. "Your genes are perfect for my taste."

Had Feather set her sights on Carlos now? Sigmund wished him luck. "For starters, you said."

"Geniuses should know how to prioritize." Wheeze. Carlos ran splayed fingers through his thick black hair. *Carlos* at a loss for words? "Medical science hasn't improved much in my lifetime. I've had ideas for years how autodocs could be made *much* better." Wheeze.

And had you concentrated on those, rather than cosmological esoterica, *Hobo Kelly* might have carried an autodoc that could have healed you. "What kind of ideas?"

Carlos smiled wanly. "I'm not ready . . ." Wheeze. Cough.

"Right," Sigmund said. "You're not ready to talk about it." Now Carlos could keep his secrets; they wouldn't get anyone killed. "It's something you can work on once you're out of here. Have you heard when that will be?"

"Several more days." Carlos shut his eyes, looking weary. "They're going to pop me into a standard 'doc soon. Now that the new lungs are grown."

"We should let you rest," Sigmund decided. "Come on, Feather."

Feather nodded. "Take care of yourself. We'll be back to check on you."

Leaving Carlos snoring softly, Sigmund and Feather went to the hospital cafeteria. Sigmund bought two coffees. "He had a close call," Sigmund said.

"Too close." Feather took a sip and grimaced. "You *still* don't know how I take coffee? No cream. Earth needs to take better care of him. There aren't enough geniuses to go around."

Sigmund liked and respected Carlos—but he couldn't yet trust him. Medusa had been busy since Carlos popped up on Jinx. She'd sieved through decades of e-mails, comm calls, transfer-booth records, research queries, financial transactions—of Carlos, and his closest colleagues, and their closest colleagues, and . . .

Sigmund's AIde had examined and organized millions of records, terabytes of data. The result was an affinity web of enormous scope—associates and affiliations, friends and relatives and long-ago classmates, fellow investors and former lovers—with ample room for speculation about what the connections, at various removes, of varying types, might mean. The data neither condemned nor exonerated Carlos. At the apex of Earth's aristocracy, it seemed everyone of significance knew everyone else.

Then, as Sigmund was looking at Feather, all the pieces came together for him.

Carlos had almost died, taking his precious genes with him. He needed a bodyguard. Feather was drawn to Carlos. And Carlos seemed receptive enough to Feather's flirting.

Sigmund had a natural spy—and an empty feeling in the pit of his stomach.

FIRST GENERAL PRODUCTS' abrupt withdrawal and then the Fertility Law unrest . . . Nessus had left behind an economy in serious trouble.

He had returned, it seemed, to worse. Tumbleweeds blew across the tarmac of Mojave Spaceport, between long rows of idled spacecraft. In the days since *Aegis'* return, very few ships had taken off or landed. The public databases tantalized more than they revealed. UN censors had clamped down on something big. He had to know what.

Not to mention, he needed to distract himself.

The good news was, transfer-booth abduction still worked.

"Two years," Sangeeta Kudrin said. She was newly dyed and coiffed, wearing a slinky black dress. Abduction had not been in her thoughts. "I had dared to hope you were gone for good. It's Nessus, isn't it?"

"Correct." Two tumultuous years. Nessus wasn't certain, or could not yet be honest with himself, what had brought him back to Human Space. He was afraid to know why Nike had been so quick to approve his departure. Nessus told himself his return was about duty. He worried endlessly whether it was about guilty secrets: his *and* Nike's.

On the slender reed of such ambiguity rested any hopes of a future with Nike.

Unseen behind his one-way mirror, Nessus plucked at his mane. He needed to concentrate on whatever new misfortunes had befallen Earth. "I hope to make this brief."

Sangeeta said nothing.

"You prospered during my absence," Nessus went on. Public databases now gave her title as a UN Undersecretary, no longer a mere Deputy.

"You kidnapped me before for information. Is that why you've taken me now?"

"It is." Nessus squirmed in his nest of cushions. "Information about Sigmund Ausfaller."

However reluctantly, she complied. Once he ascertained what a pirate was, the pieces began to fall into place. The seedy and idle spaceport. Julian Forward's failure to respond to hyperwave messages as Nessus approached Sol system. Ausfaller's failure to follow the clues that two years ago had drawn his attention toward the galactic north.

Once Sangeeta began, the words tumbled out. "And the Jinx government is still demanding answers about Julian Forward, information Ausfaller refuses to give." She leaned forward to whisper, "I believe Forward is dead, and that Ausfaller killed him."

"So Ausfaller is obsessed now, wondering how Forward made neutronium," Nessus concluded.

"Yes, damn you! Haven't you been listening? No one knows much more. Ausfaller simply won't talk. After he ended the pirate attacks, no one, not even the ARM Director, would dare challenge Ausfaller to reveal more than he chooses."

Nessus pawed thoughtfully at the deck. Julian's piracy had diverted Ausfaller from his hunt. Ausfaller had stopped Julian. Julian, the Citizen technology Nessus had provided, the neutronium Julian had made with it—all the evidence had vanished irretrievably down a black hole.

"Very good. You may go." Nessus transferred Sangeeta to a remote booth.

Forward's death did not bother Nessus—much. The Jinxian had made his own choice to turn renegade. But the innocent crews of eight ships? Those lay heavily on Nessus' conscience.

A soft chime eventually announced mealtime. Nessus climbed from his nest of pillows and synthed a small bowl of chopped mixed grasses. He nibbled at the greens without interest, his emotions roiling. Relief that Hearth was safe from ARM pursuit. Terror at being alone, so very far from home. Guilt at more deaths. Worry whether the apparent lifting of the siege of Earth would suffice to undo the economic damage. An enervating miasma of fear, uncertainty, and doubt.

But among the many familiar apprehensions Nessus

sensed an intriguing new idea. Another human community also weighed on his mind.

Someone like Sigmund Ausfaller could be extremely valuable to it.

·36·

A bit of computational legerdemain morphed Medusa's snake-wreathed head. Now a spider with oddly serpentine legs, she scuttled along the impossibly dense fabric of the affinity network that represented Sigmund's ongoing investigations. "Oh, what a tangled web we weave," she concluded.

"Cute." Feather also participated by hologram, netting from the guest room in Carlos Wu's house. It was night on that side of the world; Carlos was, supposedly, asleep. She shambled about the room, yawning. "I'm tired, Sigmund. Let's get on with it."

Fair enough. It was late for her. "Here's the bottom line. For a long time, General Products funds have driven much of the unrest. Oh, we can't prove it; the laundering was very good. But the correlations between asset transfers from GP, unusual income patterns, tax avoidance, and advocacy for 'reform' are too good not to be meaningful."

"Carlos likes to say correlation isn't causation." She waved off Sigmund's protest. "No, we don't discuss your investigation. He was explaining something about his medical research, for a new autodoc."

Your investigation. Feather's current dye job suddenly registered. Sigmund couldn't remember ever seeing her skin red. On *Hobo Kelly,* hadn't Carlos mentioned red was his favorite color? "Feather, the transfers attributable to GP tapered off suddenly. Why?"

"I don't know why." This time, Feather made no effort to cover her yawn. "Frankly, Sigmund, I don't know why you care. The Puppeteers are long gone. The criminals didn't just launder that money—by now, they must control it."

"The unrest continues without their money," Medusa pointed out. "Why keep subsidizing the cause once it became self-sustaining?" The AIde began enumerating nonmonetary connections in her network.

"This is ridiculous, Sigmund," Feather interrupted. "We're supposed to be paranoid, but there are limits. Here's a theory for you. A crime syndicate, not the Puppeteers, triggered the protests. It's all been a distraction so the ARM wouldn't notice their real plot until it was completed."

Bad attitude, red dye, and something else. What *else* was setting off his alarm bells? "Their real plot," he echoed.

"Futz, Sigmund. Are you really so dense?" Feather stopped pacing to glare directly into her comm unit. "Pressure a few bankers to cede control of abandoned GP accounts. Everything else is a smoke screen."

He could hardly believe what he was hearing. "Subverting the transfer booths? Stealing the Elgin futzy Marbles?"

"That's so *you,* Sigmund. Invent alien involvement, so you can ignore the injustice half the world now protests. It's a handy excuse for not doing anything about *us.*" Her eyes blazed. "Not that there is an us, anymore."

The dye job. The attitude. And now Sigmund realized what had been eluding him: the emptiness of the room. Feather was a slob, yet the guest room was tidy. No, barren. He knew without accessing the sensors: Her clutter had moved to Carlos's bedroom.

Despite the bright morning sun streaming into his office windows, Sigmund suddenly felt ineffably weary. "We're done here. Get some sleep." He broke the connection.

"You didn't give Feather our other news," Medusa

said. She was once more a conventional gorgon. The elaborate affinity web had dissolved into the cyberspace from which it had come.

"Consider Feather's only tasking to be protection of Carlos." Sigmund massaged his temples. He told himself he wished them happiness.

But given Feather's attitude, he saw no reason to share Medusa's other progress tracing laundered funds. To be reminded condescendingly that correlation isn't causation?

The Institute of Knowledge had accepted a large endowment of laundered GP funds just before it cut direct funding to Julian Forward. Julian Forward had taken *other* laundered GP funds, then laid siege to Sol system.

In his bones, Sigmund knew: Hidden Puppeteers were still at work.

· 37 ·

Nature Preserve 1 was a thoroughly Citizen world. There was no real danger here—only shame and misery.

Baedeker shivered in the cab of his hovering combine. The sounds of howling wind and the unhappy grinding of jammed machinery entered through the open window. Eventually he raised the window, colder but no wiser than when he had lowered it.

It would be easy enough to float back to town. The looming wall of black cloud, riven intermittently with great jagged strokes of lightning, was ample justification. Then, when morning came and the storm had passed, when much of the crop lay in ruin, he would be that much further behind in his quota.

Twittering unhappily, he raised the heat setting in his coveralls. The garment was bright orange—

Rehabilitation Corps orange—except for the clear, permeable portions that protected his heads. He climbed down from the cab's right-side door, to the side he had already harvested. He walked leaning into the wind, crop stubble crunching beneath his booted hooves. Even the lightest expanses of sky overhead were a sullen, featureless gray.

A bloody mass clogged the intake: the burrower he had glimpsed in his path. Cursing in minor chords, he popped open an access panel. He disconnected power to the mechanism and began hacking out the carcass with a pry bar from the combine's toolbox. If the storm held off, he might still get the field harvested today. In this, his new station in life, he had only such tiny successes to appreciate, and them but rarely.

The animal remains had lodged deep inside. He chopped and slashed, gore spattering his coveralls, brooding how far in life he had fallen.

There was a time, not that long ago, when he had been respected and well rewarded. Deservedly so: He had skills and expertise of vital importance to the Concordance. He had held a position of honor and great responsibility within the General Products Corporation. He ate natural foods from the farm planets, instead of slaving on one and living on synthesized gruel.

He wasn't Baedeker then, not until the end of that halcyon era.

He called himself Baedeker now, the better to remind himself every day exactly how—and by whose doing—he had been humiliated and banished. The better to concentrate on finding a way back.

It began with the scruffy scout named Nessus. . . .

NESSUS DOCKED AN interstellar scout ship due for overhaul and upgrades at the General Products hull factory that orbited Hearth. He teleported aboard—with three intruders.

"Scouts," these three were also to be considered. That was ludicrous. The important work of scouting belonged only in the jaws of *Citizens*. Other species should not be allowed to enter, let alone tour, this factory. Baedeker had protested, but Nessus, for all his unkempt disreputability, had powerful friends.

"My name is . . ." Baedeker began reluctantly. The translator choked on his mellifluous name. "I will be showing you"—under protest—"around the facility." *My* facility.

"For today, we'll call you Baedeker," Nessus interrupted. That didn't translate back to Citizen.

Baedeker tried to distract these "guests" with talk of coming in-cabin upgrades, trivia like adjustable crash couches and finger-friendly keyboards. He offered only vague generalities about the facility's main purpose: the construction of impregnable hulls.

The "scout" named Eric would not be dissuaded. He kept pressing for a tour of the fabrication volume.

"It is not allowed," Baedeker said. "That region is a controlled vacuum."

Eric said, "I'll wear my pressure suit. It's aboard—"

"It is not allowed," Baedeker repeated, his heads pivoting emphatically left/right, left/right, on their neck hinges. In the facility's microgravity conditions, only hoof claws hooked through fabric loops kept him on the deck. "The traces of gas and dust that cling to the outside of your suit would contaminate the process."

"I don't understand," another said. Omar? "Nessus, you told us only large quantities of antimatter could harm *Explorer*'s hull. How can a bit of dust harm anything?"

"What I told you is correct," Nessus answered. "I was speaking of completed hulls. During construction, hulls are fragile."

Eric had been attentive, and he was not without a certain cunning. "Extreme sensitivity to gravitational variations. Extreme sensitivity to trace contaminants. It sounds like a very-large-scale nanotech process."

Baedeker shrieked like a slow-motion boiler explosion. His howl did not translate. Nessus responded in like manner, but longer and even louder, threatening to call Nike himself.

In normal tones, as though Baedeker had not spoken, Nessus went on. "General Products Corporation does not often disclose this information. Given what you now know, it is best that you hear the rest. It would be unfortunate if you lost trust in your ship."

Then the dining-hall rumors were true! The Concordance was turning over a fully equipped interstellar scout ship to such as these—unsupervised. Baedeker was appalled. He resolved, during the upcoming overhaul, to integrate monitoring devices into *Explorer*'s telemetry. He would know what these "scouts" did, and where they went. And he would control explosives inside their indestructible hull, lest they stray.

Nessus had not stopped. "*Explorer*'s hull is impervious to damage. If not, would I have ventured out in it? Still, there is a fact I had not shared. The hull takes its strength from its unique form: It is a single supermolecule grown atom by atom by nanotechnology. During construction, the incomplete hull is unstable. The slightest chemical contamination or unbalanced force can tear it to pieces. That's why there is no artificial gravity here, and why communication here"—and his sweeping head gestures suggested the totality of the enormous orbital factory—"uses optical fibers."

Caterwauling in outrage, Baedeker stormed out. None but Citizens—and few of them—needed to know such details. Nothing good could come of this.

He seethed until Nessus and companions took a shuttle to Hearth. He did not calm down until sensors and remote-controlled explosives were hidden aboard *Explorer.*

• • •

WITH A GRUNT, Baedeker pried loose the last chunk of burrower rib cage. Blood and gobbets of flesh speckled his coveralls. Wind wailed, and he further raised the temperature of the garment before reconnecting power to the intake.

Explorer had gone out without Citizen supervision, and Baedeker prided himself on his foresight. He monitored its telemetry. He ran samples of surreptitiously reported conversations through a translator. He took comfort in what he overheard—

While Nessus' "scouts" bypassed Baedeker's sensors, relayed their communications through a hyperwave buoy, and disabled the detonators. Unwatched, they penetrated one of the most secret and secure facilities of the Concordance, located a weapon of great potency, and—dooming Baedeker to this place—destroyed a General Products hull to get the weapon out.

And with that weapon, Nessus' "scouts" had extorted a prize of inestimable value from the Concordance.

The cab was still warm, and the storm front had stalled. Baedeker resumed harvesting, the combine spewing a steady stream of grains through its towed stepping disc into a distant warehouse. All the chaff, dirt, bits of stalk and leaves, and burrower bits fell back to the ground.

The clatter of hailstones finally started Baedeker on the long way back to the barn. Hail could not harm him inside the cab; he twitched nonetheless, while the sturdy fabric of his coveralls frustrated his efforts to pluck at his mane.

Turning over a Concordance ship was the fundamental error. Nessus' error! The safeguards Baedeker had undertaken to install—on his own initiative—had been circumvented, but was that his fault? And how could he be blamed because three unsupervised scouts had discovered antimatter somewhere out among the stars!

But he *was* blamed. Scouts were too few to hold accountable, and someone must pay. He could not alter the past. He could not say where—no one could!—vast quantities of antimatter could be found. He couldn't be expected to—

Baedeker cut through the self-pity with a strident, double-throated blat of disgust. What *can* you do? Can anyone disintegrate a General Products hull *without* using antimatter?

To his sudden, utter amazement, Baedeker realized that, just possibly, he could.

· 38 ·

"Your money has been well spent," Ander said. He was newly returned from Jinx and still feeding his bulked-up weight. "Including the generous bonus."

"I don't remember offering a bonus." Sigmund didn't bother adding that two kilos of Kobe beef *was* a bonus.

Ander merely smiled and crooked a finger at the woman pushing the dessert cart.

The more arrogant, the better the news, Sigmund reminded himself. Once two cannolis and a slice of baklava found their way to Ander's end of the table, Sigmund took out his comm unit. "Protocol gamma," he said. Sound suppression, bug suppression, and a translucent holographic screen around the table to stymie lip-readers. Red, yellow, and green dots slowly chased one another around its screen. "We can talk freely."

"Free except for that matter of my bonus." Ander blotted his lips with his napkin. "I leave that entirely to your discretion."

Sigmund waited.

"Very well. You'll be amused to learn that I caroused our way to success." Ander tipped his head, smiling in fond memory of something. "Once one has been accepted, there's pleasure to be had even on West End. You should come back to Jinx with me."

Sigmund flinched. Since he had limped home from Forward Station, near catatonic with the flatlander phobia, the idea of leaving Earth terrified him. He'd been unable to face even the short trip to the Oort Cloud, where instantaneous hyperwave radio worked, to spare Ander a far longer voyage.

"It sounds like you've already gotten your bonus," Sigmund said.

A cannoli disappeared, pastry flakes raining onto the tablecloth. "As directed, I befriended workers employed by Gregory Pelton's project. I concede the process was not without its amusements."

"And?"

"You suck all the fun out of a story, Sigmund. I was eventually hired, of course. A drinking buddy recommended me. It didn't get me into the inner circle, of course, but I hold a responsible position in the back office. Close enough to the action to know, I think, who the inner circle *is*." Ander waved his fork. "Yes, I know. You're asking yourself why, if I have a responsible position, I could get away."

Murmurs penetrated the sound suppressors, no more intelligible than the snippets that might leak out. Sigmund said, "Stet. How?"

"That's the good thing about being middle management, just one transistor in the machine. No one thought anything of it when I said I needed some time off.

"It's my sister, you see. She got herself arrested in the flatlander riots." Ander dropped the sudden theatrical voice. "I told them I thought I could get Sis's charges dismissed—but those are the kind of favors one calls in only face-to-face."

A waitress came by with fresh coffee. Sigmund waited for her to leave before asking, "So what *did* you learn that couldn't be put into an encrypted recording?"

"Pelton's little secret. The reason he's been planning a big expedition, although, alas, not the coordinates of its destination." Ander leaned forward conspiratorially.

"And that secret is?" Sigmund prompted.

"Antimatter." A smug grin lit Ander's face. "He found a futzy whole *world* of the stuff."

THE MOST UNUSUAL world.

That I-know-something-you-don't-know smirk on Pelton's face had galled Sigmund for years. Someday soon, that smirk would come off. "Ander, you've earned that bonus after all."

"Excellent. A bit of celebratory brandy then?" Ander gestured to the waitress. "Some Cerbois Armagnac. The 2588, I think. Sigmund?"

He had no one to leave his money to, as Feather was once apt to remind him. The ache when he thought about her and Carlos was another reason to drink. "Why not."

Ander continued his report, and the challenges of Pelton's hoped-for expedition slowly became clear. No normal ship had the fuel capacity to rendezvous with the fast-moving antimatter system. And once there, then what? Antimatter solar wind had already destroyed a GP hull. Survival required entirely foolproof electromagnetic shields to divert charged antiparticles, and equally dependable lasers to target and ionize any neutral antimatter streaming their way.

Perhaps enough antimatter couldn't be captured simply from the solar wind. Sigmund let Medusa record Ander's particulars—some specifics, and more speculations—about concepts for mining the planet itself. A gravitationally levitated base camp. High-powered lasers to boil off the antimatter surface, the ionized vapors then to be captured in magnetic bottles.

"Who knows the location of the system?" Sigmund interrupted.

Ander blinked. "Gregory Pelton, of course. On-site, Barry Kellerman, Tabitha-Ann Wong, Don Cramer, and Melanie Donnatello. They're the inner circle. Our buddy Beowulf must know—like Elephant, he's been there—but I've never seen Bey at the facility."

If only he had enough proof to squeeze Pelton! Sigmund couldn't imagine going to the Secretary-General with just Ander's word. It wouldn't work. If he tried, news of the infiltration of an ARM informant might get back to Pelton. And while Pelton remained off-limits, Beowulf was, too. Tanj! He needed corroboration.

"Are the insiders you named all Jinxians? Bey and Pelton aside, that is," Sigmund said. A snifter of aromatic and obscenely expensive brandy sat in front of him, unsampled.

"Mostly. Cramer's another flatlander."

"Who in the group is official?"

"Jinxian government? No one, I think." Ander grinned. "West End is a very small, close-knit community. That's why it took me so long to get accepted. In the end, being a flatlander probably helped. Cramer handles personnel matters, and he errs on the side of caution. He doesn't want anyone from the government or the Institute of Knowledge getting in."

There was that name again. It sounded familiar, but Sigmund couldn't place it. "Medusa, what do you have on Don Cramer?" It wasn't *Medusa* he asked, of course, merely the subset he could carry around. The rest of her, cut off by the privacy screen, remained on the net.

"A longtime business associate of Gregory Pelton," she said.

That still sounded familiar. "Any relation to our . . . other investigation?" Ander wasn't involved in the Puppeteer hunt. Medusa was subtle enough to catch the hint.

"Maybe," she answered. "I can show you onscreen, if you like."

Ander had also taken the hint. He turned his attention to his brandy, pointedly looking away while Sigmund angled his comm unit so only he could see the screen.

"Go ahead," Sigmund said. A tiny representation appeared of Medusa's tangled web. She panned and zoomed until he saw only a corner of the graphical network. A few symbols near Cramer's suggested small amounts of GP money. (Correlation is not causation, mocked the voice only he heard.)

Cramer himself wasn't thought to have gotten GP funds. Because he had enough money of his own—or of Pelton's? Maybe, but Sigmund had another explanation. He knew all about off-limits Pelton associates. Maybe Cramer was too dangerous to approach.

The problem with an all-but-omnipresent AIde was coping in those rare instances when she wasn't around. Like years ago, inside the electronically suppressed domain of an exclusive, private Manhattan club. Pelton's words came rushing back: "Not me, not my friends, not my associates. There will be no further interest in Dianna Guthrie, or Beowulf Shaeffer, or Sharrol Janss, or Don Cramer, or *anyone* close to me."

Sigmund remembered making a mental note that day to track down who Cramer was. Too much had been going on; the matter had slipped his mind. "Are there other overlaps?"

The affinity web expanded to incorporate buddies and co-workers Ander had mentioned. Most showed only the simple white icon that denoted "nothing unusual known." A few icons, all close to the so-called inner circle, showed varying degrees of the purple tinge of suspected Puppeteer funding. Sigmund asked, "Medusa, what's your guess?"

Serpents writhed. "We're not the only ones trying to locate the antimatter solar system."

• • •

SIGMUND ROAMED CENTRAL Park, the evening breeze tugging at his suit, fallen leaves swirling about his legs and crunching beneath his shoes. A copseye floated overhead, indifferent to his off-key whistling.

Almost certainly, Puppeteers and Jinxians knew no more about Pelton's plans than *he* did. That left Pelton himself as a threat. Finagle only knew what Pelton planned to do with antimatter. It hardly mattered. If Pelton's purpose was somehow utilitarian and benign, the mere presence in Human Space of antimatter in large quantities remained unacceptable. Whether Pelton, or a corrupt colleague, or lurking Puppeteers took possession, the danger was intolerable.

But harvesting antimatter would be difficult indeed. Much could go wrong.

This time, Ander traveled to Jinx with his prospects for a bonus quite unambiguous. To earn it, Ander had only to see to it that a few things *did* go wrong. . . .

· 39 ·

Not until Achilles had lived among humans and learned to speak Interworld did he discover a word to truly describe himself. He was a *rebel.*

Disagreement was rare among Citizens. There were differences of opinion, certainly: concerning art, music, fashion. On matters of public policy, the Concordance had long consisted of the two great political organizations. Experimentalists championed courses of action that no Conservative could ever advocate.

But Achilles had *seen,* among humans and Kzinti, real politics and true struggles for power. Hearth had neither. Responsibility for Hearth's governance shifted between Experimentalists and Conservatives only after an overwhelming reversal in popular consensus. Even then the shifts often changed nothing. No matter who was Hindmost, managing Foreign Affairs remained primarily an Experimentalist duty and social justice a Conservative role.

So how different could the parties be?

Achilles dug a forehoof indulgently into the meadowplant that so thickly carpeted the deck. It was a rare Hindmost who left Hearth, but the vessel maintained at the ready for him, for that remote contingency, was luxurious.

He thought about the mental flexibility required to leave the home world, and adjusted his cynicism: *There* was a difference between parties. No Conservative had ever left Hearth.

Achilles awaited the imminent conference in the bustling comfort of the ship's relax room. In the privacy of his thoughts, he sneered at this crew. They thought themselves strong, and yet they ventured little farther than a routine shuttle run to one of the farm worlds. They need never make the jump into hyperspace. This trip took them only barely outside the singularity, for a hyperwave consultation with Nessus.

Once, before knowing the word, Achilles had hoped Nessus was a fellow rebel. Now Achilles knew Nessus was only a screwup.

Crew came and went, fluting and warbling to one another. A few apologized for disturbing Achilles' thoughts. Most did not bother, or took no note of him. He ignored them all.

On the relax room's main viewer, one star blazed far brighter than the rest. Giver of Life, it was called, and so it once had been. Its expansion into a red giant had nearly extinguished all life. Only moving Hearth itself had saved the herd—while driving many permanently catatonic.

Now they fled the slow-motion death not of a sun, but of a whole galaxy.

He stared at Giver of Life, remembering a walk on the beach. A communion with, he had believed, a kindred spirit. A great red spark had hung low on the horizon, a thousand reflections glittering on the waves. . . .

"EXPLORING HAS ITS rewards," Achilles said. "That includes unparalleled privacy here on Hearth." It was a partial truth. Pastoral reservations such as this also encouraged scouts to keep their disturbing, manic-depressive selves away from their well-adjusted betters.

A protégé cantered at Achilles' side, sand flying from his hooves. The young one still toyed with his choice of scout name, favoring for now the obscure centaur name of Nessus. "I could get used to this."

But you won't, Achilles thought. You'll spend most of your life off-world, with little-enough companionship even from your fellow misfits. And for nothing. Unless you join with me, that is. "A beautiful setting."

They ambled along the shore, warm waves easing up the shallow slope to swirl about their hooves. To their left, towering arcologies ringed the beach and blocked out the sky. To their right, to seaward, the view was entirely different. Stars sparkled above ocean swells that extended to the horizon.

Achilles let the vista speak for him.

"It's very peaceful," Nessus finally said. "When I graduate and ship out, I shall remember this as part of what we protect."

"And yet," Achilles said. He paused to stare out to sea. He always did. It was best that he not seem to be recruiting. "Never mind."

Nessus chanted delicately, with harmonics of trust and respect, "Yet what?"

Achilles swept his gaze across the sea. "Look how empty it is. We're told the planet is full. That's why so few are permitted Brides."

"Surely it *is* full," Nessus replied. The answer was swift and orthodox, as he had been taught, but puzzled undertunes sounded through.

His confusion was predictable enough. At this point in their training, scouts were at their most vulnerable. Loners and misfits all, they saw the possibility within their grasp, some for the first time in their lives, to *belong*. Most would do anything for acceptance into the fraternity of explorers.

Now was the moment, with deftness and skill, to recruit Nessus into another community. Several young allies watched from a distance, awaiting the signal to greet their newest fellow.

Achilles stopped walking. He straightened a neck, pointing out the brightest star in the sky. "Giver of Life. It nurtured us. Then, when we were ready, it did what good fathers must. It encouraged its offspring, us, to take responsibility for ourselves."

Nessus was mute for a long time, struggling with the metaphor. "A stern parent. To leave Hearth in its natural orbit would have meant incineration. Extinction."

Achilles raised his heads and assumed a confident, wide-legged stance. "The simplest course would have been to move Hearth very gradually, as Giver of Life expanded. Next simplest would have been to move Hearth immediately to its final distant orbit, and ring the planet with artificial suns. But what *was* done?"

"The oceans were seeded with genetically engineered, infrared-photosynthesizing plankton," his student said. "At the rim of the solar system, away from the danger, our sky became dark."

"The herd did more than relocate far from danger," Achilles clarified. "*This* is the history we're not taught. Our world was at risk before the sun showed its first instabilities. Hearth was baking in the waste heat of a half-trillion occupants and their industry."

As they resumed their stroll, Achilles brushed flanks with the young scout. In the teeming arcologies and pedestrian malls, such casual contact was unavoidable, reassuring but impersonal. Here on the empty beach the touching was freighted with meaning. "We freed ourselves of heat as a limit on our population. In a few generations, the number of Citizens doubled."

They walked on in thoughtful silence. "There were consequences," Nessus finally said. "It is said that many went mad."

So some had, but almost exclusively among Conservatives. That ancient history would matter more to Nessus than to most of his recruits. Achilles had studied the would-be scout's file; he came from a long line of Conservatives.

"But the world is surely full now," Nessus went on. "Isn't it?"

A wave crashed onto a pile of surf-smoothed rocks, splashing them both with spray. Achilles locked eyes with his protégé. "Not the ocean floor. Most of the world's surface is ocean."

Of a trillion Citizens, all but a few lived in stacked cubicles deep in the bowels of vast structures, the very air they breathed replenished by filters bonded to stepping discs. What sky they saw they experienced by holovision or by teleporting elsewhere. How would their lives change if those boxes lay under the sea?

Achilles now poured out his vision, of the ocean floor covered in arcologies built of impervious hull material. Surely Hearth could support two, even three trillion more Citizens.

More young ones waited nearby, all previously initiated. Achilles had honed the process. First, the approach: overwhelming an eager-to-please protégé with his charisma. Individual attention from a high official at the academy was usually enough. Then, the warm welcome from a few peers. Finally, the group assembly, bonding the recruit—a lonely misfit, as every scout trainee was—into Achilles' growing sect.

The initiates he had designated sidled closer, eager to perform their parts. Vesta, tall and lithe, with his booming contralto voices. Clotho, of the dancing green eyes and striking russet patches. Nyx, of the boldly striped coat. As they approached, Achilles rhapsodized about their wondrous future, his voices thrumming with enthusiasm—

And Nessus recoiled! "I don't understand. What of such arcologies' waste heat, bubbling up from the seabed?" A nervous whinny escaped him. "The oceans remain the lungs of the world."

"Plankton was genetically engineered once." Annoyed undertunes crept into Achilles' voices. Had they not just discussed that? And his disciples might hear Nessus' impertinence. "The plankton can be reengineered, if need be, for greater heat tolerance."

"I see." Nessus tugged at his earnestly plain mane, the reflex putting the lie to his tentative words. "In theory, that is."

Nyx edged closer. "Respectfully, sir, I had begun to wonder about the implications of disturbing seabed methane clathrates. . . ."

"Methane clathrates?" Achilles snapped back, warbling in anger. "What is this trivia?"

"Methane trapped in ice in the ocean-floor sediments," Clotho said. "How would its release affect—"

"Silence!" Achilles trilled, his undertunes demanding immediate obedience. "I know what they are," he lied. None of this mattered. His true interest wasn't trillions more theoretical Citizens. Of course there were questions and unpredictable implications.

All that mattered was that a single arcology be deployed to the ocean floor as an experiment. Such a test would require a cadre of volunteers. Scouts were the obvious source—as soon as enough had pledged their loyalty. And surely the research population must include a Harem House of potential Brides.

He would be their Hindmost, master of the ocean floor, commanding them all.

Now *four* trainees buzzed around him, discussing uncertainties. Higher up the sandy slope, others milled about, confused by the delay.

"Leave us," Achilles thundered at Nessus. "I have no patience for your juvenile failure of imagination." Achilles *had* to deal with the swelling murmurs all around. In his mind, he was already the Hindmost of a seabed arcology. There *must* be respect for his authority.

Nessus had introduced doubt. Like a pebble rolling downhill, the disturbance grew. Unable to still the cacophony, Achilles ordered the cadets back to their dormitory.

Soon after, the Ministry of Foreign Affairs reorganized the scout academy. And so he was first sent to Kzin.

A COMMUNICATOR TRILLED discreetly from a pocket of Achilles' decorative sash. "Achilles," he answered softly.

"You are summoned to the Hindmost's suite," a resonant contralto said. "We have established hyperwave communications with Nessus. The conference begins momentarily."

Dismounting from his padded bench, Achilles pivoted heads and looked himself briefly in the eyes. Some disciples remained true.

It warmed Achilles' hearts that loyal, pliant Vesta now headed Clandestine Directorate.

•40•

Ian Girard hunched over his little-kid table, lips pursed in concentration. He labored away on his electronic tablet with a stylus gripped in his chubby fist.

Sigmund sat beside Andrea on the sofa in her LA apartment. She was dye free, scrubbed clean for space. (Until last night, he'd had no idea she was blond.) Guilt didn't remove so easily; it was plain on her face as she watched her son sketch. Amid that guilt of abandonment bubbled hints of excitement. This would be her first long-range mission.

Sigmund stood for a better perspective on Ian's art. He saw two sort-of stick figures, their arms and legs emerging directly from enormous heads, separated by a triangle of similar height. "Who are they, champ?" Sigmund asked.

Ian glanced up. "Mommy and you."

Andrea chortled at his double take. "Just because you're here, Sigmund."

Not because he had spent the night, or any childish expectations thereof. "Who's who, Ian?" he asked.

Ian pointed. "This is you in black, silly. Mommy wears colors."

Andrea laughed again, eyes twinkling. "It's a beautiful picture, Sweetie. Sigmund just isn't used to your style."

Sigmund wondered what he'd gotten himself into. He'd happily return; he felt warm and uncharacteristically relaxed here. Andrea's intentions were the mystery. For all he knew, last night was only about preflight jitters. "Is this a house?" he asked the boy.

"No way!" Ian scribbled vigorously beneath the triangle. Flames? "It's a spaceship. Like Mommy is going on."

Hobo Kelly would launch on thrusters, of course. It also had a fusion drive, which doubled as a weapon, but launching from Earth on fusion drive would send a pilot straight to the organ banks—assuming he was caught.

Andrea's headshake, peripherally glimpsed, closed Sigmund's mouth. No three-year-old needed to hear that. "Great spaceship," Sigmund said.

"Good save," she mouthed.

What a simple joy it must be to raise a child. Andrea experienced paranoia only through chemicals; she'd had no trouble getting a birthright. Even though he knew only a short-term marriage contract had been involved, Sigmund thought the departed father was a fool.

A few hours around Ian, and Bey raising Carlos's children suddenly made sense. Maybe Feather's obsessions did, too. And maybe also Feather's anger at Sigmund.

Now Sigmund felt guilty. Guiltier? That Andrea might diagnose his uncertainty made him guiltier still.

Andrea waved at the bulging backpack by the door. "Sweetie, your aunt Tina will be here in a minute for you. Save your great picture and put away your tablet." When he only scribbled that much more furiously, she added, "Seriously, Ian. Finish up."

"Stay home, Mommy," Ian said. He circled the triangle/rocket with the stylus, and dragged the symbol over the black stick figure. "Sigmund, you go."

Sigmund froze. His heart pounded. He had begged *his* parents to stay, and he'd been ten at the time.

"Ian, Mommy has to go now." Andrea brushed past Sigmund, pressed the save button on the tablet, and picked up the little device. "Sigmund would come if he could."

But he couldn't! Childhood nightmares mingled in his mind's eye with autodoc alarms glowing red, Carlos dying inside. Sigmund shook, and thought he might puke. Could he ever leave Earth again? If so, it wouldn't be on *Hobo Kelly.*

"You'll have fun with Aunt Tina." Andrea used a this-time-I-really-mean-it tone, and Ian scooted.

Sigmund held it together until Andrea's sister and Ian departed.

"I'm looking forward to this," Andrea said. "I know why you won't, but there's plenty of room aboard if you decide to join us."

Us: an ARM naval crew and marines. They'd probably find nothing, "north" being rather vague as a clue. They could almost surely outrun and outgun anything hostile they encountered.

None of which halted Sigmund's trembling. "I don't think so."

They went to the building's roof. He unlocked his rental air car for the short jump to Mojave Spaceport. "Any last-minute questions?"

"Only one. Will we celebrate my triumphant return just as enthusiastically?" He must have looked surprised, because she patted his arm. "I *do* plan to return, you know."

"That's an order," he said. "And the answer to your question is yes."

HOBO KELLY ROSE noiselessly, swung slowly to orient itself into the spaceport traffic pattern, and accelerated. In a moment, it was invisible to the naked eye.

Sigmund peered into the cloudless desert sky for minutes after the ship disappeared. "Godspeed," he whispered. Then he set out for the commercial terminal, for the short, suborbital flight back to New York, there to practice the skill he was worst at.

Waiting.

• 41 •

Baedeker struggled to grasp how his life had so suddenly changed. A sumptuous private cabin had replaced the communal hardship of the Rehabilitation Corps. He once more enjoyed a proper grooming and a professionally styled mane. He was in space, again.

One change eclipsed all others. He was suddenly, if tentatively, in the confidence of the Hindmost himself, observing great affairs of state.

Observing, but not participating. The Hindmost had directed Baedeker to monitor in secrecy from his cabin. He stood and watched—and wondered why.

The Hindmost seemed to think nothing of the casual informality with which the two scouts addressed him, simply, as Nike. It was well known that scouts were insane; surely, this proved it.

And one of those scouts, the one participating by hyperwave radio, had ruined Baedeker's life: Nessus.

The Deputy Minister, Vesta, kept the social niceties short. "Nessus, you requested an urgent, real-time consultation."

Nessus bobbed heads. "The problem is urgent. My most highly placed agent has informed me of an ARM exploratory vessel traveling in your direction."

"Then you have failed," Achilles said. The bass harmonics oozed disdain.

"It wasn't *my* neutronium traps that drew ARM attention," Nessus snapped back.

"At least I tried. How much accumulated General Products wealth have *you* squandered failing to distract the ARM?" Achilles rebutted.

As the scouts quarreled, Baedeker struggled to understand why he was here. Through his family, he had sent word from exile to onetime colleagues at General

Products: "It doesn't take antimatter." Everything after that happened with amazing speed.

"We need recommendations, not argument," Vesta interjected finally.

Baedeker had never considered himself socially skilled. Banishment and near isolation on Nature Preserve 1 changed that. There, often with only memories for companionship, he had endlessly revisited past conversations. His newfound ear for nuance sensed ulterior motives and strained relations. Why did Vesta act so deferentially toward Achilles?

"Here's a recommendation," Achilles said. "Destroy Earth. *That* will distract the humans. If we had begun accelerating a stealthed ship when Ausfaller first began snooping—"

"You're insane," Nessus screamed. "It would be genocide, and it would solve nothing. Suppose the ARM ship locates us. If harm comes to Earth, or even to every human world, that ship alone can likewise shatter Hearth."

Achilles shouted back, "They won't, not if we make it seem Kzinti are behind the attack."

"Meaning double the genocide." Nessus trembled in rage.

"What is your alternative?" Vesta challenged.

"Lead them astray." Nessus' necks trembled, as he fought not to pluck his mane. "We know approximately where the ARM ship will emerge from hyperspace. Have our ships waiting. When the humans emerge, subtly lure them in a safe direction."

"There's no harm in trying," Vesta commented.

"No!" Achilles stretched to his full height. "If they're not misled, they can hyperwave back what they see."

"They might anyway," Nessus retorted.

Baedeker pawed at the deck in confusion. The tension between the scouts was palpable. Did the fates of worlds turn on their past hatreds? And why did Vesta seem to defer to Achilles, his subordinate?

The Hindmost watched in silence. "Do you have an alternative?" he messaged Baedeker privately.

With that challenge, the pieces fell into place. Baedeker messaged back, "I do. May I join the conference, Hindmost?"

The Hindmost fluted for attention. With a quick wriggle of lip nodes, he expanded the holo conference. "I've asked a technical consultant to participate. Baedeker?"

Nessus twitched. In that reaction, Baedeker read the scruffy scout's thoughts. I gave him that name. Does he use it now to mock me? Let him wonder. Baedeker said, "We destroy the human ship, not their world."

"Surely ARMs explore with an indestructible General Products hull." Nessus looked himself in the eyes. "Or have you finally found antimatter?"

"I have finally learned that our hulls can be destroyed without antimatter." Baedeker straightened, hoping to project more confidence than he felt. "Nessus, your alien scouts learned too much about how we build the hulls." Because *you* told them. "But let us learn from that fiasco.

"Recall that the hull is a single supermolecule, the normal interatomic bonds reinforced with energy from an embedded power plant. Shut down the power plant and simple air pressure will blow apart the hull."

"I thought the power plant was sealed," Achilles said.

Baedeker bobbed heads. "True, the embedded power plant has no external controls. But since the hulls are transparent, laser signaling can turn them off."

Vesta whistled with confusion. "Surely not. Why embed an off command?"

"Humans are very good with math and computers." Nessus seemed to be thinking aloud. With a shiver, he returned his attention to the conference. "There is no off switch, but there *are* embedded processors. Optical computers, embedded in transparent hull material.

That's it, Nike. Obviously they found a way to optically hack into the controls and shut them down."

Hack? Baedeker guessed that was a wild-human word. Its meaning was clear. "Obviously?"

The Hindmost trumpeted for attention. "Let us return to the current danger. Baedeker, advise us how best to proceed."

· 42 ·

"Do you see anything interesting?" Sigmund asked.

Carlos glanced up from the mission highlights Sigmund had brought him here to discuss. "Other than that all the astronomical data has been scrubbed? That, by the way, doesn't surprise me. I *was* surprised, after walking from a public transfer booth a quarter kilometer away, to encounter a private transfer booth in your foyer."

"Mine is out of order." The ability of Cerberus to tamper with the teleportation system being an undisclosed feature, in a manner of speaking Sigmund had answered truthfully. Any public-booth destination must be safer than his personal booth.

Their attempts at small talk had been painful. Sigmund didn't want to hear any anecdote that involved Feather. Carlos, in his usual way, wouldn't say much about his R & D on an advanced autodoc. The approach involved nanotech, Sigmund inferred. Direct questions got him only an enigmatic smile. "I'm making progress," was all that Carlos was prepared to share.

"About that data scrubbing," Sigmund began.

Carlos shrugged it off. "Classified. I get that. You'd be surprised, however, to know just how high my security clearance is."

You wouldn't be here, Sigmund thought, if I didn't know that.

Carlos rubbed his hands briskly. "All right then. Let's dig in. Are the beacons directional, distant, or both?"

"Mildly directional," Sigmund answered. "Semi-spherical emissions." The mysterious beacons broadcast only to the galactic north of their positions. They were distant, well beyond the ill-defined region considered Human Space. He wasn't about to give clues, however vague, to the location of *Hobo Kelly.* "Why did you ask?"

"It had to be at least one. Otherwise, someone would have discovered them long ago."

Sigmund stood and stared at his living-room window. He did it only from habit, the view having been set opaque for privacy.

Hobo Kelly had been prowling farther and farther to galactic north. Andrea's orders were to remain far from stars, using only passive sensors, the better to observe undetected—and the better to escape on short notice into hyperspace.

No solar system they had surveyed revealed any signs of technology in action. No radio leakage. No obvious atmospheric pollution. No artificial energy sources. As they hid from nothing at all, it had begun to seem to Sigmund that he had his explorers behaving more like Puppeteers than like Puppeteer seekers.

Until Andrea hyperwaved back about the array of beacons.

Sigmund turned abruptly. "You're right," he said to Carlos. "I can hardly have the benefit of your insight without sharing information."

"Thank you." Carlos smiled, as if to ask: Was that so hard? "So there's an ARM ship out exploring. It's in virgin territory—no evidence of intelligence. Suddenly, it gets to a place humming with hyperwave signals. All messages are unintelligible and of the same short length. What else?"

Sigmund considered. "A few occasional hyperdrive

traces, ripples of ships entering and leaving hyperspace. Those could be from anywhere, of course."

"Hyperwave navigational beacons?" Carlos mused. "I mean the signals, not the drive ripples."

"You mean like global positioning satellites." Sigmund had used Global Positioning System locators in Alaska. Much of the state remained empty and wild.

"Loosely speaking. With GPS, you calculate your position from the slight differences in arrival time between signals from different orbiting clocks. Hyperwave radio is instantaneous; you hear all transmitters at once. You have to calculate your position from your bearings to a number of transmitters."

"Beacons. That's what the crew decided."

"No signs of settled worlds, but hyperwave signals." Carlos closed his eyes and leaned his head onto the back of the sofa. He was quiet for a long time.

Something grated on Sigmund's nerves. It might have been Carlos's tuneless humming, but Sigmund didn't think so. "Talk to me. What's on your mind?"

Carlos opened his eyes and leaned forward. "Why not just use *stars* for beacons?"

"You tell me."

"I can't." Carlos resumed his tuneless humming. "Advanced tech in an apparently unoccupied region. And the signals are directional, so that we don't normally receive them."

"Border markers?" Sigmund asked. Maybe *Hobo Kelly* had finally found its way to Puppeteer space.

"Possibly."

"But you don't think so," Sigmund prompted.

"I don't know." More humming. "Sigmund, don't you ever deal with *easy* problems?"

Under other circumstances, knowing about Carlos and Feather, Sigmund might have found some obscure satisfaction in baffling the certified genius. But an ARM military crew and Andrea were in harm's way. This was the wrong time to stump Carlos.

"An alarm, perhaps," Carlos finally said. "When someone crosses your border, you want to know about it."

"Our ship has every type of sensor imaginable. There's been no contact, Carlos. No radio, laser, maser—nothing on any wavelength. No neutrino pulses. Nothing."

"*Not* nothing," Carlos rebutted. "Your ship has sensed hyperwaves."

An unpleasant truth hung just beyond Sigmund's grasp. "Where are you going with this?"

"Radar," Carlos said in wonder. "It could be hyperwave futzy radar."

"There's no such thing." But if there were, it would locate things instantaneously, wouldn't it? "Is there?"

"There could be." An eerie assurance settled over Carlos. "Well, not radar exactly. Hyperwave pulses travel instantaneously, as do their echoes. You can't calculate a distance from the round-trip delay time. But if you were to take bearings on a *bunch* of echoes . . . and if the receivers compared notes instantaneously . . ."

Then you have hyperspace radar.

Those hyperdrive ripples! Those were the tracks of vessels stalking *Hobo Kelly,* chasing after it as it hyperspace-hopped around! "Medusa," Sigmund shouted. "Send the recall code immediately."

But *immediately* could not negate the light-speed crawl out to Southworth Station. It would be hours before the recall got to *Hobo Kelly.*

He could only hope it wasn't already too late.

ANDREA GIRARD PEERED from the relayed message streaming from Southworth Station, oblivious to the cheering in the ARM war room.

Relief washed over Sigmund. It wasn't too late.

"We got the recall notice. Sigmund, this ship has a Generals Products hull. We know all about the black-hole trick now. And there aren't any neutron stars around. If we find one, we'll stay far away. So I ask you: What can anyone possibly do to us?"

Someone ruddy and blond leaned into the camera's field of vision. Calvin Dillard, the pilot. Sigmund couldn't make out what Dillard said, but obviously Andrea did. "I'm getting there, Cal. Sigmund, we're going to stay a little longer.

"It looks like we all made one seriously bad assumption. We've been exclusively scanning systems around G- and K-"—yellow and orange—"class stars because Puppeteers walk around on Earth without sun protection. Now look at—"

"Look at what?" Sigmund shouted helplessly to the receiver. Then proximity alarms shrieked, and he knew why Andrea had paused.

"Company," Dillard yelled. He suppressed the alarm. "Radar says fifty klicks."

"Get out!" Sigmund shouted back in vain. No innocent purpose justified emerging from hyperspace so near another ship. "Go to hyperspace now!"

"We're sensing a laser. The light is highly modulated. Seems like data." Dillard spoke to the bridge crew more than to the camera. "Comm can't parse it yet, but it's definitely low power. Not a threat."

Andrea shook off her paralysis. "I'm sending a recon image for you to enjoy later. For now, we need to focus on this contact. We'll keep transmitting on hyperwave."

"Get out," Sigmund repeated helplessly. "They're too close!"

"Still no luck translating," Dillard continued. "They're not using any known signaling protocol. Evidently there's someone out here we haven't met."

New sirens. Sigmund froze. Anyone who set foot on a spaceship was trained to react instantly to *that* ululating sound. Pressure loss.

"Futz!" Dillard yelled, diminuendo. "The hull—"

At least that was how Sigmund read Dillard's lips. The words weren't audible over whistling wind and clamoring alarm, all fading toward silence.

And then the message dissolved into static.

· 43 ·

A happy throng, dressed and dyed in every color of the rainbow, crowded the theater lobby. The Broadway revival of *The Count of Monte Cristo* was pre-sold-out for weeks after this, its opening night. Light globes and disco balls wafted overhead, bathing the area in shifting illumination.

A few of the floating devices were disguised copseyes. Sigmund wondered how many of the audience suspected.

Max Addeo had queued up for the lobby bar. A statuesque woman in a shimmering green gown, her skin aglitter in silver dye and gold jewelry, clung to his arm.

"Max," Sigmund called. No response. "Max!"

Addeo turned. Only the brief narrowing of his eyes revealed his surprise. "Sigmund. How good to see you. Allow me to introduce—"

"Hello, Cassie," Sigmund interrupted. Only close friends called her that; her given name was Felicia. Max wouldn't miss the significance that *he* knew it. Let Max start worrying what else unexpected Sigmund might have learned. "I need to borrow Max for a little while."

"Stay in line, Cass, and get us some wine," Max said smoothly. "I'll find you in a bit. Come, Sigmund." Max plowed through the crowd, with Sigmund following. Reaching a quiet corner, Addeo whirled. "What the futz do you think you're doing?"

Sigmund took the comp from his pocket. "Protocol gamma." A translucent privacy screen wrapped around them.

"If something has come up, Sigmund, why not just a call to go back to the office?"

"Max, you won't want any record of this conversation."

"Is that a threat? You need to adjust your meds." Addeo began brushing past Sigmund. "I have a play to—"

Sigmund shoved Addeo back into the corner. "Max, just listen. You're going to deliver a message for me. To Nessus."

"Nessus?" Addeo's eyes darted about, seeking an escape. "How could I possibly do that?"

"Look familiar?" Sigmund offered a slip of paper. It held only a row of digits. "It's an anonymous account at the Bank of Ceres, Antigua branch." Addeo had the sense to keep quiet. "It's received some impressive deposits, very indirectly, from General Products funds. Payoffs, I should say. I'm guessing you can bypass the middlemen and contact Nessus directly."

"And if not?"

"You *don't* want to disappoint me, Max." Sigmund shook his head. "Really, you do not." A wavering chime sounded, the privacy-shield-scrambled notice that the overture was about to start. "Well?"

Addeo wilted. "For sake of argument, what's the message you want delivered?"

"To start, a picture." Sigmund took a holographic print from his pocket. The format was archaic, by intent, the better to obscure any unintended details. In the main, it was truthful.

In other ways, there was less there than met the eye.

Five like-sized spheres floated above the print, corners of a pentagon. Five planets! Four were blue and white, Earth-like—except for their necklaces of tiny suns. The fifth world glowed on its own, its continents afire amid midnight-black oceans. No one in Sigmund's team had any idea why the one was so different.

Sigmund broke the silence. "We lost a ship and a lot of good people to get this."

"What *is* it?" Addeo asked in wonder.

"The worlds of the Puppeteers, Max." Sigmund let that sink in. "They've reached a speed just below three percent light speed. At their current acceleration, that's consistent with eight years from a standing start. After news came of the galactic core explosion, they said they were leaving. It seems that they truly are. Of course we imagined a fleet of *ships.*"

"Where are they headed?" Addeo asked. His voice shook in awe at whole worlds in flight.

"Take it." Sigmund held out the holo print until Addeo accepted. Northward, of course. "You don't need that information, and the Puppeteers already know."

"And you having this image demonstrates that the ARM knows." Addeo took a deep breath. "What does Puppeteers leaving have to do with me?"

"General Products paid you a lot, Max. It's not just you, either. They've spent lots of money since they disappeared. Some went to people more unsavory, even, than you.

"Puppeteers are cowards, Max. Everyone knows that. They've stayed hidden for as long as anyone in Known Space has known about them.

"Then we all learned about the core. Suddenly, the Puppeteers had to leave their hiding place. Coming out meant someone might find them, when being found is the last thing they can abide. The situation makes them *very* determined to distract us."

"I still don't see—"

"Then shut up and listen," Sigmund growled. "Your days of giving orders are over.

"GP money is behind the Fertility Law unrest. How many people died in the riots? GP money was behind the piracy two years ago. Eight innocent crews killed. All to throw us off their scent."

And when I picked up their trail anyway, everyone aboard *Hobo Kelly* died.

Sigmund flicked the print still in Addeo's hand. "Here's the deal, Max. *You* are my best bet of getting a message to the Puppeteers. You give Nessus the picture. You prove to him we know about this . . . fleet of worlds. You tell him the ARM believes they're truly leaving Known Space. We'll allow them to retreat in peace—if they leave *us* in peace."

He gave Addeo one last piece of paper. It named more than a dozen banks around Sol system. This sheet bore no account numbers; Sigmund's purpose wasn't to give Max access to new wealth. "Here's where GP hid its money, the fortune whose only imaginable use is interference on the worlds they're leaving behind. So I have another job for you: convince Nessus he must release these accounts to the UN. General Products can consider it a small reparation for the damage it's caused."

GP had other laundered funds, stashed in banks Sigmund hadn't listed. If the Puppeteers didn't know he knew, he might be able to detect any future meddling.

"You have ambitious plans for me, Sigmund." Max's cheek suddenly had a tic, but he held his voice steady. "Why would I do any of this, even presuming I could contact Nessus? Because you fancy you know something about a numbered account in a bank haven?"

Sigmund sneered. "Since no one admits to owning that money, I'll see that it gets transferred into the ARM survivor's fund." Most of Sigmund's wealth had already gone in trust, anonymously, for the benefit of Ian Girard. Sigmund felt no better for the gesture.

"But to answer your question, Max, there is a very good reason why you'll obey. It's quite simple, really. Unless the Puppeteers do as I ask, I'll blame you." He stared until the traitor looked away. "If that happens, you have my solemn word.

"I will hunt you down and kill you."

• • •

SIGMUND WALKED OUT of the theater, utterly drained. Scattered notes from the overture followed him down Broadway.

He went into a deli, took a stool at the counter, and got a beer. His meal, a gyro platter, eventually arrived. It grew cold, untouched, his attention elsewhere.

Max had no choice but to contact Nessus—and then, his corruption revealed, to run like a cockroach when the lights came on. After Nessus reported home, the Puppeteers had no good options, either. They would know the ARM had found them. They would know the ARM knew all about their cynically lethal interventions.

Puppeteers could move worlds! They could destroy indestructible ships. Yet that power could not *guarantee* their safety. Their only hope to depart unscathed was to leave Earth alone.

And then Andrea's sacrifice would have served a purpose.

Feather had moved on. Andrea was gone. Even the Puppeteers, for so long the focus of Sigmund's existence, must soon disappear completely.

Sigmund went back into the night, wondering if Jinxian intrigues still mattered enough to him to get him out of bed in the morning.

BETRAYED

Earth dates: 2654–2655

• 44 •

"You don't handle success well, Sigmund." Calista Melenkamp smiled, to show her words weren't critical. "You might at least *try* to look happy."

The Secretary-General invited few enough guests to her mountain retreat. Intellectually, Sigmund appreciated the honor. He just didn't give a damn. Depressed as he was, he knew better than to say so. "Quite the view you have here."

Aside, that was, from the laser-cannon batteries that protected her aerie. They looked horribly out of place.

"I'm glad something pleases you." Melenkamp perched on the stacked-stone fence that rimmed the slate patio on three sides. Even her casual jumpsuit was in her signature turquoise. She turned her head to admire the view from the summit of Mount Pisgah.

The national forest was at its autumnal peak, a fiery sea of red, yellow, and orange sweeping to the horizon. The ruins of Biltmore castle peeked through the trees in the distance.

She said, "Our people can never know what you've accomplished. We always knew Puppeteers had capabilities beyond our own, but their cowardice made it acceptable. We didn't suspect even a fraction of their power, nor that their fear could mask such hostility."

Pisgah: at almost two thousand meters, among the highest elevations in the Appalachians. A different Pisgah was the biblical mount from which Moses glimpsed the Promised Land. He died without entering it. Alone, Sigmund recalled.

Sigmund had been offered iced tea. Condensation ran down the glass and tickled his hand. The tea had been prepared southern-style, cloyingly sweet. "And now they're leaving us alone."

"Thanks to you," she said.

Had the Puppeteers not killed Andrea, Sigmund could almost have missed them. He did miss the focus they once gave his life. They had been gone for a year now. He was almost ready to consider using transfer booths again. Real soon now.

Neither Jinxians nor Kzinti had made trouble in years. Ander's subtle interference had tied preparations for Pelton's expedition—the one topic Sigmund still dare not discuss with Melenkamp—into knots.

"Sigmund?" she said.

"It's magnificent." He pointed at the eagle gliding majestically over the treetops, and wondered if it felt alone.

Melenkamp sighed. At his obstinacy? She said, "It's good to feel safe for once."

Safe? Sigmund managed not to stare. That things *seemed* secure only meant Earth's enemies had succeeded in hiding their latest evil plans. . . .

TENSION CLAMPED BAEDEKER'S throats too tightly to speak, almost too tightly to breathe. He circled his office, shaking with rage. The too-familiar hologram above his desk mocked him.

He finally composed himself enough to make a call to Achilles. "I've discovered something of critical importance. Can you come?"

Achilles stepped through almost immediately. He chirped with bitter undertunes at the hologram. "I hate the humans. If only we dared . . ." He brushed heads with Baedeker in belated greeting. "My apologies. I know you share my beliefs."

"Be comfortable." Baedeker motioned at the guest hassock before lowering himself, his leg muscles trembling, onto his own padded bench. "Tell me what you see."

Achilles studied the holo, the surely all-too-familiar

digitized version of Ausfaller's physical print. Five worlds floating in the void against an obsidian backdrop: a small part of the Cone Nebula. A few stars penetrated the cloud of interstellar dust. "The Fleet, of course."

"Authentic?"

"Absolutely. Those are our worlds," Achilles fluted impatiently. "Why am I here?"

"Bear with me, please," Baedeker answered. "Of what else regarding this image are you certain?"

"That the original used an alien format, its manufacture distinctly wild human. That the image looks to galactic south. That the image was captured without our knowledge, by a probe we never detected."

Baedeker leaned forward. "And if the latter two certainties are mistaken?"

"Then we have been duped." Achilles froze in thought. "And the humans' ability to endanger us has been greatly overstated."

WITH VESTA AS escort, the route to the Hindmost's private office bypassed enclosed and lethal security booths. Achilles, Baedeker, and Vesta still crossed three stepping-disc vestibules, two lined with armed guards, before reaching their destination.

Achilles stepped through last, into an area more like an indoor park than a workplace. His apartment would have fit inside it ten times over. The one thing he missed since Vesta had accomplished his recall was *room.* There had been breathing room to spare on a ship of his own. Baedeker looked surprisingly unimpressed by the vast, natural setting—until Achilles remembered where the engineer had been banished.

"Greetings," Nike warbled. The undertunes waiving formality were for Baedeker's benefit. For the rest, all Clandestine Directorate veterans, informality in private was a given. "Make yourselves comfortable."

Achilles prodded Baedeker.

"If I may, Hindmost." Baedeker set his pocket computer on the nearest padded work surface. He pawed nervously at the meadowplant carpet, ill at ease despite Nike's melody of welcome. "Computer, display file 'Latest ARM Surveillance.' "

The familiar still hologram appeared: five worlds caught against a black background. "It's a fake," Baedeker blurted.

"How can that be?" Nike asked. "And if so, why is that only now being discovered?"

Baedeker flinched at the harsh harmonics. "It is an authentic image of the Fleet. That is what makes the forgery so insidious."

Achilles said, "Nike, the tampering involves the *background.* That subtle change misguided our interpretation."

"Go on," Nike fluted.

"We know the humans found us. One thing only makes this image shocking: that it was taken well after we destroyed their scout ship." Achilles set his hooves far apart, in a no-thought-of-flight stance of utter confidence. "We believe the scout broadcast this picture. The alterations make the image *seem* more recent."

Nike untangled the scarlet and purple tendrils of two adjacent shrubs as he considered. "Misdirecting us into thinking the ARM can observe us undetected."

Vesta cleared his throats. "Exactly, Nike."

"Vesta," Nike said, "I accepted your experts' opinion before about the timing of the image. What has changed?"

Vesta froze. Expecting to replace Baedeker on Nature Preserve 1 for his failure?

"It's a complex problem," Achilles interjected. "The stars in the background are all familiar, blue-shifted by the camera's motion toward them. That let us derive the ship's velocity. The suns orbiting the Nature Preserve worlds are blue-shifted further, by the Fleet's motion toward the ARM ship. Since the Fleet has been steadily accelerating, its velocity when the image was taken demonstrates when that image was taken."

"What has changed?" Nike repeated, adding grace notes of growing impatience.

Achilles prompted, "Baedeker?"

"I began to think the calculated timing was very coincidental," Baedeker said. "Too coincidental. From my hyperspace detector array, we know precisely when the ARM ship appeared near the Fleet—viewed from galactic south. We also know when the ARM ship was destroyed. Between, there was only a brief interval during which its crew could have taken any detailed, high-resolution images. Call that Time Zero.

"The suns that orbit the farm worlds mimic Hearth days, because our flora evolved for that. We have no cause to remember that the rotations of the Fleet's worlds differ. The worlds roughly align only about every thirty-three days." Baedeker let them consider his tunes before extending a neck at the hologram. "This image, with *very* high probability, matches the image at Time Zero, with clouds conveniently obscuring regions that would not have been visible then."

Citizen clocks continued to define a day by Hearth's rotation; their calendar still used its eons-ago planetary revolution as a year. Both were mere convention, on a sunless world long gone from its primordial orbit. Who but far-ranging scouts—and Baedeker, to give well-deserved credit—considered such things?

Vesta sidled forward. "Nessus received the image only seventy-one Hearth days after we destroyed the ARM ship, so you can see how implausibly coincidental that matchup is."

"The differing length of days," Nike mused. "How extraordinary." He spaced his heads far apart, the better to examine the image. "This view is from galactic north, since we see the Cone Nebula as background, but I understand the synchronization principle is the same."

A different apparent vantage point to imply a different sighting. Adjusting the original image, from red-shifted by the Fleet's velocity away from the ARM ship, to blue-shifted consistent with capture by a sensor in the Fleet's path. Shifting the spectra of the few visible stars, to impute a velocity to an imaginary ship.

"If we could only be *sure,*" Nike said. "Undetected ARM ships, especially ahead of the Fleet, are unacceptable. If we could only be certain the image was a fake."

The boundaries of cloud seen from great distances were indistinct, and some areas were prone to persistent cloud cover. Statistical analyses of the apparent cloud cover were rather subtle for a politician. As Achilles and Baedeker murmured to each other, trying to frame a succinct argument, Vesta again cleared his throats.

Vesta had many virtues. Technical insight was not among them. Achilles wondered what his acolyte thought to contribute.

"I think," Vesta said, "we've made convincing ourselves more difficult than we need to."

NESSUS WORKED AT a drink bulb, too preoccupied to notice what he was swallowing. He replayed Vesta's message three times, its implications ever darker.

That Ausfaller had tricked Nessus again was the least of them.

The possibility of undetectable ships dropping undetectable objects into the Fleet's path had enforced a tacit truce with Earth. The Fleet had reached three percent light speed. Even a small mass impacting at that speed would be a fearsome thing. And who was to say the ARM, if provoked, would limit itself to a small mass?

At least that might be how Ausfaller saw it.

Aegis hung deep in the Oort Cloud, stealthed, scanning from a safe and hopefully invisible distance broadcasts from across Sol system. Or was *Aegis'* invisibility as illusory as the hologram a terrified Max Addeo had provided?

The bulb went dry. Nessus finally noticed he'd been drinking plain water. He circled the relax room to the synthesizer, this time selecting warm carrot juice.

Ships appearing undetected in the Fleet's path would be perilous. Then there was the matter of what ARM ships might discover, a provocation far beyond anything *his* meddling had so far created.

How would Ausfaller react if he learned what lay ahead of the Fleet? Nessus quivered at the thought. With his unencumbered head, he plucked deep inside his mane.

Had Achilles, in his limited time in Human Space, ever seen a house of cards? Nessus guessed not, although peace among worlds had become as wobbly as that. One world safeguarded by the intimations of antimatter it must control—a defense Baedeker had cast into doubt. Another world deemed untouchable by reason of its undetectable ships—a digital sleight of mouth Baedeker had now also discredited. Between, the anxious worlds of the Fleet.

And now, the house of cards had flown apart.

Much cautious planning must take place before any action could be initiated against either world. For that long, at least, peace would remain.

Sixty-two days after the destruction of the ARM ship, the largest volcano on Nature Preserve 3 had erupted. Had Mount Granthor not stained the skies with smoke and ash, Ausfaller's deception might still be raising doubts on Hearth. Still be protecting Earth.

Sometimes luck just ran out.

Nessus sipped his carrot juice pensively, wondering if Ausfaller's talents could somehow be used to save that *other* world.

• 45 •

The head of Special Investigations could go anywhere he chose. If people wondered why Sigmund chose to spend so much of his time visiting ARM squad rooms, they didn't ask. The truth was pathetic. He was substituting secondhand camaraderie for lost love. Someday, he'd get past it.

Sigmund told himself there was more to his roaming than that. For one, shifting around helped to obscure his surveillance of Beowulf Shaeffer. Bey hadn't worked a day on Earth, at least not legally, in three years. Tax records would have shown it. What the Puppeteers had paid Bey to explore the core (the last money he had gotten from General Products, Sigmund was almost certain) was long gone. Carlos was wealthy enough, but there were no signs he had transferred anything to Shaeffer, and Sigmund couldn't imagine Bey accepting money from that source. If Bey couldn't father his own children, he would tanj well support them.

Nor was the happy family surviving on Sharrol Janss's money. Sharrol had never had much money or been paid much, and she'd stopped working when Louis was born.

That left Gregory Pelton. What, Sigmund wondered, was Bey doing to get money from that source?

"YOU'LL FIND THIS interesting," Medusa said.

Sigmund lifted his head from his arms, folded on a mildly scuzzy table. He was in an ARM off-duty lounge. They all looked alike; it took a few seconds to remember he was in London. By body time, it was after midnight. "What's that?"

Serpents slithered. "I intercepted a call to Mary Ortega's pocket comp from Sharrol Janss."

Across the room two off-shift ARMs sat, their feet up on the battered coffee table, arguing about rugby. They must have come in while Sigmund dozed. It took him a moment to remember Ortega was Sharrol and Bey's babysitter. There had to be more to Medusa's news than a mother checking on her kids. "Continue."

"The packet headers show the call originated in Prosperine."

Sigmund sat up. Prosperine, Australia, was the nearest community, a town only if one was feeling generous, to Carlos Wu's home in the Great Barrier Reef. A fiber-optic cable into town was the logical way for Carlos to get comm service. Not even Carlos could swing a radio antenna sticking up from the reef. "Is Mom having a little action on the side with Carlos?"

Medusa's smile bared fangs. "If so, it's most interesting. A wrong-number ping on Stepdad's comp puts him there, too."

Whatever they were plotting, Sigmund wanted to stop speaking in circumlocutions. He could order the off-duty pair away, or commandeer an office, or go elsewhere, or—

"Protocol gamma," Sigmund ordered. The privacy screen surrounded him.

The underwater dwelling teemed with microbugs, relayed by Feather's comm link. Sigmund could not remember the last time he'd peeked in, only why he had stopped: He trusted Carlos.

Be honest with yourself. He had stopped lest he see Feather and Carlos together.

"Medusa, give me your latest visual," Sigmund said.

Four bodies moved in the hologram. They wriggled and writhed in an evidently room-sized sleeper field, amid a floating profusion of discarded garments. Everyone was dyed, and mercifully he couldn't see faces, but the beanpole with a Belter-style crest was surely Shaeffer.

And that energetic, lithe figure . . .

Feather rolled over and stared straight at a sensor. Sigmund told himself it had to be coincidence. "Kill video playback." His voice shook. "Medusa, when were Shaeffer and Wu last together?"

Medusa said, "That we know, not since Carlos was released from the hospital with new lungs in 'fifty-two."

Two years. Sigmund had to know if anything other than an orgy had brought them together. Why *now*?

What Sigmund's imagination painted onto the audio playback was, if anything, more painful than watching. He heard moans, sharp cries, urgent directions, inarticulate sighs, and then—

Silence.

"At that point, I lost signal," Medusa said. "Standard ARM jamming."

Discretion at last, Sigmund thought. "Keep monitoring for as long as Bey and Sharrol are there."

FEATHER CALLED MIDMORNING. "Sigmund, I have a major case of cabin fever. How about I flick over to New York? Carlos is tucked in for the night."

It was a bit after one in the morning for her and Carlos, and the reports Sigmund was writing could wait. "Will Carlos stay put if he wakes up and you're gone?"

"He takes direction well, Sigmund."

He'd seen ample proof of that a few days earlier. Sigmund spoke as calmly as he could. "Sure. We'll go out for a drink."

As things turned out, they had several. They barhopped through the East Village, with a lunch thrown in. Asked about food, she said, "Anything but fish. I am *so* sick of seeing fish." They got Italian.

At the fourth bar, she leaned over and gave Sigmund

a hard kiss. "Finagle, this feels good," she said. "There's not a lot to *do* at Carlos's place."

You found a way to entertain yourself. Sigmund kept that comment to himself. "It's good seeing you. Maybe it's time to rotate assignments. Now that Carlos is accustomed to protection, chances are he'll accept someone else."

"Hold that thought." Feather jumped out of her chair onto the karaoke stage. She jived and sang for a while with an Elvis hologram, her voice flat, and then rejoined Sigmund. "That was fun. A new assignment? Maybe, Sigmund. I don't know."

His thoughts churned. Did he want them to get back together? Just want her away from Carlos—and now also Shaeffer? As long as Feather wanted children, Sigmund didn't see how she could be happy for long with anyone.

"Maybe," she said abruptly. "Carlos and I have gotten past purely professional. I need time away to know how I feel." She touched Sigmund's arm. "Can I get away for a while without giving up my current assignment? Can you arrange that?"

He could arrange most things in the ARM. "What did you have in mind?"

"I heard about something that would be a real change." She paused to drain her vodka tonic, then keyed an order for another. The bar was too noisy for speech-recognition mode. "There's an ARM ship mothballed on Mars that needs shuttling to the Smithsonian. Fourth War vintage, believe it or not." He must have looked puzzled, because she added, "I'm not surprised you haven't heard of the transfer. The museum folk think the Belters would object to moving it, which is probably the case. They're keeping it quiet. Carlos told me. He knows because he's on the museum's board of directors."

Mars was an unattractive bit of real estate: resource

poor and too small to hold a useful atmosphere. Hardly anyone lived there. Mars was UN territory mostly because the Belters didn't find it worth claiming. They did claim an interest in anything moving outside normal Sol-system shipping lanes; Mars qualified.

"That sounds like Belters," Sigmund said.

"I don't know." Feather smiled. "Some Belters are all right."

He remembered that glimpse of Feather wrapped around Beowulf. Feather going off-world for a while sounded better and better.

Fourth War made the ship almost Sigmund's age. A dinosaur. It belonged in a proper museum. Spiting Belters was icing on the cake. "I'll put in a word for you. Who do I talk to?"

"You're a prince." She leaned over the tiny table and kissed him. "Knowing that, I brought the information with me."

Feather prodded her pocket comp, calling up requisitions for the ancient lander and an ARM transport ship, *Boy George.* "If this meets with your approval, just okay it. Carlos will take care of things from the Smithsonian end."

Amid the din of the bar crowd, Sigmund had to resort to protocol gamma to make his voiceprint understood. Then Feather dragged him up to the karaoke stage, and the day got even wilder.

· 46 ·

The advisory stared at Sigmund. *Boy George* was overdue. There had been no distress call, and its traffic-control transponder was not to be found.

Feather had played him like a fiddle. And for a fool.

It didn't take long—a few comm calls, and netting into the hidden sensors at Carlos's underwater lair—to confirm what Sigmund's gut told him. Carlos and Feather were gone. So were Beowulf, Sharrol, and the children. In both homes, the agents Sigmund sent found the chaos of hurried packing. Carlos's custom autodoc, the supposed nanotech marvel, was missing.

A big piece fell into place when Medusa dredged up the records on the ancient lander. "Feather neglected to mention it had full stealth gear."

"I thought she was someone I could trust." And that hurt.

So: *Boy George* hadn't landed because the ancient lander had secretly retrieved the escapees. Lander and transport ship would rendezvous, and then they'd be off to—where? Wherever they were headed, they could land just as stealthily.

"I don't understand," Medusa said. "Why steal ships? Why not just emigrate? Bey isn't even a Sol-system resident. And any world would happily welcome Carlos."

The same question nagged at Sigmund. He crossed his living room, to peer into a holo cube of himself and Feather, taken at a happier time. "What was on your mind?" he asked.

Bey and Sharrol would have left Earth long ago, only she was a flat phobe. That's why Carlos had had to father the children. "Here's a theory. Of all of them, only Feather can't emigrate. As an ARM, she knows too much. When she retires, she has to stay in UN territory. The problem is Feather wants to have children and she can't. Not here. That's why *she* wants to escape. To change names and disappear."

"That doesn't answer my question," Medusa said.

"I know." Sigmund began to pace. "Here's a theory. She wants *Carlos* to father her children. She convinced Carlos to run with her." She'd say the UN feels it owns his genes, and the new autodoc he was so proud of. She'd tell him her orders were to keep him on Earth. Why wouldn't he believe her? Hence, he would skulk away with her, misguidedly grateful.

"But Carlos cares about Louis and Tanya"—and Sharrol, too—"and wouldn't go without them and Beowulf." That required convincing Shaeffer he was no longer permitted to leave Earth. Sigmund presumed *he* was the ogre of whatever tale Feather spun. "Here's where my imagination fails me. How was a rampant flat phobe persuaded she could handle the trip?"

The trip, followed by a new life—off-world. Sigmund broke into a cold sweat. He knew with grim certainty that resolving this mess would take him off-world. His misplaced trust had made possible the theft of the lander, and with it what was, effectively, Carlos's kidnapping.

Perhaps all trust was misplaced. Sigmund intended, nonetheless, to rescue Carlos. He would need help to do it.

"Medusa," Sigmund said. "Send a recall notice to Ander. We have a new mission."

· 47 ·

"Ta-da," Ander said, dropping *Seeker* back to normal space.

A star shone straight ahead. It was older and hotter than Sol, but its yellow-white hue wasn't too different from Sol at a like distance. Sigmund sighed with relief.

Ander had handled most of the piloting. He had talked as nonstop as on that long-ago trip to Jinx; this time, Sigmund welcomed it. He welcomed any distraction from the hungry nothingness. Frequent drops from hyperspace, compelled by Sigmund's need for reassurance that the universe still existed, made an already-long trip interminable.

"Here goes nothing." Ander tapped a button on the main console. A shadowy sphere formed in the deep-radar display, slowly expanding.

With an imminent return to hyperspace not weighing on him, Sigmund felt better than he had in weeks. He managed to work up some amusement. "You hope to find a stasis box *here*? It's not like this is an unexplored system."

"It can't hurt." Ander smiled. "And the reward if we *do* find one is enormous."

Eons ago, two ancient races had waged a war of galactic extermination. Little remained of their epic struggle beyond a few artifacts preserved for eternity within stasis fields. Most items recovered from stasis containers defied comprehension. All embodied technology of frightening power. Conventional wisdom had it that the caches were weapons stockpiles. Not surprisingly, every race in Known Space offered rewards for new stasis boxes. A man could live a long life in princely style on the standard ARM bounty for one. To Sigmund's knowledge, it was a rare decade that saw the ARM making that payout.

Stasis fields reflected everything: light, radio, even the neutrino pulses emitted by deep radar. It was second nature for pilots approaching a solar system, any solar system, to do a deep-radar ping—and hence it was hardly a surprise that no undiscovered stasis containers awaited them in this long-settled system. Sigmund couldn't begin to guess how many times this system had been scanned by optimists like Ander.

"Oh, well," Ander said eventually. "Looking cost us nothing. Next stop, Fafnir."

TRANSFER BOOTH ABDUCTION ALSO worked on Fafnir.

"You'll be all right," Nessus told the panicked man in the isolation booth.

The man spun toward the disembodied voice. He must not have liked his reflection in the one-way mirror. He shuddered once, and forced himself to be still. "Show yourself."

That would hardly help. "You are Logan Jones, director of facilities at the Drake Hotel?"

"I am." Suddenly, the man beat on the impregnable—well, under ordinary circumstances—walls. Fists certainly couldn't harm the hull material. "I have no money worth mentioning. No one close to me does. You might as well release me."

"All in good time, Mr. Jones." Nessus paused to let that sink in. "My hope is to send you on your way somewhat wealthier for this inconvenience."

Jones's eyes narrowed. "In return for doing what?"

How much easier things would be if Ausfaller used transfer booths. He drifted from one ARM office to another, and through a few very public venues for variety, unapproachable. Any criminal force Nessus might hire to grab Sigmund might accidentally harm him, or worse, even if such action could be initiated in secrecy.

"We're done," Sangeeta Kudrin had said. "Sigmund is too smart. I'm tanj lucky he traced General Products money to Max Addeo, not me. Nessus, you can't tempt me any longer."

Nessus had answered, "But I can arrange for Ausfaller to learn about your past help . . . unless you continue to support me."

She'd nodded, fear and misery writ plainly across her face. Information continued to flow, including the report that Ausfaller, finally, was going off-world again. New surroundings meant at least the possibility of safely approaching the ARM.

"In return for doing what?" Jones repeated. "Tell me!"

Nessus found himself half-wrapped into a ball. I'm terrified of meeting faces to face with Sigmund. He forced himself to unroll. "Two flatlanders, Sigmund Ausfaller and Ander Smittarasheed, will check into your hotel soon."

That was to say, an abducted desk clerk said they had yet to check in. Despite Ausfaller's head start, Nessus had arrived first. To hear Sangeeta, the marvel was that Ausfaller could drag himself aboard another ship. Nessus imagined *Seeker* dropping frequently from hyperspace.

"Look to your right, Mr. Jones. You are to hide one of those flat devices"—stepping discs—"under the carpet in each of their rooms before they arrive. For your services and silence, after I have electronically confirmed the discs are properly installed, you will receive ten thousand Earth stars."

"Are they explosives?"

"They are teleportation devices," Nessus said. "You're standing on one just like them."

Jones's glance wavered between the booth floor and the nearby stacked discs. "The hotel *has* transfer booths. In the lobby, not in the guest rooms, but still . . ." Jones's voice trailed off in confusion.

"I mean neither man any harm. You have my word. Do you want to know more than that?"

"All right," Jones said. "I'll do it."

WELCOME TO FAFNIR.

The sign suspended over the customs counter made Sigmund's skin crawl. He focused on his breathing. The gravity wasn't far off, and he was indoors. You can cope, he told himself.

Behind him in the debarkation line Ander chatted up a pretty brunette passenger from a newly arrived starliner. Ander was always ready to mix business with pleasure.

The customs officer was a Kzin. His fur was mostly gray, with a jagged scar down one arm. A veteran, Sigmund guessed. Did *you* eat my parents?

Sigmund finally reached the head of the line. The Kzin gave Sigmund's civilian ident a desultory scan. "Welcome to Fafnir. What brings you here, Mr. Ausfaller?"

A year of increasingly desperate data mining. A large-caliber gun gone missing from an ARM weapons locker around the time of Feather's disappearance. An odd police report on Fafnir's public net, months old, of a man rescued at sea. His flotation vest had large, ragged holes front and back. The man claimed a sea creature had torn his jacket.

"Sightseeing," Sigmund said.

"The water wars," Ander piped up from behind. Water war was *the* Fafnir sport, an underwater free-for-all among mixed teams of people (wearing breathers) and dolphins. Ten teams chased or herded three native creatures sort of like turtles. It made a weird kind of sense on a world that was almost all ocean.

The ratcat wrinkled his muzzle. He apparently felt the same way as an Earth cat about water. "Your timing is good, sirs. A big tournament is coming up in Pacifica."

"Thanks for the tip." Sigmund picked up his luggage.

Once Ander cleared customs, they took their gear to the Arrivals area. Sigmund shook his head when Ander started toward a row of transfer booths. "We're tourists, Ander. Let's take a cab." They got into a taxi floater. Sigmund told it, his eyes closed against the too-pale sky, "The Drake."

"Excellent choice, sirs," the AI said. "I'm told it's one of our finest hotels."

And most expensive, surely. Ander had done the research and picked it.

They settled into their rooms, the connecting doors open, Ander disapproving still of Sigmund's insistence on rooms without ocean views. Sigmund ignored the complaints: The cityscape ten floors below felt almost like home. He began configuring a computer rack and display arrays. ARM sensors that Ander would be spreading would fill those displays soon enough.

Ander came through the connecting doors. "You think we'll find them?"

"Honestly? I don't know." Feather's paranoia, Carlos's genius, Beowulf's savvy. A year's head start. Perhaps Bey had access to Gregory Pelton's off-world wealth. The odds seemed awfully long, even if the stolen ship had been here. They had come very far in the hope that gunshots, not sea monsters, explained a tattered vest.

"It's fair to say we're due for a little good luck."

· 48 ·

Sigmund could almost fit in on Fafnir. He refused to use transfer booths; the natives seldom bothered. They saw no need to hurry.

A transfer booth could absorb only so much kinetic energy, and any two points on a rotating globe had different velocities. Earth's system daisy-chained transfer booths; for long-range travel, the passenger jumped from booth to booth too quickly to notice. Way stations aboard constellations of satellites enabled teleportation across oceans.

Not so Fafnir. Except within its one small continent, still called by its Kzinti name of Shasht, the natives mostly traveled by boat and dirigible.

Given what two weeks' intensive searching had accomplished, Sigmund might just as well have undertaken an around-the-world dirigible tour. Not that he could have left his cabin. . . .

Medusa had quickly hacked into the Fafnir comm networks. She found no sign of the refugees. The only encouragement was another negative: no signs in almost a year of Persial January Hebert, the rescued mariner claiming to have encountered a vest-hating sea monster. That suggested an alias.

The ambiguity was that people here sailed for months at a time. Many lived independently on the myriad islands that dotted the vast ocean. Either way, they dropped off what passed on Fafnir for the grid.

Ander had seeded most of the major public spaces on Shasht with sensors. Then he sailed to some of the nearer, more populous island settlements and did it again. He did it wearing ARM surveillance gear, transceiver earplugs like those Sigmund had once lent Shaeffer and Wu, and even more wondrous repeating contact lenses. Sigmund could pull up on a display whatever Ander saw.

So far, that had been nothing helpful.

"Ander," Sigmund called. A slight up-and-down movement on the Ander-view display showed Sigmund had been heard. The view was of a small shopping mall. "Go on to the next island."

COWARDICE IS A virtue among Citizens. Nessus was here on Fafnir, light-years from Hearth, because he had slightly less of that virtue than most. He was still a coward.

And Sigmund Ausfaller was still very, *very* scary.

Nessus could call Sigmund's room at any time. He could step right into the room. He could interrupt Sigmund's pacing with a trip into an isolation booth here on *Aegis*.

And say what?

Ask for trust from the raving paranoid he had stalked for years. Tell the raving paranoid that a world of strangers needed his help. Reveal the darkest secrets of the Concordance to its most formidable adversary.

Nessus sped up his own pacing, trying desperately to energize himself. He remained far from the level of mania that would permit him to act.

• • •

SIGMUND LOST COUNT how many islands Ander visited. Medusa strained to monitor thousands of data feeds from the sensors Ander had already scattered. Sigmund surrounded himself with sample feeds to feel he was doing something helpful. They had yet to find a clue. They might have already left but for Sigmund's dread of the return flight.

One sleepless night, it struck Sigmund. Beowulf Shaeffer was a born tourist. The biggest tourist attraction on this benighted, soggy world was the water wars. Sigmund sent Ander to Pacifica to check it out.

Pacifica was an ocean-floor village, established for the staff of some kind of underwater zoo. Water wars had been an afterthought, an adaptation of a Kzinti land-only hunting game—but it brought prosperity to the sleepy domed settlement.

Predictably, Ander found a food court before entering the nearby stadium dome where the fans gathered. Sigmund watched through Ander's eyes as Ander studied the posted menus, scanned the adjacent storefronts, glanced up to the second-floor balcony, looked back at the menus, picked a line—

"Ander!" Sigmund shouted. His heart pounded. "Look upstairs again. Is that . . . ?"

As Ander searched the balcony, Sigmund backed up the lens feed a minute and fast-forwarded. He knew that face! "It's Shaeffer! Get up there!"

ANDER TOOK THE slidestairs three at a time. He found Shaeffer in a phone/transfer booth, holding a pocket comp. It *was* Shaeffer—facial-recognition software was as sure as Sigmund—except he was almost half a meter too short!

Shaeffer exited the booth and bumped straight into Ander. "Aggh!"

"That sounded fake," Sigmund said. So Shaeffer had also recognized Ander. "Don't let on I'm listening."

"Sorry. Beowulf, how you've changed!" Ander didn't move to let Shaeffer out of the booth.

Shaeffer feigned a cringe. "Sorry, man, I didn't mean to nudge you."

"How strange, Ander. He's pretending not to know you. Tag him."

Ander grabbed and pumped Shaeffer's hand. "Ander Smittarasheed," he bellowed over the crowd noise. Ander's bone-crushing grip, almost like a native Jinxian's, would cover the prick of inserting a subcutaneous bug.

Sigmund checked a display. "Medusa has signal from the tracker. Well done."

Ander was still talking. "We made two travelogue vids together. Beowulf, all I can say is you must have a hell of a tale to tell."

"Hide. Hell of a tale to hide, Ander."

"Not anymore," Ander answered.

"Yeah. Right. Are you with anyone?"

Ander remembered his lines. "No, on my own."

"Come watch the game with me. I think there's an empty seat next to mine."

"Ander, get me a good look at the seat numbers," Sigmund said. "Medusa can probably find who bought the tickets."

For certain, the tickets hadn't been bought under the name Beowulf Shaeffer. Learning Bey's local alias would give them a lead on all the refugees.

Ander and Shaeffer approached a cluster of transfer booths. "Ander, grab Shaeffer's arm. Act worried he'll dash off, and then he'll never suspect we can track him."

"Why a phone booth to use a pocket comp?" As Ander spoke, his hand closed over Shaeffer's skinny upper arm.

Shaeffer looked amused by the question. "Noise!"

On cue the crowd closed around them, sweeping them onto the slidebridge to the game dome. Sigmund settled into a massage chair. Eavesdropping on an unsuspecting Beowulf Shaeffer was getting to be a bad habit.

"GOT THEM, SIGMUND," Medusa said.

"Them?"

"The seats Bey and Ander are in. Two tickets in the name Martin Wallace Graynor."

Shaeffer babbled on about the finer points of water wars. "Methinks Bey is killing time while his seatmate gets away."

Medusa smiled. Even the snakes smiled. "It gets better. The Graynors, a family of six, emigrated a couple years ago from Fafnir to Wunderland. Two men, two women, two children."

"Including Martin, I take it?"

"Right."

Sigmund thought. "Who else is in two places at once?"

"Milcenta works at Pacifica. John and two children, Nathan and Tweena, took an iceliner from Shasht a year and a half ago. To Home."

Sharrol Janss had lived underwater with Carlos, making babies. Major flat phobe that she was, Pacifica was perhaps the best spot on Fafnir for her. Sharrol equals Milcenta? Carlos was also a bit flat-phobic. Little Tanya, too, if hints from indirect surveillance could be trusted.

But they might fly frozen to Fafnir, there to become the Graynors. Fly on, frozen again, to Home, the most Earth-like of colony worlds. Things were beginning to make sense. But why had they split up?

"Medusa, you've accounted for five. What of number six?"

"Adelaide," Medusa said. "There's no sign of her here."

A chill ran down Sigmund's spine. Something *bad* had happened here.

Which woman was unaccounted for? Sharrol or Feather?

• • •

THROAT CLEARING FINALLY caught Sigmund's attention. Ander wanted advice. That was okay. Medusa could data mine for a while on her own.

Shaeffer was talking. "Ander, what are you doing on Fafnir?"

"Do *not* admit I'm off Earth," Sigmund said.

Barely perceptibly, the scenery edged up-and-down: Ander nodding for Sigmund's benefit. Ander said, "Looking for you."

"Yeah," Shaeffer said. "I thought so. You're with the United Nations police."

It didn't sound like Beowulf liked the United Nations very much. Or perhaps, Sigmund thought, it's just me. "Ander, do *not* claim to be official."

"Not . . . exactly," Ander drawled. "I'm not an ARM. I'm with Sigmund Ausfaller, and Sigmund is an ARM, but he has his own agenda. By which I mean to say I'm not here to bring you back, Beowulf."

"That's good. I don't want to go back." There was a pregnant pause before Bey continued. "Why, then?"

"Ask about Feather," Sigmund prompted.

"Can you tell me what happened to Feather Filip?"

Shaeffer grimaced. "It's long and ugly."

"No problem," Ander said. "I'll take you to dinner."

Sigmund trembled, with nothing to add.

"Thanks." Shaeffer leaned forward and whispered conspiratorially, "There's an item of great value involved, Ander. One I can't touch myself. That, and Feather, and the way I look: They're all linked."

"Ander, keep an eye on Shaeffer. Go to dinner. Get him talking." Getting Shaeffer to tell stories wouldn't be hard. "Medusa and I will keep digging."

WHILE SIGMUND CONTINUED to eavesdrop on Ander and Beowulf, Medusa sought Carlos's personal autodoc.

Calling it an autodoc failed to do it justice. It was a nanotech miracle, able to grow organs, limbs, whatever, on demand. So Carlos claimed, anyway. The United Nations had invested a small fortune in the device. It was massive: too large and heavy to move without a lift plate. The cargo manifest for the *Zombie Queen*—great name, that, for an iceliner—showed nothing even close to its size and weight. The 'doc had disappeared from Earth with Carlos. Would Carlos willingly go on to Home without it?

"Keep Bey talking," Sigmund ordered Ander. "I need more time."

To his AIde, Sigmund added, "Medusa, a new priority. Find Milcenta Graynor." If Shaeffer was also stalling, it would be to cover an escape.

"And there you were in Sirius Mater," Beowulf said to Ander. They had been talking about the core explosion. "All ready to write my story for me. I guessed then that Ausfaller must have sent you both times."

"So why did you hire me?"

"I didn't care much. The galaxy was exploding in supernovae. The big question was, How do I tell the human race? How do I make them believe? I hoped you were an ARM. Maybe you could do something."

It sounded more and more like a stall. Sigmund said, "Let's rattle our friend a bit."

· 49 ·

The water war was down to five teams, not all at full strength, and Sigmund saw only two faux turtles. Apparently that was a big deal. Fans were on their feet, screaming. Sigmund shouted to be understood. "I've downloaded a vid to you. Show him."

Ander nodded, then set his pocket comp in Beowulf's lap. A holo appeared.

Five marbles rotated against a black background, an animation extrapolated from *Hobo Kelly's* brief foray into Puppeteer territory. They blossomed into worlds as the simulated camera zoomed. Four were so Earth-like, looking past their tiny orbiting suns, it made the throat catch. The mysterious fifth, starless, glowed like a world on fire.

Sigmund described; Ander echoed what he was told. "The Puppeteers are still in Known Space. Receding at relativistic speeds, and they took their planets with them." Ander snapped the comp shut. "Five worlds all about the same size, orbiting in a pentagon around each other. Do the math yourself. You'll find that you can put a sun at the center, or not, and the orbits are stable either way. They understand tides just fine, Beowulf. That's what they hid from you."

Shaeffer had looked surprised. He asked intelligent questions. He didn't visibly react to the comment about relativistic speed. Because he considered three percent light speed relativistic? Or because he didn't know?

Regardless, Shaeffer was on a roll. *He* brought up the '45 expedition with Gregory Pelton. *He* volunteered that they had found an antimatter solar system. For that information to have become expendable, Shaeffer was protecting something very dear to him. Some*one.*

It had to be Sharrol Janss.

BEOWULF LED THE way to the Pequod Grill. (Sigmund had seen 3-V ads; the Pequod was the premiere tourist trap in Pacifica.) Ander crammed into the transfer booth with Shaeffer, miming concern Shaeffer would bolt. At the restaurant, Ander accompanied Bey to the 'cycler.

Bey talked almost nonstop, even after the food came. Along the way, he speculated about the Puppeteer worlds and where they might be headed. He theorized about how Outsiders would adapt to the core explosion.

In different circumstances, Sigmund would have been fascinated. Medusa was recording; he would process all this another time.

Ander, at Sigmund's prompting, told several whoppers about Pelton's research program on Jinx, and what had derailed it.

Shaeffer didn't react visibly to that, either.

Medusa interrupted. "I've got her, Sigmund. Milcenta. She just checked in at Outbound Enterprises."

"What's that?" Sigmund asked.

"An iceliner company. The one Carlos and the children used. And one more thing. . . ."

"Yes?" Sigmund prompted.

"If you de-opaque your window and look down, Outbound Enterprises is that low green building just down the street."

SHAEFFER FINALLY SLOWED down. It might be exhaustion, the hour being late in Pacifica, or he might have decided he'd stalled enough for Sharrol/Milcenta to get away. He hadn't, despite earlier comments, said much about Feather.

"Is this what you came for?" Beowulf asked.

"Beowulf, I believe I can tell Sigmund it was worth the trip. Now, will you tell me what happened to Feather Filip and Carlos Wu?"

"Yeah." Bey leaned forward. "And Carlos Wu's autodoc?"

"Feather Filip vanished from the same time and locale as you and Carlos Wu and Sharrol Janss. I'm supposed to find out who's dead."

Sigmund flinched, but Ander was almost certainly correct. And if anyone was dead, logic said it was Feather. Sigmund studied Beowulf through Ander's lenses.

A hand flew up to Shaeffer's throat, massaging it nervously. "Nobody should have to eat with you, Ander."

"Who's dead?" Ander repeated bluntly.

"At least Carlos. You want it from the beginning?"

Carlos had gone on to Home. What else would Shaeffer lie about?

"So there you have it," Bey finally summarized. "Carlos is dead. I saw Feather shoot him before she shot me. Sharrol and the children must have gotten away. Feather stayed to put me in the 'doc, then used the other boat.

"She left me marooned on a desert island. I think she'd already given up on catching Sharrol. Otherwise, why would she need me for a hostage? I can't guess where they all are now, but if Feather was holding Sharrol, I think I'd know it."

Amid the lies, parts of the tale rang true. Sigmund knew the principals and enough of the background to penetrate the fog of deceit. Getting the transport and lander, sneaking to Fafnir to take over the lives of the Graynors, treachery at a remote island landing . . . that all fit. A stolen weapon, and big holes blown through a nautical survival vest, had brought Sigmund here.

Only some of the roles had been changed.

Feather was gone forever. That she'd clearly gone over the edge didn't make it any easier. Sigmund was suddenly sick to death of Beowulf Shaeffer's voice.

That didn't stop Shaeffer. "On another matter, Carlos Wu's experimental autodoc is a very valuable item. I propose to sell it to you."

"We really want that back," Sigmund managed to say. "Play it casual."

Ander took his time commenting. "Your bargaining position isn't that terrific."

"Cheap," Shaeffer assured him. "I can't touch it myself, after all, and you can't afford to lose it. Look at me! That thing rebuilt me from a severed head!"

Sigmund's stomach lurched. He finally pictured it. How long had Feather gone without meds? Long enough to see her shipmates as enemies?

Then what?

Shaeffer blown apart, slaughtered first, as potentially the most dangerous to Feather. The others managed to kill her, putting Shaeffer's head into the autodoc before fleeing in their boat in flat-phobic blind panic. Shaeffer shortened by almost a half meter, because the autodoc's intensive-care cavity couldn't accommodate his natural height.

The room spun. "Ander. Make a deal to buy back the 'doc. I'm dropping off."

The final, unbearable truth registered. Regrowing Shaeffer from his head would take a lot of biomass as input. An awful lot.

Feather's dead body?

Sigmund retched and retched until his stomach ran dry.

• 50 •

In satellite weather imagery on Fafnir's public net, Sigmund watched a small dot meander from island to island. The dot was the dirigible *Wyvern;* the end of the line was a mooring tower just a few kilometers from Shasht North Spaceport, the Outbound Enterprises Terminal, and Sigmund's hotel.

One of the passengers was named Martin Wallace Graynor. The tracker Ander had planted confirmed it.

After Shaeffer "escaped" from Ander, he followed at a discreet distance. Alas, Shaeffer didn't go to recover the autodoc. The last island on *Wyvern*'s itinerary was within transfer-booth range of Shasht, and Ander flicked the rest of the way ahead of the dirigible.

Ander had coaxed Sigmund out of his room, as far as the Drake's main dining room. Sigmund sat with his back to the window wall that overlooked endless waves and not-quite-right sky. They traded seats, ocean and sky suddenly not the worst view in the room, when a pair of Kzinti came in. Did *you* eat my parents?

"It's almost cruel," Ander said. "Letting Bey think he got away from me."

Where except to Outbound could Beowulf go? Sharrol was already frozen solid for the next iceliner to Home. Before following, Ander had checked out the abandoned apartment of the Graynors, and the just-rented hotel room of Persial January Hebert, sea-monster survivor. Presumably Sharrol had rented the room for Bey on her way out of Pacifica.

Ander hadn't found anything, not so much as a holo of Sharrol and the children. The few personal effects had been sanitized. As to the whereabouts of the autodoc, there was no trace.

Maybe Ander should just "find" Bey again, to complete the under-the-table purchase charade. If Ander talked Bey down to a reasonable price, Sigmund was inclined to let Bey keep it—and to let "the Graynors" go free. Shaeffer was guilty of countless technicalities, from immigration rules to identity fraud to traffic-control infractions. So what? It was more Feather's doing than his own.

The bit of Sigmund's mind not still paralyzed with grief wondered how Shaeffer would take being caught again. Might he trade the coordinates of the antimatter system for freedom?

Ander leafed through the wine list, in a section marked "Ask the Sommelier" in lieu of price. "Sigmund, I feel we did very well here. Perhaps a magnum of—"

Feather was dead and Ander wanted to celebrate? Sigmund couldn't discuss it, but he wasn't about to order champagne. "We'll apply the cost of a bottle to what you owe me. Those surveillance lenses and earplugs you lost aren't cheap."

"I didn't lose them." Ander closed the wine list, looking wistful. "Sigmund, those things can't be worn without interruption for days. My eyes and ears were killing me. I took them out and left them on a counter for a while."

"Forget it." Sigmund didn't feel up to more complaints about the housekeeping at Ander's hotel in Pacifica.

"HE'S THERE," MEDUSA said.

There was the lobby of Outbound Express, ten stories below Sigmund and just down the street. The AIde monitored through sensors Ander had planted there hours earlier.

"He didn't waste time," Sigmund said. Shaeffer's dirigible had docked only an hour earlier. "Show me."

The new, flatlander-sized Beowulf Shaeffer stood talking with the woman at a circular desk in the main reception area. He had dyed his hair red and taken tannin pills, but without doubt that was Bey. As he turned from the desk, the check-in formalities apparently complete, Sigmund said, "Medusa. Connect me to the lobby."

"Outbound Express. Ms. Machti speaking."

"My name is Ausfaller. I need urgently to speak with the red-haired man who just registered." Ms. Machti caught Bey's attention, and transferred the call to a lobby phone pedestal beside a window wall. Talking eye to eye with Shaeffer felt odd.

Shaeffer apparently thought so, too. "Long story. Ask Ander."

"So your name is Graynor now?"

"Braynard," Bey overenunciated. Nice try. "Where are you?"

"Where should I be?" Sigmund asked back.

"Retrieving Carlos Wu's autodoc?"

"In due course. It shouldn't be left here." He was toying with Shaeffer. It didn't make Sigmund feel very good about himself. Habit? Misplaced blame? An ineffable weariness settled over him. It was time to end this.

Sigmund stepped to the window. Looking down wasn't too bad. He waved. "Look outside, Bey. Turn left. Farther. Look up.

"I'm right on top of you. It would take you hours to freeze yourself, perhaps days to be stowed and launched. I need only cross the street to stop you. Let us reason together, Bey."

"You always seem to have an offer I can't refuse. Why are you picking on me, Sigmund? I told Ander everything he wanted to know."

"I haven't heard from Ander," Sigmund said. Not since breakfast.

"Feather. Carlos. Puppeteers."

"You'll still have to come home with me, Bey." They went into a dance, Bey sticking to his story and Sigmund pretending to believe it. "Bey, are you sure about Carlos?"

"Feather blew a hole through him. But the nanotech 'doc is his last legacy, and it's UN property, and I might arrange to put that in your hands."

Sigmund held all the cards, but Shaeffer would still play it out to the bitter end. I'm going to miss you, Sigmund thought.

EYES SQUEEZED SHUT, heads held tightly against the underside of his belly, rolled into a ball, within the all-but-impregnable hull of *Aegis,* undetected at the bottom of Fafnir's ocean . . . Nessus cowered.

He dared not confront Ausfaller. He dared not return home without trying. All the while planning advanced, as Achilles so antiseptically sang it, "for reclaiming that which was so carelessly set loose."

With great effort of will Nessus unclenched. Babbling grew louder, mostly unintelligible, relayed from the sensors that rimmed the stepping disc beneath the carpet in Sigmund's room. Ander's room remained silent. *Aegis'* computers only accessed a fraction of what transpired, having to overcome defensive jamming and encryption. But "going home," whether it referred to Earth or Home, showed clearly enough Nessus was running out of time. Sigmund expected to leave soon.

Nessus had come all this way to enlist a champion. Fear had paralyzed him ever since. If he were ever to meet faces to face with Ausfaller, it must be soon.

Then why not now?

Trembling, Nessus climbed to his hooves. Sensors said Ander's room remained quiet. Nessus mouthed the transport controls and stepped through.

He drilled a pinhole through the connecting wall, pulsing a flashlight laser dialed to narrow beam. Sigmund was alone, talking to a vidphone. Nessus gathered his strength for the step through to the hidden disc in Sigmund's room.

Faintly, Nessus heard a ping. Through his pinhole, he saw the hall door into Ausfaller's room open, and then—

He dove for the stepping disc and the safety of *Aegis*.

A BELL PINGED, followed by soft knocking. Tap. Tap-tap-tap. Tap-tap. Ander, back finally from running the prelaunch checklist on *Seeker.*

"Open the door!" Sigmund called to the room automation. He turned back to Bey's holo image. "And Feather? You know, we never intended to turn her loose on an alien world. We want some weaponry back, too." He had to ask, although Feather's stolen punchgun was probubly at the bottom of the ocean, encrusted in the Fafnir equivalent of barnacles.

An elephant kicked Sigmund in the back. Fat spatters of gore suddenly dotted the vidphone and the shattered, sparking remains of his computer array. He twisted as he fell, his head flopping to face the door.

Ander! He held a punchgun, its stubby barrel still

smoking. Feather's? Lethal weapons weren't easy to come by.

Inconceivable pain faded, even more terrifyingly, to no feeling at all. Sigmund's thoughts swam in syrup. What was—

A yank on the hair lifted Sigmund up off the floor into view of the camera. Shaeffer's eyes were round. In the window, Sigmund's reflection had a gaping hole through its chest.

Had he heard Bey protest? Sigmund wanted to think so.

From a great distance, Ander said, "Beowulf . . . can hardly sell . . . nanotech machine without Sigmund knowing how . . . got it."

Betrayed. . . .

There was scarcely time to think, I always knew it would end horribly, before everything dissolved into a maelstrom of darkness.

THE OUTSIDERS

EARTH DATES: 2656–2657

• 51 •

Ausfaller! The man plagued them even in death.

Achilles watched the recording from Earth, unable *not* to paw at the meadowplant carpet in Nike's office. In the holo, Nessus wore his mane pulled back into a few uneven braids. The token effort made him look, if such a thing was possible, more disheveled than usual.

The message ended. Nike settled astraddle one of the thickly planted hummocks that served in this office as benches. His mane glittered with sequins and orange gems. He asked, "Your impressions?"

He's asking me, Achilles decided. Vesta and Nike had viewed the recording before summoning him, but that wasn't the main reason. *He* had spent years immersed in the information cacophony of human worlds. *He* knew most of the principals—if not personally, like Beowulf Shaeffer, then by direct observation and extensive study of their profiles. Ander Smittarasheed was the only player new to him. *He* was the indispensable expert as long as Nessus remained in Human Space.

What did he think? That awareness at this moment of mane coiffure, like the hoof with a mind of its own, was a defense mechanism. A distraction from an intractable problem they could neither hide from nor flee. Achilles struggled to arrange the salient points from Nessus' report. "Ausfaller's murder gives credibility to his event-of-my-death message." That had always been the fear, or Ausfaller would long ago have been eliminated by hired criminal elements.

Ausfaller had assumed, brilliant paranoid that he was, that he could trust no one. His suspicions about Gregory Pelton—among other people—had been delivered to many officials besides Sangeeta Kudrin. There was no way to contain it.

Achilles continued. "The bigger complication is *who* killed Ausfaller. Before joining Ausfaller for the trip to Fafnir, Smittarasheed worked on Jinx for Gregory Pelton, in the facility planning a return expedition to the antimatter system."

Vesta stared into the distance. After a long silence, he said, "It's rather unfortunate the Fafnir police killed their suspect."

"But not surprising," Achilles said, "not after he shot at police trying to capture him."

Maybe Kzinti police coming at him had rattled Ander. Achilles shivered—it would have terrified *him.* Who in their right mind attacked a squad of armed Kzinti? "Ander Smittarasheed had an illegal weapon, and he was covered in Ausfaller's blood."

"I wish we knew more," Vesta said.

"The authorities on Fafnir aren't releasing details," Achilles reminded them. To be fair, neither Vesta nor Nike had ever visited Human Space. How could they understand wild humans and their ways? "The police clearly believe Smittarasheed had an accomplice. They don't want that person to know what they've learned." And the maid who heard the shots, found the body, and ran screaming from the room had disappeared into Witness Protection. Whatever that was.

"Forget Ausfaller," Nike warbled abruptly. "The issue is the antimatter solar system. We let ourselves be comforted that only two humans knew its location. And now . . ."

Now Shaeffer has disappeared, and Pelton has taken asylum on Jinx to avoid questions.

Achilles thought, inanely, of dominoes falling. The metaphor had meaning only to him—but it fit circumstances exactly.

Ausfaller locates the Fleet of Worlds. He demonstrates knowledge of past Citizen meddling on Earth. Smittarasheed kills Ausfaller. Conveniently, Smitterasheed is then killed. Their deaths, in separate ways, implicate Pelton. Pelton flees, removing all doubts. The Secretary-General authorizes the ARM to locate and secure the antimatter system.

Which domino would fall next?

Vesta murmured softly, "We must find the antimatter first, whatever it takes."

"Whatever it takes," Nike agreed.

IT WAS DELEGATED to Achilles to prepare the first draft of an order directing Nessus to Jinx.

Achilles began several times, his mind wandering. Maybe fear had been burnt out of him by the news of the core explosion, and the long isolation until his recall. Maybe he had come to embrace his own bravado about being vulnerable only when he presented his heel.

Or maybe, with Ausfaller gone, Achilles could no longer *truly* see Earth as a credible threat.

A very real opportunity kept chasing theoretical dangers from Achilles' thoughts. While Nike worried about the peril behind the Fleet, no action would be taken to reclaim the lost world. Its status was, the Hindmost decreed, "a deferrable crisis."

Let Nike stay distracted! Achilles would use that time, exploit that preoccupation.

His destiny, Achilles now realized, did not lie on the ocean floor. Seabed arcologies were too grand a concept for lesser minds.

But none could deny that the world once called Nature Preserve 4 had been governed too laxly. When the time came for its reintegration into the Concordance, the need for strict control would be obvious. Who better, on that glorious day, to become that world's Hindmost than he who had masterminded its recovery?

And who better to keep far away than the one who had betrayed my previous plans?

Achilles returned to the task of drafting orders, now with a clear purpose. He detailed all the ways Nessus might observe, infiltrate, or influence Pelton's organization, specifics neither Vesta nor Nike could know to question.

The longer Nessus stayed on Jinx, the better.

NESSUS STARED AT the orders from Hearth. Ausfaller had never managed to acquire Pelton's secret. Realistically, how would he?

Stars glittered through the bridge view port. Nessus tried to enjoy them while he could as he readied *Aegis* for flight, and tried to ignore the mass pointer. Soon enough he would look at nothing else.

Only three words in his instructions truly made sense: *at all costs*. Nessus decided *they* were his orders. The bulk of the message was only copious impractical advice. Such minutiae, despite Nike's electronic signature, could only have come from Achilles.

A bowl of stale synthed grains sat on the adjacent bench. Nessus grabbed mouthfuls as he worked, begrudging the time for a meal. He would travel to Jinx as directed.

However . . .

Explorer had been bugged and fitted by Baedeker with a remotely controlled bomb. *Hobo Kelly* had been destroyed remotely. Nessus dare not imagine *Aegis* free of undisclosed modifications. He would presume everything he said, heard, and did aboard would be transmitted back to Hearth.

So he would go to Jinx—first. From there his actions must go unseen, lest anyone or anything interrupt his mission, including ARM ships that were surely out hunting.

Find the antimatter system, at all costs. That was his duty. That was what Nike intended him to do. That was what he *would* do. Gregory Pelton had learned of the antimatter system from the Outsiders.

He must go to the same source.

· 52 ·

"Look at that," Anne-Marie Papandreou said. She had said it at their first glimpse, when *Court Jester* dropped from hyperspace, and three times since. The closer they approached, the more wonderment sounded in her voice.

Nessus could only agree.

Light-years from anything, the Outsider ship/city hung before them. An artificial sun marked one end of a pole, a drive capsule the opposite end. Between, countless ribbons swept and curled and interlaced in a pattern too elaborate for Nessus to grasp.

More intimidating was the ship's behavior. It had dropped from nine-tenths light speed to zero relative within seconds of *Court Jester*'s appearance—somehow without any apparent release of energy.

Related technology moved the Fleet of Worlds. How those drives worked, from where the drives tapped energy, and where they released it upon braking remained Outsider trade secrets.

The Citizen community had once believed in technology independence. That faith evaporated quickly when a swelling sun threatened to exterminate all life on Hearth. In all the ages since, there had been no experiments on what they had bought from the Outsiders. The planetary drives controlled far too much energy to tamper with.

"Four kilometers." Anne-Marie looked up from her bridge console. "The pole is four klicks long. Amazing."

Jason Papandreou merely grinned at her obvious delight. Technically he was a flatlander, but he had traveled far more than most of his breed. Jason had certainly been around more than his wife, on whom he doted. It wasn't all commercial travel, either: He was a veteran of the last Man-Kzin War. That, and the assurances of Nessus' minions on Jinx that the Papandreous often ferried nonhuman passengers, made Nessus comfortable on their ship.

Well, *comfortable* overstated things a bit.

A light began flashing on Jason's console. "Incoming message from the Outsiders. Nessus?"

"On speaker, please," Nessus said.

"Welcome to Ship Fourteen." The Interworld words were crisp and without accent. "We ask that your ship remain ten kilometers away from us. Please wait for your escorts."

"Acknowledged." Jason turned to Nessus. "You're sure you don't want company?"

Nessus began pulling on his space suit. The task gave his mouths something to do besides pluck uselessly at his mane, and an excuse not to answer. His business with the Outsiders was not meant for human ears.

After a while, Jason shrugged. He had grown accustomed to such nonanswers. "Fine, then. Anne and I will stay aboard. Radio if you need anything."

Nessus sealed his space suit. A tongue flick activated his radio. "Testing, one, two, three." At Jason's nod, Nessus strode to the air lock with more confidence than he felt.

THREE OUTSIDERS FLOATED beyond the air lock.

They were creatures of superfluid helium, adapted to the vacuum and utter cold far from any star. Nothing that had ever lived on Hearth served to describe them. In earthly terms, they resembled black cat-o'-nine-tails with grossly engorged handles. Brains and sense organs hid somewhere within the handles. The whips were clusters of motile roots.

All three Outsiders wore metallic exoskeletons. Two offered Nessus a tentacle to grasp, and then he understood their garments. Had they been unprotected, the body heat radiating from his suit would boil them; the tug of his inertial mass might well rip them apart.

In other tentacles, they held gas pistols. They jetted the short distance to Ship Fourteen, the pace agonizingly slow.

Nessus studied the ship rather than dwell on the conversation to come. He had little curiosity; that was a human trait. The universe offered perils enough without looking for more.

Details emerged as they approached. The ribbons were enormous, intertwined ramps, kilometers long and several meters wide. Outsiders beyond number lined the ramps, branched tails in shadow, handles in the faint artificial sunlight, thermoelectrically charging their systems. Many trailed roots in bowls. Nessus guessed at nutrients dissolved in liquid helium.

That's why the Outsiders don't use hyperdrive! Outsiders had invented hyperdrive, they sold it, but (to the best knowledge of other species) they never used it. Now Nessus saw why. Light became—what, exactly, Nessus could not say, but you couldn't *see* anything in hyperspace—something quite different there. In hyperspace, Outsiders could not bask in artificial sunlight. Perhaps they'd starve.

His boots touched down, finally, on one of the tangled ribbons. Nessus' escorts moved toward a nearby door, employing a sinuous, many-limbed perambulation for which he had no name. The artificial gravity seemed inadequate to hold him down. He activated boot electromagnets before he dared to follow.

"Please go inside," Nessus heard on his helmet radio. Nothing suggested which alien had spoken. Perhaps none of them had. He closed the door. Lights came on and air rushed into the room. The transparent dome in one corner was the cubicle's only feature. Within the dome an Outsider waited, sheltered, Nessus inferred, from light, heat, and pressure.

"Undress and be comfortable," Nessus heard. The communication was acoustic, not by radio. "This climate is suitable for your kind."

The chords were as unaccented as the previous Interworld words had been. Outsiders lived in vacuum, so they obviously communicated without sound. Nessus glanced about, looking for a hidden speaker, radio antenna, or infrared sensor—and stopped himself. How they spoke hardly mattered.

"Going silent," Nessus transmitted back to Jason and Anne-Marie. He tongue-flicked his radio to off. This conversation was not for their ears.

To the Outsider, Nessus sang, "Thank you, but to remain suited is more convenient. Changing is time-consuming." And he would lose the option to flee this room—assuming its door would open for him—unless he remained in his space suit. "I am called Nessus. I am here for the Concordance." Not officially, he continued in his thoughts. "What shall I call you?"

A long pause suggested puzzlement at the question. "Fourteen will do." More silence. "We encounter few Citizens or humans in this region. We were surprised to receive your hail. Did you have difficulty finding us?"

"Yes," Nessus lied.

A thousand generations of observation had revealed little about the Outsiders. That ignorance was not all the aliens' doing. They ranged freely where Citizens, even insane scouts, feared to follow. One of the very few certainties was that Outsider ships followed starseeds—for reasons yet unknown—on their epic migrations.

That Citizen scientists could summon starseeds was a secret of the highest magnitude. Enough starseeds had been observed for long enough to make a correlation: They set sail for dying stars. That was probably how the Outsiders had first come upon Giver of Life, not long (in solar terms) before its imminent senescence became evident to Concordance specialists.

Astronomers eventually isolated the spectra and intensities to which starseeds responded. Physicists learned to induce transient instabilities in stars to produce such emissions. Engineers created a compact device—the starseed lure—to project the destabilizing force beam. Now starseed lures stealthily orbited many stars, remotely controlled by hyperwaves, to keep a few Outsider ships always within reach lest a planetary drive need maintenance.

Humans might call it insurance.

"Yes," Nessus repeated. "It took a while to find you, Fourteen."

"Very well," Fourteen said. "Your hail indicated the intent to purchase information. What information do you seek?"

Nessus took a deep, calming breath. "Visitors, or rather, customers, asked you once for the location of the 'most unusual planet' in Known Space. That was an antimatter planet. I would also like to see it."

The Outsider considered. "It seems a rather hazardous destination for one of your kind."

"From afar." The grace notes of ironic understatement weren't totally necessary; Nessus wondered if they would translate. "I came to purchase the location and trajectory."

"You already know much about the matter. Why not ask those earlier visitors?"

What would Ausfaller have done? Nessus asked himself that more and more. Offered some disinformation or half-truth, surely. Having come on a human ship, he could hardly claim total separation from Human Space. "Beowulf Shaeffer and Gregory Pelton prefer to keep it their secret."

"We charged them a significant sum. Perhaps they are entitled to having the secret kept."

Perhaps? "Unless you promised exclusivity, why not also sell me the data?

"I, however, wish to purchase exclusivity henceforth: of the system's location and even its existence." What else could he ask to safeguard the Fleet? "Also, as part of my purchase, I will require that you not provide anyone with transportation to that system."

The translator fell silent, but under the clear dome roots squirmed. Did his interlocutor consult with unseen colleagues? Writhe in anger? Convulse in amusement? "We accept your point. Our price, inclusive of such exclusivity, is five million Earth stars."

Only the tough material of his space suit stopped Nessus from burrowing his heads deep into his mane. Five million stars was a significant sum, but once it would have been doable. That was *before.* Before General Products abandoned its export business. Before a fortune in penalties and termination fees for broken contracts on so many worlds. Before funding Julian Forward's supremely expensive experiments. Before endless bribes and extortions and the purchase of behind-the-scenes influence. Before seizure of most of what little remained, when Ausfaller discovered the meddling. Before an enormous warranty payout to Gregory Pelton for the destruction of his GP hull. . . .

Which is why I must pay. We must find the antimatter.

The price would not change. Outsiders did not bargain or negotiate. Five million stars would empty General Products' accounts on We Made It, Down, and Plateau.

But Nike's orders had been explicit: At all costs. "I accept."

The actual transaction—exchanging a string of digits in the form of bank credits for a few navigational parameters—was eerily anticlimactic. Then Nessus truly *saw* what he had bought.

The "most unusual planet" had barely grazed Known Space, receding at nearly light speed. Inaccessible normal-space velocity; the ultimate in hazardous material; and now a vast, ever-growing distance: No wonder Pelton had yet to undertake a return mission. The United Nations, should they locate this system, would have similar difficulties. And having bought exclusivity to the data, Nessus knew, he had made such a discovery much harder.

It had been a fortune well spent. Nessus returned his comp to a space-suit pocket, sealed the flap securely, and turned to leave.

"As it happens," Fourteen said, "we have other merchandise you might find of value."

Nessus turned back. His comp was almost emptied of credits, and his psyche of energy. Aching for the comparative familiarity of *Court Jester,* he managed to ask, "What sort of information do you offer?"

Fourteen's roots wriggled; a shiny artifact appeared inside the dome.

The object's purpose was not obvious. Nessus sidled closer, but no details emerged. He saw only a shiny cylinder with a handle, entirely reflective.

Entirely reflective? Nessus had never heard of a stasis field following such a complex surface, but he was obviously looking at a stasis field. That often meant a weapons cache. "Fourteen, where did you get this?"

"We found it considerably closer to the galactic core."

Considerably closer was admirably imprecise. Unless the item had been awaiting sale for longer than Nessus had been a scout, it had been retrieved in or near Known Space. Starseed lures had kept this ship in the interstellar neighborhood for that long.

The one thing scarier than the unknowable contents of an ancient cache was the possibility of another species acquiring it. Trembling, Nessus asked, "How much?"

"Fourteen million stars."

Fourteen million stars for Ship Fourteen . . . it hinted at whimsy Nessus had never expected of an Outsider. Moments ago, spending *five* million had almost paralyzed him with doubt. None of which mattered. "I don't have that much money on call."

"That is understandable," Fourteen said. "We will accept your word of honor as a Citizen."

Fourteen million stars! To settle that debt would erase what little remained of General Products' wealth on Earth—and yet what choice did he have? He had come to keep antimatter from the hands of the ARM; whatever secret lurked within the stasis field might be as dangerous.

If he did not buy it, to whom might it be offered next? Kzinti?

Delivering the artifact to Hearth meant first bringing it aboard *Court Jester.* To his surprise, Nessus realized that that didn't bother him. He had trusted Jason and Anne-Marie to bring him here and get him back to Jinx. He would trust them with this unique cargo.

His voices wavering, Nessus said, "You have my word of honor."

The mirror-bright artifact materialized outside the dome, a neck's length from Nessus. It was too big for his pockets; he tied it securely to his suit. Once more, he turned to leave.

"One more thing," Fourteen said. "Since you are here representing the Concordance." He/she/it climbed from the repose it had maintained throughout the negotiations. Changing posture required flexing the handle end—the torso—as well as a scurry of tendrils. "We have noticed something most interesting.

"We understand why your worlds are in flight. At some point, we will follow. But the danger is millennia away, hardly an emergency." Fourteen paused. "We expect past agreements to be honored."

"Certainly," Nessus said. Was this *something* casual

or very, very serious? So little was known about the Outsiders. The meaning of their body language, assuming they had body language, was not part of that knowledge. The new stance might signify anything, or nothing.

"The planetary drives were sold *only* to the Concordance. For acquiring farm worlds. For moving Hearth and its colonies from its sun." Swirling tendrils might convey agitation. "Not to be made available to other races." Pause. "That long-ago arrangement *was* exclusive."

And extraordinarily expensive. Installments would continue to be paid long after Nessus was dead and forgotten. "I do not understand."

Tendrils waved. A hologram appeared of the Fleet—comprised of *six* worlds. The Fleet as it had been until a few years ago. In an elaborate dance, one world emerged and pulled ahead, while the others lagged and re-formed into a pentagon.

Nessus pawed the hard deck, for a shuddering moment unable to stop himself. Proximity did more than keep Outsider ships close for support. Proximity meant Outsider ships at all times had a good view of the Concordance worlds.

An opportunity the Outsiders had obviously grasped.

"Scouts," Nessus managed to say. "As we flee the galaxy, that world, Nature Preserve Four, will encounter any dangers first. They will warn the rest of us."

"So we speculated initially. Their communications, however, are puzzling. The language clearly isn't Citizen. It sounds almost like Interworld." When Nessus failed to respond, Fourteen added, "If the Concordance transferred the planetary drive, dishonoring its pledge of exclusivity, the consequences will be dire."

"Nothing of your systems has been transferred. Nature Preserve Four is in custody of our representatives,"

Nessus stammered, his tune marred by trembling. What was the meaning of *dire* to beings so powerful? "Too few of *us* are able to explore."

"Of that, we require convincing." Fourteen waggled tendrils once more. Air whooshed, this time into unseen reservoirs. The door opened. "Bring proof."

· 53 ·

Nessus crept from the air lock, barely able to move. He scarcely remembered being towed to *Court Jester* by two Outsiders.

Jason stared at the object strapped to Nessus' chest. "Finagle. Is that a stasis box?"

"Yes," Nessus answered dully. He was at—past—the limits of his endurance. The mania that had sustained him seemed less than a distant memory. "It must be stowed."

Anne-Marie noticed his fumbling with the straps. "Let me," she offered. She opened the fasteners, and then blinked at the artifact's surprising weight.

Jason relieved her of the cylinder. He turned it over and over, studying it from every angle. "I'll put it in the forward locker. Anne, help Nessus out of his suit."

Nessus thought nothing of giving such a treasure to Jason. To open a stasis box required a special apparatus private ships would never carry. He hardly thought at all. As from a great distance, Nessus bent and twisted and writhed free of his space suit. Fear and overload had nearly paralyzed him; it took both humans to extract him.

"Back to Jinx," Nessus called over his shoulder, wobbling to his cabin.

The hatch slammed shut, vibrating from the sharp blow of his hind hoof. The lock engaged with a satisfying click. Nessus dove to the deck, rolled himself tight, and sought, for a little while, to forget.

EAT. EXCRETE. DENY.

Bodily functions occasionally dragged Nessus from catatonia, and the dirty plates stacked near his personal synthesizer represented a calendar of a sort. By that crude standard days had passed, but he would not guess how many.

A loud, echoing scream yanked him into the present. It was the amplified ululation of a human female, shrill and panicked. Nessus threw the hatch open and raced to the bridge.

"What is wrong?" he demanded.

"There's nothing wrong," Jason said.

"Have a look out the window. This window," Anne-Marie added.

While Nessus had cowered, they had dropped from hyperspace. Two stars, one yellowish and one eye-piercingly white-violet, blazed in the view port. Glowing red smoke in a many-ringed coil looped around them. The outer end of the coil lashed and flailed, diffusing into a red veil spread across half the sky.

So much beauty! It displaced, for a little while at least, the dread that had immobilized him. He had chosen his crew wisely. "I recognize this star," Nessus said. "Amazing. I really should have suggested this stop myself. Had I not been so depressed, I certainly would have. Thank you, Jason."

"My pleasure, sir," Jason said. "We'll be on our way again whenever you're ready."

Anne-Marie bent over her control console. "I'll scan with deep radar."

Jason laughed. "Can you imagine how many ships have scanned this system already?"

Anne-Marie persisted. "Just for luck."

• • •

THERE WAS A beep. "I don't believe it," Jason said.

"Two in one trip," Anne-Marie shouted. "Jay, that's some sort of record."

Nessus' mind reeled. Beta Lyrae, as the humans called this system, was one of the wonders of Known Space. Doubtless many pilots had detoured, as Jason had, for the view. Just as surely, many had scanned for stasis boxes. It *felt* wrong. "I suggest that we locate the box, then leave it. You may send a friend for it."

"You hired my ship," Jason said. "If you order me to go on, I'll do it."

On the other head . . . if they retrieved this new stasis box now, he could buy their shares. Nessus doubted they'd expect as high a price as the Outsiders. Nessus wasn't ready to agree, but perhaps this merited more discussion. He extemporized, "I will not. Your species has come a long way in a short time. If you do not have prudence, you have some workable substitute."

"There it is," Anne-Marie said. "A little blob of a world about three billion klicks out."

Nessus craned his necks to study the new deep-radar image. The object rested on or slightly within the translucent sphere that represented the planet. He surreptitiously checked radiation meters and saw nothing out of the ordinary—and finally understood what his subconscious had been warbling about.

Pilots searching for stasis boxes counted on one thing: the complete opacity of a stasis field to neutrinos. What none would consider—and why would they?—was that neutronium was almost as opaque. That was why Achilles, curse him, had scattered large neutronium masses in desirable solar systems within the Fleet's wake. Spot an apparent nearly priceless stasis box, race to retrieve it, and then, when it was too late, fall prey to its deep, steep gravity well.

Three human ships had been lost to exactly such traps. Rather than protect the Fleet, the disappearances had *drawn* Ausfaller's attention. Nessus tasted bitter cud remembering his desperate attempts to create a similar neutronium artifact to redirect Sigmund's gaze. Julian's black hole, bulked up with a comparatively small mass of neutronium, had accomplished much the same.

This couldn't be one of Achilles' traps. A large neutronium mass set onto the planet's surface would eat its way through, oscillating around the center of mass, growing and emitting massive amounts of radiation.

Jason moved alongside, also studying the deep-radar image. "Shouldn't be any problem. All right, I'll take us down."

Nessus said nothing, knowing his silence represented a decision.

"I DUB THEE Cue Ball," Anne-Marie said.

Nessus watched her follow Jason through the pressure curtain now projected over the doubly open air lock. They rode the escalladder down to the frozen surface of the small world. The great, red-glowing arch of star stuff, source and replenisher of the thin local atmosphere, shone overhead. Through the main view port, Nessus watched with one head as they cautiously surveyed the landing zone with a portable deep-radar unit. A radio-linked auxiliary bridge display repeated the deep-radar image: an opaque cube buried in the ice.

The cube disappeared.

A steam geyser burst from the ice. A massive figure emerged. It was an armed and armored Kzin! Jason and Anne-Marie ran for the ship, only to be cut down. Nessus slapped the air-lock control; the doors began to close—

Too slowly.

The Kzin, taller than and easily twice as massive as Jason, splintered the bridge door with a single blow. "Come," he snarled.

NESSUS HUNG LIKE a bug in amber, immobilized by a police restraint device. Jason and Anne-Marie, roughly stripped of their vacuum suits, remained stunned and unresponsive. Both dangled in awkward-looking poses within their own force-field restraints. Their pressure suits had been removed to another cabin. Nessus had had only moments to dress for the trek to the Kzinti ship hidden beneath the ice.

A single Kzin, with few markings on his bright orange fur, shared the room with them, impatient for the stunned humans to return to consciousness.

Nessus tired of waiting. "What is the purpose of this action?" he demanded in Hero's Tongue. Scouts learned all the languages of Known Space.

The Kzin ignored him.

Nessus guessed the Kzin was a warrior. He would be loath to speak to an herbivore.

Jason groaned. "So none of us made it."

"No," Nessus said. "You may remember I advised—"

"How could I forget? Sorry about that, Nessus. What's happening?"

"Very little at the moment."

The restraint field as set left only heads free to move. Jason turned his head toward their captor. "Who are you?"

"You may call me Captain," the Kzin said. "Depending on future events, you are either my kidnap victims or my prisoners of war. Who are you?"

"Jason Papandreou, of Earth origin."

"Very well. Jason, are you in possession of a stasis box, a relic of the Slaver Empire?"

Only the restraint field kept Nessus from collapsing

in horror. A very few Kzinti were latent telepaths; a tiny fraction of those could tolerate the drug that awakened their powers. Kzinti warships often carried telepaths. By treaty, Kzinti no longer *had* warships, nor were they even allowed lethal weapons—but nevertheless this was surely a military vessel.

How but with the aid of a telepath could Captain even suspect *Court Jester* carried a Slaver relic?

The Kzinti—before it was their misfortune to encounter humans—had once ruled an empire. The races Kzinti subjugated were slaves. Those who had, eons earlier, left behind stasis containers called themselves Thrintun. Wielding telepathic powers far beyond the Kzinti variety, the Thrintun held whole worlds in bondage. It was no wonder the Kzinti revered their memory. Only Kzinti would feel that calling them Slavers was an honor.

A Thrintun superweapon could rekindle the Man-Kzin Wars, even imperil the Fleet.

The horror of the situation so shook Nessus that he hardly heard Jason's denial. Captain's question was a formality, of course. The telepath who had sensed thoughts of the artifact would peel the humans' minds like onions.

Captain would not talk to him. Could any Kzin bear to read a mere herbivore's mind?

A conditioned response to any such attempt would instantly kill him. Nessus was not afraid to die. He *was* terrified of the information that would die with him, and of the many lives at stake. That must not happen. He must await his opportunity to escape.

What would Ausfaller do?

"The trap you stumbled upon is an old one," Captain said. "One ship or another has been waiting on this world since the last war. We have been searching out Slaver stasis boxes for much longer than that, hoping to find new weapons. . . ."

A second Kzin, ill groomed, appeared in the doorway.

He waited deferentially for his Captain to finish talking. The telepath?

Captain ignored the newcomer. "Only recently did we hit upon this idea. You may know that ships often stop off to see this unusual star. Ships of most species also have the habit of sending a deep-radar pulse around every star they happen across."

It was easy to remember Achilles ranting about humans, and scheming to bolster the Patriarchy as a counterweight against them. Not even Achilles would conspire to help the Kzinti acquire Thrintun weapons—but had Achilles' meddling inspired Kzinti to seek on their own?

"Several decades ago we did find a stasis box. Unfortunately, it contained nothing useful, but we eventually found out how to turn the stasis field on and off. It made a good trap. For forty Kzin years we have waited for ships to happen by with stasis boxes in their holds. You are our second catch."

The echo of the deep-radar pulse sent "for luck" had masked an answering ping from the planet. They had revealed themselves and disclosed their precious cargo long before approaching within telepathic range.

Anne-Marie had also revived. At Captain's explanation, her eyes grew round. "Sorry," she mouthed to Nessus.

"You'd have done better finding your own boxes," Jason said.

"We would have been seen. Earth would have acted to stop our search." Done explaining himself, Captain turned to the unkempt Kzin in the doorway. He snarled orders in Hero's Tongue.

The rumpled one was called, simply, Telepath. Captain turned out to be Chuft-Captain, a nobleman, entitled to a partial name. Cringing deferentially, his face scrunched in misery, Telepath set to work reading Jason's mind.

The force field still held Jason. He gritted his teeth

and squeezed his eyes shut until Telepath turned his painful attention to Anne-Marie. She also endured the ordeal stoically.

Telepath shuddered before reopening his own eyes. "Chuft-Captain, they have not hidden the stasis box. It may be found in a locker to the left of the control room."

Chuft-Captain howled in frustration when he heard the humans knew almost nothing of Nessus' dealings with the Outsiders. He did not direct Telepath to probe Nessus' mind. Perhaps reading prey was too demeaning even for a no-name Kzin. Perhaps Chuft-Captain knew the attempt would kill Nessus without revealing anything of value.

Either way, Nessus was grateful. While he lived he could plan to escape.

Telepath finally left, drained by his psychic exertions. More Kzinti soon replaced him, wearing pressure suits with their helmets not yet sealed. They brought the prisoners' pressure suits. Chuft-Captain addressed the one carrying the stasis container as Slaverstudent.

"Open it," Chuft-Captain ordered.

Slaverstudent set down his load. The mirrored, cylindrical container obstructed Nessus' view of whatever the Kzin operated to break the stasis field. The mirror finish vanished to reveal a dull bronze-colored box, which opened automatically. Slaverstudent removed a three-clawed alien hand, what appeared to be a slab of raw meat inside a transparent wrapping, and a small sphere on a sculpted handle.

The hand had belonged to a Thrint. A souvenir? The handgrip on what certainly *looked* like a weapon was entirely wrong for it. What little hope Nessus had allowed himself vanished.

These were artifacts of the Tnuctipun, the most talented of the long-gone empire's subject races. For generations, Tnuctipun slaves had developed the most advanced technology of the Thrintun Empire—while secretly developing other technologies for themselves. When, at last, the Tnuctipun rose in rebellion, they and their former masters warred until all intelligent life in the galaxy was exterminated.

These Kzinti now possessed the first Tnuctipun stasis box ever recovered.

· 54 ·

Nessus and his crew stood on the surface of Cue Ball. They were there for any insights they might offer as Chuft-Captain and Slaverstudent tested the weapon. When the prisoners ceased to be helpful, they could serve as targets. As they were immobilized by portable restraint fields, the matter was beyond their control.

No! Nessus chided himself. Do not give in to fatalism. Stay alert for an opportunity to escape.

Court Jester sat nearby, a squat cylinder atop the ice, tauntingly out of reach. Nessus wondered if it could attain safe hyperdrive operating distance from Beta Lyrae before the Kzinti ship—*Traitor's Claw,* he now knew it was called—could free itself of the ice.

"I wonder why we're still alive," Anne-Marie said.

Nessus answered cautiously, "The Captain wants our opinions on the putative weapon. He will not ask for them, but will take them through the telepath."

"That doesn't apply to you, does it?" Anne-Marie asked.

"No. No Kzin would read my mind. Perhaps no Kzin would kill me; my race holds strong policies on the safety of individual members." Their captors had set everyone's space suit radios to a common frequency. Nessus had hinted at the power and long memories of the Concordance without implying any threat Chuft-Captain might feel honor bound to defy. Citizens did not fight back, not in the Kzinti sense. But they had the power of commerce, the influence to make and break worlds. Had, in the past tense: The wealth and influence of General Products were all but gone now. "In any case, we have some time."

"Time for what?"

"Anne-Marie, we must wait. If the artifact is a weapon, we must recover it. If not, we must survive to warn your people the Kzinti are searching out Slaver stasis boxes. We must wait until we know which." As though they could do anything *but* wait.

The restraint field kept Nessus from pivoting his heads. That was frustrating. His urge was to look himself in the eyes. The Kzinti would surely find Puppeteer bravado amusing. Would his amusing them argue for his life?

"*Then* what?" Anne-Marie persisted.

"We will find a way," Nessus said.

Jason finally joined the discussion. "We?"

"Yes. Our motives coincide here." That was true, taking escape as a motive. Nessus' foremost goal thereafter was to get word to Hearth of the Outsiders' demands. Even Kzinti pursuit of ancient weapons paled in comparison. "I cannot explain at this time."

Or ever.

CHUFT-CAPTAIN SYSTEMATICALLY EXAMINED the controls of the ball-and-handle artifact. He pointed it into the distance and squeezed what might be a trigger. Nothing happened. He gripped a small mechanism at the base of the handle, edging it upward—

The mirror-faced sphere writhed like a living thing, changing and flowing into a long slender cylinder with a red ball at one end and a toggle at the other. The handle had not changed.

When Chuft-Captain engaged the toggle, the red ball lit up and shot far across the ice. The Kzin swung the artifact; the glowing ball moved in concert. "Variable sword," Chuft-Captain guessed. He moved the artifact toward a distant rock spire. The top of the rock slid off.

Nessus knew what a variable sword was: an invisibly thin monofilament reinforced with a stasis field. One would slice through almost anything. The red ball marked the end of the filament, for purposes of aiming.

"A variable sword," Chuft-Captain repeated. "But not of Slaver design. Slaverstudent, have you ever heard of a weapon that changes shape?"

"No, Chuft-Captain, neither of the past nor of the present."

"Then we've found something new."

"Yes!" Slaverstudent snarled enthusiastically.

The slider in the artifact's handle had eight settings. One had turned the ball into a variable sword. Chuft-Captain set out to find the purpose of the other settings.

Setting two morphed the device into a parabolic mirror and a sonic projector. In the tenuous atmosphere of Cue Ball, even its strongest setting transmitted only a faint hum. Nessus knew that personally, as Chuft-Captain used *him* as a target. Slaverstudent had already reported very limited energy discharge. Chuft-Captain knew that. The Kzin must have already deemed Nessus expendable.

The third transformation produced a projectile weapon. Slaverstudent provided bullets that had also been in the stasis box. Chuft-Captain grunted appreciatively when one type proved to be powerfully explosive.

The next setting again set the device to writhing. It spat out the remaining bullets before settling into a new sphere, smaller than the original. Test firings at target rocks did nothing, although Slaverstudent reported energy discharge. Chuft-Captain fired at each of his captives. This time, Nessus felt nothing. "I grow weary of these duds," Chuft-Captain growled.

The fifth setting produced a stubby barrel flanked by

flat metal projections. It looked dangerous even to Nessus. Chuft-Captain fired at his target rock.

Everything happened at once. Chuft-Captain spun around, as though he were holding a fire hose, struggling to control the weapon. A glowing beam lashed about. Telepath screamed as hot plasma touched him, a sickening wail of pain and fear that faded quickly. Two Kzinti grabbed Telepath, dragging him toward the ice tunnel back into *Traitor's Claw.*

Anne-Marie was running for *Court Jester*! Telepath's flailing had knocked her off the grid of the portable restraint. Nessus felt the stirrings of hope—

Chuft-Captain, almost casually, brought her down with a stunner. He trudged after her as she bounced and slid, paralyzed, across the ice.

"It's a rocket motor," Slaverstudent said. He'd returned from flash-freezing Telepath for emergency care back on Kzin. "The flat projections on the side may be holds for feet."

Position six produced a telescopic sight and a communications laser. Nessus consulted quickly with Jason while the Kzinti continued their experimentation. The rocket mode had seemed far too powerful for the artifact's size. Unless—

"It must use total conversion of matter," Jason said.

Nessus had already concluded that. Slaverstudent surely would also. Nessus' depression deepened. A compact device able to totally convert matter to energy . . . by comparison, even antimatter was a trivial peril. Such technology promised yet *another* way to destroy General Products' hulls.

"Things weren't bad enough," Jason said. "Can you see Kzinti warships armed and powered with total conversion?"

"Futzy ratcats," Anne-Marie said suddenly. The restraint field defeated her attempt to sit up, and she swore some more.

"Nice try," Jason told her.

Chuft-Captain moved on to the seventh setting. It yielded an enigmatic cylinder and wire grid. Slaverstudent reported an energy release, but the device affected nothing.

Nessus didn't feel anything when, again, Chuft-Captain aimed it at him. Nessus thought the grid looked like a microphone.

So did Slaverstudent. He took the weapon into his ship. He returned with it in a short time. "I was right. The artifact answered me in an unknown speech. Chuft-Captain, I believe it to be a computer."

Computers didn't impress Chuft-Captain, not unless they could be taught Hero's Tongue. He went on to the eighth setting, which produced a weird shape that defied naming. Nessus thought he'd seen something like it long ago in an old topology lesson, and wondered what it could be.

It certainly did not *look* like a weapon. Chuft-Captain aimed it at a rock and pulled the trigger—

JASON TOPPLED. HE gave Anne-Marie a shove toward *Court Jester,* then turned to charge at Chuft-Captain.

The restraint grids were off! The eighth setting absorbed energy. Something came over Nessus. Desperation? Mania? A form of insanity, surely. He did not stop to analyze it.

Nessus charged past Jason, directly at Chuft-Captain, who was still puzzling over the Tnuctipun artifact. The Kzin looked up just as Nessus reached him. Nessus spun as he moved, straightening his hind leg and locking its joints. He sank the hoof deep into Chuft-Captain's side.

Ribs shattered beneath Nessus' hoof. The blow jolted his leg up to his hip. Chuft-Captain, screaming, dropped the artifact; Jason scooped it up as he ran.

Nessus pulled his hoof free and galloped on. Long before he reached *Court Jester* he saw the air lock had been welded shut. Tools in his suit pockets would free it, but not before the Kzinti would recapture him.

A Kzin had grabbed Anne-Marie. Another aimed a stunner at Jason, doubtless wondering why it was not working. Jason looked about helplessly. The instant Jason switched the Tnuctipun artifact to a weapon setting, the stunner would paralyze him.

Anne-Marie bellowed, "Run, dammit. Jay, run!"

Nessus and Jay pelted for the distant hills.

· 55 ·

"Jay!" It was Anne-Marie. "Have to talk quick; they're taking off my helmet. I'm not hurt, but I can't get away. The ship's taking off. Bury the weapon somewh—"

Nessus heard Jason swearing helplessly. "Jason, turn to the private band." He had not dared before to communicate privately, sure it would enrage their captors. "Can you hear me?"

"Yeah. Where are you?"

Nessus said, "I do not know how to describe my position. I ran about ten kilometers east."

"Let's think of a way to find each other."

"Why, Jason?" As long as he stayed in this ice cave, he could not be seen even from above, and the unavoidable heat emissions of his space suit would be greatly diffused. Moving only gave the Kzinti an opportunity to spot them.

"You think you're safer alone? I don't. How long will your suit keep you alive?"

"Several standard years." Nessus meant Earth standard. He knew no human space suit could match its recycling capability. "But help will arrive before then."

"What makes you think so?"

"When the Kzinti pilot entered the pressure curtain, I was calling my people for help."

"What? How?" Jason asked.

"Despite recent changes in the fortune of my people, that is still most secret." Beta Lyrae was one of the stars with a starseed lure hidden in its cometary belt. The lures, of course, could be controlled remotely. His coded radio distress call, once it reached the lure, would be forwarded by hyperwave to the Fleet.

These weren't secrets for human ears. Nessus admitted to Puppeteers remaining still within Known Space to keep up Jason's hope of rescue. On Earth, the ARM knew that much already; most of what Nessus said or implied thereafter was misdirection. If Jason despaired, he might seek to trade the artifact for his spouse.

TRAITOR'S CLAW SOARED skyward on a blue-white column of fusion flame. It receded to a blindingly bright spark high overhead, a brilliant dot in the red arch of celestial smoke, hovering.

Or so Jason described it. To see the sky risked being seen from the sky. Nessus remained in his ice cave.

Jason said, "One thing we do have is the weapon itself."

"True," Nessus agreed cautiously. "We have a laser, a flame-throwing rocket, and a shield against police stunners. But not simultaneously."

Slaverstudent had taken careful readings of the energy output from every weapon setting. The warship's altitude must have been set with that knowledge in mind. Over enough distance, even laser beams diverged. They could not harm the Kzinti—even if, as Nessus thought unlikely, Jason would fire on a vessel in which Anne-Marie was held prisoner.

"I think we may have overlooked a setting," Jason said.

"Wishful thinking, Jason, is not a Puppeteer trait."

"Neither is knowledge of weapons. Nessus, what kind of weapon is this? I'm talking about the whole bundle, not any single setting."

"As you say, I am not an expert on warfare."

But Jason *was*. And Jason felt certain that a warrior would not want such a weapon—he would be defenseless while it transformed—but that a spy might see benefit in combining so many capabilities so compactly. Together, they pictured a Tnuctipun spy, hiding out, perhaps among slaves of his race, plotting against the Slavers.

The undetected setting Jason hypothesized made sense only for a spy. The device must have, Jason insisted, an autodestruct.

JASON PUSHED AND prodded controls, twisted parts of the device in every configuration, talking as he worked. Unable to see, Nessus could not entirely follow.

Meanwhile, the artificial star brightened. Closer to the surface? A hotter flame? Nessus guessed both, with a gravity planer pushing opposite the fusion drive to maintain the low hover. He couldn't guess why—until Jason reported he was deep in meltwater.

Soon after, the flame went out. Jason froze into place. And then—

"I've found it, Nessus. I've found *something*."

"A new setting? What does it look like?"

"Like a cone with a rounded base, pointing away from the handle."

"Try it. And if you are successful, good-bye, Jason. Knowing you was pleasant." Nessus was only slightly surprised by his own sincerity.

"Good-bye, Nessus."

Huddling within the minimal shelter of his ice cave, Nessus sensed nothing as long seconds passed. There was a rumble. Then the ground shook, tossing him against the roof. He fell, and the waves threw him again. And again. And . . .

He blacked out before the bouncing stopped.

• • •

NESSUS AWOKE INTO what sounded like negotiations. Jason and Chuft-Captain were on the public channel. Clearly Jason had found a hidden weapon mode, no more. There was no self-destruct; Jason had surely despaired.

Nessus willed himself to listen. He must survive until rescued. He must inform the Fleet about the Outsiders' ultimatum.

Chuft-Captain said, "You have discovered a new setting to the weapon."

"Have I?"

"I do not intend to play pup games with you. As a fighter, you are entitled to respect, which your herbivorous friend is not."

"How are your ribs feeling?" Jason asked.

Nessus looked himself in the eyes. His kick had more than injured Chuft-Captain. It had humiliated him. Chuft-Captain would refuse to summon any help until he had dealt with Nessus personally.

That obstinacy might allow Nessus to survive until rescue came. But if Chuft-Captain acquired the Tnuctipun weapon . . . nothing would stop him from using that last, secret setting. The Kzin would destroy the planet to take certain vengeance.

"Do not speak of that again," Chuft-Captain snarled. "We have something to trade, you and I. You have a unique weapon. I have a female human who may be your mate."

On the private channel, Nessus shouted, "You cannot trade, Jason. You must not."

Jason ignored Nessus. "Well put. So?"

"Give us your weapon. Show us where to find the new setting. You and your mate may leave the world in your ship, unharmed and unrestricted."

"Your name as your word?" Jason asked. Among Kzinti, a name was hard to come by. Most would die rather than shame their families.

The radio waves fell silent.

"You lying son of a . . ."

"Do not say it. Jason, the agreement stands, except that I will smash your hyperdrive. You must return to civilization through normal space. With that proviso you have my name as my word."

"And Nessus?"

A wordless snarl. "The herbivore must protect itself."

Something wasn't right. It wasn't the personalized hatred. *That* Nessus understood. Chuft-Captain seemed too agreeable. Would he really let witnesses go?

Jason asked, "Is she all right now?"

"Naturally."

"Prove it," Jason insisted.

"You may hear her."

"Jay, darling, listen." Anne-Marie spoke very quickly. "Use the seventh setting. The *seventh.* Can you hear me?"

"Anne, are you all right?"

"I'm fine," she shouted. "Use the seventh—" Her voice cut off.

On the private channel, Nessus said, "Seventh? That's the Tnuctipun computer. I don't understand."

There was a despairing curse.

"Jason? Jason!" No answer. Nessus' mind raced. All the talk: It was for distraction. Jason was trapped in ice, and now the enemy had recaptured him—and the weapon.

Nessus shivered in his ice cave. He had never felt more alone.

· 56 ·

Nessus crept across the ice toward the only nearby radio emissions. His suit gear could detect the signals but not decrypt them. Kzinti private-band chatter, presumably.

Every instinct demanded that he turn and gallop in the opposite direction. Citizens fled predators; they did not attack them!

On the other head, Citizens did not stray from the herd at all. They did not scout. If he was insane enough to accomplish those feats for the well-being of all, he must be insane enough to recover the Tnuctipun weapon.

And even infant Citizens knew how to kick.

Nessus recalled Achilles' legendary boast: to being vulnerable only when he presented his heel. Once more, Achilles had gotten things backward. Chuft-Captain would remember Nessus' hind hoof for as long as he lived.

Trekking over the barren ice, Nessus struggled with Anne-Marie's rushed words. The seventh setting. What use was the computer? It didn't respond to radio signals; Slaverstudent brought it into his ship to get it to respond—unintelligibly.

Spies. Weapons. Long-lost languages. Nessus had no skills with any of these things. Truly, he was insane. Delusional.

Sigmund Ausfaller was an accountant. See what *he* accomplished.

Some mania kept Nessus struggling forward. His instruments kept him on-course to the Kzinti ship. A glow came over a nearby hill, and he realized he was almost there. He stretched his necks over the crest. There was *Traitor's Claw*, its outer air-lock door open. The light came from the air lock. He wondered if Jason and Anne-Marie remained alive.

A lone Kzin in a vacuum suit stalked across the ice. Though the device protruding from his gloved paw was unfamiliar to Nessus, the awkward grip was not. It was Chuft-Captain; he was holding the Tnuctipun weapon in its hidden, deadly configuration.

Weapons. Spies. Long-lost languages. Was he overlooking something crucial, or was he—exhibiting rare, if subconscious, rationality—putting off charging again at an armed Kzin?

What would Ausfaller see? Nessus stared at the weapon in Chuft-Captain's hand. Its barrel was cylindrical. Jason had mentioned a cone. Even if there were two hidden settings, when had Jason found the second?

Chuft-Captain took a marksman's stance.

And still Nessus could not move. What would a talking computer do when spoken to in an unknown, obviously not Tnuctipun, language?

How would Ausfaller design a spy's weapon?

To respond to an unauthorized language by directing the activation of its self-destruct setting!

Nessus yanked his heads below the crest. As the world flashed blindingly bright, Nessus was already rolling himself, as well and as quickly as he could in a pressure suit, into a tight ball. The ground tossed like the ocean in a storm. It threw Nessus high into the thin air, caught him as he came down, and flung him again. And again. That time he landed directly on his cranial hump.

Once more the world went black.

NESSUS WOKE ON his back, with his legs in the air.

He climbed stiffly to his hooves, his body one giant ache, and saw he had been thrown far from the crest behind which he had sheltered. As he looked back, *Traitor's Claw* soared silently and majestically up over the crest, slowly spinning, then crashed down onto the frozen plain. One side glowed red-hot. Amid ever-thicker steam, the wreck began melting its way back into the ice from which it had so recently emerged.

No one aboard could have survived.

Nessus approached cautiously. The outer air-lock hatch was gone, ripped off. Only the beams from his helmet lit the air lock, its interior lighting presumably destroyed. The inner hatch still held pressure; he had to override safety interlocks to cycle it.

He pushed through a howling gale into the ship, then closed the inner hatch behind him. The whistling dropped but did not stop, as the environmental system labored to replace the air he had released. He searched cabins, holds, and corridors methodically, finding nothing until—

Splattered masses hardly recognizable as Kzinti clung to the walls of what Nessus remembered as the interrogation room. Orange gore dribbled down and pooled. In the center of the room, suspended in midair by the police-restraint field, hung Jason and Anne-Marie.

Both were unconscious, and they clearly labored to breathe. The restraint must be encompassing even their heads—fortunately, or the crash would have snapped their necks. Nessus tried to ignore the carnage as he sought out the release for the police restraints. Finally, he found the control. Jason and Anne-Marie dropped.

Utterly spent, Nessus followed them into unconsciousness.

THE WELL-REMEMBERED BACKGROUND whirrs, clicks, and hums of *Court Jester* enfolded Nessus. In the familiar safety of his cabin, behind a locked hatch, he breathed deeply of artificial herd pheromones from a portable synthesizer.

Cowering within a tightly rolled ball of self.

The Kzin in a nearby cabin was the least of Nessus' concerns. Frozen solid, Telepath had survived the wreck. The authorities on Jinx, now only days away, would decide when to defrost him. Another Kzin haunted Nessus—

If only he could forget the satisfying crunch of Chuft-Captain's ribs beneath his hoof.

More troublesome was the message to be sent, once he was safe and private aboard *Aegis*. True, the shadow of the antimatter solar system would no longer hang over the Fleet. It had been replaced by the longer shadow of the all-powerful Outsiders.

Momentous events lay ahead. Quivering, Nessus yearned for Hearth. He *belonged* on Hearth, to contribute to the coming debates.

But before he could go home, he had one more urgent duty to perform. . . .

REVELATIONS

Earth date: 2658

· 57 ·

Brimming with energy, shaking with trauma, utterly disoriented, Sigmund awoke.

He was flat on his back, his face scant centimeters beneath a clear dome. Beyond the dome all was black. Readouts reflected in the curved plasteel kept his eyes from adapting to the darkness.

I'm in an autodoc!

Sigmund turned away from the display in which the list of his treatments scrolled on and on. Images—too many pictures, all horrible and confusing, crowded his mind's eye. He had been here before, hadn't he? He would climb out and meet Feather. . . . It made no sense. How could he know Feather if he had yet to meet her?

What's the last thing I remember?

Unbearable pain. A gaping hole blasted through his chest. An autodoc couldn't repair *that*. . . .

Another memory gelled, of Beowulf Shaeffer telling Ander, "That thing rebuilt me from a severed head!" That thing: *Carlos Wu's* autodoc.

Reality crashed down on Sigmund. Shaeffer trying to buy off Ander with the miracle autodoc. Ander, the smoking punchgun in his hands. Shaeffer staring over the vidphone as life drained from Sigmund.

Only I'm *not* dead. Did Bey rescue me? Save me in Carlos's autodoc?

Sigmund pounded on the panic button. The lid, indifferent to his urgency, retracted with glacial slowness. He clambered out of the 'doc—feeling more limber than he had in how long? a century?—to find himself in an utterly ordinary forest glade. Stars twinkled in a moonless sky. The constellations were unfamiliar, but he hadn't been away from city lights since arriving—

On Fafnir! That memory had eluded him. How many more did likewise? He trembled with chills that had no connection with night air or his fresh-from-the-'doc nakedness. Every rustling leaf suddenly became a Kzin stalking him.

More than Sigmund had ever wanted anything, he yearned now for Earth.

Someone had rescued him and spirited him away from Shasht's capital. That someone, Bey or not, would not lightly abandon him or the incredibly valuable autodoc. This wooded clearing, however unfamiliar, was unlikely to be immediately dangerous.

With two deep, shuddering breaths, Sigmund calmed himself. As his eyes adapted to the darkness he surveyed his surroundings. He slipped on the heavy robe he found draped over the foot of the 'doc.

"Good. You're up."

Sigmund's head whipped around toward the voice. A man, short and stocky with a long ponytail, stepped from the woods. By starlight Sigmund could not discern his features or the pattern of his jumpsuit. The stranger appeared to be unarmed.

"Sorry if I startled you," the man said. "My name is Eric Huang-Mbeke. Please call me Eric. May I call you Sigmund?" The words came from Eric's mouth and, slightly clearer and delayed, from a device at his waist: a translator.

"Hello, Eric," Sigmund answered cautiously. Eric's device rendered that, too. "Can you turn that off?"

Eric did something to the device; Sigmund couldn't see what. "How is that?" Eric asked.

How *was* it? Thickly accented and oddly familiar, Sigmund thought. Not Interworld exactly. Not even Spanglish. What came before that?

The stranger's words almost reminded him of . . .

Shakespeare in Central Park. "Are you speaking *English*?"

White teeth flashed in the dark. "Exactly."

Only it wasn't quite as dark as when he first woke up, Sigmund noticed. He now sensed that Eric was swarthy, with thick lips. His hair was black, his eyes brooding and intense.

With the coming of dawn, life stirred in the woods. Sigmund twitched at every noise. He thought about rattlesnakes, mountain lions, grizzly bears—and Kzinti. "Are we safe out here?"

"Safe?" The question puzzled Eric. "Certainly."

The sun would soon rise over the trees. As the sky brightened, surprisingly quickly, Sigmund studied Eric's face. Eric looked on edge. He looked . . . expectant. Sigmund tensed.

Bright sunshine lit the glade. Sigmund glanced up.

Above the trees, an arc of tiny suns stretched across the sky.

He couldn't breathe! His new heart thudded in a chest suddenly painfully tight. His limbs had become extraordinarily heavy. The world spun around him.

Sigmund blacked out before he hit the ground.

"SIGMUND? SIGMUND? IT'S all right."

Sigmund stayed limp, wondering if *here* had opossums. Eventually, Eric sighed. Faint noises suggested pacing. Sigmund watched through eyelids scarcely parted. When Eric was across the glade, his back turned, Sigmund surged from the ground.

A twig snapped under Sigmund's bare foot. Eric turned as Sigmund dove into him, sending both crashing into the underbrush. Sigmund landed on top, and Eric deflated like a balloon.

Someone owed Sigmund answers, and Eric was here.

With the sash from his robe, Sigmund tied Eric's

arms around a tree. Beneath the dawn glare of so many suns, the ordinary pine seemed anything but normal. Sigmund reached around Eric from behind to remove his belt. "Heels against the tree," Sigmund directed, and then he secured Eric's ankles to the sturdy trunk.

"It's time for some straight talk." Sigmund gathered his flapping robe around himself. "For starters, how did I get here?"

"For starters"—the expression sounded awkward coming from Eric's mouth—"untie me. I mean you no harm. No one here does. Quite the contrary."

With a shudder, Sigmund glanced at the necklace of suns. A hint of more suns glimmered through the leaves. Another memory shook him: Andrea had *died* acquiring a glimpse of worlds like this. "I'll be the judge of that."

"Judge?" Eric said tentatively. "I don't know that word. Maybe with the translator."

Sigmund ignored the suggestion. The translator was probably also a pocket comp and communicator. He needed answers before encountering anyone else here.

Four worlds wreathed with suns. One world afire. "We're on one of the fleet of worlds, aren't we?"

Inexplicably, Eric smiled. "Not anymore. Now we call this world New Terra. We hope—"

"It *is* one of the five Puppeteer planets?" Sigmund interrupted.

"Until a few years ago, it was one of six worlds," Eric corrected, "back when it was called Nature Preserve Four. It's now separate from the Fleet. I don't understand about Puppeteers. Sigmund, do you mean the Citizens?"

"Two heads on long necks. Three legs. Voices like orchestras—or a sexy woman."

"Citizens," Eric confirmed. "I should say, that's what we were taught to call them." Bitterness lurked beneath his words. "We, their 'Colonists.' "

Something crackled in the underbrush. Sigmund

whirled but saw only trembling leaves. *Anything* could be out there. "What's that?"

"A deer, maybe? Squirrels? How should I know?" Eric sighed. "Untie me, Sigmund. Let me help. Nessus warned me this might be hard for you."

"Nessus!" Sigmund snapped. "You know him? What does he have to do with me?"

"I know him well," Eric said. "He brought you here."

· 58 ·

Citizens beyond counting packed the vast courtyard. As one, they peered fearfully upward at apparitions that towered to a thousand times their height.

Arcology walls that normally lit the plaza with simulated sunshine now glimmered with unworldly visions. Six arcologies bounded the plaza; on their immense sides loomed six *things* dark and ineffably alien: Outsider city/ships. Tiny by comparison, the General Products #2 hulls in six foregrounds only underscored the insignificance of the Concordance's works.

A low keening claimed Baedeker's attention. His necks swiveled, searching in vain for the source of the lament. It came, he decided, from all around, like the enervating heat of the crowd and the miasma of fear pheromone. Phantom ships on every side left nowhere to flee. In such a multitude, to hide oneself in the illusory safety of one's belly risked trampling.

A stentorian chorus booming from the walls silenced the throng. "On whom can you rely to restore the trust of the Outsiders? Those who would have never dealt with them? Those whose inaction would have had Hearth swallowed by the fires of Giver of Life? Those whose rigidity would have left us all helpless before the catastrophe onrushing from the galactic core?"

In other chords: Never depend upon the Conservatives amid an existential crisis.

Baedeker glanced surreptitiously about the plaza. In normal times, badges and medallions, ribbons and sashes, accessories of all colors and types would advocate for every imaginable hobby, professional affiliation, and social interest. But times were not normal, and adornments of orange and green predominated. Orange, for the governing Experimentalists, seeking the reaffirmation of a mandate amid this latest crisis. Green, for the out-of-power Conservatives, claiming their Experimentalist rivals, having brought on this latest crisis, could not now be expected to resolve it.

More every day, crowds gathered in plazas, malls, auditoria, communal dining halls, and parks across Hearth. It could hardly be otherwise: Desperate times called for proven measures.

Since time immemorial, Citizens had gathered in moments of change and crisis. Baedeker tried to imagine them, primitive and still living in tiny bands, assembling to consider a move to new grazing grounds or whether to adopt fire.

They met again now, in numbers and surroundings those forebears could never have imagined, confronting a disaster in the making. With familiar ritual and comforting tradition, as they had convened and communed in the faces of crises across the ages, Citizens in their myriads again sought consensus.

The Outsider ultimatum, all the more frightening for its vagueness, must be given an answer. And so, the public mind and mood must be assessed, informed, shaped, manipulated, consulted . . . until, ultimately, it coalesced overwhelmingly in favor of one party. For a short time, at least, all would wear one color. It looked increasingly likely the new consensus would be Experimentalist orange.

"As daunting as are the Outsiders' demands, yet more challenges lie before us." Undertunes of hope and possibility echoed across the plaza in a familiar cadence.

On alternate arcology walls, the scene from deep space faded into a new image. It was the Hindmost! His likeness slowly emerged, as large as the Outsider vessels that remained on three walls. His mane was breathtaking, variously curled, braided, and teased, thickly woven with golden ribbons, rich with orange garnets and fire opals. Such poise and resplendence bespoke a serene confidence not even the most resonant chords could convey. The crowd sighed.

"We continue our escape from the core explosion. We continue to rebuild our cadre of selfless scouts to forewarn us all of possible dangers in our path. These, surely, are also tasks to which Experimentalists are uniquely suited."

"What of provoking the Outsiders?" someone whispered in the crowd. He was insistently shushed, and given no answer.

Neither party alluded to recent events surrounding Nature Preserve 4, the proximate cause of the current emergency. Baedeker knew that neither dared: Both had left their tongueprints all over the last crisis.

And yet any solution to the present emergency must involve that errant world . . .

With a jolt, Baedeker realized how unreal this process had become to him. Maybe every consensualization was like that. Maybe all campaigns were decoupled from events, if one knew what was really happening, or any of the actors.

But he *did* know. Early in the crisis, the Hindmost himself had sought his opinion. So, amazingly, had the once and would-be Hindmost from the Conservatives. Neither wished to hear what Baedeker had to say: In this emergency, he had no miraculous technical solution to offer.

Once he had craved the attentions of the elite. For rehabilitation. For vindication. Now, those goals achieved, he wanted only anonymity and tranquility. His sole ambition was to abandon all ambition.

If only, years ago, Nessus had sought his opinion about bringing his "scouts" aboard the General Products factory. How different circumstances would be today. Baedeker restlessly pawed the resilient surface of the plaza. Nessus had precipitated this emergency, too, and yet he remained conspicuous by his absence. Not Achilles, not Vesta, not even Nike had admitted to knowing Nessus' location.

Despite his newfound search for quietude, Baedeker could not help wondering: Where *was* Nessus? What was he doing?

"My fellow Citizens," the Hindmost continued, "the time for a momentous decision will soon be upon us."

The wonder was that the time had not already passed. Baedeker studied the tiny-seeming vessel that had taken Achilles to negotiate for a reprieve. As enigmatic as the Outsiders were, they understood Citizens. They had accepted without comment Achilles' argument for forbearance as the Concordance went through its deliberations.

Understanding. Was anything ever that simple?

Perhaps delay served some alien purpose. The Outsiders might still accept the possibility that New Terra remained under Concordance control. Given the distance to the nearest Outsider ship, what could they truly know? Only what hyperspace technology revealed: Chance interception of hyperwave radio chatter. The divergence of NP4 from the Fleet, glimpsed in the repositioning of singularities in mass detectors.

"These are a wise and capable race," the Hindmost intoned. "We value their friendship. More, we must maintain and strengthen that friendship. I ask again for your trust."

Up/down, down/up; up/down, down/up . . . across the plaza, paired heads alternated in bobbing agreement.

Even now, the incontrovertible truth from the

Colonist crisis propagated outward at light speed. The chaos of the Colonists freeing the ramscoop. Their threat to deploy its fusion flames against Hearth. The consensualization that granted New Terra its freedom. Everything was revealed in those old radio broadcasts. In a few years' time, the wave front would reach the nearest Outsider ship.

So perhaps the Outsiders agreed to delay waiting for the truth they suspected must be coming, the better to validate the terrible retribution they meant to take. Was *that* the alien purpose?

It was too depressing to contemplate.

A few Hearth years could hardly matter to those who moved at the less-than-glacial pace of liquid-helium beings. . . .

All around, his fellow Citizens focused on their civic duty, intent in the moment. They communed; Baedeker observed. He was back on Hearth, but not at home. Having once resigned himself to the loneliness of exile, he wondered if he would ever again fit in. Voices rose and fell all around, and he stood, mute, unable to share.

Liquid-helium beings. That was another way he differed. He understood cold. He *remembered* cold. Now, though dripping with sweat, he shivered.

For ages, the industry and body heat of a trillion Citizens had warmed sun-less Hearth; it was the rarest of snowflakes that survived here to reach the ground. Nature Preserve 1 was entirely different, the earliest and most conservatively engineered of the companion planets. Its equatorial-orbiting suns and their annual emission cycles evoked all the climates and seasonal variability for which Hearth flora and fauna had evolved. Even as a burgeoning population had claimed the entire surface of the home world, caution ruled, and so—at a safe distance—NP1 preserved all possible Hearthian ecosystems.

From his years of banishment, Baedeker understood climate, seasons, and weather. He had seen one blizzard after another heap snow in the mountains. He had seen a single sound set off an avalanche that claimed everything in its path.

Avalanche. *That* was the nature of a consensualization. Random and inexorable—and, if you knew enough to stay *far* away, avoidable.

The herd milling around him could not begin to understand what was about to hit them.

A STRIDENT BUZZ yanked Baedeker's thoughts back to the plaza. Pavement vibrated beneath his hooves. Their haunches already pressed together, alarmed Citizens shoved back at the crowd. The discordance swelled to tooth-rattling levels.

The Hindmost's oration continued without interruption.

Bone-jarring dissonance opened a space near Baedeker, growing as the noise swelled, a cluster of stepping discs marking its center. An emergency override! The vacated discs could now be accessed by the Department of Public Safety.

Three Citizens materialized in the plaza—only not from Public Safety. All were burly. All wore the gray-and-black sashes of foreign ministry security and the slightly crazed look of bodyguards and thugs. A new buzz broke out, this time the sound of confusion.

One of the strangers spotted Baedeker. "Come with me," he said.

· 59 ·

Could *Nessus* have saved me? Had he conspired with Beowulf? Sigmund never finished working through the possibilities.

"Step back," a stern voice commanded. Another

man—no, two men—emerged from the woods. They wore camouflage jumpsuits similar in cut to Eric's.

Sigmund froze. Why wasn't he hearing people approach? It might be the distraction of his roiling thoughts, but he did not believe that.

"We mean you no harm," one of the newcomers said. "Now move away from Eric." The man who spoke was tall and wiry, with sloped shoulders. He had pinched features under a thick mop of unruly brown hair, and he spoke with quiet assurance.

The second newcomer might have stood as tall had he not stooped; he appeared soft and professorial. His hair was colorfully dyed and braided, almost like a Puppeteer. Neither carried any obvious weapon.

ARMs received extensive training in martial arts. If they were unarmed, Sigmund guessed he could take both men. Then what? Fight everyone on this world one by one? In truth, he had tackled Eric in a panic. Sigmund withdrew three paces and sat on a boulder, resting his hands, palms up, on his thighs. Grass tickled his bare feet.

The academic-seeming one shuffled over to free Eric. He peered at the knotted bathrobe belt, his expression dubious, wringing his hands.

His companion smiled. "Thank you, Sigmund. Your cooperation makes things easier. I'm Omar Tanaka-Singh. Call me Omar. My knot-challenged friend is Sven Hebert-Draskovics. Sven, just *cut* the thing off."

Sigmund flapped a lapel of his robe. "Or let me untie it. I'd like my sash back."

Omar chuckled. "You'll get real clothes soon enough. Nessus said the robe on the 'doc would be a familiar touch."

Eric was now unbound, stomping his feet and massaging his wrists to stimulate the circulation. He paused long enough to bend over and flip his belt to Sigmund. "Use this."

Sigmund suddenly noticed that he did not cast a

shadow. Neither did Omar. Eric and Sven, nearer the trees and thus out of sight of one line of suns, each had several shadows. Sigmund's chest tightened; he dare not look up at the fireballs hurtling overhead. "I want to know how I came to be here. I want to speak with Nessus."

"As he wants to talk with you. As for how you came here . . ." Omar shrugged. "Only Nessus knows.

"He meant to be present when the 'doc finished with you. He thought seeing familiar faces would be helpful. Something urgent came up elsewhere." Omar peeled the bark from a fallen twig.

Why was *Omar* nervous?

Omar threw down the denuded twig. "If it matters, Sigmund, I apologize for the shock of this. We had to awaken you somewhere. By night, at least, we hoped the woods might seem . . . normal. Nessus said our buildings wouldn't."

Sigmund cinched his robe closed with Eric's belt. "Normal. You mean, Earth-like."

"Tell us about Earth," Sven said eagerly. "There's so *much* we want to know."

"All in good time." Omar clapped his hands. "First, let's get our guest clothes and a meal."

They were Nessus' henchmen. Sigmund wondered why they expected him to tell them anything. Perhaps it was best not to dwell on that. He followed Omar into the woods, Eric and Sven falling in behind. As Omar walked, he removed something from a pocket of his jumpsuit. It looked like a controller or computer of some kind.

They stopped after a few paces. "Step after me," Omar said. He tapped at the device from his pocket, stepped onto a thin, polished disc resting on the ground—and vanished.

The disc, scarcely a meter across, worked like an open transfer booth! No wonder Sigmund had not heard anyone approach. "Where are we going?" he demanded.

Eric sighed. "For clothes and food. Sigmund, you'll get answers much faster if you can suspend your distrust. Just go through the stepping disc after Omar."

Ander had betrayed and shot him. Someone had kidnapped his dying body. Trust was a lot to ask. "And the autodoc?" Ander's greed for the 'doc had almost gotten Sigmund killed. Just as surely, that apparatus must have saved Sigmund. He would not abandon it lightly.

"I'll arrange for its storage," Eric said. "You and Sven should move along."

Sigmund stared at the disc. He couldn't remember when he had last used a transfer booth. And yet—if Eric spoke the truth—that caution hadn't kept him from the mouths of the Puppeteers.

Sigmund flicked into a dimly lit space. It was an ordinary warehouse . . . almost. The under-eave windows were oddly shaped. In shadowy corners, unfamiliar mechanisms droned with an unpleasant pitch. The colors—everything—seemed subtly wrong. He scarcely noticed Omar take hold of his elbow and guide him off the stepping disc. The floor felt strangely warm and resilient. Moments later, Sven flicked through.

A wall-mounted mirror showed Sigmund looking even younger than he felt. He could pass for twenty! Nanotech, Carlos had said. That meant Carlos's autodoc could have repaired Sigmund down to the cellular level, could have undone a lifetime's transcription errors in every strand of DNA. His sudden rejuvenation was a miracle Sigmund was too numb to take in.

In a fog, Sigmund put on a jumpsuit and boots like those worn by his escorts. The material felt eerily slick. Somehow, pinching the fabric, he set off a kaleidoscope of colors. Dynamically programmable nanocloth! Sven did something to configure the garment to a sedate and static pattern.

A bowl of fruit, mundane as could be, sat on an oval table. Sigmund extracted a random piece from the middle of the heap. It was, unambiguously, a green apple.

Suddenly he was ravenous. He devoured the apple and two bananas, then chugged a tall glass of water. He wiped his mouth on the back of a hand. "That, at least, was normal. So what now?"

"Now we give you a tour." Omar discarded the core of the pear he had been eating. "Before you'll accept anything else, we have to convince you New Terra is a *human* world."

WITH OMAR IN the fore, Sigmund flicked—

To a bustling town square, where men and women scurried about dressed in every color of the rainbow. Earth bowed to no world in its palette of clothing and skin dyes, but these buildings! Their colors clashed horribly, and the shapes and textures troubled the mind. Sigmund tore away his gaze, and followed Omar to another stepping disc—

To a park, where strolling families enjoyed the suns. (No! I can't think about that.) He focused on the people. Men and women alike wore much more jewelry than flatlanders. Adults with children wore the most. And so *many* children. . . . Sigmund stepped after Sven this time—

To a farm, where workers piloted floating conveyances across a sea of corn that stretched as far as the eye could see. Where were the birds? Sigmund wondered, as Sven led the way—

To a schoolyard, where boys and girls ran around the playground, shrieking in glee. But that playground equipment! Everything was low and soft and rounded, the Puppeteer influence undeniable. Before Sigmund could comment, Omar stepped ahead—

To a shopping district ringed with storefronts, people (and a few Puppeteers) streaming in and out of the shops, and flicking in and out of sight from an array of stepping discs.

Sigmund surely saw thousands, more likely tens of

thousands, of people, across many locations. Some places it was midday and the sky was rife with suns; other places were experiencing dawn or the approach of dusk. Sigmund had no idea where on this world he was, or how much time had passed since his revival.

Flick. On to yet someplace else. Another park, Sigmund guessed, as his eyes adjusted to the sudden dark. A brilliant object shone overhead, streaking across the sky.

"An orbital station?" Sigmund surmised.

"An orbiting ancient ramscoop." Mixed notes of pride and anger rang in Sven's voice. "It's where our story begins—and how we obtained our freedom."

"Of course we also have more modern starships," Omar added.

These strangers controlled starships! Then he could go back to Earth! Andrea and *Hobo Kelly* had searched toward . . .

Toward what?

It was *so* simple, *so* on the tip of Sigmund's tongue. The harder he tried to articulate it, the faster the answer skittered away. It was as though—

"Nessus erased my memories!" Unfamiliar stars sparkled overhead, mocking Sigmund. He smacked a fist into his other hand. "I can't find Earth."

Omar flinched. "Then we have *all* lost newly reawakened hopes."

SIGMUND'S GUIDES (OR captors?) stepped him to yet one more bustling public square. Here it was midday, and three strings of suns shone overhead. Passersby went about their business, ignoring Sigmund and his guides.

Whistling tunelessly, Sven shuffled up the broad front steps into a sprawling low-rise building. He led the way down a long corridor to a large office suite, where a discreet sign announced: New Terra Archives.

Office of the Archivist. Inside, Sven was greeted warmly, and even deferentially.

It finally occurred to Sigmund to wonder who, other than minions of Nessus, his escorts were.

"This way," Sven said. He palmed an ID pad at the end of a hallway, and a door fell open. He retreated behind a cluttered desk heaped with untidy stacks of printout. Odd images, low-quality holos and oil paintings and framed handicrafts Sigmund could not characterize, hung on the walls. Old artifacts lay jumbled on shelves. "Make yourselves comfortable."

Sigmund took a chair. "Are you *the* archivist for this world?"

"Indeed." Sven picked up a watering can and tended to a sickly potted plant sitting on the windowsill, not meeting Sigmund's eyes. "You can imagine how eager I am to talk with you."

The shy deference was too surreal. *Everything* was. "Tanj it, I want answers! Why was I kidnapped? When will Nessus explain himself?" Sigmund turned to glower at Omar and Eric. "How are you all involved with Nessus? Are you also in the government?"

Eric canted his head. "Tanj? Kidnapped? I'm not following. Sigmund, I'd like to reactivate the translator. Whatever you speak isn't English, exactly."

But *kidnapped* was English. The Lindbergh baby had been kidnapped long before Spanglish or Interworld. "What happened here? Your version of English has been purged."

"Our language?" Eric said. His eyes blazed. "Our language? That's the least of our losses." He turned to Sven. "Show him."

THE MAN IN the vid was dark: eyes, hair, and complexion. He was of indeterminate age, his face creased with worry lines. The tartan jumpsuit he wore only emphasized a pudgy body build. His expression was worldly wise and weary, and yet it somehow gave a hint of humor.

He spoke. "I am the navigator of starship *Long Pass*. I have a story to tell.

"My name is Diego MacMillan.

"I speak human to human, ancestor to descendant. Despite everything that has gone wrong, I retain hope humans will find this message. I had to hide the key in plain sight, trusting my ability to make the clues meaningful only to humans.

"And yet . . ."—Diego scowled—"I cannot depend on that. If our descendants are viewing this, I know how you must yearn for the location of your home, the planet Earth. To leave you *that* information would risk revealing it to the Citizens and leading these murderers to Earth itself. That I will not do."

"How?" Sigmund interrupted. He was an ARM, tanj it, and this was a crime against Earth. A crime against humanity.

Sven tapped a control pad and the holo froze. "It's a long and twisty tale, but a few years ago we recovered that recording. It had been hidden, disguised and encrypted, in the bridge computer of the old ramscoop. *Long Pass*."

"We?" Sigmund prompted.

Sven nodded. "Omar, Eric, and Eric's spouse, Kirsten. They weren't yet mated. And, in a small way, myself."

"And it was all in plain sight, orbiting this world," Sigmund said skeptically.

"We're not such fools," Omar snapped. "We were raised to believe Citizens had salvaged embryo banks and a few damaged computers from a derelict long adrift in the void. Our mere existence was a testament to their patience, skill, and generosity of spirit."

"Only the ship had been seized. It was almost intact, hidden inside a General Products Number Four hull." Eric bared his teeth. "Until I busted it apart."

Sigmund twitched. "You destroyed a General Products hull?"

"We're getting ahead of ourselves," Sven interrupted. "Hear what happened after they reached the Fleet of Worlds." He jumped the recording ahead.

Diego MacMillan unfroze. "There our nightmare became far worse. *Long Pass* carried more than ten thousand passengers, mostly frozen embryos. Our masters say their Concordance took pity, that they could not let so many perish. A few Citizens admit—but only to us, the few forever trapped onboard—that they intend to turn our helpless passengers into a slave race. I believe they're at least being honest." Tears glimmered in his eyes. "Two of those little ones are Jaime's and mine.

"The Citizens removed our onboard hibernation tanks to the world they call Nature Preserve Three. They lied to those they awakened about a derelict found adrift. Even so, most people had their doubts. When Citizens encouraged them to start their planned colony, the women resisted immediate implantation with embryos.

"*Long Pass* also carried embryos of mammals, cows and sheep and such, we meant to introduce on New Terra. Of course we had artificial placentas for those animal embryos. The Citizens were determined to have their colony. They experimented with implanting human embryos into artificial animal placentas. They 'refused to accept our voluntary extinction.' "

Sigmund shuddered. Every worry or doubt he had ever had about Puppeteers . . . this was worse. This was an abomination.

"There were spontaneous abortions, horrific birth defects, and developmental problems." Remembered tragedies brought Diego to an eye-blinking halt. "To our masters, those were 'experiments.' To us . . . each was someone's child. Several women agreed to be surrogate mothers to stop the 'experiments.' "

Diego got himself back under control. "And the men still aboard this ship? We counsel our masters how to structure a human society. We try through our advice to alleviate a bit of the suffering. We're trying to reduce forced pregnancies, especially by brain wiping. All the men insist that the mother's active role in child rearing is critical. Two centuries of gender equality is a small sacrifice to save women's minds."

"Two centuries?" Sigmund echoed. "*Long Pass* must have left Earth in the late twenty-second century. This travesty has gone on for more than four hundred years."

"Five hundred by our reckoning." Eric shook his head. "That's in Hearth years, of course. We don't even know how long an Earth year is."

Then the bigger implication left Sigmund speechless. *Long Pass* was captured long before Puppeteers first appeared in Human Space. No wonder the aliens were quick to understand humans: They had had decades of practice. Puppeteers indeed. . . .

The recording had not stopped. "We do what else we can. Sometimes that's in the vocabulary and concepts we try to retain in the sanitized English taught to the children. Sometimes it's undoing the effects of Citizen mistakes." Diego smiled, almost despite himself. "Citizens are hardly beyond error. They wear no clothing, so they considered Colonist clothing a waste of resources. They learned quickly enough that nudity does not go with their disapproval of birth control *and* their hopes of controlling the bloodlines."

The smile faded. "I fear they suspect our indirect interference. We've been told of a new colony, this one on NP Four, started with only children under Citizens' supervision.

"All that remains for me is hope for the children. If you viewing this recording are like me, are human, know this: You descend from an accomplished people. We settled our whole solar system. We planted colonies, *peacefully*, on the worlds of other suns." Diego swallowed hard. "I wish I could give you the way home. Earth is a beautiful world.

"And if you viewing this recording are Citizens, I wish you go straight to hell."

SIGMUND STARED AT the ceiling, afloat in a sleeper field, with no hope of sleeping anytime soon. The dim glow of a lighting panel was his only company, his three guides having left him.

There was much yet to learn of the dark and twisted history of the New Terrans. Sigmund and his new friends had talked and talked—until he found himself slumped on the floor of Sven's office. Exhaustion or hunger? Flat-phobic overload or post-'doc rebound? Any or more likely all of them; it hardly mattered.

They ate. Sven brought Sigmund home, clucking sympathetically. He shooed the others away, and established Sigmund in his guest room. That helped, but short of drugs, Sigmund could not imagine sleeping.

He wrestled with the day's revelations like a terrier worrying at a rat. Millions enslaved for centuries. Heroes recovering their suppressed past against all odds. A trillion Puppeteers held at bay by the threat of fusion fire from a hovering ramscoop. Nessus, his bane for so many years, an advocate for New Terra.

Deep into the night, as he at last faded into restless oblivion, Sigmund's final thought concerned Nessus: *his* nemesis and yet the ally of the New Terrans.

Why had Nessus abducted Sigmund and brought him here?

. 60 .

The Hindmost's retreat hugged a verdant coastal mountainside, the setting spectacular and extravagantly private. Behind a weatherproof force field, the veranda afforded a breathtakingly panoramic view of rocky strand and crashing surf. The mansion itself was luxuriously spacious, impeccably decorated, and sumptuously furnished. I will have one built to rival it, Achilles decided, once . . .

First things first. It was too soon to be designing his official residence.

He and Vesta shared the veranda with a floating holographic Outsider ship. "It keeps me focused on the true problem," Nike had volunteered, before stepping to his broadcast studio.

Nike stepped back immediately after his speech, and Vesta was quick to update him. Instant-reaction focus groups had responded favorably. Semantic analyses suggested the media trending to the Experimentalist point of view. Real-time scene analyses, sampling public-safety cameras across Hearth, showed crowds ever more orange in their adornment. Counterrallies of the Conservatives had been poorly attended. Surely the Experimentalists' support was reaching the tipping point.

To all of which Nike said, "A mandate is not a policy."

Vesta took the words as a rebuke. He pawed the floor, the marble tile ringing softly under his dainty hoof. "Of course, Nike. Understood. We still need to placate the Outsiders. Since it is impossible to prove NP Four remains under our control, we'll end up paying to transfer control of the drive. That will take serious money. Human or Kzinti money," he added unhappily.

"I need new choices, not complaints," Nike chided. "We have a year, and are fortunate the Outsiders allowed us that. Then what?"

Vesta lowered his heads submissively.

While poor Vesta struggled to explain himself, Achilles wondered: With whose currency did Vesta expect to make payment? As the herd galloped away, of course the Outsiders lost interest in Concordance money. *Whose* currency hardly mattered; the amount was the problem. The price of the planet-moving drive was enormous.

Achilles prided himself on his realism. The Concordance could not afford to pay. The troublesome refugees on their ill-gotten world could not even comprehend the size of the payment—not that anyone proposed to involve them. That left somehow reclaiming Nature Preserve 4 for the Fleet—whether anyone on NP4 wanted back in or not.

Or, to be complete, obliterating NP4 would also remove the Outsiders' grounds for complaint. Destroying it *safely* was the challenge. True, the Concordance need no longer fear antimatter. The ex-Colonists still had General Products ships of their own. They had their ancestors' ramscoop. Even the rubble of a successfully shattered NP4, strewn in the path of the Fleet, would be fearfully dangerous. Only utter desperation could justify that course of action—

And besides, I can hardly rule NP4 if I allow it to be destroyed.

A soft vibrato sounded from a pocket of his sash: success chimes from Pan, the senior acolyte tasked to retrieve Baedeker. "Nike, Vesta, I've arranged for an outside expert to join us."

Baedeker entered a moment later, walking stiffly, indifferent to the grandeur around him. Four of the Hindmost's personal guards escorted him.

"Our reclusive master engineer returns," Nike warbled. His undertunes hinted at surprise and disapproval. Dropping off the net was legal, certainly, but it was unusual. Unavailability for the summons of the Hindmost . . . that was, if *still* not illegal, unprecedented.

"Indeed." Achilles saw no reason to mention Vesta's abuse of his position to have Baedeker tracked through the stepping-disc system, nor the guards sent to intimidate the engineer. "You asked for new options. We all remember the wild humans catching sight of the Fleet. With Baedeker's insight, we remotely deactivated the hull of their ship. The Outsider grievance is the world that ranges freely ahead of us. Let us fix the problem as directly.

"I challenge Baedeker to duplicate his past triumph by remotely disabling its planetary drive."

TO CAST A world adrift!

Baedeker's blood ran cold, and yet an insistent voice in the back of his hump wondered: Can it be done? The planetary drives were perhaps the most closely guarded resources in the Concordance. To have access to them, to study them, perhaps to discover how they worked . . .

No! His instinctive revulsion had been correct. "You would leave New Terra floating in the void to placate the Outsiders?"

Achilles' heads swiveled; he stared himself in the eyes for a mockingly long time before commenting, "So you don't think you can do it."

"That's not the point," Baedeker trilled, using a minor chord to emphasize his dismay. He had been a slave on NP1. That changed a person. Nessus' three "scouts"—Baedeker had issues with *them*. But to sacrifice an entire world for wanting its freedom?

Anyway, where was Nessus? The ex-Colonists needed their advocate more than ever. "Nessus understands the New Terrans better than most. Perhaps he can offer a suggestion."

Nike whistled dismissively. "He also is slow to respond to a summons."

Baedeker flinched. "This action would endanger millions."

"Excellent," Vesta fluted. "You imply it can be done. Once we render these ingrates helpless, they will beg to rejoin us. We will dictate the terms." He glanced meaningfully at Achilles, for what reason Baedeker had no idea.

Were they not listening, or was their desperation so great? Baedeker said, "This is evil. I will not take part."

Across the gallery, trays of cracked nuts and freshly chopped grasses were arrayed on a low table, in front of an assortment of juices in crystalline decanters. Achilles strolled to the refreshments and poured a beverage. "It is impossible to pay the Outsiders. It is unacceptable to live with armed New Terrans in our midst, even if they would agree to rejoin the Fleet. And yet we must do *something*, lest the wrath of the Outsiders fall upon the herd."

Achilles paused for a leisurely sip, his conscience untroubled. "Let us be reasonable, Baedeker. *You* would do evil to leave us without options. Without another alternative, Clandestine Directorate will instead, when the moment is right, disable the drive by more direct means: a surprise bombardment from space." He took another long drink. "The physicist in me wonders what will happen then."

The Hindmost stepped forward. "This is promising, Achilles. If their world can be set adrift in space, the New Terrans' few ships become lifeboats, too precious to squander on revenge attacks."

Mysterious technology. Unknown energies, sufficient to move a world, unleashed in an instant. *Anything* could happen. And who could say that the effects might not reach even to the Fleet?

That plan was evil *and* reckless. Unhappily, Baedeker said, "Give me access to one of our planetary drives. I will see what I can learn."

IN THE PRIVACY of Vesta's Clandestine Directorate office, Achilles raised a goblet. "To progress."

"To progress," Vesta agreed. "The question remains: Will Baedeker succeed?"

Achilles drained his glass and sprawled across a pile of cushions. Alone, there was no need to pretend he took direction from his earnest disciple. "Baedeker will succeed. With his misplaced concern for New Terra to motivate him, I am more certain of that than ever."

So certain, in fact, that Achilles decided the time *had* arrived to design the official residence of his future domain on Nature Preserve 4.

. 61 .

Everything on Hearth was old.

The marble frieze that ringed the office *looked* old—and magnificent. The honey-colored stone, aglow with a soft translucence, had been transformed by an undisputed master. Gods, men, horses—each perfect in every aspect, from the least detail of musculature to the subtlest nuance of draped clothing and flying hooves and streaming manes—commanded the viewer's awe.

Had Lord Elgin left these superb carvings in place upon the Parthenon, they would long ago have been destroyed. And if I had not had them taken from the British Museum?

Nessus told himself that Phidias' masterwork was safer here than on Earth, ignoring that Citizens had become the biggest danger to Earth. And that his motives for transporting the marbles had involved not one shred of altruism.

Perhaps it boded well that Nike had brought the marbles with him when he became Hindmost. So much remained unspoken between them. Nessus had only signs and inferences to go on, and yet his passion for Nike had, if it was possible, grown in the years he had been away. If Nike ever suspected that he did more than advocate for the ex-Colonists . . . Nessus smoothed an unruly braid as he waited for the guards who had escorted him to the office to leave.

"It is good to see you again, Nessus." Nike brushed heads in greeting. Welcoming, certainly, but reserved.

"It has been a long time," Nessus trilled. How he wished for a small fraction of Nike's poise.

Nike gestured to a mound of cushions, before settling onto another. "I noticed you admiring the marbles. They *are* unique. I value your gift as a token of our friendship."

Friendship! The possibility had been there once for much more. Before New Terra went free. Before doubts and suspicions about how far each had been prepared to go to ensure a desired outcome.

Nessus held his pain inside. "My friendship is always yours."

"I wonder: Why so long a time?" Nike straightened in his heap of pillows; undertunes of formality sounded in his voices. "It is unlike you to disregard a summons home."

So much for personal matters. "My apologies, Nike. I returned as quickly as I could. Attending to General Products interests on so many human worlds . . ." Vagueness was not a lie, Nessus told himself. He was *so* tired of lying.

"What matters?" Nike probed. "Which worlds?"

"Earth, Jinx, Down . . . you name it." Just don't name Fafnir.

"And you couldn't come faster?"

Not even the Hindmost pressed scouts very hard. The Concordance had too few misfits capable of doing what Nessus did, fewer still since the lost ships and mass insanity that marked the onset of the Exodus. "I came as soon as I could," he said sincerely. After surveying thousands of the flyspeck islands in the oceans of Fafnir to find Carlos Wu's lost autodoc. "I came to you directly from the spaceport."

The summons had been urgent. What had Nessus missed through his delay? "About the Outsiders," he began. "Of course I am aware of the consensualization." During *Aegis*' final approach to the Fleet, he had immersed himself in the broadcasts. They told him little. "Understandably, speeches disclose nothing of the proposed policy."

"Understandably."

An unsubtle reminder of my own evasiveness, Nessus thought. "I was the first to know the complaint of the Outsiders. You must understand my interest."

"The matter is in strong jaws," Nike answered. More evasion.

Behind Nike, a tableau on the marbles caught Nessus' eyes. Zeus, Hindmost of the gods, and Athena, the goddess of wisdom.

What wisdom counsels this Hindmost?

The Concordance was in debt to the Outsiders far into the future. Surely the Outsiders would accept no more promises now that the Fleet was in full flight. If taking on more debt wasn't credible, what options did that leave the Fleet? "What will we do?"

"Achilles and Baedeker are collaborating on a solution." Nike fixed him with a frank, two-headed stare. "Had you been on Hearth—"

"Achilles is reckless and selfish," Nessus blurted. And Achilles hates humans. "You *must* know of the cult he once tried—"

"Stop!" These were the harshest of insults, and Nike blinked in surprise. "Know this: Achilles has the favor of the Hindmost. *He* has been most helpful." The tremolo in Nike's voices forbade further interruption.

"We have too few scouts. I ask you to reinvigorate the training program." Nike stood abruptly: meeting over. "Others will tend to matters with the Outsiders."

"You once trusted *me*," Nessus sang desperately.

"And you see where my trust got us," Nike said icily.

• 62 •

As he had for days, Sigmund woke depressed. Routine got him out of the sleeper field and Sven's guest room. Fiddling with the still-awkward controls of the sonic shower, Sigmund wondered how best to fill the day. You could be dead, he lectured himself again. Snap out of it.

And convinced no one.

He had lost his life, his love, his purpose, even some of his memories.

Not that long ago women here had been brainwiped, the better to serve as unwilling wombs. Doubtless the Puppeteers had learned from their experiments how to excise memories more selectively. That possibility tainted with guilt every *intact* memory Sigmund had.

I'm entitled to mope, tanj it.

Sigmund was in no hurry to see his host. Sven was unfailingly polite, even deferential, brimming with questions about the worlds *Long Pass* had left behind. Prehistory, the archivist called it.

From what Sigmund remembered, English was an irrational-enough language to start. Purged by aliens for a political agenda, stripped of its historical context . . . no wonder New Terra's linguists were so often at a loss.

A dreary existence stretched before him, of endless pedantic interrogation about events long before his time. He recalled trivia and odd facts when only the whole historical record would ever satisfy them.

Sigmund got dressed, his New Terran jumpsuit programmed to a familiar black. That was something else Sven babbled endlessly about: clothing colors. Sigmund had never wasted his time worrying about fashion; he refused to start now.

Cheerful whistling from the kitchen interrupted his

brooding. Not Sven: He couldn't carry a tune. Seeing Sven's cousin as he rounded the corner, Sigmund felt better. "Good morning, faithful Penelope."

Penelope Mitchell-Draskovics was as tall as Sigmund. She bubbled with enthusiasm, and moved with the easy grace of an athlete. Soccer, was it? She had big blue eyes, usually twinkling, and rosy cheeks. She asked as many questions as anyone. From her Sigmund did not mind.

"Good morning!" Penelope said. "It's about time. What's for breakfast today?"

He considered. "A Denver omelet." She understood omelets, but of course not Denver. They talked as he assembled his ingredients. (On Earth, he would merely have ordered a meal from the synthesizer. Once he got the proportions just right, he would give the synthesizer a sample.) They talked about everything and nothing. Denver, the mile-high city. The Rockies. Grizzly bears. Skiing.

They didn't ski here. They didn't have much in the way of winter, he finally realized. The climate was much the same everywhere, optimized for agriculture by the polar-orbiting suns. It made him strangely sad.

Breakfast was finally ready. He scooped a heaping portion onto her plate. "A Denver treat for faithful Penelope."

She paused, her fork in midair. "Why do you always call me that? Faithful, I mean."

That led to the *Iliad* and the *Odyssey,* of myth and legend and epic adventure, of Odysseus' long-delayed return to Ithaca and the wiles of his wife, Penelope, turning away the unwelcome advances of suitors. . . .

"Something smells good," Sven said.

Sigmund had not noticed his host enter the kitchen. Without losing the thread of the story—he had backtracked to the Cyclops—Sigmund loaded up a plate for Sven.

Sven attacked his serving with gusto. "It's good that we're having a hearty breakfast," he said. "We have a big day ahead of us."

NESSUS ACCEPTED A bulb of warm carrot juice. "I'm flattered you remembered," he told Kirsten.

She patted the synthesizer. "How could I not? We four spent a lot of time together here."

The synthesizer was familiar; everything else about *Explorer* had changed, with most signs of onetime Citizen presence removed. The Y-shaped bench of his onetime crash couch was gone from the bridge, along with the mouth-friendly console. Padding had been stripped from hatchways throughout the ship. The relax room had only human exercise gear.

His onetime scouts had also changed. Omar, his once-obsequious captain, now calculating and assertive. Eric, his once-loyal engineer, now openly suspicious. His hair, a few years ago colorfully dyed and arranged in Citizen style, was now all black in a simple ponytail. Kirsten, computer virtuoso and his former navigator, now mated with Eric and the mother of their two young ones.

None of which mattered. The fruition of years' work was upon Nessus, and it was all he could do not to flee. "I am ready," he said.

Kirsten took out her pocket comp and placed a call. "They're ready, too."

In preparation for this meeting, a second stepping disc had been placed in the relax room. Nessus positioned himself on it. "Proceed."

Sven appeared on the disc at the opposite end of the room. He stepped aside.

FROM THE VILLAGE square near Sven's house, Sigmund stepped after Sven—

Into a spaceship.

Only familiar faces kept him from freaking out. Omar and Eric. Sven. A woman Sigmund had not met stood by Eric. With a shudder, Sigmund moved off the stepping disc—

And caught sight, across the crowded room, of a Puppeteer. His eyes did not match, one red and one yellow.

Nessus! All the bottled-up rage erupted, and Sigmund lunged. There was a crackling noise.

He woke on the deck, limbs tingling from the aftereffects of a stunner.

Omar helped Sigmund up. "Nessus is here to talk. Can we trust you?"

Sigmund nodded. *They* could trust him. Nessus was the one who should fear him. And yet who but Nessus could possibly explain? "Why am I here, Nessus?"

Nessus edged closer. "You don't trust me, with good cause, but that must change."

Sigmund said nothing.

Nessus picked up a drink bulb and sipped something orange. Whatever it contained seemed to calm him. "Yes, I brought you here. I followed you to Fafnir—for reasons that you can only now begin to appreciate." Another calming sip. "You were unapproachable on Earth."

"Because I stopped using transfer booths. Because *you* were behind the Cerberus extortions."

"Yes, to both." Nessus made a noise like a balloon deflating. "But it is the paranoid brilliance of your insight that makes you so necessary *here*."

Avoiding sudden moves, Sigmund sidled to the synthesizer and got a bulb of coffee. "I don't understand the abduction or the flattery, Nessus. Why am I here?"

Nessus backed onto his stepping disc. One head plunged into a pocket of his utility belt. Sigmund had been on New Terra long enough to guess the Puppeteer held a transport controller. He was ready to step out.

Whatever Nessus had to say was going to be unpleasant.

NESSUS SPOKE FOR a long time. "You're pawns," he concluded. "All that matters to the authorities on Hearth is that the crisis be settled."

"And that means paying off the Outsiders for New Terra's use of its own planetary drive," Sigmund summarized. "Only you can't. New Terra can't. And your government obviously sees no chance of reconciliation. If they thought otherwise, they would have opened negotiations. Instead, they kept the situation to themselves.

"Hence the pawn analogy—these people are going to be sacrificed. So what will it be? Their independence crushed? Their drive destroyed? Their *world* destroyed?"

"So I fear, Sigmund." Nessus' voice was thin, one throated. He still had one head deep within a pocket, the controller there one quick tongue thrust away from activation. "I don't know another answer. I can't imagine how to stop them."

As the only Puppeteer in reach, he *should* be afraid.

The New Terrans were stunned. They had more to absorb, even, than the threat. Sigmund gathered this was the first they had ever heard of the galaxy's elder race. The Outsiders also traded with Earth; naturally no Puppeteer had ever mentioned their servants to the Outsiders.

Eric was the first to shake off his shock. "Then we'll take Hearth down with us! I'll crash this ship into Hearth myself!"

"Your death helps no one!" Kirsten shouted. Her voice softened. "I need you. Your children need you. We need another way."

"Nessus," Sigmund said softly. His hands yearned to

crush the life out of someone; he clutched them fiercely behind his back. "Let me contact the ARM."

Nessus' exposed head swung from side to side as though hinged. Maybe it was. "If I thought that an option, I would have told you long ago. To involve Earth would mean disclosing our former colony. It's why we struggled so hard to keep secret the location of the Fleet."

"And you failed." Sigmund considered. Not, damn you all, without cost. "The ARM would go to war to protect these people."

"Then stealthed General Products hulls would pummel Earth," Nessus said. "All human worlds. There will be no hesitation and no mercy if Hearth is endangered."

Sigmund thought about his dogged pursuit of the Puppeteers, and all the attempts, from bribery to Fertility Law riots to space pirates, to distract him. "Up until now you've tried to dissuade us by more subtle means."

Nessus judged it safer to admit nothing.

"You kidnapped me. You've tampered with my memory so I can't get help from other human worlds. What, exactly, do you expect me to do?"

"I do not know." The head not deep in a pocket plunged deep into Nessus' mane, plucking furiously. In a muffled voice he said, "For everyone's sake, I hope you will figure something out."

Sigmund took a deep breath. "Before I do anything, Nessus, you're going to answer some questions for me. For, for starters . . ." He stuttered to a halt, the anger that filled him refusing to stay down any longer.

"For starters, why in the name of Finagle aren't I dead?"

"I WAS TOO late," Nessus said.

Nessus struggled to keep the fear from his voice. I kicked an armed Kzin, he told himself. I can talk with an unarmed human.

Without Sigmund's help, this world would die. Eric and others would take many on Hearth with them. Sigmund's price was answers. Truth. As with the ordeal on Cue Ball, he *must* live through this.

Maybe not the whole truth.

"You were too late," Sigmund repeated.

"I bribed a hotel manager to hide bugs and stepping discs in your rooms. My only purpose was to talk to you about aiding New Terra." That his actions preceded the Outsider ultimatum was a detail best glossed over. Too much truth would only cloud the issue. "I stepped to Ander's room just as you were shot."

Fear had kept him from making his approach for days. That was another truth best kept unarticulated.

"Ander grabbed your money and fled the scene. A maid ran in, saw . . . you, and ran back out." A body with a hole blasted through it larger than one of his heads. Blood everywhere. "Later I got access to the police report. The maid went for ice to chill down your head. If you had had a lesser wound, she might have even saved your life.

"I stepped into your room the moment she left, dragged you to the disc, and got you out. By the time the maid and hotel security got to your room, all they found was too much blood." And patches of ash, after the rigged stepping discs in both men's hotel rooms incinerated.

"Leaving the police to assume Ander had an accomplice." Sigmund cocked his head. "Perhaps he did. You."

"No!" Nessus said. "I cannot prove that, but no. Ander acted out of greed."

"You're not beyond bribery, are you, Nessus? You bought my boss once. Why shouldn't I believe you worked with Ander to get Carlos's magic autodoc?"

Nessus resisted the urge to vanish. He dare not imply guilt—however much he felt. "I corrupted officials more than once. That's how I got access to the Fafnir police report on your apparent death. But no, I did *not* have anything to do with the attack."

"Cops aren't big believers in coincidence. Paranoids certainly aren't. So explain: Somehow you had Carlos's autodoc."

Nessus shifted weight between his hooves. "The thing is, Sigmund, I didn't. Right at the end, though, I was in the next room. I heard Ander and Beowulf talking. I heard that the autodoc was hidden on an island, and the approximate longitude. After that, I had to search."

"My heart had been shot out." Sigmund inched closer. "I wouldn't have survived any search."

Nessus somehow stood his ground. "No, you wouldn't. We went straight from your hotel room to my ship. I put you into a stasis field. It's where you stayed until I retrieved the 'doc."

After he was ordered to Jinx, and went with the Papandreous in search of Outsiders. After, in his desperation, he assaulted a Kzin. After he defied the summons of the Hindmost to first scour a thousand islands, one by one. Nessus kept to himself how he had hesitated even then, unsure how Sigmund would respond.

Now Nessus would find out if all that had been for naught.

Sigmund stopped his advance. "And what of Ander?"

"Dead in a shoot-out with Fafnir police." Nessus surrendered to nerves, pawing at the deck with a hoof. "A squad of Kzinti."

"Serves the bastard right," Sigmund snarled. "And Bey?"

"Beowulf Shaeffer?" For once, Nessus could answer without evasion. "His name does not appear anywhere in the investigation report."

"What names do?"

"Hotel staff, waiters, bartenders, and bar customers. The authorities were thorough enough. They even pulled someone out of deep freeze just before his iceliner was going to leave. The man had had dinner with Ander a few days earlier. It turns out they met at the water wars."

"And this corpsicle's name?"

Nessus needed a moment to remember the name. "Martin Graynor. Does that mean anything to you?"

Sigmund pondered, then slowly shook his head. "It doesn't."

For once, Nessus thought, I'm not the one pretending.

· 63 ·

"You'd like to believe, Sigmund," Kirsten called out. "So far you don't."

Sigmund had been stuck in the corridor, steeling himself to move. Spaceships still terrified him; on the bridge, there could be no pretending he was anywhere but. Willing himself forward, he went onto the bridge. "Sensors in the halls?"

"Good ears—and skulking in the halls. It had to be you." She patted the seat next to hers. "Sit."

The crash couch might have come from the bridge of *Hobo Kelly* or *Seeker*. Thinking of either ship made him queasy. Still, the couch really *could* have come from ships he'd been on. On the armrests, the layout of controls was identical. The fabric crinkled as he squirmed, no different from a thousand times before. It made sense: Why wouldn't the Puppeteers import human-engineered equipment for their servants?

It meant he could hot-wire the emergency protective field of the crash couch into a restraint field. There was no one he needed to restrain just now, but the idea was comforting.

"Do you want to talk about it?" Kirsten prompted.

Did he? Sven said Kirsten was a genius. She had

found the first hints of the colony's true past hidden in the computer of this very ship. Surprising himself, Sigmund decided to give it a try. "Believe what? That some Puppeteers aren't evil?"

"Most are like us. They want nothing more than to be left alone to live their lives."

"Why did Nessus want to meet me *here*? On a ship?"

"You really dislike ships, don't you? People here are descended from explorers. I couldn't quite believe it when Nessus told us about flat phobes." Kirsten did something with the console, and the bridge screen de-opaqued. A tarmac stretched before them, with surprisingly few ships on it. "See, we're on the ground.

"To answer your question, it wasn't you Nessus had in mind when he picked the ship. He chose this place to reassure Eric, Omar, and me. Understand this, Sigmund: We can't entirely trust him, either. Yes, he's been an intermediary, sometimes arguing our case. He's still a Citizen. If circumstances ever came down to a stark choice between Concordance interests or New Terra's—"

"That's an excellent point," Nessus said. He stood in the hatchway, as though ready to bolt—as he probably was. "Sigmund, your task is to see to it such circumstances never arise."

BALANCED ON A knife's edge. It was a quintessentially human saying, but apt. The question remained: Could Sigmund be turned from adversary to ally?

Nessus said, "You still have doubts, I think."

"With cause, certainly." Sigmund got out of his crash couch to face him. "You have much to answer for."

More than you know, Nessus thought. More than he could possibly reveal without inciting an attack. The problem was, only information could bring Sigmund to trust him. After much agonizing, Nessus had decided what secret he could disclose. "As a show of good faith, I'm going to tell you about Gregory Pelton and the antimatter."

Sigmund *and* Kirsten twitched at that statement. Antimatter had that effect on sentient beings. "Go on," Sigmund said cautiously.

"I'll start with what I think you know. Pelton wanted to do something spectacular. He and Beowulf Shaeffer took Pelton's ship, *Slower than Infinity,* to an Outsider vessel. There, they bought the coordinates of the 'most unusual world.' How am I doing?"

"Max Addeo earned what you paid him," Sigmund said.

As did Sangeeta Kudrin, a detail Nessus did not plan to share. "You also know that Pelton and Shaeffer made an emergency call to Jinx after their hull dissolved. What you don't know is that Pelton contacted one of my colleagues, in hiding on Jinx. It was he who deduced what had happened. The most unusual planet and its star are made of antimatter. The antimatter solar wind eventually destroyed the hull. General Products paid the warranty in full."

"Who is this colleague?" Sigmund asked.

"He's sometimes known as Achilles. Foolishly, he revealed what had happened. Fortunately, Pelton remained obsessed with a spectacular personal accomplishment. He kept what he knew secret from the government."

"But not from *me*," Sigmund said.

Let him feel smug, Nessus thought. "Pelton's adventure came soon after the discovery of the core explosion. The Concordance was already in a panic. Because Pelton's crippled ship entered Sirius system at relativistic speed, the antimatter system must also be moving at like speeds. That meant he must have gotten a lift from the Outsiders. It was deemed enough to just monitor the problem, until, with its terrific speed, the antimatter receded beyond human reach."

Sigmund nodded. "My expert reached the same conclusion about Outsider involvement. It didn't make me any less vigilant."

Nessus did *not* want to explain having left Sigmund, dying, in stasis for almost three Earth years. He chose his next words especially carefully. "Then, seemingly, you died. Your mysterious murder and disappearance gave your 'in-the-event-of-my-death' messages great credibility—even before Pelton fled to asylum on Jinx. Suddenly the ARM is in an emergency effort to find and secure the antimatter system."

"Suddenly?" Sigmund folded his arms across his chest. "I'd say it's about time."

No, it was one more reason to consider a preemptive strike against Earth. "The Hindmost deemed it urgent that we find the antimatter before the ARM did. Buying the coordinates from the Outsiders no longer seemed a waste of resources. For technical reasons"—fearing my ship was bugged—"I hired a human ship and crew for the mission. We found Ship Fourteen. . . ."

Sigmund looked skeptical.

Sigmund was unique, but this was all so beyond the scope of his experience. Was even this carefully edited glimpse of the truth too much? What would you think, Sigmund, about the Outsiders having a Tnuctipun stasis box?

Keep it simple, Nessus told himself. "I had means at my disposal human ships do not. I gave my crew the coordinates to search for the Outsiders. Once we rendezvoused, I spent much of General Products' remaining wealth purchasing the location of the antimatter system. Unlike Gregory Pelton, I also thought to buy their silence. They will not disclose this information to their next visitors.

"Happily, it's barely grazing Known Space. That course, combined with its great speed, will make exploiting the antimatter virtually impossible."

"And that's supposed to comfort me, Nessus?"

"Probably not," Nessus said, "nor is it my intent.

You're of no use to me or New Terra if you feel comfortable."

"YOU WERE QUIET," Sigmund said. "What do you conclude?"

Kirsten brushed unruly bangs from her forehead. "That Nessus knows more than he shared."

"He always does. Nothing he said contradicts what I know." Sigmund jammed his hands in his pockets. It was that or try to put a fist through a plasteel bulkhead.

What in his head, besides the location of Earth, had the Puppeteer messed with?

· 64 ·

"There," Eric said unnecessarily.

An image floated before Sigmund, downlinked from an orbiting telescope. The instrument's normal assignment was scanning for space junk as New Terra sped through the interstellar darkness. Now, at Sigmund's request, it displayed a much more likely threat.

Five balls hung in the center of the room, rotating about their center of mass. Sigmund had seen something like it once before—but not quite like this. Not so close. Not so real.

Hobo Kelly had glimpsed the Fleet of Worlds from a distance of light-years. (From what direction? he asked himself. The answer still defied him.) New Terra was only 0.03 light-years out in front of the Fleet. (Defined in Hearth years, of course. The length of an Earth year was too valuable a clue for the world they sought. Of course it was gone.) New Terra pulled ahead slowly, using their planetary drive at full acceleration. The Puppeteers, not surprisingly, ran theirs well below the rated capability.

"It's the only sky we ever knew," Eric said. "And now, except through a 'scope, we can't see it at all."

Sigmund blinked, unable to grasp *that.*

Five worlds, four ringed with tiny suns, one on fire, as before—but not *just* as before. On four worlds, the continental outlines were crisp, whorls of storm cloud wispy and sharp. And on the fifth . . . "Eric, what's wrong with the image of Hearth?"

Eric peered. "Nothing."

Sigmund put a finger into the holo. "Don't you see this interference? It's like a diffraction grid."

Eric shook his head. "It's not interference. There is diffraction, but it's from real structures on the surface."

"A trillion Puppeteers." Eric nodded confirmation, but the number was too large, without meaning. The pattern in the holo made it terrifyingly real. "On a world propelled through space, buildings so large, covering the planet, that we see a grid from"—it was awkward, but Sigmund knew he had to start thinking in English units—"185 billion miles away."

With a savage twist, he turned off the projection. If he dwelled too long on the power of the Puppeteers, he would never be able to act.

SIGMUND, FEELING LIKE a condemned man, zigzagged to his appointment with the governor of the world. Penelope accompanied him more for support than as a guide. Everywhere, strangers came up to them and greeted him warmly. He was news here.

Terrific, he thought. More people to disappoint.

Stepping discs transported them to fields and valleys, mountaintops and pedestrian malls, to every corner of the continent of Arcadia. There was much of this world he had yet to see, but Arcadia was where Puppeteers had settled their human servants. He was in no hurry to encounter the Puppeteer exiles and prisoners who had chosen freedom on New Terra over repatriation to a prison elsewhere.

Arcadia was a bit larger than Europe, with climates ranging from Hawaiian to Northern Californian, and a population below that of Greater Peoria. This place could be heaven, if the Puppeteers weren't about to—

No, tanj it! He was here to stop that. If only his mind weren't so . . . off.

Here and there something triggered a flash in his tortured memory. Worlds uninhabitable except in the depths of their deepest rifts or on the tops of their highest plateaus. A planet scoured by winds so fierce they drove the population underground for much of the year. Another world, of crushing gravity. Fafnir, a world almost drowned, the place he wished he could forget, was clearest in his mind. Death made an impression on a person, he supposed.

He wasn't sure exactly when arrangements had been made for this meeting, only that Omar had decided it was time. Sigmund's new friends all worked for the government one way or another. Coming up to the appointed hour, he and Penelope stepped to the courtyard within the modest government center. Before heading off to her lab, there to match wits with an emergent plant pest, she wished him luck and pointed out the building where he was expected.

Any big-city mayor back home would have turned up his nose at the complex. Sigmund dredged up a memory of the Secretary-General's mountaintop retreat. This was much better.

Sigmund walked into the lobby and gave his name to the receptionist. He did not wait long before a young man approached. "This way," he said, escorting Sigmund a short distance to a modest office. "Governor." The aide closed the door on his way out.

A woman with striking violet eyes came out from behind a massive desk to greet Sigmund. Her office was devoid of ornamentation other than a few plants and what seemed like family holos. "Sabrina Gomez-Vanderhoff."

He couldn't remember seeing anyone on New Terra wearing such a variety of colors and textures. Clothing and jewelry here signaled position and status and—well, he was not entirely sure all they could represent. With the nanotech here, jewelry could be generated on a whim. The appearance of clothes was programmable. He just didn't get it.

Clothes on Earth reflected more than a download, and they were wildly idiosyncratic. Rainbows of clothes and skin dyes—those were crystal clear in his memories.

Probably because those memories were useless.

His own sweater and slacks were programmed to black. It occurred to Sigmund he hadn't seen much black here. What message was he sending?

Sigmund offered his hand. She looked at it, puzzled, and he returned it to his side. "Sorry, it's an Earth custom. Governor, I am very pleased to meet you. Sigmund Ausfaller."

"Except at state occasions, we're informal. *Sabrina* is fine." She eyed him appraisingly. "I'm told you've been through a lot. Are you ready to talk? Have you had time to acclimate?" She motioned to a conference table and chairs, whose padded legs betrayed a Puppeteer influence.

Time was a luxury he doubted they could afford. "Now is fine, Sabrina."

"So tell me about yourself and Earth."

He talked until he was hoarse. They paused while an aide brought ice water, and Sigmund talked some more. Sabrina's curiosity was insatiable.

And her interest changed nothing. "Sabrina, I can't reunite your people with Earth. I've lost it all. Where Earth is. What sort of sun it circles. Its planetary neighbors." An image flashed through his head, tantalizing and impossible, this time of people living on an Easter egg. His mind was hopelessly jinxed. "What *any* human world, or its sun, looks like. Everything is gone. Nessus saw to that."

Disappointment was plain on her face. "Still, we have to keep looking. What else can we do? Anything you remember is more than we had before. Maybe you'll recognize something that will bring back more memories."

Fly randomly about interstellar space, hoping to recognize something. If that was the best available course of action, New Terra was doomed. No, tanj it! If it killed him—again—he would *not* sacrifice a world to the Puppeteers.

Sigmund's mind seethed, unable to transform defiance into a plan.

"If I do find Earth, it would probably mean war. Nessus has clear limits on what he'll do to help us. It excludes anything that will harm his people. That's why my brain was scrubbed."

"War was the resolution of conflict between political entities by coercive, even lethal means. Sociological maturity and a sufficiency of resources made war obsolete."

Sigmund looked all around, without seeing who spoke.

"Thank you, Jeeves," Sabrina said. "Sigmund, this is a copy of the artificial intelligence resident on our ancestor's ramscoop. His English is unedited."

Of course the Puppeteer-approved dialect lacked the word *war.* The concept would have implied a possible recourse against tyranny. "I have more bad news," Sigmund said. "Your ancestors left Earth at a very special time. Those 'political entities' had combined into one world government. Technology and spaceflight provided ample food and resources."

And the Fertility Laws had kept people from outgrowing those limits. Sigmund let that go. He had made several attempts to understand New Terran sexual politics. Sometimes he got blank looks, other times red faces. By Earth standards, these people were prudes.

Sabrina leaned forward. "War was obsolete among our people? That hardly sounds like bad news, Sigmund."

"Not long after your ancestors left, we met the Kzinti." Sigmund shivered. "Starfaring carnivores and imperialists." (Jeeves volunteered a definition for *imperialism.* It would have been quaint had it not been so naïve.) "Think eight-hundred-pound, intelligent tigers."

Sabrina scratched her chin. "Tigers?"

"Jeeves," Sigmund said. "Do you have *tigers* in your database?"

"I do, Sigmund." A holo tiger materialized over the table, poised to pounce, its eyes glinting and fangs bared.

"Shit!" Sabrina jerked back in her chair, shivering. "I've never seen a big predator before."

"Point made, Jeeves." The image vanished. "Sabrina, the one thing Kzinti want more than additional worlds and new slaves is . . . prey."

And they eat their prey, Sabrina.

"I see." Sabrina swallowed. "War isn't so obsolete in the galaxy."

"If one of your ships should lead Kzinti back here, you'll see that very quickly. Though it would serve the Puppeteers right."

Sabrina sighed, and then squared her shoulders. "So scouting is out. Sigmund, tell me what we *can* do."

Nessus didn't know. Sabrina didn't know. Why the tanj did everyone think he would? Well, he *didn't* know.

An icy resolve settled over Sigmund. He was good—very good—at one thing, and *that* Nessus had not touched.

"What we can do," Sigmund said, "is establish an intelligence service."

· 65 ·

"Puppeteers," Sigmund said, "can certainly pick worlds. I'll give them that."

"Citizens," Penelope corrected from across the dinner table. The pink of her dress brought out the rosy glow in her cheeks.

"Puppeteer."

"Citizen." Penelope raised a finger delicately—hold on for a minute—while she took a sip from her mug. Irish coffee was another of his innovations. "Unless *Puppeteer* actually means something."

Perhaps it was time to introduce something else. "Wait here." He dashed off, returning from the bedroom wearing a sock over each hand. He'd drawn an eye and a mouth on each.

"What are these?" she asked.

"Puppets." He sat on the floor behind the sofa, hunched so that only the top of his head peeked over the top. He raised his sock-covered forearms over the sofa back. In a falsetto he said, "I'm Nessus, and I'm afraid of my shadow."

Laughing, Penelope came closer and tousled his hair. "*Now* you can be Nessus."

"Hold that thought," he said. He'd also retrieved a favored old rag doll from her collection, and tied long pieces of string around its wrists. He dangled the figure over the sofa back, by strings clasped in hands still dressed in sock puppets. Humming, he marched the floppy doll from one end of the sofa to the other.

Penelope wasn't laughing anymore. And that tune. What was he humming?

"Funeral March of a Marionette," by Gounod.

Reality crashed in. New Terra did not have dresses.

Penelope's unisex outfits remained the pale gray he had come to learn meant: not committed, not unwilling, but currently not looking. The pink he had pictured would have been quite provocative.

With a groan, Sigmund opened his eyes to a lonely ship's cabin. "Sleep field off," he called, and the collapsing field gently lowered him to the deck. He washed and dressed, wondering if Penelope would ever be more than a friend.

He found Eric in *Explorer*'s relax room, attacking a moo shu burrito. Judging from his expression, Mex-Man cuisine, another of Sigmund's innovations, was an acquired taste. Sigmund just wished the young man would stop imitating him.

"Morning, Eric."

"Hello, Sigmund." Eric raised his plate. "Excellent."

"How long until dropout?" This mission was almost surely futile, which only made knowledge of the ravenous *nothing* outside the hull that much worse. Still, New Terra's pathetic navy, of which *Explorer* was the first armed to Sigmund's specifications, had to be tested. New Terra's databases had specs for comm lasers, so *Explorer* now carried five of them. At close range, they would serve as weapons. No fusion drives, of course. The only hope of a fusion drive anytime soon was to salvage and reverse-engineer technology from the old ramscoop.

Looking stoic, Eric swallowed the last bit of his breakfast. "Anytime. I've been waiting for you."

Sigmund filled a bulb with coffee, and they headed for the bridge. The mass pointer showed only a few short lines. They were remote from anyplace. "Eric, do the honors."

Stars filled the screen, and the gnawing fear in Sigmund's mind receded. A little. "Passive scan, please."

"Nothing," Eric said. "Radar now?"

"In a moment." Sigmund sipped his coffee, waiting

for a cosmic shoe to drop. When none did, they emitted a ping. Radar found nothing nearby. "All right, deploy the targets."

Their purpose was a semirealistic test of the new targeting systems, although Kirsten, who had done the programming, thought it unnecessary. She had lost the virtual coin toss—guessing evens or odds on a random number—and stayed on New Terra with little Diego and Jaime.

Eric commanded an air lock open. Escaping air tugged the drones, modified buoys, out of the ship. "Thrusters on minimum. I'll get them dispersed."

On the radar scope, the blips that represented the drones slowly pulled away. Sigmund armed the weapons console. "That's far enough. Drone one, evasive maneuvers."

In the radar display, all the blips continued their stately, and very linear, retreat.

"Tanj," Eric said affectedly. "Defective. Try another?"

Sigmund nodded.

Eric leaned closer to his console. "Drone two, evasive maneuvers."

Nothing. "Too bad Kirsten didn't program the drones," Sigmund said.

As drone after drone proved unresponsive, Eric reverted to English expletives. They seemed more satisfying. "Maybe it's no accident they're like that. Could someone have intentionally introduced a malfunction?"

"*Sabotage.* That's the word you want." Spy School 101, Sigmund thought. "True, someone could have tampered with the drones. I don't think that's how they'd do it.

"Any saboteur presumably knows the purpose of the drones. They would be better served to subvert the evasive-maneuver code, make it less random. The fire controls would be less rigorously tested than we think, and we might get overconfident."

"I have so much to learn." Eric hung his head, embarrassed. "I'll work at it. I promise."

That reaction made Sigmund feel worse than the bug in the drone software. "Just bring them back aboard. Kirsten can figure out what went wrong."

STARS AGAIN FILLED the main screen. This time, one shone visibly brighter. "Passive scan, Eric."

Eric studied his instruments. "Not a thing. Radar?"

"All right," Sigmund said. "Find us an ice ball."

They were far outside the star's singularity. A ping went out. They waited. And waited. Sigmund's skin crawled, although in a different way than in hyperspace. There's no danger here, he told himself. Nessus and his friends had explored the system ahead, before independence. It was unoccupied and inhospitable. And while *he* had no idea where Kzinti were likely to be found, the Puppeteers did. *They* had set this course for the Fleet. New Terra was simply a little way out in front, along the same path.

And, by the same token, it was highly unlikely they could encounter an Outsider ship here.

They got a radar return well over an hour later. In the main scope, it looked like just another ice ball. "All yours, Eric. Take us closer."

Eric dropped into a crash couch and took the thruster controls. They crept closer, until Sigmund called, "That's close enough." Sigmund took the other couch and rearmed the new weapons console. He centered his crosshairs on the image. "Three . . . two . . . one . . . fire."

A geyser of steam erupted from the target, glowing luridly with scattered laser light. He released the trigger. "You take a try." They took turns, with the three bow lasers and, turning, the two stern lasers, targeting smaller and smaller chunks. "Your wife does excellent work."

They chased down and destroyed a few more Oort Cloud objects. Eric's eyes glowed. "We can do this, Sigmund. You're going to save us."

It's easy to blast ice. A Kzinti warship on evasive maneuvers, shooting back . . .

Sigmund kept his thoughts to himself.

"WE'RE DONE," SIGMUND announced. They had learned what dumb targets could teach them.

"Home then?" Eric said. "We'll return more secure than we left."

But only a bit. Lasers penetrated GP hulls, supposedly in every wavelength that was visible to any customer species. Then we paint over them, lest hyperspace drive us mad.

Yes, lasers penetrated the hulls, but the Puppeteers could *destroy* them. *Hobo Kelly* was gone in seconds.

Sigmund said, "You're sure you don't know how Puppeteers could remotely destroy a hull? Couldn't they do what you did to extract the ramscoop? Couldn't you do it again?"

Eric shook his head. "*Long Pass* was hidden inside a General Products hull, held rigidly in place. We knew exactly where the reinforcing power plant was. That's why I could fry it with *Long Pass*'s comm laser. The odds of a laser destroying the power plant in a moving target . . ."

"Right." Sigmund paced the tiny bridge. The main sensor panel continued to show . . . nothing. It meant he had failed. Laser-arming New Terra's few ships would raise spirits; it could do nothing against the overwhelming might of the Fleet.

"The ramscoop is still a potent weapon," Eric said. Tone of voice added, "Isn't it?"

"Not anymore, I think." Sigmund ceased his pacing to squeeze Eric's shoulder. "It worked the first time because *Long Pass* was kept right in the Fleet for convenient study. When you broke it loose, the Puppeteers had no time to react. Now it's orbiting New Terra. Its fusion drive would make it visible from billions of miles away. Lasers or collision by a remote-controlled ship would demolish it before it got close enough to be a threat."

Only the Outsiders had the power to save New Terra. *That* was the reason *Explorer* was out here. Sigmund had revealed his purpose to no one, not even Eric. Eric might tell Kirsten; Kirsten might tell Nessus—and Nessus, surely, would have a different opinion than Sigmund, whose new home world was, in the final extreme, sacrificial to the wrath of the Outsiders.

Sigmund circled the bridge again, checking the sensor panel as he passed. Nothing.

His spirits drooping, Sigmund told himself that random exploration for the galaxy-roaming Outsiders was slightly less pathetic than randomly looking for Earth.

"SURPRISE!"

Sigmund sat up with a start. He was napping in a crash couch on the bridge, not in his cabin. Close to home meant close to Puppeteers. "We're back to New Terra?"

"Just slightly past." Eric pressed a button and the main view port de-opaqued.

Five worlds, the size of quarter-sol coins!

"You brought us to the Fleet?" Sigmund screamed. "Why?"

"Relax, Sigmund. We're stealthed and zipping past at almost two percent cee, relative. Kirsten, Omar, and I sneaked back into the Fleet on this very ship, when we were supposed to be away scouting. It's how we found *Long Pass*. I thought you'd like to see it up close."

The worlds ballooned as Sigmund watched. In one aux display, hundreds of ships made themselves known by their traffic-control beacons. Another display showed

Hearth in close-up, a world seemingly paved in monstrous buildings.

From many billion miles away, it was frightening. Now, Sigmund could almost reach out and touch it. His heart pounded. And Eric grinned ear to ear, delighted with himself.

I never asked for hero worship. Now it's going to get me killed.

"Lots of hyperwave chatter," Eric commented.

In the mass pointer, five lines aimed themselves at Sigmund. *Explorer* was only seconds away from their singularities. Sigmund slammed his palm against the control console—

Do *not* look up!

Staring grimly at his feet, Sigmund groped around until he found the view-port control. Eric gazed straight forward, unfocused. "Eric," he called. "Eric!"

With a shudder, Eric came out of his trance. "What happened?"

Carlos Wu happened. A genius like *Carlos* was what New Terra needed.

"I dropped us back into hyperspace. You were staring right into the blind spot. That hyperwave chatter . . . was probably hyperwave radar." As had betrayed *Hobo Kelly* to its doom.

Eric turned white. He volunteered nothing, and responded only in monosyllables, for the short flight back to New Terra.

. 66 .

They delayed landing for a few extra loops around New Terra. Sigmund hoped the opportunity to play tour guide would do something for Eric's shattered confidence.

Beowulf Shaeffer would have given a better tour.

From low orbit, Arcadia was even more utopian than Sigmund's stepping-disc forays had suggested. Vast stretches of farmland, alternating with lush forest. Great river systems. Natural harbors on three coasts. A long mountainous backbone, gentled by the eons into rolling hills. Scattered cities—towns, really, by Earth standards. None of the ugliness of long-abandoned highways and railroads, the colony having been built from the start around a stepping-disc system.

Arcadia was the smallest of three continents.

Life thrived as well on the larger continents, Elysium and Atlantis, but it was *wrong*. The dominant red Sigmund could almost handle, pretending it was fall foliage. But the purple, the magenta, the dusky yellow, the blends . . . all Hearthian life.

Elysium was the youngest of the continents. Its mountains soared, sharp edged and peaked. A major fault line, with active volcanoes anchoring both ends, snaked across one corner of the triangular landmass. An immense basin, one end drifted with gypsum sands, had collapsed deep into a high arid plain. Most of the continent was forest and prairie, a tame version of primeval Hearth. Before independence, Puppeteer tourists had frequented its parks.

Atlantis had the shape of a mitten. The side with the thumb rose far above the ocean. Four great rivers, each with many tributaries, ran downward from that mountainous edge. The jungle they watered was vibrant with every color but green.

This was not one world ranged against the Fleet. One small, scarcely settled continent! Whatever this detour may have done for Eric's confidence, it further shook Sigmund's own.

PENELOPE AND SIGMUND strolled to the restful sounds of waves lapping the nearby shore. Sigmund's jumpsuit remained its customary black, but (after consultation with Eric) he had set the placket and cuffs to a pale blue. Solid black, it seemed, sent a message of "not looking" far more emphatic than Penelope's standard gray.

It pleased him that she seemed pleased.

They shared the boardwalk with many couples and families. He caught Penelope smiling at a pair of boisterous little boys randomly zooming around the adults.

"It's a beautiful day," he said. It always was, when you could simply step to the nicest weather.

"It is." She smiled shyly. "Thanks for inviting me on a walk."

"You're quite welcome. Woman cannot live by crop pest alone."

She patted his elbow. "Tell me about crop pests on Earth."

They touched a lot here. It was strictly companionable. He was accustomed to reproduction being ruthlessly controlled, with free sex as the outlet. On New Terra, they took things slow; when something finally happened, they bred like rabbits.

Penny remained in just-friends mode.

Sigmund said, "I'm partial to corn on the cob. Does that make me a corn pest?"

"Seriously, Sigmund."

He looked again at happy couples. He tracked a little girl ramming around the boardwalk, shrieking with innocent glee. He could marry here. He could, for the first time in his life, truly imagine starting a family, despite everything that was happening.

Sigmund froze. I'm out of whack.

Concentrating, he felt an unfamiliar serenity. An ARM autodoc would be dosing him up right now. It made no sense. He was paranoid naturally.

He had been wandering in a fog of unwonted feelings and unexpected behavior. He had blamed it all on the near-death experience, the shock of his abduction, and flatlander phobia. None of those could have helped.

And none was the real problem. Carlos's autodoc

treated paranoia. It wasn't an ARM model. Sigmund had emerged on this world with his biochemistry reset. After years with his paranoia fixated on the safety of Earth, brainwashing had left old habits without an immediate focus.

No *wonder* he'd felt off his game.

"Sigmund? You've gotten very quiet."

"Sorry." He took Penny's hand. "It'll pass."

What would pass was this unfamiliar tranquility. Old habits were belatedly reasserting themselves. He could sense that, too. A ghost of Old Sigmund had gotten *Explorer* away from the Fleet in time. Stress and reflexes were pulling him back down the labyrinthine pathways of paranoia.

ARMs dated ARMs because usually no one else would have them.

He spotted a refreshment stand a short distance up the boardwalk. "How about some ice cream, faithful Penelope?"

"That would be nice."

It would be so simple. Make excuses to keep using the autodocs. Woo Penelope. Have a family. New habits would eventually replace old.

Except . . .

If nothing changed, everyone on New Terra was doomed. Obliteration of the planet? Futile resistance and mass slaughter? Surrender and reenslavement? He didn't know.

One thing Sigmund *did* know: He was the only one on this world who could possibly stop it. And he could only do that as . . . himself.

He squeezed Penelope's hand. "Let's get you that ice cream."

Actually, Sigmund knew a second thing. After today, his clothes would go without any trace of color for a long time.

• • •

DIEGO SKIPPED ONTO the patio holding a toy spaceship over his head, vrooming although ships were equally silent on thrusters and hyperdrive. Jaime dashed after, leaping in vain for the toy. "*I* want to be Sigmund," she shouted as both children pelted back into the house.

Kirsten shot her mate a glance. Eric's hero worship must irk her, too, Sigmund thought.

Tanj, *I* don't want to be Sigmund.

He, Eric, and Kirsten had gone round and round on this. The bottom line never changed. Puppeteers feared the Outsiders—quite rationally—more than they feared anything New Terra might do. While that was the case, nothing he did could help the situation. Any credible threat New Terra could pose would only make things worse by moving up the inevitable attack. The Concordance was clearly unwilling to offer terms they thought the humans might even consider.

Sigmund guessed the Puppeteers would offer terms after something awful happened.

Not even surrendering the drive was a viable option. It would leave New Terra adrift in space, prey to the gravitational influence of every star they passed.

Introducing Russian roulette as a metaphor for that strategy had not helped.

"So what will it be?" Kirsten asked softly. "Outright destruction or slavery?"

Inside, the children squealed happily. They deserved peace and freedom, they and all the innocents like them.

Sigmund shoved back his chair and stood. "Neither one, tanj it. Neither one."

". . . THE HINDMOST IS most anxious. He was unhappy even before an alien ship intruded on the Fleet. Now *I* lose patience with you. You do not want that."

With heads lowered in submission, Baedeker let Achilles' rant wash over him. From what Baedeker had been told, an intruder had emerged from and vanished into hyperspace. That meant it wasn't an Outsider. The wild humans had kept their distance since learning their ships weren't safe here. That left the ex-Colonists. "Why do you suppose they—"

"Stop," Achilles roared. "Your job is to forge us a new weapon, not to speculate."

Baedeker had been regularly reporting his progress. Or was it progress? The planetary drive appeared to tap the zero-point energy of the vacuum. Somehow, it shaped an asymmetry that was inherently propulsive. The energies involved were beyond staggering.

Each time that he entered his lab, the mere notion of tampering with the drive made Baedeker tremble. The eagerness with which Achilles embraced such meddling made Baedeker want to hide forever beneath his belly. Not that a mere bulwark of flesh would protect him.

Achilles continued to rage. ". . . Or perhaps I should have you returned to Nature Preserve One to pick weeds. The fields have inspired your creativity before."

The serenity of the fields felt strangely alluring. Return was not the worst fate Baedeker could imagine.

If a planetary drive was damaged, how far would the effects travel?

There must be another way to bring the ex-Colonists to their senses. Baedeker fluted obsequiously, "I will redouble my efforts."

"DO NOTHING, AND wait for the Concordance to destroy us. Do something, and bring on their attack even sooner." Sabrina looked as grim as the report she echoed. "Neither is a very attractive option."

"No, they're not," Sigmund agreed. Behind Sabrina, a holo cycled through panoramic images of Arcadia. Every politician's office he'd ever seen on Earth was filled with images of . . . the politician. Never Sabrina's.

"Not for us, certainly. For the Puppeteers, the choice should be easier. Why don't they get it over with? Waiting only increases the possibility we'll try to do something to them."

Sabrina spun one of her many rings around a finger, considering. "They don't know Nessus told us. They don't know we know."

He shook his head. "They're Puppeteers. They'd worry we might, somehow, find out."

"Then I don't *know* why, Sigmund."

"They would delay, Sabrina, for only one reason: to make use of the time. I don't know what they're doing with it. And because delay risks us finding out and acting, the Puppeteers must be watching us closely."

She stopped turning the ring. "Watching us. How?"

That they continued to have such conversations, however futilely, suggested the electronics experts Eric had recruited had done what Sigmund had asked of them: They had properly shielded Sabrina's office. "The modifications we're making to our few ships are no threat to the Concordance. Not when they can dissolve General Products hulls from a distance."

"I know," Sabrina said. "They're for morale, or in case a scout runs into these Kzinti."

He had lied even to her. He trusted her integrity, but he knew nothing about her acting ability. "The truth, Sabrina, is I assumed we were being watched. Confirming that meant giving any spies something to do."

"Persons employed to surreptitiously ascertain secrets," Jeeves offered.

The color drained from Sabrina's face. "Our own people?"

"There are millions of humans on New Terra. Some might be loyal to the old ways. Some might have been informants before independence; they would have no choice but cooperate if threatened with exposure. They wouldn't necessarily know the consequences of their actions. However . . ." Sigmund smiled. "People here aren't very *good* at spying."

Not to ARM standards.

He had had Sabrina order Arcadia's largest spaceport cordoned off for the new navy. The facility employed thousands, in every capacity from technician to cargo handler to perimeter guard. Invisible to all, operating from a control room accessible only by stepping disc, a few specialists watched all the rest. Sigmund had personally vetted and trained them all.

The naval yard teemed with spies. They lurked about, watching. They copied files without authorization. To the limited extent Sigmund had reliable staff to follow them while off-base, they skulked about at night to rendezvous secretly and to radio messages.

On *Explorer*'s return from its "weapons test" flight, Sigmund had confirmed what he was sure he would find: coded hyperwave chatter. The signals had only one possible source: stealthed buoys that trailed or distantly orbited New Terra to relay the reports of the spies.

"I don't understand." Sabrina paused to pour ice water from a carafe. "You make this sound somehow good."

"Yes, it is." Sigmund accepted a glass, nodding his thanks. "My business is to find—or keep—secrets. That's made me a student of how, in the past, very big secrets have been kept. Whatever we do to save ourselves, we must prepare it in secret." Where no one will think to look.

"So arming our ships is all for show. Something to divert the spies from . . . what?"

Sigmund had a course of action in mind. It was far too flimsy to call a plan, but even governors deserve to be left a few rays of hope. "Let's just say, possibilities."

REDEMPTION

Earth date: 2659

· 67 ·

"I admit I foresaw no options for your people, Governor," Nessus said.

"Believe me, we've been looking. We do appreciate having the chance to look." Sabrina Gomez-Vanderhoff, in whose modest office they met, seemed not to have slept for a week. She gestured at a colleague just joining them. "Nessus, do you know Aaron Tremonti-Lewis? I asked him to join us. He is our Minister for Public Safety."

Lewis sat on the edge of a small sofa. "Public Safety deals in putting out fires, cleaning up after storms, and handling parties gotten a bit rowdy—not handling the enmity of your people. The Concordance could squash us like a bug. How can we plan for *that*?"

Don't overdo it, Sigmund thought. He watched from a darkened room adjoining the governor's office. Lest Nessus have bug detectors, the surveillance was very low-tech: a one-way mirror built into a decoration newly hung on Sabrina's office wall. Amplifiers in earplugs boosted the scarcely audible sounds from next door.

Nessus sat astraddle a proper Citizen couch. Such furniture would have been standard in the governor's office before New Terra got its freedom. The couch restored to its place symbolized bigger changes soon to be undone. "I had expected to see Sigmund Ausfaller, and possibly some of my former scouts."

"Pfft." Sabrina said. Sigmund couldn't parse that, but it sounded dismissive. "Nessus, I know you meant well, but Sigmund is mentally ill. Deranged. He worries constantly about these Kzinti beings finding us. If they find us, they find the Fleet, too, I keep telling—"

A timid knock interrupted Sabrina's outburst. "Come in," Sabrina said impatiently.

The door opened. A junior aide rolled in a cart piled with snacks and beverages. "Apologies, ma'am." She backed out quickly.

Aaron wandered over to the cart. "Coffee, tea, and an assortment of juices. No beer."

Don't overdo it, Sigmund thought again. Cue Sabrina.

Sabrina came out from behind her desk and poured herself a cup of tea. "There's carrot juice, Nessus. If I recall correctly, that's your drink."

Nessus dismounted the Y-shaped couch and filled a glass. "Then Sigmund will not be joining us. I had hoped he might be the saving of you."

"He's a nutcase," Aaron said.

"Enough, Aaron." Sabrina sighed. "Nessus, we asked you here for guidance. We few cannot resist the might of the Fleet. It saddens me, but New Terra must enter a new relationship with Hearth. Once the Outsiders' deadline makes the Concordance act, it will be too late."

Sigmund heard without listening. Get on with it.

Another knock at Sabrina's door: the same junior aide. "My apologies. I'll get the mess out of here." Cringing under Sabrina's stare, he gathered empty and partially filled glasses.

A moment later, there was a knock at Sigmund's door. The aide came in, no longer cowering. "This is it, Sigmund. Nessus' glass."

"Good work," Sigmund said. They stepped to a lab. Eric and Kirsten were waiting for him, with a bunch of technicians most of whom Sigmund had yet to meet.

He could scarcely bear to breathe as a tech lifted Nessus' lip- and tongueprints from the glass. Sigmund had given Eric the idea—it wasn't a big leap from fake fingerprints—but making it happen required skills Sigmund lacked.

The tech walked around a larger-than-life holo of the lifted prints, peering this way and that. "Looks complete," the tech said. "You'll have your copies in five minutes."

Kirsten smiled, showing more confidence than Sigmund felt. Maybe she was faking it, too. She said, "That's good enough for me. Let's do it."

They stepped back to Sigmund's stakeout. In Sabrina's office, depressing talk of surrender continued. Nessus straddled his couch, facing Sabrina's desk.

Sigmund pushed against the back of the mirrored ornament. It swung out silently on well-oiled hinges.

Nessus crumpled from a stunner blast, never knowing what hit him.

"I'M IN," KIRSTEN said. "The right-side tongueprint worked."

Text scrolled in a holo above Nessus' pocket computer. Sigmund could not read a thing, but Kirsten could. Everyone in Nessus' ill-fated Colonist scout program read the Concordance script. Teaching them to read had been easier for Nessus than translating everything a scout might need.

"How long will Nessus be out?" Aaron asked nervously.

Sigmund had been asked that repeatedly since proposing this plan. The answer remained the same: best guess, based on comparative body weights of humans and Puppeteers, a few minutes. "We're going as fast as we can."

"Searching . . . searching . . . searching," Kirsten muttered. (She had access only to basic operations reachable through the touch screen. Pocket comps did not have full keypads, and no human's voice would ever be confused with a Puppeteer's. Apparently they had three pairs of vocal cords per throat.) She frowned. "No navigational data on the comp. That would have been too easy."

"He's twitching in his sleep," an aide called from the next room.

Tanj! The effects were wearing off fast. Sigmund was loath to risk a second zap. "Kirsten, look for—"

"I know. The way aboard *Aegis*. I've got stepping-disc addresses and security codes." Kirsten tapped the touch screen of Nessus' comp, now pointed at her own. "Transferred. And we're logged out."

An aide dashed off with the comp, to restore it to Nessus' pocket before he woke.

Kirsten transferred a copy of the data from her comp to Sigmund's. "We're set."

Seconds later, he and Kirsten were aboard Nessus' ship. With luck, the stolen tongueprint would also give Kirsten access to the bridge navigational computer.

HANDS JOSTLED NESSUS. Who? Why?

His eyes flew open. He found himself slumped half-off a couch in the governor's office; Sabrina was shaking him. His legs and necks tingled. "What happened?" he asked.

"I don't know. You just passed out," she said. "Aaron went to find a Citizen autodoc. We put them in storage." She looked embarrassed by the admission. "Should we contact someone on Elysium?"

Nessus struggled into an upright position. "No need. I feel better." For all Nessus knew, the Concordance had spies among the refugees and émigrés on Elysium. He would have. Achilles would have thought of it, too.

"We still have a Citizen synthesizer handy. Perhaps you would like to order something for yourself. Food or a tonic?" Sabrina hovered over him.

Something nagged at Nessus. What had he just been thinking? Achilles would have spies. . . .

What about *Sigmund*?

Nessus stiffened. Sigmund unaccounted for. Nessus had gotten no answer, he now realized, to where his former scouts were. Sabrina acting nervous.

What if *Sigmund* was up to something?

How? What? Why? Had he broken Sigmund while erasing memories of Earth, or was Sigmund . . . ?

What *would* Sigmund do?

Nessus' mind just did not work this way—that was why he had brought Sigmund to this world.

His right front hoof tore at Sabrina's carpet. He *must* run. *Now.*

"On second thought, I don't feel well." Nessus got off his couch, staggering for effect. He remembered seeing a stepping disc in the vestibule outside her office. She followed him from her office, looking ever more anxious. "I will contact you soon about resuming."

With those words, he stepped back to the safety of *Aegis.*

KIRSTEN HUMMED AS she worked, holo text flashing past, while Sigmund monitored the security system. The bridge's security cameras showed empty corridors and rooms.

"That's interesting," Kirsten muttered. Indecipherable text kept flashing.

"What?" he asked. "Nav data?"

She shook her head. "No, where we are. Nessus put *Aegis* underwater."

"Then we won't go out the air lock. . . ." Something moved on one of the monitors. "Finagle! Nessus just flicked into the relax room!" A moment later, Sigmund's comp buzzed, with a too-late warning from Sabrina.

Kirsten's hands still flew over the keypad. "Do I keep looking for Earth?"

Sigmund fingered the stunner in his pocket. Nessus at the least suspected. Stunning him again, aboard his own ship, would surely remove all doubt.

Nessus was not an ally, exactly, but neither was he an enemy. As a source of insight into Concordance thinking, the Puppeteer was irreplaceable. ARM scuttlebutt, supposedly informed by past Kzinti experiments, was that coercing a Puppeteer triggered a conditioned suicide reflex.

How about, Sigmund, that Nessus did not leave you on the floor to bleed to death? How's *that* for a reason not to threaten him?

Sigmund said, "Do we have a way off *Aegis* besides the stepping disc in the relax room?"

"There are probably other discs; I pulled several addresses off Nessus' comp. Check the cargo holds. *Explorer* had stepping discs in its holds, for loading."

He panned several cameras. "Here, too."

She grimaced. "I'm not finding anything about Earth or Sol system."

"Widen your search," he said. He watched Nessus looking for something on the relax room's shelves. A weapon? "Very quickly."

Kirsten's holo flashed even faster, the effect almost stroboscopic.

"How long do you need to cover your tracks?" No one had ever hunted on New Terra, so the metaphor got Sigmund another blank look. "How long to purge the audit trail and log out?"

"A minute or so."

If Nessus started their way, they had maybe 30 seconds to get off the bridge and down the other corridor to the hold before he would see them. Decision time. Confrontation meant losing whatever help Nessus might willingly provide. Get out now, Sigmund thought, before Nessus can truly know he has been spied upon.

Nessus picked up something and walked out of the relax room.

"Kirsten! Start your cleanup!" Sigmund hurried to the nearest hold, moving as quickly as he could without making noise. He stepped through to the relax room. Nessus would be halfway to the bridge by now.

Sealed packages sat on a shelf beside the synthesizer. Sigmund couldn't read the labels, but he guessed these were emergency rations. Puppeteers would have backup synthesizers and presynthed food in case the backups had problems.

What they were didn't matter. Sigmund swept several packages to the deck.

In the stone-silent ship, the splats were deafening.

When Nessus found the mess, he'd think he bumped the shelf. Wobbling packages that took a moment to topple was surely an easier explanation than intruders. They could come back the next time Nessus met with Sabrina.

Sigmund stepped back into the cargo hold. He called Kirsten on her comp. "Check the monitors. Did Nessus turn around?"

"Yes, he went back to the relax room. What's the mess you made?"

"The cargo hold. *Now.*"

"Yes, boss," she said.

They rendezvoused in the hold. Sigmund waved Kirsten through first. Sigmund flicked after, emerging to find Eric and Kirsten hugging.

Sigmund could not help thinking of Penelope—but nothing had changed. New Terra needed him to be *him,* and Penelope deserved someone . . . normal. "We're no closer to Earth than before," Sigmund said bitterly.

Kirsten slipped free of Eric's arms and turned. Inexplicably, she was beaming. "On the other hand, Sigmund, the trip wasn't a total loss.

"I found the Outsider ship Nessus visited."

· 68 ·

"Time is up."

Baedeker flinched at the intrusion. Few knew the access codes for his lab. Fewer still would arrive here unannounced. He turned and confirmed his fears. "Hello, Achilles."

Achilles gazed about at rows of lab instruments and computers. His mane coif was more elaborately garish than ever. "We have not stinted on resources for you."

The subtext was hardly subtle: Any lack of success will be blamed on me. No matter that generations of Concordance researchers had feared even to try reverse-engineering the drive technology.

"We'll be more comfortable there." Baedeker motioned toward his small office area. The short walk, a little settling-in time, offers of refreshments . . . it all took time. Achilles had come unannounced like this to rattle him—and had succeeded.

He needed to gather his wits.

He had learned a few things about the drive. The underlying technology *did* tap zero-point energy. The energies involved *were* extraordinary. Beyond that, he had dared to perform only a few noninvasive scans. The readouts hinted elliptically at far more than they revealed.

Baedeker guessed at quantum logic—and he quailed at the consequences of disturbing it. If he was correct, an unknowably complex real-time computation channeled and directed vast energies. Every probe he undertook risked collapsing the computation into an unintended state. What would happen then . . . ?

This was frighteningly far beyond Citizen science.

Achilles waited for Baedeker to settle onto a mound of cushions—and remained standing. "The situation with the ex-Colonists requires resolution. Your reports have been less than forthcoming. Have you found a way to remotely disable their planetary drive?"

"Respectfully," Baedeker began, "the energies involved are—"

"Answer the question." Achilles' undertunes pulsed with impatience.

Baedeker stood, setting his hooves far apart in a confidence he did not feel. He *wanted* to flee. But the forces with which Achilles was so eager to meddle made flight meaningless. . . . "I found no remotely accessible controls." Nor had he found any unsuspected weakness that he might exploit. How could he, when so little of the design made sense?

"That is unfortunate," Achilles warbled. "The Hindmost has decided we will wait no longer."

"Because of the ship that flew past the Fleet?"

"That is not your affair," Achilles snapped. "Because of your failure, it appears we must disable their planetary drive another way."

Baedeker plucked at his mane. The other way was bombardment. The more he learned of the drive, the more the notion terrified him. "That could mean genocide."

Achilles craned a neck to more closely study a small decorative holo. "Provoking the Outsiders *would* mean genocide. Ours. Something unexpected happening on our old colony? That would be merely unfortunate."

Somehow, the casual apathy rang false. Baedeker allowed himself to hope. "There may be another option." Most of his recent investigations had been directed to finding something—anything—safer to attempt.

"Oh?"

Baedeker heard the faint grace note of interest under the feigned indifference. "We had thought to disable the planetary drive by surprise, making the New Terrans' ships too precious to use against Hearth. What if we turn the plan on its heads? What if we destroy all their ships by surprise? They would be defenseless. Then, a threat to damage their planetary drive might suffice."

"Interesting," Achilles whistled. "*If* you have a way to destroy all their ships."

Baedeker bobbed heads vigorously. "We need only generalize how we can destroy individual hulls. Imagine a network of stealthed comm buoys deployed around New Terra. At an opportune moment, those satellites beam the 'power-plant off' command to every General Products hull on the surface or in nearby orbit."

Achilles' eyes gleamed. "Opportune?"

"We would act when all their ships are located. If I recall correctly, they were left with very few ships under the agreement of separation. General Products will have the records. If we know how many ships there are, we concentrate on finding them." Baedeker had in mind remote sensing.

"Oh yes," Achilles chanted. He seemed, suddenly, *very* happy. "We have ways to locate the ships. You may have done it yet again."

IN THE MAIN bridge display of *Remembrance,* a world shimmered.

Sparkling blue oceans. Continents rich with forest and fields. Swirls of white cloud. Round it all circled tiny suns, like necklaces of brilliant yellow topaz.

For most of Achilles' life, this world had hung in the sky over Hearth. As it would once again—only he would not see it. He would be *on* it, ruling. His reward. Nike had promised.

Achilles stood tall. "Ready?"

Baedeker fidgeted on the other command couch. For all he had scanned his console obsessively for much of a shift, he checked everything again. "Three ships on the ground, at their main spaceport. Two ships in synchronous orbit over Arcadia." There was a flurry of whispering to his console, and five small holos formed. Each centered on a remotely viewed General Products hull. "All five accounted for."

As his spies had reported. "And are you prepared to take them all out?"

A hoarse, bass whisper. "Yes, Achilles. All buoys have target lock. I am ready at your command."

At my command. I can get used to that.

Stealthed, *Remembrance* was invisible except to hyperwave radar—a technology the humans lacked. He felt like Zeus, ready to smite the puny humans below with his lightning.

Perhaps, when his reign began, he would change his name.

Achilles opened a sixth small image. It centered on a ship also stationed to guard the human continent, for all the good it would do them. This target was freighted with significance: the old ramscoop with which the Colonists had extorted their—fleeting—freedom. This hull had not come from the factories of General Products.

"On my count," Achilles sang. "Three. Two. One. Now."

The laser sliced through the old hull. Ululating with joy, Achilles retargeted on the largest fragment . . . and the largest after that . . . and after that. . . . Eventually, he hit the small onboard supply of liquid hydrogen. It flashed to gas and plasma, exploding the ruptured tank. Most of the debris was invisibly small, but it rocked the larger wreckage.

Beside him, Baedeker gaped. In his displays, from the subtle touch of five stealthed comm buoys, five hulls had vanished.

Three irregular heaps slumped across the tarmac. Smoke billowed from one heap, from who knew what cargo set aflame. It was impossible from this distance, especially through the smoke, to characterize the rubble, but Achilles' imagination offered details: decks and interior walls, cargo and supplies, thrusters and hyperdrive shunts, life support. . . . And a few bodies, doubtless.

As for the suddenly hull-less ships in orbit, air pressure had burst every interior partition. Clouds of debris surrounded the wrecks. Every loose or ruptured part had gotten a little push from air escaping as the hulls came apart.

The rebels' fleet destroyed in a moment. The Fleet

once more safe. A world—his world—left with no option but to submit.

Basking in Olympian invincibility, Achilles broadcast the Concordance's ultimatum to the planet beneath his hooves.

• 69 •

Among the legacies purged from New Terran culture was poker. Digging deeper, Sigmund found that the New Terrans had *no* games of chance. Mentions of "bluffing" and "shell game" had gotten him only blank stares.

With luck, the concepts were as foreign to Puppeteers.

Even as a chemical payload billowed into a smoke screen over Arcadia's main spaceport, his handpicked crew assembled, flicking across the world unseen.

SECRETS FASCINATED SIGMUND—and to uncover secrets, one studied how others hid theirs.

He knew of no better example than the years-long clandestine development of the atomic bomb. With only his (hacked-at) memory as a resource, he had merely the broad outlines to guide him: a secret so closely held that scientists and technicians never learned what Project Y was until they were escorted to their new jobs, in a place where no one would think to look, amid desolation where nobody lived.

Centuries and light-years distant, in the midst of the First Atomic War, that had meant deep in New Mexico's mountains. A whole town built in the wilderness, too remote to approach without raising suspicions, its very existence denied. The babies born there during the war shared a post-office box in another city as their official place of birth.

His Los Alamos was a system of caverns, in the side of a cliff, in the vast sunken basin at the desert tip of Elysium, in a desolation shunned by Citizen tourists and émigrés alike. After the unavoidable first visit by aircraft, everyone and everything came by stepping disc—*if* they knew how.

Like transfer booths, stepping discs could absorb only so much kinetic energy. Discs handled more energy, but still not enough for transoceanic jumps. Without orbiting relays, Colonists were kept on Arcadia, where they could not surprise or discomfit Puppeteer tourists.

But relays at sea worked just as well, and "oceanographic research" was a credible cover story. The oceans of New Terra remained preserves of Hearthian sea life. The ships now deployed were ostensibly to investigate whether plankton, krill, and other earthly biota from *Long Pass*'s cargo could be introduced, as part of a longer-term plan to add still-frozen fish eggs.

The public disc network had no record of shipboard relays or the endpoint discs on Elysium. The very few Arcadian discs that knew those secret addresses were tuned to different frequencies than the public network, hidden inside secured buildings, and responded only to classified access codes.

MAKING BABIES TAKES time. Sigmund never expected the registration of births to become an issue. Today's events proved him correct.

Half a world apart from the sneak attack, Sigmund watched with pride as his crew flicked from cavern to starship. The ship glittered before him, its plasteel hull hopefully immune from whatever attacked GP hulls, its mirror coating proof for at least a few seconds against lasers. Every part—plasteel panels, thrusters and hyperdrive shunt scavenged and disassembled from a grounded decoy at the main spaceport, control consoles, life support—had come through the secret disc system. Everything was assembled in haste, by teams working around the clock. Just days earlier, the ship had passed a pressure test: two atmospheres of pressure within, simulating one atmosphere with vacuum outside. Supplies were still coming when the Puppeteers struck.

His communicator crackled. He recognized Eric's voice. "We're ready, Sigmund."

"Be right there." Sigmund looked once more about the cavern, then signaled to the ground crew to remove the giant camouflage tarps that hid the cautiously enlarged opening. He took two paces to the nearest stepping disc, flicked aboard, and strode to the bridge.

Eric and Kirsten looked at him expectantly. Sigmund nodded. "Let's do this."

With the eerie silence of thrusters, the great ship floated from the cavern floor and drifted sideways into the mountainous basin. It hovered there for a moment, as Sigmund waited to be struck down.

Nothing happened. Maybe the Puppeteers *didn't* know about shell games. "Engage," Sigmund said.

The New Terra starship *Why Not* leapt skyward at maximum thrust. In hours, it had left the planet's singularity and vanished into hyperspace.

• 70 •

Achilles had an epiphany: He had confused reigning with governing.

Reigning was pomp and privilege. Governing was annoying detail. Once he had imposed order on the ground, he would import administrators. Vesta cared about such trivia—let him handle it. Let him handle *her.*

In the bridge display where Achilles had so recently enjoyed the destruction of *Long Pass,* a woman earnestly and endlessly prattled. "I have a team of my best people working on it," she said. Sabrina Gomez-Vanderhoff exuded an obsequious sincerity. Doubtless, she thought to make a spot for herself in his court.

As though he would forget who had led these rabble during their independence.

Let her imagine whatever she wished about her future. For now, he needed on-the-ground cooperation. If only he could keep her on-topic. "All that will wait," Achilles snapped. It made his brain ache that all her minutiae *would* come back. "Focus on the matter in our jaws." On surrender, quickly accepted, but never quite implemented. "What of the planetary drive?"

"I apologize, Achilles. A moment." She leaned out of the field of her camera for a whispered consultation. "I have dispatched technical personnel I consider extremely trustworthy. They will assume responsibility from the custodial staff. There is a problem first."

There always was. "I do *not* like problems," Achilles shouted.

She averted her eyes submissively. At least she remembered how to behave around Citizens. In more conversational tones, he prompted, "What is the problem?"

"Securing the drive. The staff at the drive facility refuses to relinquish it. We know they have stunners, stolen from an office of Public Safety. We will remove those who resist, but it may take time. The drive is on Atlantis, beyond stepping-disc range, so it will take a while to get sufficient loyal staff to Atlantis by boat."

Of *course* the drive facility was off Arcadia. No sane Citizen would have permitted even tame humans free rein on the same continent as a planetary drive. Only now even the pretense of docility was gone. Now, suddenly, onetime caution had become a problem.

Below the view of his camera, Achilles pawed at the deck in frustration. All human spaceships were destroyed. Victory was in his jaws. That insubordinate humans might damage the drive *now* was intolerable. "Proceed with caution," he said. "But once that is done, I expect action."

Her head bowed. "The question is . . ."

"Is *what*?"

Her shoulders slumped and her voice fell. "The question is, What then? What do we do *with* the controls? Match course and speed with the Fleet? Slow down, or stop, and let the Fleet catch up with us?"

Comm delay made every exchange that much worse. *Remembrance* remained stealthed, because (as Baedeker was so quick to remind Achilles) ground-based lasers were a threat if humans spotted the ship. Lest *Remembrance* be revealed, transmissions went through a relay of stealthed radio buoys. What an annoyance a minute could be.

"This would be much easier in person," the woman said. "Is that possible?"

Was it? On the ground, stealthiness was no defense. Lasers would *really* be a threat. Concussion from a big-enough explosion against the hull could mash him, even while the hull remained intact. So: no landing for now. *Remembrance* could hover just close enough for this woman and perhaps a few of her staff to step aboard. That seemed possible—

Until he remembered Sigmund Ausfaller hiding a bomb *inside* a GP hull to coerce Beowulf Shaffer. So many years ago, the ploy had amused Achilles, then regional president for General Products on We Made It.

Would he gamble with his life that another human would not conceive the same trick?

No. Baedeker must first assemble isolation booths of hull material, and equip them with sensors, before anyone from New Terra could come aboard. "Soon, Sabrina. I am making arrangements."

Ausfaller! The man plagued him even in death.

THE UNIVERSE HAD gone insane.

Nessus listened to Nike's message, over and over. Each time, he hoped to glean some positive element. Each time he failed. His own frantic communications hyperwaved to Sabrina went unanswered.

New Terra had been attacked, its paltry few ships destroyed. Achilles poised to take over—or to destroy New Terra's planetary drive if thwarted.

It was madness. Nessus tore at his mane, waiting now for Omar to respond.

And then a reply from Omar finally did arrive. . . .

Sigmund gone to meet with the Outsiders. *They* knew where Earth was. The repercussions were beyond imagining. But Sigmund did not know *exactly* where the Outsiders were. It would take Sigmund time to find them.

The starseed-lure network gave Nessus a fairly precise location. *He* might still reach the Outsiders first.

He *had* to.

Nessus sent a belated reply to Nike—another lie, another deception, to fester between them—and then *Aegis* dropped into hyperspace. He must get to the Outsiders first.

The universe had gone insane.

WHY NOT DROPPED from hyperspace, to find . . . absolutely nothing.

Sigmund studied the bridge sensor displays, smiling with a serene confidence he did not feel. Eric and Kirsten stood by expectantly, both looking like they hadn't slept in a week. Crew across the ship waited to hear good news over the intercom. It was all they had to do, beyond waiting to repair whatever next failed on this jury-rigged hulk. They were here to support Sigmund. Endangered, because of him.

If only he and Kirsten had gotten back aboard *Aegis.* They never got the chance. Nessus changed access codes, whether from suspicion or routine. A second mysterious fainting spell was not credible. Then even the option of more direct action was lost, as Concordance business reclaimed Nessus' attention. The Puppeteer left, and Earth's location remained lost.

But we have the Outsider coordinates. Make it work.

"All right." Sigmund rubbed his hands briskly. "Spotting Outsiders on passive sensors was too much to expect. Kirsten found out where they *were,* not where they are. Eric, a radar ping."

"Aye-aye, Captain," Eric said. "Now we sit and wait."

Sigmund shook his head. "Now we use the telescope, and look around the nearest suns for starseeds. Find a starseed and the odds are good the Outsider ship is following. Just don't ask me why."

"Look near?" Kirsten said. "That's rather vague. And it's not like I understand what we're looking for."

Sigmund had Bey's description, but none of his eloquence, to go by. "Usually it's only a node maybe a mile or two across. Could be taken for a boulder, a little asteroid. We'd never see it. But sometimes . . . well, most of that ball is a gossamer-thin, silvery sail, tightly rolled. Unfurled, it's thousands of miles across. When it catches the sunlight . . ."

A lump caught in Sigmund's throat. He had been a bastard to Shaeffer. Maybe, just maybe, the man was having a decent life now, beyond Sigmund's reach. He hoped so.

"Got it," Kirsten said. "Look for light glints that don't behave like planets."

Hours later, neither radar nor random peering had found a thing. Sigmund asked a question whose answer he dreaded. "Kirsten, did you recover a date for Nessus' visit to the Outsiders?"

"You never wanted to know," she said.

"I do now. How long ago?"

She checked her pocket comp. "The coordinates on *Aegis* were last accessed about two and a half years ago, but didn't Nessus say he hired another ship? A Known Space human ship?"

Sigmund twitched: I died, Nessus scooped me up, he went to the Outsiders, and I was awakened.

How had Nessus put it? "It became urgent to find the antimatter before the ARM did. Buying the coordinates from the Outsiders no longer seemed a waste of resources. For technical reasons I hired a human ship and crew for the mission. We found Ship Fourteen. . . ."

Only Nessus had glossed over a minor detail. He waited a couple years to revive me. Why? If we get through this, Sigmund thought, I'll ask.

The key was getting through it. "Two-plus years? That's not too bad. The Outsiders don't use hyperdrive. They can accelerate to near light effectively instantaneously, so they're somewhere in a sphere of about two light-years' radius."

"Somewhere within. Do you know how *big* that volume is?" Kirsten asked.

"It's a lot smaller than the whole tanj galaxy," Sigmund snapped, "and we can cross it in days. Plot a search pattern. Err on the side of searching nearer stars. We hop, look around with radar and telescope for, I'll say ten hours, and then repeat."

"Aye-aye, Captain." From Kirsten's lips, the words were skeptical.

"All hands," Eric called over the intercom. "We'll be returning to hyperspace soon. Details to follow." Kirsten plotted their course with her usual eerie dispatch, and they did.

As the nothingness beyond the void engulfed them,

Sigmund wondered how Sabrina was faring. His final advice to her, before *Why Not* left on its desperate mission, had been, "Stall."

THE COLONIST WOMAN, safe behind an isolation partition, droned on nonstop. With no encouragement, she would segue into minutiae. The so-called rights of the people. Emergency assistance. Satellite services disrupted by debris from the attack. A sudden urgent need to erect a tall wall around the pathetic Arcadian government compound, for protection against the apparently inexhaustible supply of extremists.

Now she had somehow diverted herself onto the resumption of grain exports. ". . . So many of the fields that once grew Hearthian grains have been replanted in terrestrial crops. Cargo floaters have been dispersed to new uses. We'll need new shipments of seeds and Hearthian fertilizer. And ships, of course."

At least negotiations were progressing with the extremists who occupied the planetary drive facility. If he had to, he would return to the Fleet for a shipload of robots. They would clear the building.

But things were *so* close. He could taste success.

He would wait a little longer.

ERIC WALKED INTO the relax room, looking apologetic. "Nothing, Sigmund."

"Thanks." Sigmund managed a smile. "That's progress. We've found one more place the Outsiders aren't."

What was this, their fourth hop? For an elder race who had roamed the galaxy forever, the Outsiders were deucedly hard to find. Sigmund took a long sip of coffee from his drink bulb. "This is taking so long, you'd think we were looking for Ship Thirteen."

Unlucky numbers were as foreign a concept as games of chance. "This will take a while, Eric. Hold on." He called Kirsten on the bridge. "You're clear for the next leg of the search."

She called a warning over the intercom, and plunged them back into the nothingness.

Something nagged at the borders of Sigmund's consciousness, something he and Eric had just been talking about. He let it go. They were talking about superstitious nonsense.

At least explaining superstition gave Sigmund something to do for two days in hyperspace. Knocking on wood. Black cats (actually, any cats). Walking under ladders. Tarot cards. He had not quite exhausted the topic when they returned to Einstein space.

Once again, they found nothing.

"THAT INCOMPETENT FOOL!" Achilles raved. "He got himself captured."

Harsh discordances echoed across the ship. Baedeker cantered to the bridge. "Who?" he asked cautiously.

"Nessus." Achilles summarized the message from Hearth. "He got a short message off before his comp was confiscated."

Baedeker chose his notes carefully. Achilles in a rage was frightening. "Captured by whom? Where?"

New Terra hung in the main bridge display, and Achilles straightened a neck directly at it. "There. He sneaked back to negotiate secretly with his friends. Fool that he is, he allowed them aboard his ship. Now they control *Aegis*."

A stealthy ship, its location unknown to Achilles' spies. Baedeker quivered: He could not dissolve a ship whose location he did not know. Worse, *Aegis* would have a Fleet space-traffic-control transponder. Change the transponder's identification code and the captured ship could approach the Fleet, even Hearth itself, with no questions asked.

Baedeker shook off the horror that threatened to

paralyze him. They—he—had attacked the New Terrans. Now the humans had a weapon. "I will begin a search for the ship."

"And I will—" Achilles stopped midphrase, harmonies dangling. "I will await your success. Until then, you will say nothing about Nessus or his ship to our human 'guest.' "

STEP, STEP, TURN.

Sigmund was exhausted, but he could not sleep. He could not stay still. He could not let the crew even suspect his doubt. And so he paced about his tiny cabin.

Step, step, turn.

Six jumps already on their search pattern, and nothing found. Back and forth across the volume of space where logic said the Outsiders must be. Fear of failure gnawed at Sigmund, scarier than the nothingness on the other side of his cabin wall. This search wasn't working, and he knew of nothing else to try.

Step, step, turn.

The intercom emitted three quick clicks: a pending announcement. "Dropping out of hyperspace, in five, four, three . . ." Kirsten had the con, and it was her voice. She sounded as weary as Sigmund felt.

Step, step, turn.

Each time *Why Not* dropped from hyperspace, Eric retrieved hyperwave radio messages from a remote comm buoy. Sabrina was reportedly still on Achilles' ship, supposedly negotiating—a hostage. And Omar, out of touch with everyone when Nessus contacted him, had made a judgment call: He told Nessus about *Why Not* and where Sigmund had taken it.

What Nessus would do with that information was anyone's guess.

Sigmund squeezed water from a drink bulb into a cupped palm, and splashed it on his face. The tepid water helped, just a little.

It was time again to act hopeful and positive. Sigmund opened the cabin door, to go help man the sensors on the bridge.

A victorious cheer burst from the intercom: Kirsten shouting with glee. "I've spotted a starseed!"

• 71 •

"Calling Outsider ship. Calling Outsider ship. This is the human starship *Why Not.*"

The starseed was more or less a light-year away. That distance was an estimate, based on a guess at how much light the sail reflected. Eric had likewise approximated its velocity, reasoning from the apparent tilt of the scarcely detectable sail and the red-shifting of sunlight reflected off the sail from the nearest sun.

"Calling Outsider ship. Calling Outsider ship. This is the human starship *Why Not.*" The message repeated endlessly, recorded by Sigmund in Interworld, each time hyperwaved along a slightly different path.

Hope that the Outsiders with whom Nessus once parlayed had chased this starseed. How soon after the meeting did they start their pursuit? How fast did they travel? What might have distracted them along the way?

Finding the starseed reduced their enormous search sphere into a still-vast cone. If Sigmund allowed himself to dwell on all the variables, he would go insane.

"Calling Outsider ship. Calling Outsider ship. This is the human starship *Why Not.*"

"This is Outsider—"

The cheering was so loud Sigmund had to replay the incoming message. "This is Outsider Ship Fourteen. Greetings, *Why Not.* Can we help you?"

"We have information to trade," Sigmund hyperwaved back along the same bearing. "May we join you?"

"We are about nine-tenths a light-year apart," Ship Fourteen answered. "We'll wait for you."

How far was that? Because of Nessus, Sigmund had no idea how long Earth's year was. New Terra's calendar followed Hearth's, measuring years that had lost all physical significance ages ago. The Puppeteers' treachery was much of what Sigmund had to trade. He would not let slip that secret by asking for the distance to be specified in Puppeteer light-years.

There had to be *something* he remembered, something Nessus did not think to remove, that related to the calendar.

Maybe there was.

New Terrans were puritanical about sex, Sigmund thought. They probably got it from the Puppeteers. "Kirsten. Excuse me if this is a bit forward. What fraction of a year does it take a woman to have a baby? From conception?"

She blushed. "About five-sixths of a year."

On Earth, if you were lucky enough to get a birthright, it was nine months. Ergo: "On Earth, it's three-quarters. An Earth year is about eleven percent longer than your year."

Three days later, *Why Not* emerged again from hyperspace.

A city made of ribbons lit by its own artificial sun—exactly as Bey had once described it, the Outsider ship waited for them.

Hovering alongside, tiny in comparison, was a GP hull.

IF NOT FOR Beowulf's stories, Sigmund would never have found his way here. And if not for Bey's stories as warning, Sigmund would now, surely, have gone mad.

Giant cat-o'-nine-tails clad in exoskeletons came out to *Why Not*. So slowly Sigmund almost screamed, they ferried him back to their ship. The gas pistols they used barely nudged them along. He was miles from both ships. If they were to release his hands . . .

He closed his eyes to shut out the universe.

Subtle maneuvering alerted Sigmund to their imminent arrival. He opened his eyes and the Outsider ship loomed. So many interlaced bands! They had been woven and swirled into a convolution his mind refused to grasp. Up close, glimpsed through random loops of that Gordian knot, the central spar seemed more like a mountain than a mast.

They landed finally on a ribbon. The feeble artificial gravity seemed inadequate to the task, and he activated boot electromagnets before he dared to take a step. After his heels snapped to the ribbon with a reassuring clang—there was a lot of metal to this ship—he allowed himself to be led. He passed hundreds of Outsiders basking in light and shadow before reaching a door. One of his escorts held it open. Sigmund pressed through a weak force field, and the door closed behind him.

A Puppeteer waited inside, his mane a disheveled mess. He turned. One eye was red, and the other yellow. Nessus.

Why Not had a long head start. How had Nessus gotten here first? He obviously knew exactly where to go. But how?

A clear dome was the only feature in the room. An Outsider reposed beneath. "Take off your pressure suit and stay awhile." The voice came from everywhere and nowhere. Wall and ceiling speakers, Sigmund decided. Vacuum creatures do not use sound. "You will be quite comfortable."

"My name is Sigmund. What shall I call you?"

"Fourteen will do."

Sigmund removed his helmet. "We have a common acquaintance, Fourteen. Beowulf Shaeffer."

"Indeed," the room said. Inside the dome, the Outsider had not stirred. "Shaeffer has been here before you. Now as to the information you wished to sell?"

NESSUS' HEARTS SKIPPED beats as a human entered. The human turned toward him: Sigmund, of course.

It was too soon! Nessus had just arrived himself. He had had no time to . . . do anything.

The conversation veered all too quickly to business. "Now as to the information you wished to sell?" Fourteen said.

That was surely the secret of New Terra. "Sigmund!" Nessus shouted. "Stop and think. The consequences would be"—he stuttered to a halt, at a loss for words—"unknowably huge."

"Can you call off Achilles? Can you make everything as it was? Can you guarantee it will never happen again?"

Nessus lowered his heads. "You know I cannot. But this will be worse."

Sigmund bared his teeth. "For you, perhaps. That's not my problem."

SIGMUND SET DOWN his helmet. "We should talk first about price."

"What do you think the information is worth?" Fourteen countered.

The lives of everyone on New Terra. How did one set a price on that? "Fourteen, Beowulf has assured me your people are very honest traders."

"That is our intention," Fourteen said.

Now we'll test that, Sigmund thought. "Is it satisfactory for me to reveal what I know, and for you to then set the price?"

"Perhaps we cannot afford an honest price."

"I'm sure you can," Sigmund said. "If we can agree

on no other terms, I will take as payment the right to independently operate one of your planetary drives."

"Interesting." The room grew deathly quiet. Sigmund's impression was that Fourteen consulted somehow with others of his kind. "Your price is the cancellation of that part of the Concordance's debt."

"It is."

"A princely sum," Fourteen said. "We are intrigued."

"Then you accept my terms?" Sigmund pressed.

"I do. Proceed."

And so Sigmund revealed, as Nessus moaned softly beside him, the long-secret history of *Long Pass* and New Terra.

• 72 •

"I must consult," Fourteen said abruptly. "Return to your ships. We will meet again in one Hearth day."

Their own ships. Sigmund suddenly pictured Nessus' indestructible ship plunging *through* his cobbled-together vessel. Like a laser through butter.

Nessus had kept him alive—for years, apparently—within a stasis field. The Puppeteer could shelter *himself* from such an impact in stasis. If not for such contingencies, why even have a person-sized stasis-field generator aboard?

Sigmund cleared his throat. "Fourteen, I would like to moor my ship to yours."

"That is not customary. Explain."

"For the safety of my crew. Given what you have just heard, I'm sure you can understand."

"Nessus," Fourteen said. "All who visit here are under our protection. You are aware of the power we wield. For the sake of the Concordance, you should respect our rules."

Sigmund took Nessus' shiver as acquiescence.

• • •

"CALLING NESSUS. CALLING Nessus. Calling Nessus."

I must confront Sigmund soon enough, Nessus thought. Then it will be faces to face. What harm can come of talking by radio now? He rolled out of a nest of pillows.

The ex-Colonists would see the despair and panic in his unkemptness. He left video turned off. "This is Nessus."

"I suggest a secure channel," Sigmund said. "Eric tells me we use Fleet-standard encryption, from before independence. I assume your automation knows the algorithm."

So now Sigmund would keep secrets from the Outsiders. Not for the first time, Nessus wondered what depths of insanity had possessed him to bring an ARM to New Terra. "*Aegis* has the algorithm, but we will need a common secret key."

"Use the name of the man who killed me."

That should add to the Outsiders' confusion. Despite everything, Nessus could not help but look himself in the eyes. "Done." There was a moment of static while cryptographic software took over the channel. "All right, Sigmund. What else can we possibly have to talk about?"

"Starseeds."

"I do not understand." Nessus *hoped* he did not.

"Omar advised us you were coming. You were scouting ahead of the Fleet. You got a report from Hearth about Achilles' attack, and you contacted New Terra."

"Correct." Video was off, and Nessus plucked frantically at his scrambled mane. "I had hoped to help you resist Achilles. Instead I heard where you had gone. Now I must stop you."

"Ahead of the Fleet," Sigmund repeated. "We were but a few light-years from here, yet you reached Ship

Fourteen before we did. Hence, you knew where it was."

Keep it simple. Don't lie—Sigmund will find you out. Just don't tell the *entire* truth. "I was here before."

"That's the thing," Sigmund said. "You weren't exactly 'here.' You visited Ship Fourteen more than two years ago. We went to where Ship Fourteen was. We headed where you went that last time. Where the navigation computers aboard *Aegis* said it was. You came . . . here."

The truth wouldn't work. Nessus had to try lying. "I found it with sensors."

"No." Sigmund's flat tone admitted no doubt. "The sensors on this ship were scavenged from *Explorer*. Surely a Concordance scout ship had the best available sensors."

Caught in a lie, as Nessus had feared. "Why do you care?" he asked. "We have other matters to concern us."

"Call it a thirst for knowledge." Sigmund paused. "Even nonparanoid humans have it."

"Ah, curiosity." A very human trait. Wandering away from the herd got animals killed. Any semblance to curiosity was bred out of Nessus' ancestors long before the first glimmer of sentience. It was one of many reasons scouts were rare—and why, in his foolishness, Nessus once thought Colonists might serve.

The difficulty with curiosity was, it knew no bounds.

"To continue," Sigmund said. "You went straight to a distant Outsider ship. It occurred to me you might have hidden a beacon on the Outsider ship, something to report instantaneously by hyperwave. But I've seen you around the Outsiders. They terrify you. You wouldn't risk being caught."

"I can almost admire your fascination with puzzles, but this is not the time. Sigmund, our escorts are due soon to return us to Fourteen."

Sigmund would not be deflected. "Do you know how *we* found Fourteen? First we found a starseed. If an Outsider ship were in the area, it was likely to be nearby. Do you know why the Outsiders follow starseeds?"

"Truly, I don't."

"A bit of truth at last. Nessus, I would appreciate it if you'd turn on video. As you say, our escorts will fetch us soon enough. I'll see you then. Unless you have something to hide."

"No, but if I don't you will conclude that I do." Before activating the video link, Nessus looked himself in the eyes again. "See my coiffure in all its splendor."

Judging by appearances, Sigmund had not rested well, either. Despite the dark bags beneath his eyes, his eyes shone with excitement. "Here's how I put it together, Nessus. Outsiders follow starseeds. Know where a starseed is and chances are you can find an Outsider.

"Just as I don't believe Puppeteers would dare bug an Outsider ship, I don't believe you would dare bug a starseed. I don't believe you would *touch* one. One of the few things anyone knows about the Outsiders is that starseeds are special to them."

"Really, Sigmund. It's time for me to prepare for the—"

"That leaves one possibility, Nessus. Outsiders follow starseeds. And what do starseeds follow?"

Nessus was afraid to speak.

"You should not be so modest. The Concordance has some kind of bait. Outsiders follow starseeds, which follow bait, which is controlled by Puppeteers.

"What do you suppose Fourteen would pay for *that* information?"

· 73 ·

Sigmund was suited up, helmet in hand, standing in the corridor by the main air lock. Eric and Kirsten had come to see him off. "You don't have to do this alone," Kirsten said. "Either or both of us would come with you."

He never doubted that, but he had another role in mind for them. "Can I trust you?"

"Of course," Kirsten said.

"Who *don't* you trust?" Eric said at the same time. His eyes darted about, looking for eavesdroppers. He seemed not to notice his mate's worried expression.

Eric is driving Kirsten away, Sigmund thought. Emulating me is driving her away. It made Sigmund sad.

"I sent a file to both of you. It contains everything I know or suspect about Puppeteers and Outsiders. If I don't come back . . . use the information as you see fit." Things could go wrong in so many ways that Sigmund couldn't begin to be specific. "Consider immediately hyperwaving everything back to New Terra. Until then, I trust you not to look."

Then Sigmund snapped on his helmet and walked into the air lock.

Four Outsiders floated beyond the air lock. Two took his hands. They towed him at their accustomed glacial pace toward Ship Fourteen. *Why Not* vanished in the dark behind him. Stars surrounded him, impossibly distant.

It wasn't the vast emptiness that most terrified Sigmund. It was the loneliness that all the emptiness represented. His life, light-years removed from everyone else in the universe.

If they survived this, Sigmund swore, he *would* change.

• • •

SIGMUND'S ESCORTS LED him to a room indistinguishable from yesterday's. Lights came on as he entered, and air whooshed in. The clear dome, at the end opposite the door, remained dim and unoccupied. This time he was here first, and he saw Nessus arrive. They removed their pressure suits in silence.

The dome brightened, and an Outsider appeared. The dome could function as a transfer booth, or contain the equivalent of a stepping disc, or project incredibly lifelike holos. None of which mattered.

Nessus sidled closer to the dome. "Fourteen?"

As before, sound issued from unseen speakers. "We shall forego pleasantries. This will be brief."

Sigmund forced himself to be calm.

"Sigmund, you brought news and asked us to assign a fair price. Upon due consideration, the information matters only to New Terra and to the Concordance. It is without value to us."

Sigmund could only stare. "The Puppeteers are deeply in your debt. Knowledge of their duplicity surely matters."

"It is less of a surprise than you imagine," Fourteen said—at which Nessus twitched.

Intervention had been Sigmund's last hope. How could the all-powerful Outsiders react with such indifference? And why? "Puppeteers will enslave a world of humans, or destroy it, or set it adrift. Whatever happens, they do it to placate *you. We* are blameless in this. How can you not act?"

"Settle your petty differences amongst yourselves. Our interest is only the payment due to us. Who pays is your affair. Be glad we do not react to your presumption."

"Thank you, Fourteen," Nessus said. "The Concordance appreciates you leaving this matter in our jaws."

There *must* be options. "Earth would pay a fortune for this information."

"If you believe that, Sigmund, you do not need us. Go there and sell it yourself."

And what could he sell to get Earth's coordinates? The suspicion that Puppeteers could lure starseeds?

Beside Sigmund, Nessus quivered. Despite his victory, he remained as terrified as ever. A Puppeteer could never learn how *not* to be afraid. The fear was wired in his genes.

And in that instant, Sigmund finally understood. The truth had been in front of him the whole time.

"I THINK YOU will help, Fourteen" Sigmund said. "No, I'll restate that. You *will* help."

Beneath the dome, tendrils writhed.

"You will help, Fourteen, for the same reason you are so eager to remain uninvolved. For all your power, you are far fewer, and far weaker, than anyone imagined. But *I* know. My *people* know. And if you do not resolve this matter to my satisfaction . . . then *everyone* will know."

What truth he had surmised lay scattered across the files left for Eric and Kirsten. In time they might connect the dots as he just had. Sigmund hoped it wouldn't come to that.

Nessus pawed the deck. "Fourteen, I do not know what troubles Sigmund. He does not speak for me."

"Noted, Nessus. Sigmund, explain."

"What *do* we know about your people?" Sigmund mused. "Very tanj little. You live on enormous ships. You follow starseeds. You sell information and technology, always for a premium price. You lease the occasional remote planet or moon, always offering a generous payment, and you buy occasional supplies.

"You overpay for worthless real estate, flaunting your wealth, so that no one gives any thought to what you *really* need: metals. In inner solar systems where exposed metals are to be found, the briefest interruption in your protective gear and you would be boiled away.

"And then there's the fact we *think* we know, but don't: that yours is an ancient galactic civilization. Almost every question anyone ever asked about your civilization goes unanswered. The answers are priced, quite symbolically, at a *trillion* stars, effectively beyond purchase.

"I stress: *almost* every question. The 'facts' of your species' extent and venerable origins . . . *that* information is dispensed freely, and at no cost."

Had he learned to read Puppeteer facial expressions? Nessus seemed perplexed.

Sigmund pressed on. "So, what of the elder race that roams the galaxy at sub–light speeds? The civilization that in some mysterious way involves the slow migration of starseeds from rim to core, and back again? It's common knowledge—yet it's something Puppeteers and humans and Kzinti cannot possibly know. None of us have been sentient long enough, or traveled far enough, to confirm these things. What if it isn't true?"

"Our business is none of your concern," Fourteen said, his tentacles still atremble. "Dress for vacuum, and go."

Sigmund ignored the order. "A galaxy-spanning race, ancient of days. Can it be true? Humans and Kzinti traveled the stars for hundreds of years before first encountering any Outsiders. And that was all sublight travel. We didn't *have* hyperdrive until you sold it to us.

"Imagine this is the only Outsider ship in all of what humans so grandly call Known Space. How many ships must there be across the galaxy? A billion, maybe. And yet here we are on Ship Fourteen. What are the odds of such a low number? They seem, well, astronomical."

Nessus found his voice. "Sigmund, I don't understand."

"You know more than you realize, Nessus. If we have been told the truth, why aren't Outsider ships everywhere? You know they aren't. You would never have allowed *Explorer* to fly with an all-human crew if encountering an Outsider ship were a risk."

"You expect my help in return for your numerology?" Fourteen said. "This is pointless. Prepare to go."

"Ah," Sigmund said. "I should mention another thing we know. Outsiders do not haggle. Now we see why: Your take-it-or-leave attitude sustains an aura of power. It's also why you wouldn't overlook the Concordance transferring a planetary drive. Your forbearance might lead the Puppeteers to infer weakness. Any odious consequences of your actions"—of your cowardice—"matter less than maintaining your image.

"The time for posturing has passed, Fourteen. Reconsider your decision. Help New Terra."

Tendrils wriggled and twisted. "And if we refuse? Do you plan to spread these speculations around Known Space?"

Sigmund smiled. "Yes, if you force me to. But there is another alternative."

TRIUMPH AND DESPAIR chased each other in circles. Nessus had almost lost track of his mood. Only exhaustion and fear were constant.

What could Sigmund possibly hope to gain by taunting the Outsiders?

The shame of it all was, the Concordance should have seen through the pretense long ago. Citizens were dealing with the Outsiders while the ancestors of humans still swung in the trees. The mystery of it all was, why did Sigmund freely share this insight with *him*?

Sigmund spoke Interworld. He knew Beowulf Shaeffer. Of course Fourteen believed Sigmund could reveal the Outsiders' secret across Known Space. But Sigmund had lost the way to Known Space—and Sigmund knew Nessus knew that.

First starseed lures. Now this.

Sigmund expected *something* of him. What could it be?

• • •

"FOURTEEN, WHAT IF we have something *you* need?" Sigmund asked abruptly.

"Hardly likely."

"Fourteen, let's talk of starseeds."

Across the room, Nessus plucked at his already-tangled mane. He was all but catatonic. Would he have the wit to follow Sigmund's lead?

"What of starseeds?" Fourteen asked.

"The Puppeteers accepted your false history, so your race *is* older than theirs. A trillion Puppeteers now live on Hearth, while you are few. Compared to the other intelligent species, you are frail." With thoughts of Kirsten blushing, Sigmund chose his next words carefully. "Your children must be exceedingly precious to you."

Silence.

"I can only speculate how starseeds figure in your life cycle."

The Outsiders lived in the vacuum, soaking up faint (if artificial) sunshine, lying prone in scarcely discernable gravity. They must have evolved, eons ago, on tiny, cold rocks far from an ancestral sun. Sigmund imagined spores or eggs expelled from those rocks into space, *slowly* growing on a thin diet of solar wind and cosmic dust. How long would it take to become a miles-wide starseed? To what purpose did the starseeds wander? Did it require some rare cosmic event to germinate the seeds?

Sigmund had no idea. It was enough that Nessus knew. "Truly, *how* hardly matters. Fourteen, I apologize if I am being unseemly. What matters is that you follow starseeds. They do not follow you.

"Because when the radiation wave arrives from the core explosion—even sooner, if it is true starseeds migrate to the galaxy's core—your history, however venerable, must end."

• • •

IF SIGMUND WAS correct . . .

Hope once more pushed away despair. Starseed lures! With them, the Outsiders could stop their next generation from the slow-motion death of migration to the core. With them, the Outsiders could learn to modulate their own artificial suns. They could lead starseeds, rather than follow them.

And Sigmund was leaving the manner of disclosure to *him.*

The price of Sigmund's discretion remained to be determined.

Nessus set his hooves far apart, feigning a self-assurance he did not feel. He had nowhere to flee. Assuming a confident stance did him no harm. He found his voices. "Our scientists have studied starseeds."

"To what end?" Fourteen asked. Into his lack of inflection Nessus read suspicion.

"Scientists," Nessus dissembled. "Why do they study anything? The fortunate thing is that they did. They discovered stellar spectra to which starseeds are attracted." And now the lie. "They theorize it would be possible to remotely stimulate a stellar magnetosphere, thereby attracting starseeds.

"Would you consider a trade?"

"A TRADE," FOURTEEN said. "Possibly. I will need to consult."

Sigmund cleared his throat loudly. "Not so fast."

"My dealings with the Concordance do not concern you," Fourteen said. "Still, I would expect you to be pleased. If we forgive the transfer of a planetary drive to New Terra's control, your problems are solved."

That might have been true—once. Achilles' attack

changed everything. New Terra was helpless. The Fleet would try to reclaim their lost colony while they could. Or was he being paranoid?

Tanj, he *should* be paranoid. Why else was he here? What else was he good for?

"The problem will be solved, Fourteen, if you do a bit more. Support our independence as part of the deal. Grant perpetual rights to use the drive now on New Terra as we choose. And so that any of it matters, guarantee us these rights."

More writhing of tendrils, eerily evocative of Medusa. "You have high expectations of beings so feeble and few."

Irony from an Outsider. I still have much to learn, Sigmund thought. "No one on Hearth yet knows what we have discussed. They remain terrified of you."

Fourteen considered. "It is our policy not to intervene between other species."

"Policies change," Sigmund said. "Make independence and Puppeteer noninterference a condition of the trade. Then you won't have to intervene."

"And if we refuse?"

Puppeteers did not understand bluffing. If Sigmund wasn't imagining things, though, the Outsiders were consummate bluffers. Well, so was he. "Then everything we have talked about becomes common knowledge across Known Space."

Sigmund didn't know the location of Known Space, which made it an empty threat—and Nessus knew it. Sigmund glanced at the Puppeteer. The Concordance had pulled the strings of the Outsiders, too. "About certain matters you and I discussed privately earlier . . ."

"Understood," Nessus said.

More squirming of tentacles. "And conversely, your eternal silence on these matters if we reach agreement. I will need to consult with—"

"And *I* have requirements," Nessus interrupted.

Sigmund froze. What was Nessus up to?

"The conditions, Fourteen, are these: First, you never convey location or navigational data to Sigmund, or his ship, or anyone you have reason to believe comes from New Terra. Second, you withhold what you know about New Terra from the species in Known Space."

The room shrank to only Nessus' eyes. Peace and independence for New Terra. Surrender all hope of ever going home. Sigmund understood the bargain.

He kept his silence, gladly, as Fourteen finalized arrangements.

· 74 ·

Paraphernalia and supplies removed from cargo holds and never returned. Out-of-tolerance equipment awaiting recalibration. Tens of empty food trays and hundreds of abandoned drinking bulbs. Wrappers, crates, straps, padding, and packaging of all sorts. During the operation above New Terra, the corridors, cabins, and rooms of *Remembrance* had grown progressively more chaotic.

Just the thought of such dangerous clutter made Baedeker's shins hurt.

Chanting as he worked, Baedeker recycled trash, identified and sorted apparatus, repadded and repacked, and began moving things back into cargo holds. He would normally resist such work as beneath him, but this was different.

This was a step toward going home.

Somehow—the specifics remained elusive—Nessus had resolved the crisis. The last thing Baedeker had heard, Nessus was a prisoner. The humans apparently took Nessus and his ship to the Outsiders. There Nessus escaped his human captors and negotiated a three-way deal. The shape of the deal was the most nebulous of all, in all but one respect—New Terra would go its own way.

Hence: Hostilities had ended. *Remembrance* was recalled.

Baedeker was deep in song, happily stowing repackaged equipment, when odd sounds intruded. Muffled conversation? It could only be Achilles and the human woman Sabrina. She would be home soon, too. Her home. Only it didn't *sound* like conversation.

Baedeker was pleasantly surprised how quickly everything was going back into the holds. The rooms had seemed crammed on the way here. Early in the operation, whatever he needed always turned out to be behind or under everything he did not want. Like the two cargo floaters he had just found half a ship away. Like the big crates that held . . .

The two big crates were gone.

"TALK ALL YOU want," Achilles said. "Personally, I would save my breath."

Sabrina gabbled inarticulately. Invisible restraints encased her from head to toe, the same force field that pinned her to the second crash couch on the bridge. It was a Citizen couch, of course. On a human it did not look comfortable. "Mmpph. Gack."

He had set the field strength to maximum. Even breathing must be hard. She would quiet down soon enough. "This is a fascinating experiment. Very advanced science. You should be honored that your world can take part."

Her eyes never left him. With a struggle, she managed to get out, "Tssch. Jwerrf."

"Initiation sequences complete." Let no one say he was not keeping her informed. "Probes are active."

Telemetry streamed in an auxiliary display. He continued his narration. "Thrusters: nominal. Guidance: nominal. Sensors: nominal." The sensors had locked onto the nearest of the orbiting suns. He flashed the ship's comm laser against a random spot on Atlantis, and the probe sensors immediately changed their lock. They resumed tracking suns when the laser turned off. "Tracking: nominal."

The main holo showed a real-time image of New Terra. They were in synchronous orbit above the continent of Atlantis. Too small to discern at this magnification, they were also almost above the planetary-drive facility.

Veins stood out in Sabrina's forehead and neck. Her face was turning purple. Her struggle to communicate went beyond what little breath the restraint field allowed her to take. She would faint soon, and then who would see his accomplishment?

"Very well," Achilles said. He adjusted the restraint enough to free her head. "I can restore it just as easily."

". . . Don't . . . ha-have t-to . . . *do* . . . thisss," she wheezed. "Pl-plea . . . sssee . . . d-don't."

"Probes inbound," he answered.

He had parked both probes at ten planetary diameters, with Baedeker none the wiser. The probes were quite simple, really. Thrusters. A bit of electronics. And a *lot* of depleted uranium, far denser than lead.

"I *do* have to do this." Achilles monitored the probes' progress as he spoke. "Somehow, you have become too powerful."

She jutted her chin just enough to suggest pointing at herself and her helplessness. "Too powerful?"

"A few years ago, your people coerced the Concordance. Now, somehow, you have intimidated even the Outsiders. Whatever the course you choose, New Terra will be near the Fleet for a long time. You are far too dangerous to have as neighbors."

She breathed deeply for a while, gathering her strength. "But the Hindmost ordered you back to Hearth. He ordered that we be left alone. You told me so yourself."

"All the more proof that you are too dangerous. Even the Hindmost has fallen sway to Outsiders, compelled to do your bidding. I *will* destroy you while I can."

"Defy the Hindmost and you become an outcast." She spat on the deck. *"Herdless."*

Achilles twitched. The insult had teeth. She knew something of Citizen ways.

No matter. In time, the herd would see the wisdom of his actions.

The probes continued their breakneck plunge. "Accelerating at thirty gravities, the probes will impact in another seventeen minutes. By then, they will be traveling about 217 miles per second.

"It will be instructive to observe how a planetary drive shuts down."

BAEDEKER DID NOT know how long he had stood, paralyzed, just outside the bridge. This was madness.

The energy from the collisions alone would be stupendous. The energies that might be unleashed by a wrecked planetary drive—those were beyond imagining.

The death of everyone on New Terra and on this ship? That he had no difficulty at all imagining. And he did not think the catastrophe would confine itself to the planet's surface.

He wanted, more than anything, to run. To hide. Neither running nor hiding could possibly save him.

Disaster *would* happen . . . unless *he* stopped it.

WITH GROWING EXCITEMENT, Achilles tracked the probes' descent. His prisoner raged. She begged. She finally fell silent.

"Three minutes to impact," he told her.

Nothing.

"Two minutes to impact."

"Stop it," she shouted. "Stop it now. You win. I surrender the planet to you."

Would she? Could it possibly work this time, or was it another ruse? There were no notes, no chords, no symphonies, for the hunger he felt. To rule a world!

But the Outsiders demanded its independence. Nike would never let him rule here. The human was merely stalling until help could arrive from the Fleet.

"Laser illuminating the drive facility." He spoke over her scream of protest. "Probes locked on target. Ship's instruments on and recording. Ninety seconds to impact."

EDGING *FORWARD,* ONTO the bridge, was the hardest thing Baedeker had ever done. That way lay madness and death.

Could any argument prevail? Achilles already had defied the Hindmost.

Baedeker stood there, numb, the final seconds dribbling away. Could any action at this late moment even stop the cataclysm?

Somehow Baedeker managed two steps forward. "Achilles. You must not do this! I cannot predict the consequences. No one can. You endanger even the Fleet. You endanger the life of every Citizen!"

Achilles swiveled one head around. The other remained fixed on his console. "I *will* do this, and I do so *for* the Fleet. Our former servants have somehow manipulated even the Outsiders. We must destroy the New Terrans while we are able.

"So be thankful you are here to observe the drive shutdown. Watch and learn." The head that tracked Baedeker turned momentarily to check a timer. "Forty-five seconds."

The restraint field arched the human prisoner around a crash couch. It must be excruciating. She said, "*You* must stop Achilles. He's insane."

"Thirty seconds."

Imminent death. An implacable stare. The entire herd in danger. The impossibility of flight. What could he do?

"Twenty seconds."

Baedeker spun on his front hooves as though to flee the bridge. He didn't.

Heads turned backward, spaced far apart for perspective, Baedeker lashed out with his massive hind leg. Just before impact, he locked the hip and knee. The jolt up his leg snapped his jaws shut and rattled his teeth.

All his weight struck Achilles on the cranial dome. Baedeker's hoof sank into the mane, through the mane, into . . . bone fragments.

Achilles collapsed like a popped balloon.

"Turn off the laser. Now!" the woman shouted.

Baedeker teetered in a fog. Nothing could stop the probes. The projectiles were too close to stop. Too close to miss. Even an ocean impact—if he redirected the beam and the probes could veer that far off their present course—would cause massive tidal waves.

"Trust me! Do it!"

The timer showed 15 seconds. There was no time to think! Baedeker cut the laser beam.

Ten seconds to impact. Five.

The main display flashed impossibly bright. His eyes snapped shut, but even the afterimage was blinding. Tears streamed down his faces and necks.

But he was alive!

Blinking through the pain and tears, Baedeker opened his eyes. Safety interlocks had cut out the bridge's main viewer. He reached over Achilles to release the human from her restraints.

She sat up, groaning. "Show me," she whispered.

Baedeker reset the external optical sensors and the main bridge holo—and there was New Terra! It looked . . . untouched. And yet something was different.

In the skies over Atlantis, two suns were gone.

EPILOGUE

Earth date: 2660

The suns hot on his back, his mane a sweat-sodden, bedraggled mess, Baedeker crouched over his work. He painstakingly untangled weed stalks from redmelon vines. When the whole row was freed, he picked up a small trowel. Working slowly—it was an edged tool in his mouth!—he dug out the weeds, one by one.

Four more rows of redmelon remained. After that, nine rows of rebicci. Then a thick patch of steppe grass.

Once he had craved the attentions of the elite. For rehabilitation. For vindication. Then he wanted only anonymity and tranquility.

And now?

Now, for as long as the humans would have him, Baedeker wanted only to putter here in his garden.

A THOUSAND DANCERS, fleet-footed and lithe, glided about the stage. Sometimes they moved without a sound. Sometimes every hoof struck the floor in the same instant, like a clap of thunder. When they sang, it was in voices so pure and poignant that hearts could break. Rhythm and movement and melody became one. Time slowed.

And beyond the incomparable glories of the Grand Ballet, Nessus thought, I am here as Nike's guest.

Nessus leaned closer. Nike leaned closer, still. They touched, and somehow their necks were twined. And so they remained until intermission. . . .

Nike sighed. "In time, we'll have more scouts."

And New Terra would once more have ships of its own. And I won't be sent, yet again, far from Hearth and herd and . . . you. "I know," Nessus said.

And yet.

Words sung in anger could not be unsung. Trust lost was not easily rebuilt. Rejection still hurt. Lies and deceptions hung between them, making the past off-limits and obscuring the future. Yes, the Hindmost needed him. What did *Nike* feel?

What did he feel?

They sat with their necks still twined, in safely ambiguous silence, until the ballet resumed and conversation became impossible.

THE HEAP OF onion grew as Sigmund chopped. He swept it aside with the blade of his utility knife and went to work on the green pepper. He started the butter melting as he diced the last of the ham. Someday he'd get *just* the right proportions for the perfect Denver omelet.

And maybe he *wouldn't* put it into a synthesizer. When you had the time for it, cooking was satisfying.

A Brandenburg Concerto played softly in the background. The Puppeteers had purged Beethoven, Richard Strauss, and McWhorten—all too martial?—but Bach and Mozart remained.

Bach. New Terra safe. True friends: Kirsten and Eric, Sabrina, Omar, Sven. . . .

If only.

Sigmund did not dare let his thoughts go down that path.

The butter started to brown, and he began sautéing the chopped ingredients. There was a soft knock on the door. A woman's voice, indistinct.

Probably Kirsten. She had been at loose ends since *Aegis* last set off. Once Eric and Nessus returned from their joint scouting expedition, Sigmund hoped, Kirsten and Eric would patch things up. Eric would be a fool to drive her away.

"Who's there?" Sigmund answered.

"Faithful Penelope."

Sven had finally impressed upon Sigmund the importance here of color. He checked his pants and shirt. Charcoal gray. Passionless, hiding-from-the-world gray. "I'll be right there." As the onions charred, he hurriedly set the gray much paler and the collar and placket bright blue. Was the effect too distant? Too forward? He crossed the apartment and opened the door.

Penelope, clad head to toe in hot pink, waited outside.

His jaw dropped.

"The great hero has returned, back from an epic journey across a sea of stars." She smiled. "Only somehow he forgot his last stop. Would it be all right if *I* come the last few feet?"

Life, home, and love—all lost. Rebirth, a new home, and new love. The most beautiful music ever written swelling in the background.

Sigmund found his voice at last. "Not all right, exactly. That would be perfection."

THE COMBINE FLOATED effortlessly above the field of grain. The hum of the motor filled the cab. Behind the combine floated a small trailer, into which clusters of tiny orange seeds flowed in an endless stream. The harvest disappeared instantly, teleported to a distant storage bin.

Endless harvesting. Endless fields. Endless droning. Endless menial labor. And, like the constantly emptying trailer, nothing to show for it.

Achilles stared ahead at the setting suns. Like the fields and the droning, his thoughts never varied. Power over a world like this had almost been in his jaws. He did not know exactly how, only that he had been betrayed. By Nessus—again—certainly. By perfidious humans. By Baedeker.

Day after day, Achilles struggled to remember. How had things gone wrong? What clues had he overlooked?

Would he ever know, or were those memories forever gone?

He had returned to Hearth, ignominiously, in an autodoc. The bone of his dome had knit. His mane grew back, lustrous and full. The injured lobe of his brain regenerated. But as for the holes in his memory . . .

Some things he *did* remember. The splendor that was life on Hearth. The beauty of Brides. The incredible instant in which a moon became neutronium. The adulation of acolytes.

That Baedeker once invented *his* way out of exile.

So shall I, Achilles thought. When that day comes, someone owes me a world—

And I intend to claim it.

Printed in the USA
CPSIA information can be obtained
at www.ICGtesting.com
LVHW041231170624
783358LV00002B/141